Broken Wings

Broken Legacy Series, Volume 1

R.A. Vincent

Published by R.A. Vincent, 2023.

Prologue

"Stop! Thief!"

I leaped over the stand, startling the owner into dropping a crate of apples. A string of foul curses followed me. I ran faster—darting around a mother carrying a wailing child, breaking through a troupe of giggling women covered in gaudy jewels.

"How dare you!"

"Filthy peasant!"

My feet struck the uneven, sun-scorched ground, feeling every rock and discarded trinket like lances through my bare feet. Still, I ran.

I held my prize closer, the coins digging painfully into my chest. I would not give them up.

I could still see him sauntering through the square, tossing a weighty purse of coins in the air, and scoffing as he told his friends they would have to pay for drinks and cards because his worthless father was restricting his spending.

My fist clenched as it did when I heard him, complaining while he carried enough coin to feed every child in the orphanage for a month.

I had my chance when he and his cohort stopped outside of the brothel, leering at the half-dressed women dancing on the balcony. He shoved the purse in his back pocket, I came in close, slipped it out—

—then I went flying, thrown into him by a brutish oaf on horseback, kicking the dirty peasant out of his way.

I twisted around, searching for them in the trail of destruction and angry merchants in my wake.

Ever since the brothel moved closer to the market, my hunting ground was overrun with wealthier, younger, and stupider targets. Still, I'd never gotten more than a couple silvers here and there. An entire purse of gold coins was a prize I couldn't let get away.

"Whoa!"

A cart backed in front of me. I veered right, slipping between two stalls and disappearing into the trees.

The orphanage was on the other side of the forest. My life began within these trees, for beneath a towering oak was where Sister Aven found an abandoned babe, squalling in her soiled wrappings.

I knew every inch of this forest. I bathed with the fish in the stream. I climbed the tallest trees, and fell out of more than my fair share. My first lover fumbled and stuttered his way through taking my maidenhood, under a shelter in the clearing that I made of fronds and branches. The spoiled noble would have more to complain to his father about when he returned to Golden City to be waited on by servants, and have his day scrubbed away in a lavender-scented bath. He would tell him that for all his teachings that nobles were worth ten times as much as a peasant, they forgot to mention they were also ten times as slow.

I ran until the sounds of laughter, haggling, and overworked horses fell away, leaving me in the serene quiet of my forest. Tripping to a stop, I leaned against an oak, catching my breath.

I took no pleasure in stealing, but I took even less in listening to the children cry on the floor under threadbare blankets for more food. When Velez was around, the cut of his wages that he sent back home was enough to fill our bellies and buy the occasional treat. But the money stopped coming, and he stopped visiting. To this day, we don't know what happened to him.

After Velez disappeared, I was the only one of age who could find work and help Sister Aven care for the children.

And I tried.

I responded to every stained sign seeking new barmaids. I offered my calloused and scarred hands to every builder and merchant. They all had one question for me. After the thirtieth rejection, I learned to throw myself out before they got the chance.

"This was necessary," I whispered, thinking of the day Gannon passed out in the fields—weak from hunger. "I've never stolen for myself. Only for the children."

Straightening, I began thinking of the explanation I'd give to Sister Aven for where I'd gotten so much money. I wonder if she'd believe the "a merchant paid me to man her stall for the day" excuse twice in a row?

I set off, and found I couldn't move.

"What—?"

Roots sprouted from the ground, wrapping, twisting, snaking around my legs.

"Look, guys." A man stepped out from behind the bush. His smirk was twice as triumphant as when he smacked the ass of one of the women entering the brothel. "I caught a rat."

"Let go of me." I thrashed in the grip of the climbing roots. "Let go!"

"Shut your filthy mouth." His friends followed, falling in around me. All three of them bore a blue tear-shaped mark on their foreheads. "No one gave you permission to speak."

"I told you we should've gone to the whorehouse in Parlan," said the tall, red-haired one. "Ossian is overrun with thieving trash like this thing."

"I told *you*, I've been banned from Parlan," snapped my captor. "Those whores dared to complain to the owner, claiming they refuse to serve me. At least the Ossian whores know their place. They're not in a position to turn down coin."

He carried on a conversation while wielding magic without a trickle of sweat on his brow. The strongest magic-user I knew could summon a candle's flame after minutes of intense concentration. And that assumed he was sober and well-rested.

This power—lashing my limbs, tying me to the tree, rendering me completely immobile—was something the likes of me had never seen.

"Get your coin and let's be done with this trash, Tavis," said the blond one with a thin slash of a mouth. "We must be through the gates before nightfall."

"I'll take this." Tavis snatched the purse from my grip. I broke two fingers trying to hold on. "As much pleasure as I'd take from watching the magistrate cut off your thieving fingers, he's a busy man whose time shouldn't be wasted on scuttling gutter trash like you."

He tangled in my hair and yanked my head up. Pain exploded in my scalp.

"I'll do him, and the rest of the civilized world, a favor by— Wait a moment. Verlin, Fionn, take a look at this."

I stiffened as they verged on me. Shrinking, I drew back as far as the tree would let me.

"Under that grime, you're quite pretty for gutter trash." The one called Verlin stroked my cheek. "Why are you stealing? Surely you'd make all the money you want in the whorehouse. I know I'd have paid to have those pretty pink lips wrapped around my—"

I snapped, sinking my teeth in his finger.

"Argh!" He snatched away, and slapped me across the face. "Rabid bitch!"

My head lolled, ears ringing. He did not hold back with that hit.

"Just for that, leave her, Tavis. Maybe after a few days screaming, crying, and shitting herself tied to this tree, she'll learn to respect her betters."

"Surely you're not speaking of yourselves," I said. "I see no one better before me. Only three, silly little boys so afraid of one small woman, they must gang up on her three on one."

Verlin slapped me again.

The hit made me bite my lip. Blood welled in my mouth.

"I take it back," I rasped. "Even little boys can hit harder than that."

Growling, Verlin advanced on me—fist raised.

"Stop." Tavis swung out his arm, holding him back. "Don't mess up her face. We came all this way to this garbage heap to share a whore... so that's what we're going to do."

"What? No! Don't you dare—"

"Fionn, clean her up."

The blond one raised his hand, and a blast of water struck my face. I gasped—choking and drowning in the onslaught. They were so strong. Magic like this was beyond my comprehension.

"St-stop."

The roots crawled under my shirt, and ripped it off. I screamed as the roots retreated from my torso, and only my torso—baring my body and the raggedy breastband struggling to cover me.

"Stop this!" Fear blew through my bravado. "Don't touch me! If you do, I'll—"

"You'll what?" Tavis crooked a finger. My pants were the next to go. "Go ahead, use your magic. Break free and tell anyone who'll listen that three nobles put you in your place. You'll be flogged for slander before you get a word out."

"Well?" Verlin taunted. "Fight back, peasant. Surely you can take us. We're just a bunch of silly little boys after all."

I gritted my teeth, fists clenching. I said nothing.

"Wait. Can it be?" Fionn's hacking laugh grated on my ears. "Don't tell me you don't have any magic."

The look on my face told all. The three of them burst into raucous laughter.

"Release me at once!"

"Why should we?" Tavis yanked my head back again. The roots began moving and bending, dragging me down to my knees. "You've just told us that we can do what we want to you over, and over, and over again... and there's nothing you can do to stop us."

"Get away from me," I screamed, fighting and flinging to free myself of the roots.

Their pants hit the dirt.

"Help! Someone, help me, please!"

"Oh, do keep screaming." The roots crawled under my breastband and slipped the lining of my undertunic. "That's my favorite part."

"Don't do this! Help!"

Help!

Pain shot through my skull. I screamed, agony shredding my throat and ratcheting my cries to heights I didn't know I could reach.

"Fuck's sake, we haven't even touched you yet."

My mind was on fire. Lit aflame and reduced to ash within my skull. No one had known pain like this. If the world knew suffering like this existed, babes would not leave the safety of their mother's womb.

I flung my head back—screeching, shaking, sobbing my lungs to shreds. *What is this magic! What have they done to me?*

Heat blasted my face, carrying the echo of my screams.

No... not mine. Theirs.

The pain went on for an eternity, blinding me to their next strike.

Suddenly, the roots fell away—dropping me face-first into the dirt.

"Uhhh..." I groaned, straining to peel an eye open. "Ahh!"

I scrambled back and rammed into the tree. Lying before me were Tavis, Verlin, and Fionn, but their mothers wouldn't know it to look at them. I gaped at the burning corpses, my vision doubling—tripling them through my head-splitting haze.

"How— Ah!"

I doubled over, clutching my head. It felt as though someone drilled a hole in my skull and poured scalding water through it.

A boom shook the earth, toppling me over. A shadow blotted out the sun, its presence towering over me.

I forced myself to my feet and met her eyes. The dragon forced herself where she did not fit, flattening the bush and crushing mighty trees that lived long before her under her girth. Sunlight caught her gleaming red scales and melted within them, trickling down her body as brilliant red faded to molten orange on her legs and feet. Her long, narrow head was the length of my body and topped with a row of ivory horns from the tip of her nose to her crown.

She was beautiful. So wonderfully magnificent, I wept to look at her. I wasn't meant to be in the midst of such radiance, but for some reason, she came to me.

I glanced at the men that were. *She saved me.*

I couldn't say how I knew she was a she. I sensed it in the rightness in which her name came to me.

"Reyna."

Stepping forward, fear like I'd never known shook me to my core. I brushed a finger on my forehead, feeling the tear-shaped mark beginning to form.

"Oh my gods," I breathed, crying for an entirely different reason. "You've killed me."

Chapter One

"Walk straight, Ainsley." Rosaleen jabbed my spine. "Royalty doesn't slouch."

I drew back my shoulders, attempting to follow her order. The very act felt wrong. A thief moves through a crowd unseen. Head down. Face shadowed. Leaving behind a trail of witnesses who could swear to nothing.

That isn't your life anymore. Before you risked your fingers, now you tempt your life.

"This is a terrible idea." A curious glance passed over my face, and I instinctively ducked my head. "I can't do this. No one will be fooled."

"You don't have a choice. It gets worse every day. You can't hold a conversation or complete a task without—"

"Ah!" I clutched my head. Knocked off-balance, I crashed into Rosaleen.

"Without that," she finished, putting me back on my feet. "You have to learn to control the bond, or it'll kill you."

"It's because she's bored." I massaged my temples, as though that could soothe the fierce, foreign mind invading my consciousness. It wasn't scalding heat that poured in my mind that day, two full moons ago. It was Reyna. It was the mental bond forging between a lowly orphan thief and an all-powerful fire dragon.

My dragon.

"She hates hiding. She hates that she has to keep her distance from me. These spells are her tantrums." I cried out again, rocking to a stop. Felt like someone lit a whip on fire and lashed it across my skull. Reyna did not approve of the word "tantrum."

"She is quite unforgiving with you," Rosaleen mused. "I've tumbled many a new rider who wasn't put through this much pain."

We shuffled forward in the line, nearing ever closer to Golden City.

"Those riders were allowed to proudly boast and show off their new bonded dragons." I dropped my voice, looking around. "They had no fear of being killed on sight. Reyna saved my life, and sentenced me to death."

Rosaleen squeezed my hand, saying nothing. What could she say that hadn't been said by every commoner for a hundred years, ever since the new laws were handed down, banning us from bonding with dragons?

Dragons were wise, powerful beings with the ability to set a city ablaze all at the command of their human. Such power did not belong in the hands of the weak, the infirm, the poor, the lazy, and the uneducated. Especially because when one such commoner was given that power, that is exactly what she did... set Golden City ablaze.

Ever since the revolution, peasants were allowed nowhere near dragons, but if one poor human peasant had the misfortune of being chosen by a dragon anyway, the Renders corrected the creature's mistake. Only two ways to break the bond between dragon and rider. Either the dragon chose to end the bond of their own free will, or the human died.

The Royal Renders roamed the country, carrying out option two.

"There's no use mourning what isn't," Rosaleen said. "Yes, this seems a misery now, but think of what could be. When you complete training, you'll have a proper home and a salary that'll care for the orphanage. Your brothers and sisters will want for nothing. And, because it needs to be said, you'll be a dragon rider, Ainsley. Do you know what everyone we know would give if they could fly away from all this?"

I hugged my best friend, pressing my cheek to hers. It was as smooth and lovely as the rest of her, bringing shame to my dry, river-washed skin. One could only count their flaws when they stood next to Rosaleen. She was the kind of beauty you looked at again and again, and always found something new to admire.

From her unending curves, trickster's smirk, bottomless green eyes, and ebony curls forever smelling of honey and jasmine, it was no surprise that even when I made an effort and wore my single nice dress, my bony form, stringy blonde hair, and too-big eyes didn't get a second glance from the men that flocked us when we went out.

Even so, I was half of me without her. We'd been inseparable since we were three. Rosaleen did not grow up in the orphanage with me, though she was an orphan too. She was taken in by an aunt who set her life on a different path.

We didn't speak as we moved up the line, our feet bringing us closer and closer to Golden City. Breaking free, two children chased a small wooden dragon across the dirt, laughing as one of them used her earth magic to make it rear on its hind legs and dance.

I looked over their heads to a woman gathering the wind, letting it cool her and the man whose arm was around her. Past them, a water-user kept the heat at bay with a fine spray of mist shooting from his palm.

None of it was particularly strong or thrilling magic, but it was magic. Far more than had ever graced me.

"Oh no." Rosaleen smoothed the wrinkle between my brow. "What are you overthinking now?"

"I was simply wondering how they'd do it. Firing squad? Arrow through the heart? Have a dragon lift me above the city and then let go? It'll surely be one of the above after they discover that not only am I an impostor, but that..."

I thought of all the doors slammed in my face. Of the shopkeepers and pub owners who laughed in my face. Of the wailing sobs I cried on Sister Aven's shoulder when she had to sit me down and tell me the truth.

"I have no magic."

"Ainsley," she hissed. Rosaleen snapped around, making sure no one heard. "You believed you didn't but now we know that can't be true. Dragons can't bond with the magicless. The bond is magic itself. You must have some kind of firepower, or Reyna wouldn't have chosen you. Now is your chance to discover what it is."

"Fire magic doesn't exactly hide itself, Rosie. Besides, I've tried for weeks to summon something—*anything*—and nothing happens."

"It will," she said firmly. Her optimism continued to astound me. "Give it time."

"I shall give it ten minutes." The gates loomed before us. "That is when this charade comes to an end."

One by one, the common folk passed by the watchful eyes of the Golden Guards, flashing their bands for judgments. Peasants were not allowed to set foot in the royal city unless they had business there, and that business was inked on their right forearm. A green band for household staff—maids, cooks, and gardeners. A purple band for entertainers—dancers, comedians, acrobats. And a blue band for Rosaleen—

Whore.

"We didn't have a choice," Rosaleen said, unnecessarily rolling up the sleeve of her sheer dress. The gauzy material gave a clear view to the spiderwebbing lingerie that served as her underclothes. "Only a royal or noble can be a dragon rider, and in all of Adalinda, there is only one royal line unaccounted for. You can hardly show up and say you're the long-lost, illegitimate daughter of General Ivo. We needed origins that can't be traced."

"Yes, I know this, but still," I whispered as she flashed her arm and was let through with a nod.

"Wait, stop." A golden gauntlet dropped in front of my face, bringing me up short. "You have no band. Out of the line, peasant."

I darted from the guard's unsmiling, bearded face to Rosaleen's huge, beseeching eyes.

Say what I told you, she mouthed. *Do it!*

Steadying myself, I raised my chin. "Who are you calling peasant, boy?"

His eyes bugged. "Excuse me?" He scrambled for his sword. "How dare—?"

"How dare *you*?" I was proud of my voice for not trembling. "Know your place, pet soldier. You stand in the presence of—" I flicked to Rosaleen, standing on the edge of the moment that would change everything.

I straightened, looking him in the eye. Royalty doesn't slouch.

"You stand in the presence of Princess Ainsley, descendant and lost heir of Queen Kisandra, ruler of Adalinda."

Chapter Two

The tips of my shoes skidded over the cobblestone path, when they weren't hanging in the air. I ordered the guards a dozen times to put me down and let me walk on my own, but my cries fell on uncaring ears. Their grips were iron around my arms, lifting and carrying me through Golden City.

All my life I dreamed of what existed beyond the twenty-foot stone wall that separated Golden City from my town. My dreams did not include this.

"Put me down. I'm not resisting. I will go with you willingly."

No acknowledgment that they heard a word I said.

I blew out a breath and glanced behind me, searching for Rosaleen. I caught her darting under a shop's awning. It wouldn't do for the guards to know we were together.

A growing doom crowded my chest, stealing the air from my lungs, and forcing the sense back into my brain. Desperation turns even the wisest into a fool. This lie was my only hope to enter dragon training and learn to control my bond with Reyna. It was my only choice, and of course it wasn't going to work.

What did I think would happen when I announced I was the long-lost heir to the throne? The guards would bow, kiss my feet, and summon a litter to carry me to the palace?

Rosaleen spent far more time around royals and nobles than I did—though they were unclothed at the time. She spent two months teaching me their ways and mannerisms. She drilled all she knew of Golden City and the Royal Rider Military Academy into my head. All to keep her best friend alive long enough for two guards to carry me through the city to my execution.

I choose death by height. Let a dragon carry me to the heavens and drop me. A grim smile twisted my lips. *At least for a moment, I'll fly.*

The three—*four*—of us wound through the twisting streets, converging on the citadel. We passed curious glances and raised brows as we went, drawing as much attention as they were getting from me.

Golden City was night and day the town that was my home. In Ossian, the townsfolk dressed in simple, comfortable fare with nary even a wedding band to call jewelry. They were made blander in comparison to the wealth and riches around me. Every person I laid eyes on was adorned in silver rings, gold necklaces, shiny circlets, and heavy jeweled earrings.

Golden City was not made out of gold—anymore. When Queen Kisandra and the House of Boreen ruled, the city was a shining monument on the horizon, seen for miles around. Then, the traitor attacked and burned everything to the ground. No one knows what happened to the queen amid the carnage. Some say she escaped and went into hiding. Most say she died.

All I knew was the city that sprang up in the ashes of the wreckage was no less grand.

Fancy shops spilled out with laughing, pampered nobles. We passed by a group of women perusing a storefront that was all shoes. Not the weathered, leather sandals that adorned my feet, but strange ones that covered the entire foot, and boasted useless baubles and flourishes.

My escort took me around an eatery. A proper one where they sat at tables under the sun and food was cooked and brought to them. The closest I'd come to that was Sister Aven slicing and sharing out the bread I stole from the market that day.

The last time anyone cooked a whole meal for me was when I was a child. I couldn't conceive of having so much coin, I could pay someone to do what my own two hands were perfectly capable of.

The deeper into the city we went, the more displays of wealth blew my brows further up my forehead. Jewelry shops, dress shops, shoe shops, dance halls. Just a few miles away was a whole different world.

I stopped struggling as we neared the citadel gates.

"Open," the guard barked.

They carried me through to a courtyard milling with people.

No, not just people.

I swept over a crowd of varying sizes, ethnicities, and genders, but all sharing one thing in common. A teardrop mark.

Dragon riders.

That day marked the first day of training. Rosaleen and I hoped those in charge would be too overwhelmed with the hundreds of newly bonded nobles traveling in from all over the kingdom to devote too much time verifying one peasant's lie. I was about to discover if our gamble would pay off.

I peered over my shoulder one last time, watching the gates close on the flash of ebony that was Rosaleen.

I was on my own.

Inside, the men carried me up a flight of stairs. I had no earthly idea where we were going. They stopped speaking to me after I ordered them to bow and let their princess pass.

"—not possible!"

Crash!

I jerked, head snapping to a room on the right.

"How are you going to stop me?"

The door flew open, nearly taking my face off. Storming out, our eyes met.

My chest squeezed, and not just because another blast of pain soared through the bond, scrunching my muscles tight. I was certain as my blurred vision enveloped him, I had and would never behold someone so gorgeous in this life or the next.

Amber eyes flecked with gold raked me up and down. Full, dusky lips flattened, no doubt taking in my plain, worn dress; raggedy shoes; and lack of shiny baubles. He himself had much less than the nobles we passed on the way in.

A single diamond stud in one ear and a dragon cuff on the other was all the puffery he allowed himself. The rest of him—gray pants; tight, sleeveless tunic; and black-scaled boots—said utilitarian in every stitch.

I lingered on his boots for a second, then was quickly drawn back to his face. Sharp cheekbones and a firm square jaw, one could cut themselves caressing him.

The thought went through my head and heated my cheeks. The stranger frowned like he read my mind.

"What's this?" he demanded.

"A commoner, sir. She claims she's Queen Kisandra's lost heir."

"What? Queen Kisandra?" He looked me up and down, lingering on my dragon's mark. "Ridiculous. She's obviously lying because she'll be put to death for bonding to a dragon without royal or noble blood."

I stiffened. He saw through me so quickly, I wondered if the truth was written on my face.

"We suspected as much, sir," the guard replied. "We thought it best to bring her to the commandant and let him sort it out. He may wish to make an example of the peasant. Make sure none of the others make the mistake of claiming royal blood to escape their crimes."

A chill climbed my spine. I did not wish to discover what it meant to make an example of me.

"I see," the stranger said. He bent and pressed his forehead to mine, shooting my heart into my throat. "Goodbye, little trickster." His breath was warm and minty on my lips. "I respect the attempt, if not the execution. *Latumire.*"

Farewell.

My tongue stumbled over a reply. He walked off before I got a word out. He so easily sent me off to my grave, as if there wasn't a question that I was a liar minutes away from meeting my end.

The guards brought me inside, making the man behind the desk look up. Face handsome, but grizzled—a long, vicious scar raked from his crown to his chin, tugging his mouth down on one side. It was difficult to guess his age. He could be forty or one hundred and forty. A dragon bond slowed normal aging.

Finally, I was released and dropped in a seat.

"What's this?" asked the commandant, echoing the stranger. "The Royal Roll begins shortly. I don't have time to hear how this recruit is particularly special, and her parents request that I hold her hand through training."

"She's a peasant, Commandant. A peasant who claims she should be allowed to join the recruits because she's Princess Ainsley. The daughter Queen Kisandra gave birth to after fleeing into hiding during the revolution."

"No." The commandant whipped his coat off his desk chair and strode off. "She's lying to escape punishment. Send her to the Renders."

The guards hauled me up, toppling the chair.

"I'm not lying, and I can prove it!"

His footfalls didn't slow.

"I'll submit to any questioning you choose. They say those bonded to blood dragons have magics that let them tell a lie from the truth. Have them test me. They'll tell you I am who I say I am."

"I'll not have you waste their time, girl. Take her away."

"What are you so afraid of?" I yanked out of their grip. "If the Heart Readers deem me a liar, the result is the same. If they say I'm telling the truth, then you'll be saved from making a huge mistake and ending the life of your queen's heir.

"Or is that your goal? To kill your sovereign? You've grown proud and rich in her absence, and you won't stand to answer to her descendant about why I had to come to you, when you should've spent your life looking for me.

"Traitor."

Commandant ground to a halt.

"Treasonous rebel. My mother would weep for what has become of her kingdom."

Slowly, he turned to face me. I locked my knees, refusing to let them shake. Refusing to let them buckle. Never in all my days did I want to inspire the expression on his face again.

"I will give you one chance to take that back, girl."

Hold firm, Ainsley. Everything is going to plan so far. Rosaleen said I must do and say everything it takes to get before a Heart Reader. If I didn't, I was dead.

I lifted my chin. "I will take it back *after* I speak to the Heart Reader."

He stared at me for so long, sweat stained the raised hairs on the back of my neck.

"Very well," the commandant said. "Danvers, fetch Master Whelan. On your way, tell the recruits there's been a delay, and tell them why." He trapped my gaze in humorless pools. "Either our blessed princess has returned to us, or today marks the first execution of the season."

Chapter Three

"Do you understand the consequences of lying to me?"

Master Whelan both was and wasn't what I expected. The air of power, refinement, and seriousness—yes. The bright-pink tunic and more of those odd, overly embellished shoes—no.

"I do," I replied. "Believe me, sir, I've waited a long time to tell my story. I'm ready to begin when you are."

It was just me, Master Whelan, and the commandant in his office. Master Whelan was surprisingly kind. He invited me to sit on the couch, and offered me tea he poured himself.

Master Whelan leaned back, smiling at me over the rim of his teacup. "We've already begun. Tell me about yourself, Ainsley."

I swayed, body feeling heavy. The elixir I knew he'd put in my drink began to take effect. "I am Ainsley. I'm twenty years old and from a town called Ossian."

"Who are your parents?"

My reply was immediate.

"My mother is Queen Kisandra," I said, tone flat. "I do not know my father."

Whelan and the commandant exchanged looks. "Who gave birth to you, Ainsley?"

"Queen Kisandra of House Boreen."

"When?" Commandant snapped.

"Twenty years ago. I am twenty."

"You expect us to believe Queen Kisandra has been in hiding all this time? Why wouldn't she have returned to reclaim her throne?"

"Commandant, please." Whelan leveled a mild smile on him. "If you'd allow me..."

Growling, he agitatedly flapped a hand for him to continue.

"What proof do you have of your parentage?"

"I have no proof," I said honestly. "I was abandoned in the forest when I was a babe. A kind woman found and cared for me. Tucked in my swaddling was a letter explaining who I am—"

"Where is this letter?" Whelan and the commandant asked at once.

"Gone. It burned in the fire that took my adoptive mother's life."

"Unfortunate." Whelan cocked his head, studying me. "Did this letter explain why our queen did not return after the usurper was killed?"

"No."

His brows drew together. "Did it explain why she left her heir in the woods to die?"

"I expect because I was a disappointment to her. Most parents do not welcome the arrival of a magicless child."

A hard, pressing silence filled the room. My gaze was calm and unfocused.

"You have no magic?"

"No."

"But you bear the dragon mark?"

"Yes."

"A dragon chose you despite having no magic?" he repeated, for his clarification or my own, I did not know.

"Yes."

"Impossible."

"No."

Master Whelan's kind smile was rapidly disappearing. I could tell he did not believe me, even though his own magic said I wasn't lying. "How can that be?"

Again, I answered honestly. "I don't know."

"This makes no sense," Whelan said to the commandant. "She is answering truthfully but... she can't be."

"Her having no magic would explain why Queen Kisandra did away with her. A powerless bastard is a smear on the House of Boreen. Nothing short of proof that the line is cursed." He spoke like his callousness was mere fact. "But then again, she can't be powerless if a dragon chose her. I suspect her magic level is so low, it took more concentration and discipline than she possessed to access it. Rider training will solve that."

"Does this mean you'll accept her among this season's recruits? From her own lips, Queen Kisandra rejected our supposed princess. She clearly did not intend for her to rule."

"I do not want to rule," I spoke up, drawing their attention back to me. "I want to train and learn to control the bond. Such is my right as a dragon-marked royal."

"Then, I have one last question. Have you come here under false pretenses with a fairy story of queens and princesses to cover your true station as a common peasant and dragon thief?"

"No. I am who I say I am. An abandoned child... who wants to learn to fly."

He flicked off me. "What say you, Commandant? She is completely truthful."

"The general must know of this."

"Yes."

"He will wish to question her himself."

Whelan nodded.

"But."

Hope soared. Days bled into weeks while Rosaleen trained me to fool a Heart Reader. Slow my heartbeat, still my fidgety hands, maintain enough, but not too much eye contact. Again and again we practiced, our anxiety a growing ball in our chest knowing I had no way of testing it beforehand. I wouldn't know if my efforts paid off until my life was on the line.

I closed my eyes, sending silent thanks to my friend, and the Heart Reader that made such frequent visits to her bed, he deluded himself into thinking they were true lovers, and taught Rosaleen how to fool him so that he need never wake up from the lie.

"But," finished the commandant. "It is her right to train. Report to the courtyard, recruit, you're already late."

I jumped up, rushing to leave before he changed his mind.

"Although, let me say this." He stopped me in my tracks. "If I discover that you're an impostor, I will rend your head from your shoulders myself." His breath rolled over my ear. "That is my promise to you, *Princess* Ainsley."

I tore out, refusing to chance a reply. I was in. By the gods, our ridiculous, silly, impossible plan worked.

We did it, Reyna. Soon, my beauty, we'll be together.

THE COURTYARD WAS TWICE as packed when I returned. I fixed on the gates, wondering if Rosaleen was still on the other side, awaiting news of if our gamble worked.

"—dragon finally took pity on you in the end, eh?"

Someone went flying across my vision. I reacted instinctively, catching them before they hit the ground.

"Wager it was a fire dragon. A common peasant beast for the useless piece of trash. How fitting."

I followed the nasty voice to a group of guys. It was the jewelry that drew my attention first. Diamond-, emerald-, and ruby-crusted rings on every finger. Jeweled studs through their lips, ears, and brows. Gold chains and bands around their necks and arms.

I quickly put it together. *Status.*

Only nobles and royalty were allowed to live in Golden City. They all had station of birth. They all had money, so naturally, they needed another way to put themselves above each other. Going by the obscene number of jewels the group was wearing compared to the guy they were tossing around, I found who ranked higher in the rider order.

"Are you ok—?"

The guy shoved away and ran off. I flicked from his retreating back to his tormentors. It was impossible not to think of Fionn, Verlin, and Tavis. They gave me the same lip-curling sneer. I was not wearing any jewels.

"Is there something you'd like to say?" The leader of their group spoke. I knew from his finery to the way the other guys seemed to fan around him, keeping him the center point.

Wavy, brown locks fell to his brow, shading surprising light, silver eyes. He was handsome by anyone's definition. Unnaturally gorgeous by more than a few.

"Hello? I said, do you have something to say?"

I shrugged. "Nope. Maybe I will when you become worth my time." Spinning around, I walked off.

"What the fuck did she just—? Hey! Hey, come back here."

A snort sounded to my right. Actually, more than one. Covering their faces, half a dozen recruits smothered laughs at my reply. Seemed my initial judge of character was correct. This wasn't a nice guy.

"Recruits, fall in."

I pitched forward—buffeted on all sides by recruits hurrying to the front of the courtyard. By the time I straightened, nine neat lines formed before the commandant.

"Princess," drawled the commandant, "deign to join us, or should we move on your time?"

Tips of my ears heated as everyone turned to see who he was speaking to. I quickly took my spot at the end of the line.

"Good morning, recruits. Welcome to your first day of training."

I burst into applause, cheering. No one else joined in.

Quickly, I dropped my hands but not fast enough to avoid the cold glare from the commandant. I'd been in Golden City for a whole hour and already made my first enemy.

"I see you could not wait for introductions, so allow me. Recruits, you are standing in the presence of Princess Ainsley of the House of Boreen, the only known heir of our lost sovereign, Queen Kisandra."

All eyes flew to me.

"What did he say?"

"Princess?"

"It can't be. Everyone knows she and the royal family died during the revolution."

"It appears not," Commandant Drake said, eagle ears picking up the whispers. "In direct contrast of everything we've concluded after decades of searching and investigating, the young princess tells us that our queen survived the inferno that destroyed the city and slaughtered thousands, only to give birth and abandon her almost a hundred years later."

The scorn in his voice was so clear, I wondered why he didn't skip to the part where he called me a lying bitch.

"Princess Ainsley, please, come up and address your subjects."

I started. "Oh— Uh, okay, sir."

"Get back in line!"

I ran back, face on fire as raucous laughter belted out of the recruits. That was my fault. It was hard for me to pick out the sarcasm amid the disdain.

"As I was saying, welcome to your first day of training," he repeated. "For those who do not know, I am Commandant Drake. You may address me as Commandant Drake or sir."

"Yes, sir!"

"None of you are green. You know what will be expected of you in the coming months. You've all trained and sacrificed to be here, but there's one truth you can't escape: someone must be first, and someone must be last."

A grim silence swept over the crowd, the effect of those words taking hold. I stood there nonplussed.

Someone must be first and last? Why bother stating something so obvious?

"If you'd like to leave—choose death instead of the glory and honor of serving Adalinda—that is your right. You may go now."

No one moved.

"Excellent." Something akin to approval bled into his voice. "You have chosen correctly, for no matter how your journey ends, you've picked the path of duty, loyalty, and sacrifice. There's no greater honor than serving Adalinda, and there's no higher reward than doing it alongside the great and terrible creature that dubbed you worthy above all else.

"Congratulate yourselves. You are dragon riders."

The recruits burst into applause, whooping and cheering. Happiness swelled in my chest. I didn't know what would happen, but anything was better than living under the cloud of fear and pain I survived the past several weeks. Forced to keep my distance from Reyna and her making me cry for it all the while.

I had a chance now. A chance to earn coin and provide for my two dozen foster brothers and sisters. A chance to do more with my future than steal from people who had one. I was never going back, or giving up. The citadel was where I was meant to be.

I'm a dragon rider.

"You will enter through those gates into the arena," the commandant announced. "Your first test begins now."

The recruits turned as one and marched through the gates. One didn't start dragon rider training until they bonded with a dragon.

Or at least that's what I thought. Knowing when to speak and when not to. Falling into formation without hesitation. The understanding on their faces while cluelessness was written all over mine. Everyone here knew what to expect... except me.

Following behind, I trailed my recruit class into the stadium. We filled the seats, surrounding a massive stone platform. I claimed a space off to the side by myself. I felt their eyes on me. I didn't want to know what they were whispering about the long-lost princess.

"Hey."

I glanced up as a guy with short, coarse hair and thin wire glasses dropped beside me. I knew him from the twenty minutes before when he was in my arms.

"Thanks for your help back there. Sorry I ran off like that."

"Don't have to apologize. The glare coming off that group was blinding. I ran away from them too."

"I'm Poet." Over his shoulder, two people broke off and headed our way. "A pleasure, Princess."

"Just call me Ainsley."

"If you don't mind, is what Drake said true? Are you—?"

"Shame on you, Poet." A hand clapped his shoulder. "Don't interrogate the girl." Long, reddish-gold hair; a round nose; and top-heavy lips smiled at me. "Although you should get used to it. Everyone who isn't talking about you now, will pick up the conversation later. Queen Kisandra's daughter returned."

Poet gestured behind him. "This is—"

"His favorite lay, Maili."

"I wasn't going to say that," Poet cried.

"I know," Maili teased, dropping a kiss on his cheek. "That's why you're my favorite lay. Such a gentleman."

I watched the display curiously. Orphans were scorned by society—noble and commoner alike. Some of the hatred I endured was due to old superstitions about curses and catchable misfortunes. Anyone so wretched that their mother took one look at them at birth, and cast them out to die, must be a harbinger of bad luck.

Some people believed that, but all of them saw me as a worthless drain on society—doubly so because I had no magic. None of my lovers, the few that I could count on one hand with fingers left over, were eager to announce they were tumbling me.

I didn't know what it was like to not be someone's secret. I was even Reyna's secret.

"This is my twin," Maili continued, introducing the companion who shared her face from the curve of her brow to the tiny mark above her lip. Their only difference was their hair was shorn close to the scalp. "You can call them Ormr."

"Good to meet you both."

Maili and Ormr joined us and gave Poet assistance in his task of staring at me. Nervousness rolled down the back of my neck. Thieves did not like this much attention on them.

"Mind if I ask you something?" I spoke up. "The guy that shoved you, what was he saying about fire dragons?"

Poet scoffed. "That guy's name is Keir. Total bastard. He turns everything into a competition, including who has the best dragon."

"The best dragon?"

"Yeah." Maili leaned around Poet. "Apparently, the rarer, the better. Fire dragons are the most common because they breed easily. They build their nests on mountaintops and inside volcanoes, so predators can't get at them. Not like sea dragons who have to defend their babies from all kinds of creatures down there. Or sand dragons who bury them and leave. Egg thieves dig up the nests, kill the babies, and sell the pieces of their smashed shell. They're made of pure jadeite."

I knew this unfortunately. People came to Ossian for more than the brothels and cheap pubs. If you knew where to go, a thriving underground market sold everything you'd receive a death sentence for possessing, from stolen eggs to human beings.

"So bonding with a sand dragon who was fortunate enough to survive the slaughter of their kind and grow to adolescence somehow makes you better than other riders?"

She shrugged. "According to more than just Keir, yes."

"That's completely stupid."

Ormr barked a laugh. "No argument from us. My Kenna is a sky dragon, second most common. I don't care that she has thousands of cousins. I'd sooner cut off my limbs than be parted from her."

"Silence, recruits!"

All conversations ceased in an instant. Sister Aven would give anything to learn the commandant's tricks.

"I will be brief for those who don't know." Drake looked right at me. "In the academy, you live and die by your rank. You will be assessed in these categories: battle readiness, magical accuracy, teamwork, scholarship, and special talents.

"Today is your first test in teamwork. One by one, you will step up here and summon your dragon through the bond. Sending your requests and commands telepathically is the simple part. Getting your dragon to respond is a different matter.

"Dragons are well aware that they are the superior being in the relationship. They hear your request to come, and ignore it if they're so inclined. Why not? They know your thoughts and emotions. They know you're not in danger, so why disturb their rest? But if your dragon is routinely in the habit of ignoring you, that is a failure on your part.

"It is your duty to build trust and respect with your bonded. We will find out if you've done that work today. If you haven't, you will start out with five demerits in *every* category. I have no tolerance for laziness."

Protests went up around the stadium.

"But, sir!"

Drake spun and zeroed in on the recruit. "Yes, Rider Giolla? You were about to demonstrate what I do to the insubordinate?"

Giolla sat down hard. "No, sir. Thank you, sir."

"Then, let's begin." Drake stepped off the stage and fell in beside two people I hadn't noticed before. By their uniforms and no-nonsense appearance, I assumed they were instructors. "First, Keir of House Stryker."

Poet's tormentor took his place on the stage. I wasn't kidding when I said the man was blinding. Sunlight fractured through his many jewels, making me squint.

Keir simply stood there, looking at us.

"When is he going to— Ahh!" I shrieked and flung myself back, landing none too gently on my ass.

My noise swung his massive, obsidian head around. He roared—blowing my skirt up and flattening my ears against my skull. Ormr, Maili, and Poet clapped their hands over their heads, screaming. Our shrieks only served to further enrage the sixty-foot-tall dragon that appeared within the puff of a breath.

I was a speck before his terrifying magnificence. Reyna was the only dragon I'd seen up close. All others were dots flying in the sky, far above the dirt-smeared girl hanging off a tree branch, knowing this was as close as I'd ever be.

This creature was nothing like my girl. He was slim where she was bulky—if such an adjective could be given to a dragon that was a hundred times my size. His nose was both wider and flatter. No horns sat atop his head, but instead protruded from the bends in his arms and legs. He was absolutely beautiful, and he was going to kill us all.

Rearing up, the dragon's claw raked the air, coming straight for—

The sun burned my eyes, its obstruction gone. Whipping around, the dragon was nowhere to be seen.

"Apologies," Keir said, smirking. "Suoh doesn't like crowds. Or noise. Or inferiors."

Maili helped me up. "At least this explains his insufferableness this summer. Keir bonded with a shadow dragon. The rarest of all."

"Sh-shadow dragon?" Every one of my limbs was shaking. "I've never heard of those."

"They're incredible," Ormr said. "They can fly, but they don't need to. They travel through shadows of any size. An army of them would be unstoppable. There's nowhere the enemy could hide."

"But they're extremely irritable," Poet put in. "There're so few of them because they are known to kill their mates, offspring, and riders at the slightest provocation."

I had no words. Reyna flicked me off like a gnat every time I tried to climb on her back, breaking my leg twice and my wrist once. Even so, I knew she was being gentle with me. If she truly wanted to hurt me, she'd have torn my head off. I couldn't imagine regularly fending off a dragon that would kill me for sneezing too loud.

"Rafferty of House—"

"Sit down. I'm next."

I recognized the next person climbing the platform. The heart-squeezingly handsome stranger who sent me off to my death with an honored farewell.

His muscles rippled beneath too-tight clothes, giving my eyes too many places to look. It was hard to categorize the look on his face, the set of his broad shoulders, or the slight curve of his lips when he stood up and looked directly at me.

"Dominic, I made myself clear," Drake belted. "You cannot join this season's recruits. Get off the stage now."

He didn't spare him a glance. We were locked in a stare-down that dampened my collar. "I will not."

My brows jumped up my forehead. I knew Commandant Drake for a short time, and even I knew that was an unwise thing to say to him.

"I am Dominic of House Roark."

I froze. *Roark? As in King General Roark?*

"I am not bonded anymore, but it doesn't matter. My dragon will soon return to me. Until then, start me off with as many de-merits as you wish."

One of the other instructors stepped forward. "Dominic, be reasonable. You cannot complete *dragon* rider training without a dragon. If you join the recruits, you will be held to the same stan-dards if you fail. You are needlessly throwing away your life."

"Impossible. I could be bonded with a broomstick and I'd still best everyone here. My skills are far above this class of recruits and their instructors. You'll all be learning from me in the end."

My jaw dropped. What the fuck was wrong with this guy?

"Arrogant son of a bitch," Maili muttered. "I wish I wasn't cursed to find that so sexy. No offense, Poet."

"I wasn't offended until your last sentence."

I almost laughed, but I couldn't. Dominic wouldn't let me. A mad statement, but there it was. I could do nothing while he trapped me in his amber seas.

"Very well, boy." The chill in the commandant's voice dropped the temperature thirty degrees. "Far be it from me to deny a man his choice of death."

He tossed a vague nod in his direction, then walked off the platform… toward me. I stopped breathing as his body claimed my personal space—his arm brushing against me.

"I see you survived, Princess."

I think I said something in reply. I couldn't be sure. How did someone like me react when held under the sway of King General Roark's son? Because he could only be his son. The very man who, during fifty years of subjugation and tyranny under the rebel traitor, survived the slaughter of his entire battalion and faced the usurper in a final battle.

He won that day, and wrested control of Adalinda under the military with himself at the top of the hierarchy. It was General Roark who outlawed commoner dragon riders. It was he who walled off Golden City, began a campaign to conquer neighboring lands, and increased taxes so high, the gap between rich and poor grew too wide for a sea dragon to swim across it.

"Ainsley of House Boreen!"

I hurried onto the platform—torn between happy to escape Dominic's orbit, and nervous to stand before the recruits. I very decidedly gave Dominic and Commandant Drake my back.

Taking a deep breath, I closed my eyes. *Reyna, it's time. Come to me. My beauty.*

Pain exploded behind my eyes. Crying out, I dropped to my knees.

"Uh ho." Keir's nasty voice grated. "No control, Princess? Even children learn how to stop the bond from hurting them after a week."

I gritted my teeth. If that was true, I had no idea how. What I did know is that I'd done something wrong. Irritation rolled through the bond. Reyna wasn't pleased with me.

Reyna, please. I'm sorry for disturbing you. You've waited so long to leave the forests of Ossian behind. Now is your chance.

Nothing.

What she did or did not feel about my plea, I had no idea. Nothing came through the bond.

A minute passed.

Five.

Ten.

The chuckles got louder.

"Our great and wonderful princess returned can't even get her bonded dragon to obey her." Insufferable was the right word to describe Keir Stryker. "Good news for you, Roark. Your father should have no fear of her taking the throne."

"Will you be silent?" I snapped. "Couldn't summon a breath with all your racket."

Keir shouted something back, but I wasn't listening.

Please, Reyna. We can't start behind.

Again, I got nothing back. It was said that when the bond is fully formed, I'd be able to see through her eyes like she could do mine. Until then, I made due with vague emotions and assumptions. I had another one then.

She wasn't coming.

"Princess..."

I clenched my fists, knowing what was coming.

"That'll be five demerits. Take your seat."

I shuffled off, accepting the punishment. There was nothing I could've done. The last thing I thought to do the last eight weeks was summon the dragon that'd get me a death sentence. I was forced to hide Reyna in the woods, and sneak away to visit her every day.

Don't worry, my beauty. We will learn everything we need to catch up to the rest. Underestimating us will be the worst mistake they make.

I purposely sat down next to Ormr, putting three people between me and Dominic. His direct way of openly watching me made me feel like I had stolen coins burning in my pocket while the Watch Guards patrolled the market.

"Dizir of House—"

"Wait, sir," Maili cried. "Look there."

Following her line of sight, I shot to my feet. There in the distance, winging across the sky faster than I could track, was my Reyna.

I ran up the platform as she set down, shaking the ground. I couldn't believe it. She came to me.

"R—"

"Reyna?"

I tripped to a stop. "Reyna? How do you know my dragon's name?"

"*Your* dragon?"

"Oooh," Keir crowed. "Seems I have to take it back. We will have a new sovereign. What else could it mean when the dragon of General Roark's favored son, deems the princess more worthy than him?"

"What?" I said. "I don't understand."

Dominic's *everything* changed as he looked at me. The lines of his brow hardened. Gone was mild interest to be replaced by an expression I knew well. *Hatred.*

"Commandant," he began, "your reservations about my impending end can be put at ease. I won't be going through training without a dragon. I will reclaim mine... after I kill Ainsley Boreen."

Chapter Four

I sat on my bed, watching everyone unpack their stuff, speak to their new bunkmates, and openly gossip about the day's shocking news. Princess Ainsley, heir of Queen Kisandra, had returned, and was marked for death.

"Do you think he'll do it?"

"Of course," Rafferty said. "Wouldn't you? The woman stole his dragon, then showed up to steal his throne. Unlucky for the princess, during training is the only time he can kill her and it not be treason. Who you are doesn't matter in dragon training."

"Psst, Ainsley." Maili waved from the bed she was claiming—right next to me. "Don't let them worry you. Everything will be fine."

"Will it? I've had plenty of people tell me I should die and save the world the oxygen, but no one's ever offered to take care of that for me."

"It will." Poet tossed his stuff on the top bunk above Maili. "Dom was just surprised to see his dragon appear at your summons. I don't think he'll really kill you. I mean, that is the only way to break the bond if Reyna doesn't do it herself.

"Thinking about it, she would likely go back to him if you were out of the way. Second best becomes first again when the competition is gone," he said, inclining his head. "Dom was already humiliated when Reyna broke the bond and left. Now he discovers it was for the only one who could take the throne from him. It'll appear to everyone that the dragons are naming the true heir, especially if no other dragons choose him after this."

He looked up at me. "You've trained, right? Hand-to-hand, swordsmanship, magical mastery? You can handle yourself when he comes at you?"

"Now he is coming at me?" I cried. "You just said I didn't have to worry."

"I might be wrong."

"Poet, stop talking," Maili ordered. "Ainsley is going to be fine. Of course she didn't show up to the citadel without training. She'd have to have a death wish."

I looked away, fists balling the sheets. I didn't have a death wish. I was just painfully clueless. Nobles and royals had all the money in Adalinda to spend on tutors, masters, and trainers for their precious heirs. Of course they all showed up prepared to take everything the commandant threw at them. I was the only one who didn't know what the coming years would bring.

Ormr entered the bunk room carrying their pack. They tossed it on the bed above me. "What are we talking about?"

"Anything else," I said quickly to Poet and Maili. "Please."

"We're talking about this new demerit system," Maili said. "We have to think the rumors are true."

"The demerits are new?" I asked.

Ormr nodded. "They used to give us a test or challenge, and let nature take its course. Whoever got the highest scores or won the most bouts was the best. The end. Now demerits can sink the best and drag down their points."

"Knowing Drake, that's exactly what they'll do," Poet agreed. "The man's a taskmaster. He demands absolute perfection. Half the recruits are already starting in the negative, and it's the first day."

Poet was one of those recruits. His fire dragon, Valor, did not respond to his summons.

"But if the rumors are true, they have to train us harder. I heard—" Maili looked around, then gestured for us to come closer. "The forty-fifth Ryuku was sent to the Dark Border three weeks ago. None of them made it back alive. Reports say there's nothing left but pieces of them."

I gaped at her. "The Ryuku? But they're the elite squad. Trained to defend the Dark Border and prevent another Druk invasion."

"The Druks are getting stronger," she whispered. "Experimenting. Changing. They're deadlier than ever."

I don't think I could've heard worse news than if Drake walked through the door right then, said he knew I was a fraud, and where did I want my head buried after he lopped it off my shoulders?

Druks were our worst enemy. Even worse than lone, human-hating dragons that sometimes attacked unprovoked. It was all in their name. Druk was Adalindian for *abomination*.

"If they're getting stronger, we have to get stronger too," Ormr said. "We know what's at stake."

I glanced off through the window, gazing unseeingly at the sunset. Reyna was off making a new home in the royal forest, awaiting the arrival of the first official day of training same as me.

I wasn't completely ignorant. All I wanted was to live a peaceful life with her and the only family I'd ever known, but receiving free training and learning to control the bond came at a price. Reyna and I would pledge eternal service to General Roark and the army—joining the thousands of riders who protected the nation.

I could accept this. No one lived the life I did and came away with fantasies of fairness or getting something for nothing. But Druks—

Branches snapped and tore at me, enacting their revenge for disturbing their peace. Hard pants burned my chest and shredded my lungs. I stopped breathing long ago. Nothing came in after each ragged breath out. Maybe it was my body's defense—an easy death.

A dark mouth rose in the distance, beckoning me inside. I threw my body in the cave and plastered against the walls, sinking low as I muffled my sobs.

It couldn't be here. How was it here?! We were miles and miles from the Dark Border. Close to Golden City where they dare not come for fear of the riders. It just couldn't be here!

Thud—tck, tck, tck, tck. Thud—tck, tck, tck, tck.

I flattened against the wall, vision warping through my tears. Its feet came into view—horrid and unnatural, they turned toward me. Bending down, the creature smiled into my eyes.

"Hey— No, I'm sorry. I didn't know this was your bed."

Shaking free, I twisted around, landing on my other bunk neighbor in time to see him tossed across the room. Dominic picked up his pack and threw it after him.

The general's son dropped down on his bed—right next to me. My muscles tensed as he smiled, slow and deliberate, drawing my eyes to those oddly soft, dusky lips. I didn't know why it felt like he was seeing right through me to that scared little girl in the cave. Weak, alone, abandoned. I was no one's hero.

I was no princess.

Dominic could see it all. From our very first meeting, no matter that it was only hours ago, the two of us learned one truth—I did not fool him.

"Princess."

I swallowed, feeling the weight of descending silence in the room. We had everyone's attention as wholly as he had mine.

"Dominic."

I made up my mind on the spot.

"Can we talk in private?"

He smiled. "Of course. Nothing would give me more pleasure."

"Okay. Let's—"

"No," Ormr, Maili, and Poet blared at once, making me jump.

"She doesn't want to do that," Maili said quickly. "Long day. She's tired and doesn't know what she's saying."

I yelped. Maili tugged me off my bed onto hers.

"Are you insane?" she hissed. "During training is the only time he can publicly kill you and receive no punishment, but he can just as easily murder you with no witnesses around and claim it was self-defense."

"But you don't think he really meant that, do you?" I flicked at Dominic who hadn't taken his eyes off me for a second. "He wouldn't kill me to get Reyna back. Not when he can bond with another dragon at any time. I mean, riders who lose their dragons don't just go around murdering people."

It was known there were two ways to break a bond. The rider's death or a dragon's choice. Every now and then, a dragon left their rider for someone they deemed more worthy. Of course they did. Dragon riders were gifted a longer life, but our few extra hundred years didn't come close to the thousand-year span of a dragon. Once their rider was old, gray, and tired, the dragon moved on.

Sometimes they didn't wait that long, and left a young rider for reasons only they knew, but the case remained, it wasn't a reason to kill. A young rider had no reason to believe they wouldn't form a new bond sooner rather than later. And *this* rider—son of the most powerful man in Adalinda—must be holding back potential bonds through sheer force of will. A hundred dragons would choose him.

"It's not a reason to kill, except he announced to everyone that's exactly what he's going to do," she whispered. "How eager are you to find out if he's bluffing?"

Dominic stretched out on his bed, smiling away as if he read the thoughts going through my head.

"Sweet dreams, Princess."

I DID NOT HAVE SWEET dreams. My eyes snapped open at every rustle, snore, and shake, convinced Dominic was standing over me with the knife he'd bury in my gut. Each time he was a silent, unmoving lump on his mattress.

I trudged through the hall, following behind an animated Ormr and Maili.

"It's our first real day of training. Can you believe it?" Maili had an extra bounce in her step. "Years of training, studying, and waiting to be chosen. Now we're finally here."

I grunted.

"You okay?" Ormr asked. "You disappeared last night, then when you came back, I felt you toss and turn for hours."

"Sorry about that. I went out for drinks to celebrate, and maybe calm my nerves. Didn't work. Turns out, lying five feet next to your would-be assassin doesn't make for a restful night."

"You went out drinking?" Maili asked. "Don't tell me— Are you hungover?"

"Shh!" I flapped a hand, looking to see if anyone heard. Drinking during training was forbidden. Something Rosaleen didn't tell me until after my second pint. Wasn't her fault. She assumed like I did that our instructors would state expectations. Didn't bode well for me that all of my blunders were common knowledge to the other recruits. I saw a worrying number of demerits in my future.

"I'm not hungover. I just get headaches when I don't get enough sleep. I should get used to that now. I won't sleep at all with things the way they are."

If Dominic wanted to throw me off-center, it was working. Rosaleen and I were supposed to be celebrating the success of our impossible plan. I was alive. I was masquerading as the long-lost princess, sleeping in a real bed, and looking forward to a salary for the first time in my magicless life. I'd be able to buy food, clothes, and shoes for the children, and, if she'd let me, buy Rosaleen out of her contract.

It was a time for celebration in every way. Instead, Rosaleen and I drank too much while arguing and obsessing back and forth on if Dominic was truly going to do it, and what it meant that I made an enemy of the general's favorite son.

"This is not good, Ains," Rosaleen said. "I honestly don't see how it could be worse."

"But I'm not a threat to him. I'm not deluded enough to try and take the throne. I just want to train, learn to control the bond, and live my life in Ossian."

"That was before we found out Reyna left him for you." She leaned forward, dropping her voice in the noisy pub. "I never would've suggested you pretend to be Queen Kisandra's heir if I knew. It looks like you two are in competition, and Dominic is losing. Whispers are going to spread that the heir has returned. Everyone's going to be watching, waiting to see what you do.

"We've lived under military rule for a long time, and a tyrant's rule for longer than that. What happens if the people start wishing for a return to the old ways—when we were happy and prosperous. When we were free," she said, brushing a finger over the permanent tattoo that told the world her profession. "What happens if Reyna isn't the only one who chooses you."

Her words banged around in my headlong into the night and most of the morning while I got ready and dressed in the uniform that was left beside all our beds.

The three of us entered the mess hall and joined the breakfast line. I strained to see over Ormr's shoulders. Heavenly scents filled my nose, making my stomach contract with hunger. I couldn't remember the last time I ate to bursting. My painfully thin body couldn't remember either.

"Quick march, recruits," Drake ordered. He sat at the front of the room, eating his breakfast on a raised platform that bore down over the hall. "You have thirty minutes till you report to your first day of training."

Taking a tray, I covered it in eggs, bacon, turkey, sausage, beans, rice, a bowl of porridge, toast, fruit. Everything before me ended up on my plate.

"Princess."

I almost spilled it all on the floor. I turned and bumped into his chest. How had Dominic come up behind me so fast? The man moved like a python. You didn't know one was above you until it sprung from the tree, wrapping around your throat before you got out a scream.

"Roark."

Warm honey eyes traced my face as if committing every inch of it to memory. I flushed and he stole that too, grin quirking up his lip like he knew the exact effect he had on me. It wasn't my fault. I wasn't used to anyone but my siblings and Sister Aven paying this much attention to me.

Those eyes came closer, filling my vision as Dominic erased the distance between us—and there was barely any of that to begin with.

Breath trapped in my lungs. His lips were so soft and inviting, and they were coming straight for mine. I trembled under the minty heat breaking through his parted lips and tickling me.

Eyes fluttering shut, I puckered my lips.

Crunch.

I snapped open as Dominic took a bite of his apple. The polished silver goblet on my tray reflected my blooming red cheeks.

"That friend of yours is cute," Dominic said. "What's her name? Where does she work?"

It took a minute for my brain to catch up. "Friend? You mean Maili?"

"No, the friend you snuck away in the middle of the night to meet. The tumbler."

A roaring sounded in my ears. "You— You followed me? But you were asleep in your bed when I returned."

He smirked. "Was I?"

Thinking back, I saw a mound under a sheet. No telling if a person was under there.

"So?" he pressed, voice as tempered and smooth as the hand that grasped my waist, moving me from the line and out of the way. "Who is she? Did she help you fabricate the lie that you're Queen Kisandra's daughter?"

Panic tightened my grip. Why did he keep doing that? Seeing right through me.

"It's not a lie. Commandant Drake brought me before a Heart Reader. Don't you trust Master Whelan?"

"I trust that you're smart enough to know your story would be tested in every way, so you came prepared."

I needed to move the conversation away from this topic. "The woman you saw me with wasn't a friend. We just met last night and got to talking. That's it."

"You were having quite an intense conversation with someone you just met."

"That's because we were talking about sex," I blurted. "I told her the best position is on top. She said it's on the knees and from the back. Then she went on about it being a bore when they tie you up and you can't participate in the fun, but I love it when I'm doing the tying."

Shut up. Shut up, shut up, shut up!

"Nothing like having a big, strong, sexy man at my mercy." *Dearest Zaeah, mother of dragons, let the earth open up beneath my feet and swallow me.* "It pissed her off that I wouldn't bow to her experience, but I've never been one to back down from a fight, Roark." I put extra pressure on his name.

"I see. So if I'm understanding you correctly, after lying and deceiving your way into rider training with a stolen dragon, you flouted curfew to go out drinking and argue with a random tumbler about sex positions?"

He hummed, nodding to himself. "I like this. Makes it much easier."

"What does?"

"That you're a terrible liar."

"I'm not lying," I said. "Now, why don't you answer some of my questions? Like why you were stalking me through the city in the middle of the night?"

He shrugged, crunching on his apple. "I assumed you were going out to meet Reyna. I need to see her. Find out what you did to her to force her to break our bond."

"I didn't do anything," I cried. "She came to me. She saved me. I laid eyes on her for the first time after she chose me."

"More lies."

I blew out a breath. "There's nothing I can say to convince you, but I can reassure you. I love Reyna. She protected me when no one else would. Cared for me the way no one else can. As much as I can, I will care for her too. She'll be happy with me. Know that as you go on to bond with another dragon."

His calm mask cracked, anger finally bled through. "I will not bond with another dragon. Reyna's been mine since she hatched. I was the first person those eyes saw, and she chose me instantly. I raised her. I trained with her every day for eleven years, then she was just gone.

"I will find out what you did to her, so that no other lying commoners ever dare attempt the same trick. But if I do that before or after I kill you, makes no nevermind. Either way, I will get her back."

We stood there glaring at each other, sparks shooting off us like kaminari dragons.

"Dominic? Hey, Dom."

Rouge curls broke our eye contact. I backed up as a tall, sweet-smelling figure pushed between us. "Dom, there you are. What are you doing over here? Come sit with us."

Dominic let himself be dragged a few steps. Breaking away, he advanced on me so fast, I backed into the wall, squeaking as he planted his hands on either side of my face and—

His lips crashed on mine, swallowing my cry. All the stupid silly thoughts in my head of his soft lips and calloused hands blew out of my head. The real thing was so much better.

Sweet, tangy apple painted his mouth, mixing with the minty prickle of his toothpowder to introduce me to my new favorite flavor. Dominic brushed my chin, popping goose bumps up and down my arms.

Flattening against me, he knocked my tray to the floor. The whole of him was hot, hard, and firm against me. Trapping me. Giving me no way out if I had the thought to try. A firm, almost rough nip made me gasp, parting my lips. He plunged with no hesitation or permission.

Roaring, erupting, melting—heat hotter than Reyna's flames overwhelmed me. I grasped his jaw, pulling him closer still. Our tongues clashed in a furious battle, pulling feverish moans from the both of us.

"Dominic? Dom, what are you doing!"

His hands were everywhere, and I was no better. I teased his hardened pecs, tangled in his hair, boldly grabbed his ass.

My boot came down on my fallen food and went flying. Dominic caught and lifted me, wrapping my legs around his waist. I took back everything. It wasn't his chest that was hard and warm against me. That honor went to the firm and demanding cock between my legs.

I reached down between us.

"Whoa," he said, snagging my wrist. "I like the way you think, Princess, but we are in public."

I blinked at him, mind foggier than the bond's worst attack. *What was happening?*

"I thought you were puckering up for a kiss before, but I had to be sure. You want me," he dropped. "I assume that was your backup plan in case stealing my dragon didn't work. You'd steal me."

Sighing, he put me back on my feet. Reality was catching up to me faster than my dizzying daydreams.

"All right, listen, because you'll only get this offer once. You're a beautiful woman and I have working parts. Naturally, I'd jump at the first and every opportunity to bed you. If you'd started with your seduction game first, I might have been more amenable to your bid for power."

I couldn't have been more confused.

"You wanted to leave your bleak, commoner life behind, and figured your best chance was to steal a dragon and become a rider. It's not. This is your best chance. Return my dragon to me, drop out of training, and I will make you one of my wives."

My mouth hung open, gaping wider than my round eyes.

"Our wedding will make you a noble by marriage, and our children noble by right. You'll never have to return to what you're escaping from. To prove I'm serious, I'll write up a contract, seal it in blood, and have it witnessed by the High Council. All you have to do is give me back my dragon," he forced through gritted teeth.

"You did something to sever our bond, you can do the same to sever yours. You have twenty-four hours to make the right choice."

"I—"

He walked off, taking the woman who was shouting at us with him.

I stood there in a daze, suddenly noticing the dozens of pairs of eyes on me. What did I just do? Dominic kissed me and all sense flew out the window. None of my former lovers had such an effect on me—stealing my sense of time, touch, and sight, and keeping it wholly for themselves.

I rejoined the food line, looking anywhere but his direction.

The man offered to marry me— No, he offered to make me one of his wives. I'd fritter my days in a grand manor, raising his children, while he only deigned to visit when he wanted to make more. For that, I'd receive a handsome stipend from the royal treasury and need never worry about stealing food, or feeding my brothers and sisters again.

And all he wants in return is Reyna.

Pressure built in my temples. I hissed under a vicious lash of mental pain.

No need for that, Reyna. I spent zero seconds considering his offer. You're not for sale.

I filled up my tray again, then took it to a table near the center where Ormr and Maili waited.

Maili's brows were up to her hairline. "Were you and Dominic just—?"

"No. Absolutely not."

Smiling, she flashed me a knowing look. "You're a complicated woman, Ainsley."

Commandant Drake cleared his throat, asking for silence. He began instruction with the mess hall only half full.

"Good morning, recruits. Thus begins your first official day." He gestured beside him. "Seated next to me are your instructors. They will introduce themselves at the start of your classes..."

I listened with half an ear. My attention was on my meal.

I scarfed the eggs into my mouth, so light, fluffy, and perfectly seasoned. And the bacon—ah!

Meat was expensive. Unless I caught, skinned, and prepared the kill for Sister Aven, she wasn't spending hard-earned coin on meats that cost ten times as much as bread and porridge.

Now here I was with three different kinds of meat on my plate. What I'd give to bundle half the buffet up and take it to the kids. Niamh would love the sausage. Sister Aven was teaching her how to cook. The young girl had taken to savoring every bite of her food, trying to figure out the ingredients and spices used.

And Colm. He said almost every day that he'd sell a limb to eat something other than stale bread for once. He would drool over these offerings.

But he won't have to. Immediately after I receive my first pay, I'm showing up on the doorstep with a feast.

A hand came across my vision.

"What!" I snatched my plate away. "What are you doing? This is mine."

Ormr goggled at me. "I was... reaching for the salt."

I passed it over, and the pepper for good measure. Ormr shared a look with their sister. I could see the thought going through their heads.

Complicated woman.

"—in battle readiness," Drake was saying. "Your instructors will give deeper explanations throughout the day, but I do want to say this. Special talents has undergone a change. It is now considered an entry class into the Ryuku squad. Those in the top ten percent can begin training with the squad and joining them on assignments beginning their second year."

Excited whispers broke out. I saw nothing but happy and excited faces over this news. All I could think about was what Maili said the night before. The forty-fifth was obliterated. The best and strongest of riders was no longer a match for the Druks. They needed better and stronger to fill the ranks, and they needed them now.

"As you know, your rank is the final determiner in all things. This year, we've changed how we do things with the inclusion of demerits. I must also tell you that the criteria for continuing rider training has changed as well."

Ormr and Maili stopped eating, their forks halfway to their lips. Something in their expressions made me stop too.

"Before, you had to rank last in every category to be cut from training. Now you're only required to be ranked in the bottom ten percent in three."

"What!"

"Three?"

"Bottom ten?"

I blew back at the rush of shouts and arguing.

"But, sir." One of the guys I saw with Keir jumped up. "You can't be serious. This is ridiculous. You can't—"

"Ridiculous, you say? Tell me, Rider Lonan, why is it acceptable for riders to be deficient in any area, let alone three? Which skills are so beneath you that I should be required to let you slide by? Is it teamwork? Or scholarship. Yes, our riders don't need strong, curious minds. I should let our nation's last defense be made of ignorant fools. Don't you agree, Rider Lonan? Speak up, boy."

"No, sir," Lonan muttered. "Sorry, sir."

"Bottom ten in three," Drake barked. "And be lucky it isn't less."

"Yes, sir," everyone chorused. "Thank you, sir."

"That's all for now. You have exactly twenty minutes to finish breakfast and report to your first lesson. I'm sure I don't have to tell you that tardiness results in demerits."

I finished my food, got a second helping, finished that, then followed the first-year recruits to battle readiness.

"Welcome." Cold, piercing blue eyes set under protruding brow ridges and an unsmiling face swept over us. Captain Roan was one large mold of muscles on muscles stuffed into a skintight uniform. "In this class, you will not only learn hand-to-hand combat, but all methods of surviving without your bonded. If your dragon is killed in battle, you will not lie down, expose your belly, and wait to die. You will fight, and you will know how.

"Today, you will be assessed to determine your starting ranks. In other words, if you thought this would be an easy day, you were sorely mistaken. Today will determine if you spend the rest of training fighting your way to the top, or defending your title as best."

The undercurrent of excitement in the group was palpable. Everyone was ready to show off their skills.

"First pair, Dominic Roark and Lonan Silva. You have five minutes to pin your opponent or render them unconscious. Do not use magic."

Dominic and Lonan stepped onto the mat, shedding their uniform shirts as they went. I swallowed, lingering too long on Dominic's body for more than one reason. He was a mass of scars, including one, large vicious slash across his back that could only be from a dragon's claw.

Then I was looking at him for the other reason. He wasn't overly bulky like Captain Roan. Dominic's hard, fit body was both toned and slender. The difference between a blunt hammer and a finely honed blade—he was made for beauty and power.

I warmed under my collar thinking how easily he lifted and wrapped me around that body. Which was half as warm as I got recalling that he bluntly offered me that body, tied up in his unromantic proposal of marriage.

"Been waiting a long time for this, Roark." Lonan danced on his feet. "The fourteenth son of the fifteenth wife. Long-awaited golden child of Golden City."

Dominic stood arm-crossed and feet shoulder-width apart. Perfectly still... and, by his expression, bored.

"We're all going to be learning from you, huh?" Lonan laughed. "I'm gonna have so much fun making you cry in front of—"

"Begin!"

Lonan rushed the unmovable, stoic mountain that was Dominic Roark. Bellowing, he punched Dominic in the ribs.

Snapping to life, Dominic grabbed and twisted his wrist—forcing a shrieking Lonan's arm up the wrong way over his shoulder. Dominic smashed his fist in his face and drove it all the way down, bouncing Lonan's skull off the mat.

He was up and striding off before blood from his broken nose hit the canvas. Lonan was out cold.

"Holy mother of dragons," Maili hissed. "Fuck five minutes. He put him down in five seconds. Not to mention he absorbed that first punch without a flinch. What is he?"

"He's the one to beat," Captain Roan said, smiling for the first time since I laid eyes on him. "To anyone angling for top rank, that is your new standard. Impress me."

Ormr and the red-haired woman from that morning, Nuala, were next up. Their bout did not end in five seconds. On the contrary, they traded blows in a fierce, but equally matched fight that left Ormr with a bleeding head wound and Nuala with a slight limp from Ormr's hard kick to her knee.

No holding back. They were playing to win.

"Take a break, ponder what you did wrong, then come back ready to go again," Roan ordered. "There are no ties when you're fighting to the death. Next—"

"I'll go next, Captain," Keir spoke up. "I'll take the princess, if you don't mind."

Captain Roan grunted agreement.

Slowly, I stepped onto the mat. Keir wasn't the same pompous noble from the day before. All the rings, bands, and necklaces were gone, leaving behind the parade of jeweled studs climbing both ears.

"Never put a princess on her knees before." He slowly licked his lips. "But I'm sure you're used to it."

I barely acknowledged the insult. I got called worse while walking through town, minding my own business. Many a *helpful* gentleman would inform me how much coin I'd make if I did various filthy things with them on the back of their carts, in the alleys, or on top of bar tables for the enjoyment of their drunk friends.

"What's wrong? Nothing to say? Am I still not worth your time?"

I tuned him out. Silently, I went through my options. I had no formal fighting training unless I counted the scuffles I got into with my siblings or bullies around town. I learned how to take care of myself early, but how did street fighting compare to hours a day, drilling and training with the likes of Commandant Drake?

Velez's voice echoed in my ears. *You don't need to win the fight, Ains. You just need to walk away from it.*

I nodded, squaring my shoulders and crouching low. *I'll make you proud, big brother, so come back home. See me become everything we didn't know I could be.*

"Begin!"

Keir charged me. Bouncing on the balls of my feet, I spun at the last moment—twisting away from his grasping hands. Keir reacted faster than I was ready for. He changed directions on the spot and swung.

"Ah!"

Keir clipped my shoulder, knocking me off-balance and dropping me off on my hip. My left hand flew up, striking his midsection. He drove his fist down in the same devastating move as Dominic.

I flipped on my front and rolled, nearly flying off the platform. Titters sounded as I righted myself in time to meet Keir's fist. He hit me full on—knocking me clean off my feet.

I struck the bare earth flat-backed, bones audibly crunching.

"This the best you can do, Princess?" Keir skipped away, laughing. He was playing with me now. Dragging it out. "Pathetic."

Wheezing, I forced myself up. Blood dripped from my ruined lip. I would walk off this mat, not be carried. At the very least, that would keep me from the bottom rank.

Keir rushed me again and I spun away. I was ready for the countermove and dropped, shooting through his open legs, and jumping up behind him—striking him on the back.

"Agh!" he shouted. "What the hell do you think you are? A snake dancer? Stop twirling and fight me!"

I gritted my teeth. Snake dancers were a particular kind of dancer you met in a particular kind of pub. They danced half or fully nude for men, teasing their *snakes*. Did this man despise me in particular, or was he incapable of seeing any woman as more than a sex object?

Keir charged—fist up and arm out to ram me if I spun again. *Now.*

I ducked, grabbed the belt he didn't know I loosened, and pulled it free. His unbuttoned pants fell, snagging around his knees. Keir tripped and fell on his face—bare ass up for all to see.

The recruits burst out howling. Maili laughed so hard, she dropped and took Ormr with her.

"Bitch!" Keir scrambled pulling his pants up.

I thought fast. If this guy got back on his feet, he was coming at me hard.

He was coming to kill.

I looked down at my hand. *You don't have to win. You have to walk away. Do whatever it takes.*

The leather lashed across his ass.

"Aaaahh!" Keir bent like a bowstring, cheeks clenching tight. "Crazy bitch! What are you—?"

I belted him once, twice, four times on the butt. I couldn't hear his yelps for the raucous laughter. Although, I think it was Poet screaming, "Again, again!"

Keir threw himself over, clutching his red backside. "I'll kill you f-for this. Say goodbye to the House of Boreen!"

I didn't pause to think. My enemy would destroy me if I let him get to his feet. So I wouldn't let him get on his feet.

I stomped his crotch, crunching his testicles under my boot.

Keir's eyes bugged—mouth open in a silent scream.

I looked to Captain Roan. "Sir, do I—?"

"Finish him."

He didn't need to tell me again. I wrapped the belt around my fist, buckle facing out.

"Wait. Wait, don't—!"

Grabbing his collar, I smashed the metal in his face over, and over, and over. Keir flopped back on the fifth hit—unconscious.

"Mother Zaeah, Ainsley!" That was Poet laughing and carrying on loudest of all. "That was incredible!"

"That was not incredible." Captain Roan brought silence with a single sentence. "No technique. No form. No coordination. You fight like a street urchin defending a piece of rotten fruit that fell off a cart."

I turned to go.

"But."

But? Turning back, I met his wide, beaming grin.

"But damned if you didn't just teach everyone here the most important lesson they'll ever learn. There are no rules on the battlefield. There is only win or lose. Kill or be killed. You're looking at my rank two, riders," he announced, dropping my jaw.

"From this point on, if I don't see half her ruthlessness on my mat, you'll all fall very short of three. Next!"

Chapter Five

It was a bloody and battered group that stepped onto the field for magical accuracy. The riders took Captain Roan's words to heart with frightening determination. They beat, pounded, kicked, and ripped each other apart.

Captain Roan smiled the whole way through.

"What's this?" A tall, slim, short-haired brunette stood in the middle of the grassy field. I studied her with too much interest. She wore the pale-blue instructor's uniform like the rest, but hers looked like a dragon had their fun with it. The legs were torn off her pants, leaving behind the barest scrap of fabric needed to cover half her ass.

Her top received the same treatment. Gone were the sleeves and midriff, revealing the jagged spiderweb scar traveling from her shoulder to neck.

"Where's the rest of you?"

"Thospital thing," Maili lisped. Someone stole my move and used their belt to beat her face in. She showed them by grabbing their arm and breaking it.

"Hospital wing? Of course," she sighed. "I told Drake battle readiness should be the last class of the day. Oh well, we'll have to make do. Fall in."

Again, the class ran, limped, and hobbled into two rows.

"I'm Lieutenant Colonel Phiala. Former leader of the thirty-sixth Ryuku squad, now Regent of Falkor."

Regent? My opinion of her was forming quickly. Not only did she lead the elite dragon riders, but General Roark made her regent of one of the largest townships in Adalinda. Only his strongest and most trusted were gifted their own corner of the kingdom to rule.

"But I put someone else in charge for the season and came here to teach you little bastards, because Falkor's cold as shit and twice as boring. Every day was like counting the scales on an ice dragon's ass."

I blinked. *What?*

"So don't bore me. I'll fail your pampered asses for fun."

No one spoke. What was there to say in response?

Phiala clapped. "All right, no time to waste. Magical accuracy is a straightforward class. It's the foundation of your magical training. Here, you will learn to control your bond and your power. Why, you ask? Of course you do, ignorant shitheads."

"Have we done something to offend her?" I whispered at Ormr.

Their good eye crinkled. The other was swollen shut. "Rumor is this is her in a good mood. When we offend her, we're dead."

"In battle, things get confused," Phiala continued. "Riders are flying everywhere. Your dragon is swerving, spinning, and plummeting. You're straining to see through the blood in your eyes. The last thing anyone needs in that situation is a misfired fireball blasting them in the back.

"Control is everything. Dragon riders don't commit friendly fire. They don't know the meaning of the word collateral damage. If we're going to kill our own people and destroy our cities in a fight, we might as well stand back and let the Druks wreak havoc. Got it, fuckers?"

"Yes, ma'am," we replied.

"Ugh. Ma'am? If you're gonna beg for me to kick your ass, I'll oblige. Your assessment just got ten times harder." She snapped her fingers. "Two lines. Be quick about it."

I edged to the side, coming around the lines to the lieutenant colonel's side. She was shorter up close, and powerfully built.

"Lieutenant Colonel?"

"What?"

"I have to tell you…" I trailed off, catching Dominic's eye as he physically picked up a guy, tossed him away like a gnat, then took his spot at the front of the line. He pointed at the guy next to him, his message clear. That spot was for me.

"Tell me what, rider?"

I gave Dominic my back. "I need to tell you that I don't have any magic."

Phiala frowned.

"I've never had magic. I was born that way. For a few weeks after I bonded with my dragon, I thought my ability would come. It didn't. A dragon bond boosts your natural ability times ten, but ten times zero is still zero."

She stared at me, unblinking.

"So…" I said slowly, leaving an opening. "I won't be able to take part in your lessons. I understand what that will do to my rank, but it can't be helped. No magic means no magic. I hope I can still learn from you how to control the bond." I rubbed my temples. "It's like there're nails in my skull, and every day, a dozen more are added. I'll do anything to make it stop."

I looked around. "I can get started on those bond exercises now. Where should I go so I won't be in the way of the assessment?"

"You should get your ass in line, Rider Ainsley." She scoffed. "Tenille bless us, I told you not to bore me, and you took it too far to heart. Don't have magic? That's the weakest excuse to get out of training that I ever heard."

"I'm not lying. I don't—"

"Enough." She waved and rough hands seized me.

Twisting around, I looked into dark, soulless eyes. I screamed.

Uncaring, the dirt men dragged me away, my boots skidding across the ground. They dropped me right where Dominic wanted me—next to him.

"This is how it works. The Druks will attack you. The innocent Adalindians will run around screaming, panicking, and generally getting in the way. You are to hit the Druks and only the Druks. Any harm done to the Adalindians will reflect in your rank.

"You must take out seven Druks before the next person takes your place. Speed is paramount," she said, pointing to me and Dominic. "The team that completes their run first, wins. Members of the losing team will each receive a demerit."

"Lieutenant Colonel, I can't—"

She raised a fist, and the earth shook.

Dirt creatures rose from the ground, terrifying in their likeness. The women wore dresses and flowers in their hair, details so intricate I could count the petals. The men shook loose dirt from their beards as they rose to full height, looking around as if this was the first they saw sunlight with true eyes.

And the Druks...

Thud—tck, tck, tck, tck. Thud—tck, tck, tck, tck.

I flattened against the wall, vision warping through my tears. Its feet came into view—horrid and unnatural, they turned toward me. Bending down, the creature smiled into my eyes. Its grotesque wings reached for me, shutting out the scant light.

"There you are, little mouse."

"Begin!"

Druks took to the skies, their impossible earth wings stretching across the horizon—blotting out the sun. Then at once, they dove.

Ripping through the Adalindians, they snatched dirt children from wailing mothers, lifted them in the sky, and dropped them. They tore heads from their shoulders, and sunk their claws in mothers' chests. Villagers were running, jumping, zigzagging across the landscape, mouths wide in silent screams, and coming straight at us.

Dominic took off running. Almost immediately the flying Druks dropped into the panicking mob, taking away his easy targets.

This didn't slow him.

He dodged a screaming woman trying to throw herself in his arms and grabbed a Druk by the head. The creature ignited into flames.

Snapping around, he threw the burning Druk across the field. It crashed into its comrade, ripping him free of a woman whose head was within its claws.

They crumbled into smoldering dust.

Two children leaped on him, strangling his legs in death grips. Dominic didn't pause for breath. He touched his thumbs and fore-fingers together, then broke away. A fireball grew before his chest, beating back the shadows on his face. He flicked his wrist and it shot away, claiming another victim in a fiery, painless death.

"Why are you standing there!" A hard shove propelled me forward. "Hurry up! We're going to lose."

"I can't. I don't have magic!"

My cry was a call to arms. Suddenly, the Druks turned on me—racing at me full speed.

I spun around, and my captors turned Druk raised their claws. It slashed my face, exploding pain in my right cheek. I had no doubt that if they were real instead of dirt, the hit would've taken half the skin off my face.

I ran.

Villagers broke away from Dominic and came at me, running to their savior.

Claws tangled in my hair. Yanked off my feet, I screamed as chunks of hair ripped off my scalp. The dirt Druk threw me down and punched. I rolled out of the way almost a hair too late—feeling the ground rumble beside my head.

I scrabbled to my feet. I cracked my neck whipping my head around. I had to do something. *Anything!*

Ten feet away, I lit on a rock. Barely larger than my fist, it'd make a barely useful weapon.

You don't have to win. You have to walk away.

I dove. Rolling under a swinging claw, I crawled to my only hope of a weapon. Snatching it up, I flipped as the Druk descended on me. Every ounce of strength I possessed poured into my fist.

"Ahh!" I smashed the rock in its monstrous, reptilian face.

It blew back... unharmed.

Dread leadened my bones, gazing at its unchanged hardened face. My hit hadn't so much as chipped its dirt nose.

It backhanded me across the face, sending me flying.

I skidded over unforgiving earth, leaving behind pieces of cloth and skin. I crashed into a fleeing couple. They collapsed on top of me, pinning me to the ground.

My world was pain. Blood wept from a thousand cuts on my body. Fire scorched through my mind. Reyna was worried about me. Her anxiety poured through the unrestrained bond, scrambling my thoughts.

Through the haze, I heard my team.

"What are you doing!"

"Useless fuck! Get up!"

Get up. "Get off!" I bellowed, shoving the villagers off me.

I got to my feet, and was immediately knocked down. A village mother shoved her baby in my hands and fled.

"Joke's over, Rider Ainsley," Phiala bellowed. "Use your magic. Take them down. Save your people!"

"I don't have magic!"

Three Druks took to the skies. They grew before my eyes. Claws lengthening. Wings morphing from two to four. They dove, heading straight for me and my charge.

I stood frozen, a captive in the onslaught while more mothers ran to me—carrying babies for me to protect.

"Stop this! I'm not lying. I was born without magic!"

Claws wrapped around my throat. The Druk lifted me into the air, still holding the baby. Pleas trapped behind my lips, terror filling my soul. Higher we flew, and higher, and higher. Phiala's intent was clear. She would force the magic out of me... even if it killed me.

"Don't do this!"

"Fight back!

"I can't!"

There was no hope for me. Even if my fists and nails were enough to beat back her golem monster, if I dropped this baby, it was an automatic fail. Discarding a fake innocent to save myself didn't bode well for my chances in a real fight. She was giving me two options: die disgraced, or die a rider.

Dying on the first day. Grim humor overwhelmed me, flooding a strange calm as I held my charge close. *At least for a short time, I lived my dream.*

The Druk let go.

I flew.

My head split open. Agony obliterated my mind, twisting and seizing my body into mangled coils, plummeting through the air. I knew this pain. I'd felt it once before.

Reyna.

A roar shook the very air. I blasted sideways—shock snapping me to consciousness as a Druk snatched me out of the sky.

"You summoned your dragon?! You fucking fool! I wasn't going to kill you. Send her back!"

Reyna flew impossibly fast. Slicing through the air, her powerful wings buffeted air from a mile away—flattening my ears against my head. This was the power of dragons.

"Send her away!"

The recruits ran, fleeing in a dozen different directions.

Reyna split her maw. Flames gathering in her throat—stealing heat from the atmosphere.

Light blinded me. I squinted, straining to make sense of what I was seeing.

Fire.

Balls of fire suspended in the air, blazing the field in warm light. In a blink, they shot through the sky—impaling every flying Druk. Eviscerating each rampaging monster. Destroying my captor.

It was beyond anything I'd ever seen. Power on this scale was possible for the bonded whose magic was amplified by a dragon's. But Dominic was dragon-less. If this is who he was without Reyna, with her... he's unstoppable.

I plunged to the ground, still holding on to the baby. Strong arms grabbed me. I cried out as we rolled, his arm an iron band pinning me to his chest.

Protecting me.

"Reyna, stop!" Dominic was power, strength, and command. Rising up, he ran straight at every sensible person's worst fear. A rampaging dragon. "She's safe, my beauty."

My beauty.

He offered me up to her—a peace offering on the dawn of destruction.

Reyna reeled back, and set fire to the world.

Chapter Six

"Get up. Wake up, shithead!"

Water shot up my nose. I bolted up, sputtering. Four blurred figures formed over me. Three concerned, one pissed.

"What the hell were you thinking!" Lieutenant Colonel Phiala huffed like she ran ten miles. "You summoned your dragon to get out of the assessment. Have you lost your mind!"

"I..." I trailed off. *What happened?*

I could still feel Dominic all around me, holding me up and offering me to the vengeful goddess of wind and fire.

"Where's Reyna?"

"Back where she should be. Dragons know not to interfere in training. It's vital that you learn, train, and grow to survive. For her to do what she did, you had to believe you were without hope. Moments from dying. Completely ridiculous since all you had to do was use your power."

"I don't have power!" I burst out, blowing Poet, Ormr, and Maili back. "I kept telling you. I was born without magic. My dragon bond amplified nothing, because there was nothing to amplify."

Phiala's brows furrowed. "That cannot be. The bond between dragon and rider is power itself. It's like trying to build a bridge without solid ground on the other side. It doesn't work."

"It's impossible... but it's true."

She said nothing—observing me without expression. The silence stretched so long, the guys helped me to my feet, standing me up before the judgment of the recruits.

The field was gone. A gaping crater where dirt and grass used to be were all that remained. Inside the pit, the remains of Reyna's flames smoldered, giving off such fierce heat, they turned a pleasantly cool day sweltering.

Recruits glared from the other side of the field, even more battered than they were after leaving battle readiness. Mud soaked their tatted, scorched clothes, but I didn't believe that's what angered them. Dragons were on our side. These nobles and royals never felt the pants-soaking terror of being one's enemy.

"You have no magic," Phiala said, a strange undercurrent in her tone.

"No, Lieutenant Colonel."

"Then, you're no use to anyone."

"I can't hire you. What use are you without magic?"

"Get out. I didn't think there was anything worse than an orphan bastard, then you walked in."

"You should work for me. There's good money in tumbling, dear. Don't need magic to suck a cock."

I clenched my jaw, ears ringing with the ghosts of my past. "So I've been told."

She scoffed. "Get out of my sight. Take your ten demerits with you."

I didn't argue. Unsteadily, I walked away.

"But it's not her fault," Ormr protested. "She told you over and over again that she didn't have magic. Her dragon attacked because of you."

"Exactly," Maili chimed in. "Give those demerits to yourself. Actually, pack them in your bag and take them with you back to Falkor. We don't need careless instructors like you."

"Is that right?" Phiala laughed. "Loyalty to your friend. I like it. I even like the balls on you, girl. But I didn't get where I am by taking disrespect. The four of you have Hatchery duty for a month."

"But—!"

"Say another word and you're cut."

My friends stomped off. Maili grabbed my hand, taking me with them.

"You didn't have to do that," I said softly.

"Yes, we did," Ormr said. "Maili and I had a trainer like her. Years ago. She believed you couldn't reach your highest potential... without pain."

Ormr lifted their sleeve.

I hissed, chest tightening on sight of the wicked scar. It looked like someone ripped them apart to the bone, gouging the flesh and muscle.

"We weren't bonded by then," they said. "Our dragons couldn't save us."

"Did you tell Drake that you don't have a power?" Poet asked.

I nodded.

"Then, it's definitely their fault that this happened. Either he couldn't be bothered to tell the instructors that you can't participate in magic training, or he told them and she ignored him and you. She fucking dropped you eighty feet. Of course your dragon felt your fear."

"There's a difference between pushing us to our limits, and torture." Maili had an expression on her face I hadn't seen before. This wasn't the sweet, smiling girl I was coming to know. "Torture doesn't make better dragon riders. Just makes them twisted—like her."

I was quiet taking that in. I thought it was a paradise on the other side of the wall. Looking up from my poor lonely life, the shining city on the hill held all my dreams. It wasn't that I thought royals and nobles would be kinder to a magicless woman. More that I believed their looks couldn't sting when I was a rider with hope and a future.

Then, a Druk golem sent me plummeting to my would-be death.

There's a reason dreams are short and reality is relentless. Doesn't do to dwell in a fantasy.

"Torture," I repeated as we entered the citadel through the back entrance. "Is it sad that I've gotten used to it? I've gotten this reaction from everyone who found out I don't have magic. Other than—" I cut myself off. I almost named Rosaleen and my siblings. "Other than the few friends I have, everyone treats me like I'm less than human.

"Phiala said that she wasn't going to kill me. But I saw it on her face when she was forced to accept the truth. Without magic, I'm better off dead."

"You will be."

We froze, searching up and down the hallway. No one was there.

Shaking my head, I continued on.

"You haven't seen ruthless yet, Pretend Princess."

"Who's there?" I cried.

"Roark won't get a chance."

Movement out of the corner of my eye turned our heads. My shadow moved on the wall—spinning, twisting, forming something new. Rising to the ceiling my—its—fist crumpled.

Wide eyes flicked down to the open palms at my side.

"I'll be the one who kills you, bitch," Keir's voice whispered from everywhere and nowhere. "Watch your back, because I'll be coming from the front."

I DREAMT OF DRUKS THAT night. Taloned wings beat the sky, chorusing a steady *whomp, whomp, whomp* under a battalion of ten, fifty, hundreds of Druks.

The unholy union of man and dragon, scaled feet gave way to muscled legs. Reptilian eyes set over normal, snubbed, long, or pointed noses. They dropped out of the sky, descending on the people they once were. Men, women, children threw all the power they had at their attackers, and it made no difference.

Lifting them up in the sky, they let go.

My eyes peeled open.

A silent figure stood over me.

"No!"

My foot flashed, heading swift for my assassin. My shin smacked into a hard, immovable palm.

"Excellent reaction time, Rider Ainsley. You nearly caught me off guard."

Fuzzy, sleep-induced fog lagged to clear. Rider Ainsley? Neither Dominic nor Keir would call me that. They preferred princess and bitch respectively.

"Who are you?" I croaked.

"I haven't received that question for quite some time."

His form came into focus. I bolted upright, something between a question and a greeting clogging in my throat.

Scar cut across his brow. House emblem carved on his hilt. Silver circlet woven through his graying locks. Every recruit in the room standing to attention. All of this pointed to who he was, but none of that is why I recognized him.

Dominic's eyes.

"King General Roark."

I scrambled out of bed and stood to attention. Everything in me tried not to focus on the fact that I wore nothing but underclothes.

"At ease."

I didn't twitch. What was at ease about waking up to the ruler of the country standing at my bedside?

"What can— Did you want to speak with me, General?"

"I did."

Not a trace of emotion on his ageless, handsome face gave his thoughts away. It was strange standing before him. In the darkest corners of the seediest pubs, King General Roark was cursed to hell and back. Wealthy nobles and honored riders praised him. Commoners despised him.

I never formed an opinion on him either way. No matter who ruled Adalinda, there was no place in it for a magicless orphan.

"I received a report that a recruit signed up to training claiming to be the heir to Queen Kisandra. Not the first time this has happened, and it won't be the last. I trusted Commandant Drake to address the situation, until I was informed of this."

General Roark withdrew a scroll from his pocket.

"What is it, sir?"

"This, Rider Ainsley, is a marriage contract between you and my son." He snapped it open. "It states that upon the signing of this contract, you will undo the forbidden magics you performed on his dragon to make her break their bond, and bond with you. Once done, you will become his wife, be granted regency of Nithe, receive a yearly stipend of ten thousand ryus, and have no obligation to participate in royal functions or bear him children if you do not wish to."

My mouth opened, but nothing came out.

"Putting aside for the moment that I did not approve this match, there is a very serious issue that needs to be addressed." He looked up at me, pinning me to the floor. "Did you use forbidden magics to steal a dragon, Rider Ainsley? Magic that was outlawed after the usurper stole and forcibly bonded numerous dragons to her, then used them to destroy this kingdom and everything we hold dear?"

I choked. The prickling of dozens of pairs of eyes itched beneath my skin. "N-no, sir. I would never—could never do such a thing. I was born magicless."

The barest twitch of brow was his only reaction to that. "You could have had an ally do it for you in order to grant you a place within the riders. For reasons I will determine."

"No, sir," I said firmly. "I'd never been anywhere near Dominic or Reyna before she found and bonded with me."

"You will swear to the dragon choosing you of your own free will?"

"Yes."

"Then," he said, baritone soft and deep. "Dominic has no other recourse than to kill you."

I stilled.

"If he desires his dragon back, that is. Making this contract"—before my eyes, the paper withered and crumbled to dust—"null and void."

I strangled my fingers behind my back. I couldn't have signed it. As the general said, I did not perform such magics, so I could hardly undo them. Even so, it shook me to the core that not only was Dominic not lying about the marriage, but he intended to treat me so generously.

A regency? A stipend? Letting the choice to be at his side or bear his children remain my choice?

If I was some desperate lunatic with a death wish who dared to steal the general's son's dragon, that outcome would've been more than I ever could've hoped for. I, Sister Aven, and my siblings would want for nothing for the rest of our lives.

"If the dragon chose you over my son, it would mean she found the more worthy rider. Impossible if you were a common peasant, but plausible if you are who you say you are. The daughter of Queen Kisandra."

It sounded like a question, but I answered him anyway. "I am who I say I am."

"We will see. Get dressed and meet me outside, Rider Ainsley. Five minutes."

I hesitated, glancing at Dominic's empty bed. I hadn't seen him since he demolished every Druk and saved my life during the assessment. Afterward, lessons were suspended for the rest of the day due to the overfilled hospital wing.

I dressed quickly, then found the general outside, waiting by the citadel gates. I followed his gaze up. High above our heads, an ivory-scaled dragon circled the skies.

Tizor.

I'd only ever seen General Roark's dragon from a distance. Even from where I concealed in my forest, small and unseen, I couldn't help but wonder at the majesty of Tizor. He was beautiful.

For a death dragon.

"I'm here, sir."

General Roark gave me a long, unreadable look as though he'd forgotten his request and wondered why I was speaking with him.

"Walk with me, Rider Ainsley," he said, after the discomfort settled deep in my bones.

A guard opened the gates and let us through. Stepping out from the citadel's hold, the glittery, charming world of Golden City enveloped me.

I started down the hill and the general did not follow. Turning right instead of left, he led the way to the palace.

"Do you know the history of how Adalinda came to be what it is today?"

"Yes," I replied.

"Tell me."

I gazed off in the distance, watching Tizor dive for something I couldn't see. "A hundred years ago, a thousand-year peace ended in blood and fire. The usurper allied herself with our greatest enemy, the Druks, and learned forbidden magic to sever the bonds of great dragon riders, and force them to bond with her. She and her dragon horde laid waste to the city and attacked the reigning family.

"The riders weren't prepared for this attack. They'd never fought dragon rider versus dragon before. Yes, dragons will kill people, but they don't attack unless it's to defend or protect. Not even under their rider's order."

We walked the cobblestone path—the city sounds growing quieter.

"Humankind and dragonkin are as one. Born from Zaeah, mother of dragons, and her twin brother, Parthelan, father of man. They created us, blessed us with magic, then split our souls—putting a piece of us in the other to walk the earth until we find our dragon half. It's why we can bond with dragons, but not any other creature.

"That day, her captured dragons committed the greatest tragedy in our history. They burned man, woman, rider, and child alive. The usurper stole the throne, then for the next fifty years, she quelled every rebellion and conquered the neighboring kingdoms. Edjer, Ghidorah, Hyelong, and Nehebkau all fell to her, and now make up the new Adalinda," I said.

"We lived in tyranny throughout those hellish years until you, sir, defeated her. You brought peace to the land, and—and Adalinda under military rule."

"What do you think of that decision?"

"Sir?"

"What do you think of Adalinda's military rule?"

General Roark walked stiff-backed and composed beside me. I wondered for a second what it was like to grow up with this man as a father. Nation's hero. The weight of his reputation so heavy on his shoulders, that he doesn't relax or let down his mask on a light stroll with a subordinate. Although, it's possible Dominic grew up with only the reputation, and not the man.

General Roark had thirty-two children, and the many wives who bore them. I doubt he found the time to run the country and have an active role in raising children scattered about the land.

Where the usurper used violence and murder to bring the neighboring kingdoms to help, General Roark married the displaced queens and heirs, and made them his queens and heirs.

The icy, mountain people of Edjer who walked through the Ossian square with fur-lined coats, griffin feathers woven in their white hair, and skin that refused to brown in the sun. The Ghidorian people who traditionally cooked foods with burning spices that left me stealing food from a Ghidorian stall once, and only once. My Hyelongan baby brother, so small and trusting as he gazed up at me with eyes a different shape than mine. The Nehebkan man with the obsidian skin of a shadow dragon, who always gave me more bread or fruit than my coins could buy.

I didn't know a world that wasn't as diverse as it is now, because General Roark didn't give them a choice. He kept the land that the usurper conquered. He ruled on the throne that she stole. He changed the laws and allowed men to have many wives, which his lieutenants, captains, and majors took to with alacrity. Our bloodlines were so interwoven, half a century later, the citadel was filled with young riders of two legacies—or one, as the new rule demanded.

"I don't have an opinion," I answered. "I don't know enough about war, government, or rebuilding a kingdom to form one."

"A diplomatic answer. You certainly know enough to respond with a reply that reveals nothing at all."

I also knew enough to not say anything to that.

"Would it surprise you to know that I am a hero no longer? Now, what people see is a general. And a general is not a king."

We converged on the palace gates, passing through into the courtyard.

"They say I should step down and pass the throne to one of the royal families who didn't have a claim to it when Queen Kisandra ruled, but feel they should now. They say we are no longer at war."

I tried not to visibly react as we passed under stone arches. It was magnificent.

The palace sat higher on the hill, but the citadel was built taller. It obscured every view of Queen Kisandra's lost home from where I gazed up from Ossian. Such a shame it was to be kept from this.

Turrets reached for the sky, topped with shining jade perches for the royal dragons. My gaze clung to the sandstone walls and mosaic glass, following them all the way to the great dome.

Ground level with the mortals was no less beautiful. I looked over the bridge, watching palace gardeners spray beds of hyacinth, gardenias, and roses with rainbow-reflected gentle mists. Servants blasted breezes through the courtyard, chasing away daring fallen leaves.

"When the usurper took the throne," General Roark continued, drawing my attention back. "She rewarded her allies, the Druks. You know how they got that name—abomination. Druks do not believe in Mother Zaeah or Father Parthelan. Dragons are not our kin. They're beasts like any other to consume for our strength."

I nearly heaved. Compounding my feeling was a painful backlash from the bond. Yes, I knew how those once-men came to be, and still it made me sick every time I thought about it. The legend said that the first Druk was just a desperate, starving man. He wandered lost in the desert for three days without food or water, when he stumbled on a sleeping sand dragon.

He attacked it.

Rooting and desecrating the poor creature's body, he chomped on its leg, but cracked his teeth on the scales. He drank its blood, but scorched his mouth. He cut it open, desperate for more tender meat inside, and consumed its still-beating heart.

Mother Zaeah's vengeance was swift.

Almost immediately, the change took hold. Wings ripped out of his back. Scales covered half his body. His hands and feet grew longer, reptilian, and claws. He became half man, half dragon. An abomination. A creature with human reason and dragon instincts.

He made his home in the sand—unable to leave the place. He lashed out violently, fatally, when threatened. When the urge to mate overwhelmed, he hunted women in the nearby villages.

He became a monster.

The stay from death he received by consuming the sand dragon's heart lasted less than a year. Eventually, desert warriors hunted and killed him.

This sad end was a warning to many, but not all. A small, dangerous cult formed during his reign of terror. They worshipped him as the next stage in our advancement. Man and dragon were made to bond. Born to become one.

Born to be Druks.

"Druks were a small desert community during the reign of Queen Kisandra. Vile, but not a serious threat. When the usurper took over, she not only allowed them to wreak havoc on Adalinda, but she turned a blind eye to their hunting. Scores of dragons were slaughtered. Thousands of Druks were born.

"They say we're no longer at war, but thousands of dragon riders fight to hold the line at the Dark Border, stopping the Druks' constant invasions. They stop the hunting of wild dragons, and put it all on the line to protect outlying villages from slaughter and womb raids."

"Womb raids?"

He inclined his head. "Female Druks are infertile. Those who are still human among them will wait until they are done having kids to go through the change. Those who don't feel like waiting, kidnap village women and slaughter the husbands, brothers, sons, and fathers who'd come after them."

I had no words.

"This is what my riders face every day while rich and sheltered royals tell me we're not at war."

"Sir."

"Sir."

General Roark nodded at two guards standing beside the open entrance into the castle. It was nothing like I was expecting.

People rushed about all over the place—calling orders, carrying rugs, moving furniture, cleaning the walls.

The general didn't slow moving through the chaos. With each step, servants fell back, dipped their heads, and didn't resume until we passed. I cast them one last look as we turned down a darkened hallway.

"Preparations for the Calthoon feast," he offered. "To celebrate this season's new recruits. Your sacrifices are appreciated. They should be acknowledged."

I nodded. "Thank you, sir, but if you'll forgive me, I'm not sure I understand why you brought me here."

"It's quite simple, Rider Ainsley. There are royal dissenters in my midst who feel I should cede rule to them, despite them having no claim to the throne. As a result, many have produced a long-lost heir to Queen Kisandra—"

My pleasant mood fled.

"In actuality, these poor pawns are puppets. Paper rulers for my dissenters to work through. Desperately, they continue trying to make these frauds appear legitimate despite my exposing them every time."

"That's not me, sir. I—"

"Silence."

He didn't bark or shout, and my mouth snapped shut. Something in that dark hiss, or possibly the empty look in his eyes, like he was looking at nothing—made me never want to speak again.

"Earlier, you said that no one used forbidden magics to get you this far, but it's been done before. I had knowledge of these magics struck from every book. Made it illegal to speak of them, but many royals have lived as long or longer than me. I cannot strike it from their memories. They've used those magics with little regard to the consequences all for the sake of controlling Adalinda.

"Dragons have been stolen before," he said, surprising me. "Bonds broken. Legacies forged. Accomplices and threats assassinated. All to get a little girl like you close enough to kill or unseat me. Do you want to know why I stand here before you while my enemies are decoration?"

After a beat, I nodded.

"It's because I have a simple and foolproof method for revealing a liar."

"A Heart Reader, sir?"

"Oh, no." He smiled. "They are easily tricked."

A chill climbed my spine. He knew. I don't know how, but... he knew.

General Roark stopped so abruptly, I stumbled.

I hadn't noticed we'd come up on another pair of double doors. Colored light painted the wood, depicting the flying Tizor stained on the window. I listened to chatter flowing from the other side of the door. Also... was that music?

"Let us find out if you are who you say you are, Rider Ainsley."

I had to run. Escape the castle and his all-knowing eye, and run until I was so far out of his reach, I didn't know the ground beneath me.

General Roark turned his back, reaching for the handle.

Now is my only chance. I took a step.

"If you run, you will not make it through the palace gates."

I stopped. "Run?" I injected my voice with confidence I didn't feel. "I have no intention of running, sir. I'm eager to prove the truth."

"Excellent." The door swung open, releasing a wave of music, chatter, and laughter. "After you."

His eyes met mine the moment I stepped inside. As if he'd been waiting for me all this time.

Dominic slowed his dance, hands falling off Nuala's waist. Everyone stopped when I entered the room. Ormr, Maili, Poet, a bruised and scowling Keir, and a host of other people I didn't know or recognize.

We were in a ballroom. Servants rushed around the edges of the room—hanging garlands and dusting pedestals. In the midst of it all, my rider friends danced an interrupted dance I knew well from the fun and lovely Calthoon celebrations Sister Aven threw us in our solitary part of Ossian. Teaching us the dances and songs from her childhood.

"What's this? Why have you stopped?" A woman in a heavy red gown clapped. "Again, again. You perform this dance for the glory of Adalinda, and the honor of the riders before you and to come. Again! This with feel— Oh, General." She finally saw what everyone was looking at. "Forgive me, sir."

"Please, continue. Rider Ainsley and I have our own business."

General Roark made me jump threading my arm through his. I sought Dominic again as he led me around the dancers and their watchers—parents, possibly. Poet turned back to Maili. Ormr took their partner's hands. Nuala tugged on Dominic's arms. But he followed me, as intensely, but not in the same way, as Keir.

I flicked away from them, alighting on the servants. They weaved their garlands on and around strange golden statues. I knew nothing of art, and I had no money to buy statuary if I did, but I had to think no small a price would move me to fill a ballroom with the pieces before me.

Shocked, screaming, and bug-eyed statues watched over us. A dozen to count on one wall, more surrounding the ball— *No,* I thought, following the statues to the front of the room. *Not a ballroom. A throne room.*

"What do you know of the House of Boreen's magics?"

I thought back to the lessons Sister Aven gave us. She made sure I knew all kinds of magic, so that I knew when to fight. And when to run.

"It's rare. The Boreen line is the only family known to have and pass it on," I said. "Living magic."

"Correct. It's quite marvelous to witness. The power to imbibe inanimate objects with life. It's said when the usurper attacked, Queen Kisandra turned every chair, statue, rug, and candlestick against her," he said. "It wasn't enough."

"Dom, what's wrong?" Naula's voice tickled my ear. "Pay attention."

"Her power wasn't enough to save her, but at least it helped her escape," I said.

"That isn't the only gift her power granted us." He swept out a hand, motioning to the throne.

Golden vines entwined up, around, and over the masterpiece, each kissed with flowers I'd never seen before. Big, bright delicate petals surrounded a bigger floret center.

"It's pretty," I said when we stopped before it. "Very nice."

That thousand-mile stare beheld me once again. "It's more than very nice. It's enchanted, Rider Ainsley. We'll never know for sure, but I believe Queen Kisandra's final act was to imbibe her throne with power. If anyone not of her bloodline sits on it... well..."

He turned his head. I followed his line of sight.

"Do you want to know why I stand here before you while my enemies are decoration?"

"Mother Zaeah," I breathed.

He clamped down on my hand.

"Wait, no! You can't—"

General Roark hauled me around, seizing my shoulders.

Everything stopped. The music, the dancing, the innocence, the dead look in General Roark's eyes.

"Another impostor!"

"Treason! Traitor!"

"Throw the bitch on the throne!" I knew that voice anywhere. "Let her be a mutt's toilet!"

"I will have no more of these tricks. These impostors," Roark bellowed. "Let this be a lesson to all of you. All who dare to question my rule and devotion to Adalinda. These paid chits will be executed in front of you, and then you'll be next."

It was only then I noticed not everyone was shouting. Ormr and Maili stood pale and quiet—wide-eyed like they were trapped between two impossible options of helping me, or joining me. Around them, unfamiliar faces watched rapt, but quiet. I had a nasty feeling Roark was talking to them. They were next.

"Wait!" I thrashed in his grip. Through the blur, I looked for Dominic of all people. It was suddenly so clear to me why he offered that marriage contract.

To spare me.

He knew what his father would do to the next royal impostor that showed up threatening his rule. Dominic saved me once. Maybe he'd save me again.

Then, I found him.

Dominic leaned against a side door, not moving an inch. He wasn't coming to save me. No one was.

"General, it's not what—"

He threw me.

I flew back, falling into the arms of the throne. It sprung to life. Vines lashed my arms and throat—holding me fast, dragging me back as I tried to run.

"Help! Help me!"

General Roark looked on in grim satisfaction. Why hadn't I seen it when I opened my eyes and connected with him? He's a monster.

"H-hel—" I choked, squeezing desperate lungfuls through my constricting throat. I strained against the binds around my wrists to get to my neck. Before my eyes, my skin began to change. Gold rushed up my arms and fingertips. I clawed the air as black crept into my vision.

We should've known better. Peasants don't get to live a life on the hill. This was always going to end one way.

My execution gallery cheered, applauded, laughed, or watched in silence. I fixed on Ormr and Maili. It wasn't too much to ask to gaze upon friendly faces while I died.

As they looked back, their lips parted—brows blowing up their foreheads. One after the other, the cheering ceased, the applause ended, and the laughter died on Keir's vile lips.

My chest heaved, heart racing watching gold spiral up my forearms, inking those golden flowers into my skin. The grip around my neck loosened.

Jumping, I started under the weight of something falling against my collarbone.

My wrists were suddenly freed. The vines retreated, leaving behind two ivy bracelets on my wrists. I touched my throat with gold-stained fingers, tracing the necklace's cool lines.

"No," General Roark hissed. "No... it's not possible."

"Princess." A man broke from the shocked crowd. Running through the dancers, he fell prostrate at my feet. "Princess, you've returned to us. You're home."

"Princess!"

Suddenly, everyone was running, pushing, screaming my name or cursing it.

A weight settled on my head. Shaking, I lifted it off and held it before me.

My crown.

Chapter Seven

"Where are you from?"

"Adalinda."

"Where were you found?"

"In the forest near the border of Ghidorah."

"Are you magicless?"

I sighed, head lolling forward. I was exhausted. If I closed my eyes then, I'd sleep for a year.

"Are you magicless?" she repeated forcefully.

"I've answered these questions a dozen times. When will you be satisfied?"

Seconds after I held the bestowed crown in my hands, it was taken from me.

General Roark barked for the guards and rushed me out of the throne room under heavy and harsh protest from the royals. *Where are you taking her? Release the princess. Don't dare harm her.*

He didn't have me harmed. Instead, he tossed me in a cold, windowless room with my cold and humorless companion. The Heart Reader introduced herself as Madame Sela, then proceeded to interrogate me for hours while General Roark, and then Dominic, looked on.

"I'll tell you when I'm satisfied, girl. Answer the question."

"Yes, I'm magicless."

"Did you steal Dominic Roark's dragon to gain entry into Golden City?"

"No," I said firmly, and I said it to Dominic. "Reyna found and bonded with me."

"What were your intentions in coming to Golden City?"

"Training to become a dragon rider and control the bond."

"Did you collude with a member of the royals to stage a coup against our high and just General Roark?"

I flicked down to my wrists. The bracelets were taken from me. Those along with the necklace and crown. General Roark had the guards tear them from my body the minute we were out of sight of the royals. I watched him try to destroy them with his wither magic. At will, the general could make anything he touched shrivel into nothing and die.

Anything, except my golden gifts. He gave up and had the guards whisk them away, but my new tattoos remained.

What did this mean? No. I knew what it meant, I simply didn't know how it could be real. I claimed to be Queen Kisandra's daughter to save my life. Not for a moment did I believe she had a thing to do with the likes of me. But it had to be true.

She cursed the throne with living magic to kill anyone who wasn't the rightful ruler. Her last act of defiance against the usurper, and through the years, every impostor who claimed to be her descendant. Why wasn't I one of them?

I'm a part of her bloodline, but how? Am I her daughter? Granddaughter? Did she escape that night and live long enough to have and abandon me?

"Rider Ainsley, did you—?"

"No. I did not collude with any royals. I'm here for one thing and one thing only—to train. All of this is unnecessary."

"Unnecessary." General Roark towered over me. "A hundred years, and there isn't a whisper of a whisper from Queen Kisandra.

You would have us believe she hid in isolation for eighty years, only to fall pregnant and abandon her magicless whelp in the woods?

"You were taken in by some woman, but she's dead now. There was a letter explaining your heritage, but it burned. You're hiding something, Rider Ainsley, and it doesn't take a Heart Reader to see it. This reeks of treachery."

"I am not lying, sir." I fixed on Madame Sela. "Right?"

She looked from me to him, and shook her head. I was telling the truth.

A knock sounded on the door.

Roark yanked it open. "What? I told you we're not to be disturbed."

"Master Quinlan and Master Peregrin are getting restless, sir. They demand the princess's safe release, and have summoned all the loyalist royals and nobles to ensure it."

Dominic watched me in cool silence. He wasn't like his father, hiding contempt behind an unflappable mask. I truly did not know what this man was thinking.

For a silly moment, I thought he would save me because he was willing to offer fair and generous terms in the marriage contract. I blamed my terror for that delusion. Dominic was fair and generous because he wanted Reyna back. He watched unmoving while his father threw me to my death for the same reason.

It wasn't about me. It never was.

"Those fools will not have the satisfaction of a scene," said the general. "Take her through the north gate and return her to the barracks. The usual restrictions remain. No one other than military staff is allowed in the citadel, and you"—he turned on me—"are not allowed to leave."

"But what about Reyna?" I blurted. "She's in the Royal Wood with the other dragons. I have to see her."

"You will see her when you train."

"No, I'll see her when I wish. You can't keep me from her."

The look he gave me was terrible. "What did you say, girl?"

"She will abide by your rules, Father," Dominic smoothly sliced in, cutting off my response. "I'll see to it."

He nodded sharply. It was impossible to believe of this man who'd grown to legend in the stories about him, but looking at General Roark, I couldn't help but think... he was worried.

"You're done," he told Madame Sela. "Go and confirm her story."

"What about my bracelets and necklaces? My crown?"

"There is nothing in this castle that belongs to you, girl." His voice was a low, dangerous hiss. "You'll do well to remember it."

I said nothing. I'd spoken unwisely enough for one day.

"Dominic, with me."

Dominic followed his father out, eyes lingering on me till the very last moment.

The guards helped me up and took hold of both arms. I felt like a prisoner, and that's exactly what the general wanted me to be. Confined to the citadel where I couldn't plot with any royals or nobles.

The guards half carried me out.

"—care of it," Roark finished, jabbing his son's chest. "Understood?"

His eyes found me again, gazing over his shoulder from where they stood far, but not far enough away. Dominic looked at me as he said, "Yes, sir."

DOMINIC AND I WALKED silently through the castle's twist-ing hallways. He sent the guards away, telling them he'd take me since he was heading the same way.

"What did he tell you?" I asked, shattering the peace.

"Who?"

I glared through slitted eyes. "You know who. Your father told you to kill me, didn't he?"

"Of course not." Not a hitch tripped his step. "That would be treason. My father is a good and honorable man who respects the monarchy... wherever she may be."

"I'm not fooled. He wants rid of me, and you already had rea-son to do so. Now you can get Reyna back and remove a threat to your future rule all in one stroke."

"If you die during training, Princess, it'll be because you weren't good enough."

"What is your game? You announced to the entire recruit class that you're going to kill me, and now you have amnesia?" My voice was climbing higher. "Say what you want to say, Roark. You've been nothing but honest since I met you. Don't stop now."

"I've said exactly what you need to know. You aren't listening."

I flashed. Grabbing his collar, I shoved him against the wall. I could've been Nuala wiggling and whining in his arms for all his re-action.

"I didn't want this. *Any* of it. All I wanted to do was come here, train, and be a dragon rider. I'm not a part of a plot or coup. I'm here for Reyna, and Reyna only!"

"I know."

"Also— Wait. What did you say?"

"I said, I know. You are no spy, Princess. You wear your every thought on your face. You were terrified up there," he said. "You thought you were going to die, and when you didn't, you were more surprised than anyone.

"Who are you?" he asked, shrewd look sweeping me. "Why will you still not say? The throne cannot be tricked. A distant relative of Queen Kisandra tried sitting on it, and died screaming. You are her close relation, but you didn't know it. Why did you come here, then?"

I released him. "Stop."

"Who did you think you were? Where are you really from?"

"I want to leave."

Dominic caught my wrist. The world spun.

Gasping, I blinked up at Dominic—finding myself pinned between him and the wall. "I'll tell you what you want, Princess."

His growl settled low in my belly. Who spoke like that? Who had this kind of presence? Both soothing and dangerous. It made no sense. I didn't feel the fear near him that I felt from Tavis, Verlin, and Fionn. I knew he wouldn't hurt me in an underhand, defiling, violent way for the mere fact that I slept right next to him. He had his chance. He also had his chance to watch me plummet to my death, and he saved me.

"What you want is to listen close, because I'll say this clear so that there's no confusion. Your death was decided the moment you stood on that platform and summoned my dragon. You will not make it out of training, and I'll tell you why.

"It's because I don't trust you. You're a liar," he whispered, the words turning to heated air on my lips. "You're hiding something, and it's more than peasant origins. For years, the monarch loyalists have moved in the shadows, working to unseat my father from the throne. Their many attempts litter the ballroom. At some point, they had to get their hooks into a true heir.

"At some point... there had to be you."

I swallowed hard. "I didn't collude with any royals. The only ones I've ever met spat on me!"

He scoffed, his piercing light eyes boring into me. "Madame Sela is the best, but she's only as good as the questions she asks. You may not have colluded with a royal, but it doesn't mean you haven't colluded with someone."

"I—"

"*You*," he said forcefully, "are not who you say you are. You will never have my throne, or rule my people."

"I don't want the throne!"

Dominic smirked. "Funny, that's what I said for years. The fourteenth son of his third-favorite wife, I assured my father, brothers, and sisters that I didn't want the throne. I simply wanted to serve and learn from the general. You don't know what I sacrificed to be chosen as his heir. If you think I'm going to let an obvious liar sway me with nonsense bleating about not wanting the throne while she steals it, then you're ill-equipped to enter this war."

"Wow," I replied. "You schemed and plotted to gain your father's trust. You're the manipulative liar, not me. Maybe you're the real threat against him—"

Dominic grasped my jaw. Not hard. No force. And still, I froze.

"Careful, Princess. Wouldn't do to voice such accusations."

We were so close, my heaving chest pressed on him as his pressed back. Both of us sharing our breaths.

"Why not?" I asked softly. "You're going to kill me anyway, so why shouldn't I repeat a few accusations to anyone I choose?"

"Because no one will believe you." Lightly, his calloused thumb stroked my cheek. "If anything, they'll distrust you more for trying to sow suspicion against the general's favorite son."

"You'll do that all by yourself when you come after me over an imagined vendetta. You think using our brutal training will cover you when you try to kill me? Everyone—including the loyalists you're so worried about—will see it for what it is.

"An assassination," I breathed. "Removing the true heir to keep my dragon and my throne for yourself."

Dominic smiled. "Oh, I wouldn't say so. Because no one will know it is an assassination. They'll watch. They'll cheer me on. They'll say I was good, just, and patient with this usurper who sought to take what's mine. And in the end when it's done and you're dead, they'll say there's nothing that could've been done, because not even you saw it coming."

"But... you can't—"

"Shhh." He lightly nipped my lips. "Don't waste time with curses, pleas, or bargains. You're going to lose this fight. It's inevitable. All I ask is that you make it interesting for me."

He released me, backing away. Physically, I could move. Emotionally, there was nowhere to go.

"Make your way back without me, Princess. I'll slide in next to you later."

I stayed in the hall long after he left, stupidly blushing even while I gazed at my gold tattoos. My history. A piece of truth.

And a death sentence.

Chapter Eight

I tripped over a root, dropping my bucket.

Snatching it up, I continued on, feeling my way through the wood with only the bond to guide me.

It wasn't easy sneaking out of the barracks. I was pelted with questions the second I walked through the door. Word traveled fast.

An hour after the last hushed moans ceased and the amorous couple finally went to bed, I tiptoed past a sleeping Dominic—I checked—and slipped out.

A low, huffing noise tickled my ear, drawing me to the left through some bushes.

There she was.

Reyna curled up beside a pond, as serene and still as the body of water. Moonlight glinted off her scales. My beauty shone luminous in her magnificence. My dragon. My Reyna.

"Reyna."

She opened a single eye, observing me. She knew I was coming of course. Even if it was possible to sneak up on a creature with superior hearing and smell, the bond would've let her know I was coming.

"You chose the perfect spot, my beauty." I slid down a small hill, joining her. "Lots of light and shade during the day. A pond for us to swim. Did you have to fight the other dragons for it?"

She huffed.

"Was it a close fight?"

Amusement trickled through the bond. *Of course not.*

Laughing, I threw my arms around her snout, hugging her tight. It scared me the first time I felt her emotions. How could it not frighten to feel an emotion but instinctively know it wasn't your own? Especially when it was a dragon's almost sadistic blood-lust from a kill.

That feeling I still hadn't gotten quite used to. But all the others—her joy, her amusement, her curiosity—made me happy in another way I couldn't explain.

"I brought your requested items," I said, letting go and making my way to the bank. "Sorry it took so long for me to get away."

She huffed again. Stretching out her paw, she made her wish clear.

Shaking my head, I smiled as I filled the bucket, carried it back, and began scrubbing her claws. I didn't understand her constant swims in Ossian River at first, until it dawned on me. My vain and fastidious bonded did not like to be dirty.

"You were watching, yes?" I asked, looking up through my lashes. "You know what happened."

Reyna tipped her head, meeting her eye to mine. The answer was yes whether the gesture meant that or not. She saw what I saw. She heard what I heard. She knew what I knew. I was in trouble.

"Reyna, you know I didn't have a choice," I hissed. "Rosaleen's Heart Reader told me the only sure way to fool him is for every lie... to be the truth.

"I was abandoned in the forest. A kind woman did take me in—Sister Aven. There was a letter naming me and where I came from. And it did burn in a fire when Sister Aven had me read it, then set it alight in front of me—making me swear I'd never tell a living soul."

I tossed my head. "She was right. I don't want to imagine what would've happened to me if anyone knew that my parents were Druks."

She growled—rows of terrifying teeth reflected my pale face. The only thing she hated more than the name were the abominations themselves.

"It's all so confusing, Reyna. It's not like the letter said much," I admitted. "Only that my name was Ainsley, and the only reason she left me was because my life was in danger. She asked the person who found me to love and care for me as their own and that—that one day she'd come back for me, and I'd fulfill my destiny for the glory and honor of the Druks."

Reyna snapped, scaring me off my ass and flat on my back. My fault for saying their name again.

"Sorry," I cried. "But what was I supposed to do? I thought the letter was crazy nonsense designed to stop my rescuer from looking for her, but then, when I was eight, he came." Horrid, vivid memories crashed in my mind. "A Dr— One of them found me in the forest. He chased me terrified through the woods, laughing the whole time. I hid in a cave believing I would die.

"When he found me, he simply looked at me, chuckling while he said I wasn't ready yet. Just like that, he left." My throat tightened. "Every year, on the same day, he'd come back. It didn't matter where I was, or how well I hid. He'd find me, attack me, chase me, and when I lay down accepting this was the year he'd kill me, he'd stop and say I still wasn't ready."

Tears welled, bending her lethal, ivory claws in my vision. "I know I should've said something. Broken my promise and reported the truth to a Royal Rider. They're planning something, and I'm at the center. I'd be a fool if I refused to admit I didn't find out what that was today.

"I'm related to Queen Kisandra. I have a right to the throne by blessing of the throne itself. I don't know what this means, how it's all connected, or what destiny they want me to fulfill, but it doesn't need saying that I won't.

"I hate those beasts. It's monstrous what they do to dragons for power, and innocent women for sex and children. They can't use me for any reason, at any price, but..."

I trailed off looking into her knowing eye.

"But I can't tell the truth," I whispered. "If they lock me away, execute me, or kill my monstrous tormentor, I'll never meet her."

A feeling spread through the bond. I didn't know it. It wasn't the first time Reyna felt this way toward me, but I didn't recognize it those times or now. If I had to guess, I'd say it was pity.

"It's wrong, but she's my mother. Isn't it my right to know her? To meet her even if it's just once?"

She snorted.

"Dominic sees right through me. He knows I'm hiding the truth behind my story, and that I'm a threat to his rule. Maybe all that's true. Still, I must lie until I see her and she tells me everything about who I am." I twisted, gazing up in the distance at the castle on the hill. "Does that make me selfish, Reyna? Am I a stupid child who should've let go of silly daydreams long ago?"

Reyna bumped me, knocking me off-balance again. My heart cracked. *Of course she thinks I'm selfish. I'm protecting a dragon-killing Druk because they happen to be my mother.*

Stretching over me, she bonked me on the back.

"Ow, Reyna, I get it. You don't think—"

Huffing, she kept knocking me around, bringing me closer until I was pressed against her foreleg. My eyes widened as she laid her head against me, holding me close. A feeling—that feeling—spread through the bond again.

"I love you too." I closed my eyes, pressing my cheek to her smooth scales. "Dominic really will have to kill me. I'll never let you go, my beauty."

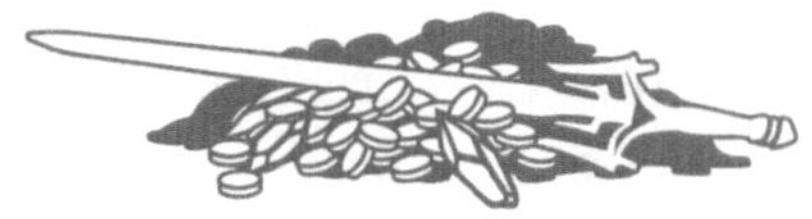

"FUCK OUT OF THE WAY."

A hard shove propelled me off my feet. I crashed to the ground, my books and parchment flying. Keir's band of walking horse-dung sacks laughed their heads off. He didn't. No trace of amusement hid behind his snarl.

Dominic won't get a chance to kill me. Keir was coming for me first.

"Back off, Keir." Ormr got between us. "You both fought. She won. Get over it."

"She didn't win! She used dirty, underhanded tricks like the street rat whore she is. That bitch isn't a princess, and I'll prove it." He pinned me over Ormr's shoulder. "Before I kill you."

"Wouldn't do for you to go around announcing intent to assassinate your sovereign." Maili helped me to my feet. "Treason isn't a good look on you, Keir, but a noose could be."

"She isn't Queen Kisandra's daughter, she's a liar. Our queen would've strangled this magicless embarrassment the moment she—"

Shooting past Ormr, I cracked my textbook on his face. Blood spurted from his ruined nose.

"You'd think you'd know better than to call someone who uses dirty, underhanded tricks a street rat whore."

"You bitch! I'll kill you!"

Keir launched at me, backed up by his friends. Ormr and Maili ran to my side.

Blast of wind slammed into us, tossing us across the hallway. I landed hard on my left arm, crying out.

"Enough. Riders will conduct themselves with pride and decorum at all times. Period." A long-necked man wearing thin-framed glasses and a scholar's robe came striding down the hall. "If we're forced to have this conversation again, you will be banned from my classroom. Rest assured, your absence will be reflected in your rank."

Conversation? I groaned getting to my hands and knees. *Throwing us across the room and barking at us is a conversation?*

"Forgive us, sir." Keir's faux charm returned in force. "I lost my temper when Rider Ainsley said these scholarship lessons are a waste of time, then threw a textbook at me."

My eyes bugged.

"I, for one, believe a strong mind makes a strong rider, but she said only flabby-bottom cunts sit around reading when there are Druks to fight."

"I see." His voice chilled the entire hallway. "Sorry to hear you have such a low opinion of the men and women who sketch your maps, chart your supply routes, record your triumphs, and expand your mind. We do our best to serve."

"But I didn't, sir," I cried. "He's lying."

"Oh? So you did not break Rider Keir's nose?"

"That was me but—"

"Already your story falls apart. Library duty," he ordered. "One month."

Maili shook her head when I opened my mouth to argue.

Fuming, I envisioned breaking something else as Keir stood up smirking. I turned my back on the foul jerk and reached for my fallen textbooks.

They burst into flames.

"What the—?"

Keir's band of horse dung laughed again, but none of them as loud as him.

"Oops. Madigan is still getting the hang of his boosted fire magic," Keir crowed. "You understand— Oh, wait. You don't."

They sauntered into the classroom, still laughing.

"What went wrong with him? So much malice in one person."

Ormr helped me up. "Keir takes being the best a little too seriously. We're all competitive, but most of us know the line. Keir never met a limit that he didn't stomp on while clawing his way to the top."

Didn't sound like the description of a decent person, and Keir wasn't one, so I'd say Ormr was correct.

We went inside, passing the threshold into a stadium-like room. Rows stacked on rows of desks, leading down to the teaching area. I landed on a guy who slept a few bunks away from me and claimed the seat next to him.

"Hey, Awnan. Do you mind sharing your textbook with me?"

He blinked owlishly. "Princess? You're speaking to me?"

"Call me Ainsley, please. Textbook," I repeated. "Do you mind?"

"No," he said quickly, shaking himself. "I mean, yes. Please, sit, Prin— Ainsley. It's an honor to share with you."

"It would be if she was talking to you." Dominic appeared out of nowhere, grabbed the hapless recruit's collar, and tossed him aside. We were sitting together with his arm secure around my shoulder before I knew what was happening.

"Rider Roark," I forced through gritted teeth. "You seem to have misplaced your hand. Get it off me."

"That isn't what you said the other day in the mess hall."

"Really? That joke is beneath you."

"It isn't," he breezed, reclining in his chair, "but you could be. Actually, you prefer the other way around. Tie me up, Princess. I'll be the big, strong, sexy man at your mercy."

A strangled noise escaped my throat. Had he done it? Had he killed me? I was fairly certain this much heat couldn't suffuse someone's body without them bursting into flames.

Dominic raked me up and down. "Interesting. You must know I'm lying, but that's not stopping the naked interest in your eyes. You're still attracted to me even after our conversation in the hall?"

"I— No— You said—"

"How often do you sleep with men who want you dead? I'm not judging, but that's a specific and risky kink."

"How arrogant are you?" It was a struggle to keep my voice down. "I never said I wanted to sleep with—"

Dominic closed the distance and captured my lips. Impossibly soft and warm, sweetness burst on my tongue, plunging me into a memory of a warm summer day when I climbed to the tallest branch of an apple tree—delighting in my treat while Adalinda spread out before me.

He didn't ravish me. Opposite of our furious clashing in the mess hall, Dominic drew out every playful nip and explored me thoroughly—as though giving me an opening to retreat. As if daring me to.

My ability to do that vanished with the moral high ground. Dominic Roark was terrible, manipulative, deadly, and kissing him did not make me forget that. I knew he was a bad guy.

He just didn't kiss like one.

Demanding and pushy, or timid and fumbly were all I'd known up to that point. It was nothing like the bold confidence of a man who stole my kiss while gentle fingers teased my cheek.

His hand continued down—skating over my shoulder, brushing my breastband through my shirt, then slipping beneath my uniform. I jerked as he tickled the sensitive flesh above my thigh.

My foot connected with the table, and it flipped.

It crashed down the stairs—scattering recruits and setting off a chain reaction that took out every table and chair on the way down. Our instructor dove out of the way, sliding across the polished wood and colliding into a bookshelf.

"No, no, no, no—!"

The bookshelf came tumbling down. Reacting fast, he blasted the falling books with wind magic—sending large, heavy tomes flying through the air. Rider Fedelma took one to the face and crumpled to the ground—unconscious.

I clapped my hand over my mouth, muffling my horrified screams as our instructor fought his way out from under the mess. Everyone turned and looked at me.

"I'm sorry," I breathed. "I'm so sorry, sir. That was an accident."

"Rider Ainsley..."

Dominic's shoulders shook. He fought hard to keep his laughter in.

"Yes, sir?"

"Leave this room."

I bit my lip. "But, sir. What about the assessment? And shouldn't I stay to clean up?"

"Now."

Under dozens of watchful eyes, I slowly stood. Dominic tossed me a wink, holding back his laugh but not his smirk.

It wasn't his fault. It's not like he knew I'd kick a table and destroy the classroom. All the same, I walked out of the classroom feeling like I had taken a test, and I failed.

"YOU'RE REALLY THE PRINCESS." Poet tossed his head, blowing out a breath. "I can't believe it."

"Apparently, you never believed it," I teased. "Did you think I was lying?"

"Yep."

"Yes."

"Absolutely."

I goggled at Poet, Maili, and Ormr. We were on our way to our next lesson—teamwork.

With nowhere else to go, I waited for them outside the classroom. We didn't leave fast enough to avoid Major Sorrel's glare.

"We thought you were a commoner trying to save your skin with a desperate lie," Poet explained. "They do that, you know."

"But we didn't blame you," Maili added. "If you ask me, that dumb law should be repealed. Who are we to say a dragon made the wrong choice? If that's who they bonded with, then it's no one's right to interfere because the person doesn't have enough money. Fucking stupid."

I could've kissed her.

"Don't say that too loud," Ormr muttered. "I heard the instructors were given orders to give extra attention to everything Ainsley says and does."

I snapped my head up. "What? Me?"

"Of course you. If anyone hears us talking about the stupidity of the social order, they may think Ainsley is stirring up dissent. I don't want to make life here any harder for you than... it will be."

"Thanks," I said, because I didn't know what else to say. I told the general in all the ways I knew how that I didn't want the throne, not even if I had a right to it. What did I know of ruling a nation?

What did I know of leading a war against Druks? The only social ill I could correct was to make enough money to feed my rough-and-tumble family.

I'd leave ruling the nation to the man who saved it. If only I could get him and his spawn to believe that.

We followed the crowd of recruits heading out to the field. I couldn't believe it when I walked out and found everything as it was. Crater filled in. Healthy bed of grass growing like it was never disturbed. For someone to right what Reyna incinerated, they had to be a fearsome earth mage.

"Gather up."

The order came from a stout, bald man whose skin was browning before our eyes. Rarely did one meet a pale dragon rider. Rarer indeed to meet a retired one.

"Welcome, recruits, to teamwork. For those who don't know, I am Colonel Kinryu."

Kinryu? The Kinryus were an old, Hyelongan merchant family that traced their line past the days of recorded history.

I knew this because Velez told me about them in length, eyes alight with excitement while he told me about his new apprenticeship. One of the last real conversations we had before he disappeared.

"Don't let the cute, pansy name fool you," the colonel continued. "This class is the cornerstone of everything you'll learn here. It's the foundation. You can learn all of the fighting and map-making skills that you want, but it means nothing if you can't work in harmony with your dragon."

I nodded along. This was the class I was most looking forward to—partly because it was one I hadn't failed right out of the gate. This was my last chance to prove myself to my instructors. I wasn't a peasant, princess, or usurper. I was a dragon rider, and I belonged here.

"We begin with the basics today, summoning and mounting your dragon. If your dragon still does not respond to your summons, that's an automatic fail for this assessment. I'm sure I don't have to explain why." Shrewd eyes swept us. "Moving forward, you can expect five demerits for each lesson where you prove you don't have your dragon's respect, or a reason to waste my time."

My gaze drifted off him and down the line. Dominic was in front and three people to the left. He refused to wait to bond with another dragon before starting training, and that arrogance came back to bite him in the ass. How did one graduate from dragon rider training without training with a dragon?

"As for the rest of you," continued the colonel, "knowing how to mount and ride your dragon is a skillset all on its own. There isn't a dragon alive that will tolerate being saddled like a pack animal. You must learn to climb on without stirrups. You have to stay seated on smooth, slippery scales in midair, while fighting. The only way to achieve this is full and total trust and cooperation between rider and dragon.

"For the purposes of the assessment, you will summon one at a time. Moving forward, all of your dragons will be on the field. Knowing how to work with other riders is just as important as working with you. No one goes to war alone."

I rocked on my heels, shaking out my hands. I was both nervous and excited. It's been less than twelve hours, and I already missed Reyna. But how much she missed me would have no effect on today's outcome. Reyna was known to toss me off her back, then spread sympathy through the bond while I cried in the dirt, clutching my broken leg.

Not this time. I'm with other riders now. I can finally see the proper way to mount her. First place may be a stretch, but I won't walk away from this field without placing top ten.

"Hear that, Reyna," I said through the bond. *"Me and you, my beauty. Top ten."*

Irritation came back. I either interrupted her wash routine, or she wasn't impressed with my low bar. We were better than top ten.

I smiled. *Agreed.*

"First up, Rider Keir."

Keir stepped forward. "Suoh is a shadow dragon, sir. He—"

"Hates sunlight. Yes, I understand that gives you both a disadvantage, but you are called to duty on a Druk's schedule, not the sun's. Summon your dragon."

Keir didn't argue. He walked a fair distance away, giving his dragon a wider berth. There were no shadows on that great open field—except one.

I leaned over, whispering to Maili. "So as long as there is even one shadow, his dragon can travel through it?"

"Amazing, right? Don't let on to him, but Keir's destined for a Ryuku squad. He can go anywhere, walk into any enemy territory, and no one will see Suoh coming."

Discomfort crowded out my awe. I hadn't thought of it like that before. Where and why did I suddenly pick up a skill for collecting the most dangerous enemies? Keir? Dominic? Commandant Drake? Major Sorrel? General Roark?

And the week wasn't over.

Keir summoned his ill-tempered dragon. He appeared and immediately reared his head back and roared at the sun. We broke formation clapping our hands over our ears, and running away in the case of a few.

Suoh bucked and swung his head. I couldn't see Keir behind him at all, let alone see what he was doing to mount him.

I squinted. "Hold on. What's that?"

A small, round object appeared in the sky above Suoh. It grew rapidly—flattening to a disk, then melting down like paint poured over my head. I stared in disbelief at a half dome floating in the sky, slowly turning pitch black.

Suoh settled instantly. Settling on his haunches, his bellowing stopped under the cool shade.

Keir leaped into sight, jumping on Suoh's back. The dragon didn't so much as flick an ear at his weight.

"What is that?" I cried. "Where did that come from?"

"Came from Keir," Poet spoke up. "Illusion magic. It's rare. Ghidorah is the only province known to turn out illusion mages. And yes, the fucker is smug about it."

"It's impressive," I said grudgingly. "No wonder they're a good fit."

I flicked to Colonel Kinryu. He wasn't smiling, but the expression on his face was pretty close. I had a feeling even that was a big deal for him.

"Next," he said. "Rider Ormr."

Ormr stepped out of line and summoned Kenna. The sky dragon swooped down lighter than a cloud. The ground didn't even shake.

Brilliant sky-blue scales rippled down her body, gradually changing colors until pure white graced her feet. She was three times the size of Reyna, but slim. Everything about her was made to slice through the heavens.

Ormr blasted the ground, using their wind magic to shoot fifteen feet into the air and hop on her back. Skillful and an automatic pass, but not a method I could copy.

"Rider Maili."

I stood a little taller. Maili had an earth dragon, so she had to have earth-type magic herself. This was the first I'd see it in action.

Cadmus arrived on the field with all this bulk. The opposite of Kenna, he had a smooshed nose where hers was long and pointed. His scales were a mottled green-brown like baby soilings, and stout little legs barely held him up. His stomach trailed on the ground. Cadmus looked better suited to burrow in the ground than soar through the sky.

Maili raced toward Cadmus and jumped. Vines burst through the earth, wrapped around her waist, and carried her the rest of the way up.

I was quickly starting to get it. This wasn't just a display of teamwork, it was also a chance to show off our dragon-boosted powers.

"Rider Dominic."

All eyes fixed on the general's son. He stepped out of line.

"I cannot complete the assessment at this time. I can't summon my dragon."

"I should say so." Colonel Kinryu looked past him, and landed on me. "Rider Ainsley. You're next."

Taking a deep breath, I stepped out of line and walked a ways from the group. I was already calling for Reyna in my mind.

"This is it, Reyna. I don't have magic to spice this up, but we're not quitting. No lower than top ten for my beauty."

A dot rose in the horizon. Pointing toward the citadel, she flew fast—heading straight toward us.

Movement out of the corner of my eye made me turn. Half my recruit class were edging toward the rear entrance. Just in case.

Reyna dropped out of the sky, her translucent wings stretching across the sun and casting reddish light over us. Setting down, Reyna lay flat with her wings partially out and ready to take off again.

Seeing the other recruits gave me an idea what I was doing wrong. They weren't clambering, climbing, and kicking their way onto their dragon's back. They used their magic to bridge the distance, then drop carefully into position.

Reyna has horns at the base of her neck. I started running, picking up the pace as I gathered my thoughts. *Jump, grab, and vault myself over. She won't feel—*

A blur shot past me.

Dominic jumped, grabbed Reyna's horn, and swung on her back. Shooting me a wink, he shouted, *"Kaja!"*

Reyna flapped her wings. The rush of wind blew me off my feet, dropping me hard on my backside. Together, they took off.

Reyna soared through the air—flipping, diving, twisting effortlessly with a rider who was not me on her back.

"Whoa. I didn't know dragons would let anyone but their bonded ride them."

"This is embarrassing."

"Even her dragon thinks she's a worthless waste of blood and bones," Keir said.

Blood rushed into my face.

"Wouldn't be surprised if she finally figured out she should dump the fake princess and return to Dom."

This couldn't be that. Our bond hadn't broken, and if she wanted back with Dominic, she always had that option. I didn't know why I was on the ground while Dominic was on her back, but it meant nothing.

After too long, Reyna touched down and bent her wing. Dominic slid off, then strolled past me—not giving my fury more than a disinterested glance. "Thanks for summoning my dragon for me, Princess, but tomorrow, be quicker about it."

I ran at him.

"Rider Ainsley," Kinryu gruffed, "you're going the wrong way. Mount your dragon."

Swallowing it, I faced Reyna as ordered. At the very least, I saw how Dominic did it, and finally knew how to mount her without getting thrown. That asshole would watch me take off on *my* dragon, and remember that no matter what he did, she chose me.

I sped at her, leaped, grabbed the horn, and swung myself over. Pure joy filled my heart as she stayed still.

"We did it, Reyna."

It was my turn to toss that bastard a wink. Settling on her back, I grabbed her horn tight. Time to fly.

"Ka—"

"Arggh!" Reyna screeched. Rearing up, her tail came flying at me from the side. I barely got out a scream before she struck me. I somersaulted through the air, falling into darkness before I hit the ground.

Chapter Nine

Ormr, Poet, Maili, and I stood in the mess hall, staring at the same thing everyone else was.

Our ranks.

"I can't believe it," Maili breathed. "Rank one: Dominic Roark. Rank one: Dominic Roark. Dominic Roark, Dominic Roark, Dominic Roark. The guy doesn't have a dragon and he still beat all of us out?"

She didn't have to say it. Everyone was whispering the same thing. Dominic cleared rank one by miles, leaving us all in the dust. The instructors were kind enough to include our point ranking, showing how demerits dragged us further down.

Dominic had perfect hundreds all the way through—including teamwork. Kinryu didn't deduct a single point for his taking off on a borrowed dragon.

I continued down, eyes sliding across the rank boards.

"Ormr, you did it," Maili said, hugging her twin. "You're rank two in every class except magical accuracy. That's only because the demerits dragged you down and Nuala took the spot."

Maili gushed over her twin, but she did amazingly too. Rank five, rank five, rank four, rank three, and rank five.

"I did good too," Poet said. "Twelve, nine, eight, fourteen, and six. The fourteen is for magical accuracy too. At least I'm nowhere near the bottom."

"Poet," Maili hissed. All three of them looked at me apologetically.

"It's okay," I said. "Rank zero, rank zero, rank zero, rank thirty-six. It's no more than I expected."

"It's bullshit," Maili corrected. "You ranked zero in magical accuracy and special talents because you don't have magic. That's not your fault. Not to mention you were thrown out of class for the scholarship assessment. You should've dropped more than a bookshelf on Sorrel's head."

"Ainsley, you've got to do something," Poet said. "You're rank zero for three classes. You're going to get cut from training."

"The good news is you've got two weeks before the first cut," Ormr said. "We'll help you. Whatever you need."

I cracked a smile. "Thanks, but there's nothing anyone can do about the magic thing. For scholarship, I'll just have to buckle down and bring the score up. But at least one good thing came out of this week..."

Battle Readiness
Rank One: Dominic Roark
Rank Two: Ormr Kaida
Rank Three: Nuala Arpina
Rank Four: Ainsley Boreen

"I can't believe Captain Roan made me rank four."

"He didn't do it," Ormr said, clapping me on the shoulder, "you did."

A silly smile stretched my lips. It looked bad now, but I wasn't discouraged. Like Maili said, two of my zeros were due to being magicless. The other was for destroying a classroom. None of that had to do with my abilities. I had two weeks to make it right in scholarship, and I will. I wouldn't be sent away from the citadel. I was meant to be a dragon rider.

"We should go," Ormr said. "Hatchery duty."

"I don't mind it as much as I thought I would," Maili mused. "They're so cute."

"Like a nest of baby scorpions," Poet muttered.

"A nest of cute, deadly scorpions," I said. "Why is that so accurate?"

An hour later, I dropped the cute. "Stop! Please, stop!"

The baby fire dragons tore at each other, opening bleeding wounds on their faces, backs, and forelegs. I grasped the hinds of the aggressor, straining to pull him off his nestmate. "Maili, help!"

"I can't! She's got this one by the arm! She's going to tear it off!"

There were only curses and shouts coming from Poet's and Ormr's directions.

When I first heard the Hatchery was where they cared for nesting dragon mothers and their babies, I wondered why anyone would give it to us as a punishment. The ignorance was literally knocked out of me with the first tail smack to the head.

Dragons were great mothers. They defended their babies to the death. What they were not, was good siblings. Baby dragons did not like sharing their mother's attention, and weren't above maiming or killing their competition.

In the wild, the fathers watched over the babies while mothers went off to hunt—putting an end to any fights. That wasn't possible in the Hatchery. Fathers had to be kept away because they were too territorial. Separating fighting dragon babies was doable. Separating full-grown dragon fathers was suicide.

That left the duty to Hatchery workers and insubordinate riders, because if a mother came back from hunting and found one of her babies dead... we would all die.

Letting go of his legs, I tackled Tiamut—jumping on his back, snapping my arms around his cool, scaly body, and rolling to the other side of the nest. He screeched and flailed the whole way—straining his neck trying to snap my face.

The Hatchery dome rattled.

"They're coming back!"

Almost immediately, the devious little bastard started whining and crying in supposed pain.

"AARRGGH!"

I released Tiamut, dove out of the nest, and ran. I was covered in Tiamut's and Shabina's blood. A moving target.

Poet, Maili, and Ormr beat it into the cage. Poet ran so fast, he couldn't slow down and smacked his face into the opposite side.

"Come on, Ains! Run!"

"AARGGH!"

The roar battered my eardrums. A shadow cast over me, harkening the angel of death. I felt her heat on the back of my neck. She swiped at me, the rush of wind from her claws blowing my hair up.

I was going to die.

"Ains, jump!" Maili's terror popped my hope of survival. "Jump now!"

I jumped, diving through the entrance. Ormr slammed the cage door shut as her claws closed on the space I was occupying. Enraged, she threw herself at the cage—roaring, tearing, snapping at the bars. We screamed our fucking heads off, cowering against the cage as far as we could go.

The workers assured us they used the best and strongest Nehebkan steel to build the safety cages. They only failed once or twice a year.

Satisfied she got her point across, Nuria's tail smacked the cage one final time before she flew back to her babies. Tiamut, the smug little jerk, happily chirped and snuggled against his mother. You wouldn't have known that ten minutes before, he was savaging his sister.

"Shit," Maili breathed. "I'm too young and beautiful for this kind of stress."

I was too busy catching my breath to agree. According to the workers, they started the Hatchery for dragons of royals and no-bles. They wanted to ensure their precious bondeds were given the best care and attention while breeding, were protected from egg thieves, and most importantly, that their children didn't bond with any peasants out in the wild.

Nuria's bonded, Master Kilzred, brought his son and daughter to the Hatchery every day to see Tiamut and Shabina—waiting for the day her twins chose one or both of his children.

I wonder if this is how Dominic and Reyna first met. The day the general brought him into this breeding pen.

If that's true, no wonder he thought he owned her. Every baby in here was already marked for a rider like tagged cattle.

"That... was close," I wheezed.

"Rookie move," Ormr said. "Shed everything with baby blood on it. Even if you have to strip naked."

Ormr wasn't kidding. They had to do the same a couple days before. The workers kept spare uniforms for us to take on the way out.

"Stay here," Poet said. "We'll get you a change just in case."

I wasn't about to argue. I stayed behind while Maili and Ormr went back to work, and Poet jogged over to get me a fresh uniform. After I changed out of the torn and bloody clothes, I resumed my duty on the other side of the Hatchery—giving Nuria a healthy amount of space.

Despite the constant threat to our lives, Hatchery duty wasn't so bad. The babies were angels when their mothers were around.

And the mothers were too content feeding and grooming them to bother with what we were doing.

I started piling hay in a barrel to take to the goat pen, smiling while I looked around.

The best likeness I could give of the Hatchery was to compare it to a large birdcage. The interlocking frame surrounding us was made with the same Nehebkan steel, and reinforced by magic. Father dragons knew they weren't allowed in here. Didn't mean they cared to take orders from humans. The Hatchery was built to keep dragons out as much as it was to keep them in.

Even so, it was beautiful.

Eight mothers were currently nesting in the Hatchery. Two were still sitting on them. The rest were looking after mischievous younglings, and would for five years. That's how long it took before a young dragon was ready to survive without their mother.

Five years in this place, the workers went through every effort and spared no expense to make it comfortable. The nests were spread out in the grand room, giving each mother space. Each nest was built on a raised platform and tailored to the natural environment for each dragon.

Sandpits for the sand dragons. Seawater tanks for sea dragons. Charcoal and burnt wood for fire dragons. Dead leaves and grass for death dragons.

My gaze slid quickly off Tizor's mate and his offspring. Their ability to drain the life out of anything that touched them couldn't affect me at this distance. Still didn't make being near their pale-green, unstaring eyes, odd stillness, or unnatural quiet any easier. It was as if the life had drained out of them long before they met humans.

Sarcany, Scartha, and Ur just lay in their nest day and night, only rousing at meal times. Even when their mother was away, they didn't fight or seem to notice others around at all. The same could not be said about their father.

They were a beacon to Tizor. The reason he kept circling the city and diving out of nowhere, was because he was assessing and attacking the Hatchery's potential weaknesses. I wanted to run in a cage every time they opened the Hatchery for the returning mothers.

He wanted in.

I loaded up the barrel, then wheeled it out to the goat pen. I peeked my head in. They were where they usually were—huddled up together in a corner, shaking. The workers built it so they didn't see the dragons coming and going, but they smelled and heard them just fine.

"Hey, guys. I know this is the natural process of life. In the end, we're all sustenance to the continued growth of all beings, but this is hell for you." I spread out their hay, then fished in my pockets for the apples and carrots I pilfered from the mess hall.

The creatures carefully left their posts, sniffing out my treats. "I wouldn't wish dying a dragon's breakfast on my worst enemy."

I stayed in for a while, petting, cooing, and feeding them all the treats I had. They weren't likely to survive the week. They deserved it.

Stepping out of the pen, I glanced at the entrance leading back into the Hatchery, and turned the other way.

One good thing came out of Lieutenant Colonel Phiala's unjust punishment. She showed me the way to sneak out.

There was a reason I left feeding the goats for my last task of the day. It'd be hours before I had to report for library duty. This window was my chance.

"Bye, guys."

Circling the pen, I grabbed the change of clothes I left behind the water trough, dressed, then took off.

The Hatchery was a part of the citadel, but it was built with many exits, so the workers wouldn't get trapped inside if anything went wrong. One of those exits led outside to the goat pen. The pen bordered the Royal Wood. If the barracks were the recruits' resting place, the Royal Wood was for the dragons.

I could go through there and see Reyna as I did every night, but my business was in Golden City.

I followed the shouting, bangs, and chatter around the high walls, and came in through the kitchen. They had a delivery entrance. The merchants carting in fruits, vegetables, and meats was the closest outsiders got to the citadel.

Slipping through the hustling workers, I went ignored. I wondered if they were too absorbed in their work to notice the returned princess, or if they did not care.

"Excuse me. Sorry. Don't mind me. Excuse me."

I weaved through the busy cooks, fixing on the delivery entrance. A figure walked past the opening. They wore a green hood pulled low over their face, giving only a glimpse of their trim beard and the small scar cutting through it.

Is that—?

"Hey!" A body slammed into me, dropping a bowl of potatoes on my feet. "What are you doing in here, rider?"

"I'm so sorry." I dropped and hurriedly grabbed the runaway spuds.

"Just leave it."

"I can help."

"Go," she said, taking the bowl. "Before I ask why you're sneaking out through the kitchens." She met my startled expression and winked. "Princess."

Seemed as I didn't move through the citadel as unnoticed as I thought. I thanked her and hurried out. Bursting through the door,

I started outraged *bwaks* out of two free-walking chickens. I looked around. He was gone.

Couldn't be him anyway. Lots of people have scars. A life with dragons ensured it.

Shaking it off, I left the courtyard and joined the busy traffic around the citadel. My destination was in the lower city. A good walk, and one I'd enjoy.

Bejeweled citizens brushed past me, many of them wearing crowns of braided flowers, and eating fried pastries on a stick. The next day were the Calthoon celebrations. Calthoon was the god of the veil. The split between our world and the afterlife.

It's said that during Calthoon, the veil is opened and he can hear our prayers. Prayers for an end to the fighting. Prayers for new babies, more coin, better circumstances. All through the day, our people dance, eat, spread cheer and thanksgiving for all we have. Then at dawn's break, we drink Calthoon wine, and slip between the worlds—into the place of unknowing.

When Calthoon comes through the open entrance, you may ask him anything and he'll grant it. If he doesn't, he saw the evil or selfishness in your heart, and relayed the *no* his absence suggested.

I passed by a stall, watching the man stopper bottles of Calthoon wine, all ready for tomorrow.

The next night would be my first time celebrating Calthoon out from under the watchful eye of Sister Aven. She did not let us partake in any kind of wine as children. Once I was of age, I followed Sister Aven's lead. Plus, if I passed out around the kids, I'd wake up with a makeover.

Would I join in this year? There's a celebration for the new recruits, but I have a feeling the general will not allow me back inside the castle anytime soon.

I put the question away for the time being. If I was going to do anything, it would be to leave Golden City and celebrate with the only family I knew. Sitting in the barracks while all the recruits were at the castle, or wandering the city by myself. Neither option compared.

"Dom! Dom!"

My head snapped up.

Three kids shot out from behind a stall, unheeding of the woman calling them to come back. They raced straight for—

No! I ducked as Dominic turned, crouching low behind a confused man whose beard was braided with gold rings. *Why is he everywhere!*

Staying low, I crab-walked out of the lane and went into an alley. I hugged the wall, peeking around the corner.

Dominic couldn't see me wandering around, blatantly ignoring his father's order that I stay confined to the citadel.

"Dom! Dom! Look what I made." A little girl in a thin, tattered brown dress and long hair held up a rather questionable-looking Calthoon treat.

She and the two little children following her were peasants. That couldn't be clearer to anyone as she stood in the middle of rich nobles all wearing an unnecessary number of jewels. While the most expensive thing she had on was worn cloth boots.

Dominic bent to her level—no doubt to deliver his scorn directly in her eyes to match that *no one is worth my time* look.

A grin split his face. Whole, beautiful, and happy—the force of that perfect smile knocked me off my feet. I wobbled and had to grab the wall to stay upright.

"Whoa. You made this all by yourself, Orla? You sure Mom didn't help?"

"She did not."

I took another look at the older woman who rushed after them. She wasn't running to save her children from the beast. By her beaming smile, she was happy to see him.

"She made it for you all by herself," Mom said. "Even added the nuts you like."

Dominic laid a hand over his heart. "I'm honored. You always give me the best gifts."

"Happy birthday."

My brow bobbed. It was Dominic's birthday? He didn't say a word about it during lessons that day, and no one said a word to him. Did royals and nobles not celebrate birthdays like the commoners do?

"Eat it, eat it, eat it," Orla cried, bouncing and clapping.

"My pleasure." Dominic tore off a bite, and groaned. "Oh, so good. Mmm. Hmm. Can't stop," he said, tearing into it like a madman.

The children howled laughing. A giggle escaped me, and I clapped my hand over my mouth.

What was I doing? Just because the guy doesn't tear the heads off children, doesn't make him a good person.

"I got something for you too," he said. Dominic reached in his back pocket and pulled out a small book. "My mother used to read these stories to me when I was small. Now you can read them to your brother and sister."

I tensed. *I was right. He's an ass.*

Little Orla shrank. "But I... I can't read."

The shame in her reply crushed my heart to dust. Was Dominic truly so far removed from the people he demanded to rule, that he didn't know families who couldn't dress their children in clothes without holes, definitely couldn't afford to send them to school?

Schooling that was free during the time of Queen Kisandra until General Roark decided educating the peasants was what led to the revolt. The usurper wouldn't have gotten such dangerous ideas in her head, let alone the knowledge of the forbidden magics, if she hadn't gone to school.

"You don't know how to read?" Dominic shrugged. "Guess that means I have to teach you."

Orla gasped. "Really? Thank you, Dom!" She smooched his cheek, then ran into her mother's skirts, squealing.

I backed away as Dominic and the woman fell into conversation. What was I supposed to make of that scene? Would he really take time off from training and learning to rule so that he could teach one little girl from the other side of the wall how to read? If he did, what did it mean? Was he a good person under the domineering, manipulative mask he showed the world?

I thought back to that morning, when he stole a bun off my plate.

"Hey!" I brandished my fork. "Give that back!"

"Why? I thought I made it clear by now. What's yours is mine. Your food, the throne, your dragon, and your..." He trailed off, looking me up and down so slow and pointed until he landed on my lips. "...everything else."

Nope, my first impression of him was correct. Terrible, arrogant bag of dragon dung.

I took the back alleys to the Silver Bucket. Wasn't worth testing this strange new side of his personality on my breaking his father's rules.

Music spilled out of the back entrance. A jaunty, happy tune that lifted my spirits. I loved to dance, and I loved Calthoon. Let Monday carry the worries of my terrible rankings. I deserved to spend that weekend enjoying the celebrations.

Rosaleen waved from her booth near the stage. The musicians talked amongst each other while they drank and took a break. It'd be impossible to talk to her when they started up again. I'd better get everything out quickly.

"Rosaleen." We hugged each other like parted lovers who hadn't seen each other for years—not close friends who spent a few days apart.

"I'm so happy to see you," she said. "And your new tattoos. Wow, you look great in gold."

I laughed. "Not as happy as I am to see you. It's so good to see a friendly face. And look." I fished in my pocket and handed her my coin purse. "We got paid today. Sixteen gold ryus, Rosie. The most money I've ever held in my hands. Half for you. Give the rest to Sister Aven."

"I'm giving *all* of it to Sister Aven," she said, giving me a look. "You know I am. Why pretend I'd do otherwise?"

"You're still over three hundred ryus away from buying out your contract. This was always the plan. Take it, Rosie. I'd give you more if I could."

"Ains, we were eight years old when you swore you'd buy me out. I don't hold you to the promises of a child."

"I do."

She looked away, almost hiding her trembling lips.

Eight years old. That's how old she was when the aunt that took her in after her parents' death said that starting on her eighteenth birthday, Rosaleen would pay back all the money she wasted on her by working in her brothel.

Two years and that three-hundred-and-fifty-ryu *debt* was only down to about three hundred and forty.

"Let's talk about something else," she said. "Ossian's been buzzing with news of the princess's return. I asked Mother Zaeah to bless our plan, but I didn't know it worked this well."

I let her change the subject.

"It did work well, though it wasn't because everyone instantly believed my lies." I told her everything about the general's visit, his withering the marriage contract, our strange walk through the castle, and the end when he tried to throw me to my death.

"It lashed and choked me, Rosie, I swore I was dead, then…"

She gaped at me, eyes wide the entire story. "…and then?" she cried. "Don't leave off there."

"Then, I didn't die. By some crazy twist of fate, the lies we told to save my life, turned out to be the truth. I am from Queen Kisandra's bloodline. A close relation. Daughter, granddaughter, I can't be sure. But the throne placed a crown on my head."

Rosaleen blew back, shaking her head. She wore the same outfit that she did our first day together in Golden City. The only difference was the bright-red underclothing that was a source of admiration from half our patrons.

I was glad she chose the spot she did. We could talk without all the blatant potential eavesdroppers, succeeding in their task.

"The general ripped the crown from me and said in no uncertain terms that he'd see to it that I never rule. His son repeated the sentiment in case I didn't hear it the first time. He said he's going to kill me."

"Who?" she hissed. "The general or his son? Not that it matters because it's *treason*!"

"The son. But I'm pretty sure the general ordered him to get rid of me too. He confined me to the citadel. I shouldn't even be here right now."

"Will you be okay? Should you go back?"

I shook my head. "Anyone looking for me will assume I hung around the Hatchery after my punishment. They restrict who goes inside so that the mothers don't get overwhelmed. My watchers can't check. I'm fine."

She squeezed my hand. I squeezed back.

"What about going into Ossian? Especially tomorrow for the celebrations. Can you sneak out?"

"I wouldn't dare try," I replied. "The gate guards would report me to the general. Plus, he'd want to know who I was sneaking out to see. I can't have Sister Aven and the kids mixed up in my lies."

"Well, they're not lies anymore."

"Even more reason." I dropped my voice. "Everyone wants to know where the princess has been all this time. I think they're hoping I'm the key to finding Queen Kisandra."

"Is that what the general is hoping? From the sound of it, he'd prefer she never return to take his throne. He can deny you while there are still so many questions, but he couldn't deny her."

I opened my mouth, then stopped. Rosaleen was right. General Roark's behavior after the throne failed to kill me was not of a subject pleased to see the usurper hadn't wiped out the monarch line as we'd all believed.

He wanted rid of me—I knew this—but after I was gone, what would he do to ensure this never happened again?

"I just want to train. Control the bond and live my life with Reyna. How did all of this happen?"

"It's fate, Ains. Mother Zaeah and Father Parthelan brought you here because there's something you must do. A peasant. A princess. A dragon rider. Maybe you're meant to bring those worlds back together again."

I snorted. "Definitely not. I'm a failure at all of those things. I couldn't find work as a magicless peasant and had to resort to stealing. I'm nowhere close to taking the throne. And, I'm doing so terribly at training, I'm ranked zero for three lessons. Poet says I'll be cut—"

"What?" Rosaleen sat up straight. "They're threatening to cut you?"

"Yes. Anyone who ranks bottom in three categories." I laughed ruefully. "Lucky me, I'm automatically at the bottom for two classes because I'm magicless— Rosaleen, why are you looking at me like that?"

"Ainsley..." she breathed. "Don't you know what it means to be cut?"

"Yes, I'll be kicked out of training."

"You'll be kicked out... and executed."

I stilled. "What? No. It doesn't mean that. It can't mean that."

"Ains," she cried, smacking the table. "Every bonded pair has to train and join the Royal Riders. No exceptions. But what do you think happens if someone washes out of training? Do they allow some incompetent weakling to go on and join our defenders? No. Of course not."

"But that doesn't mean they're killed."

"It does. Dragons are too precious to remain bonded to a failed rider who spends his days manning a silks shop. They need the dragon to bond with someone better, and the only way to force it is to—"

"—kill their rider." My lips were numb. "Why didn't I realize this? Mother Zaeah, Rosaleen! Ormr said I have two weeks to raise my rank before the first cut. What can I do in two weeks!"

"Okay, don't panic." She got out of her seat and paced our small corner of pub. Movement helped her think. "There's nothing you can do about the magic classes, but what about the other one?"

"It's scholarship. Major Sorrel said starting Monday, we'll analyze past battles against the Druks—why they succeeded, or why they failed. I'll have to write reports on it. Do I have to tell you why that's a problem?"

"It's not a problem, because you're going to cheat."

I blinked. "Excuse me?"

"You heard me, and don't get all innocent on me, Miss Trickyfingers. If you can steal to save your life, you can cheat to save your life." She dropped her palms on the table, leaning over me. "Pick the smartest guy in your class and seduce him. He'll write all your reports for you."

"I can't do that!" No one in Adalinda was more outraged than me in that moment. "First, the reports aren't the only problem. Second, the smartest guy in my class is Dominic Roark."

"Even better. He's using sex to control you. You use sex to control him."

My jaw worked. "He's not using sex to control me."

"Didn't you nearly kill this major guy and half your class just because he kissed you?"

"I need to stop telling you everything."

She laughed. "Ains, don't make a big deal about it. Sex, power, status—it's all a game. Roark has been playing his whole life, and you can bet, if the roles were reversed, he wouldn't spare an ounce of conscience about using you." She saw the look on my face. "Ugh, okay. Watch this."

Rosaleen flicked to the table of guys who'd been staring and pointing at her since I walked in. Her whole demeanor changed. Dropping her shoulder, she giggled, tossing them a flirty wink. "What's up, boys? Are you going to stare all night, or are you going to buy me and my friend a drink?"

A bulky, blond guy leaned back in his chair, smirking. The leader of the pack. "What will you give us if we do?"

Rosie's finger slid down her shoulder, catching the strap of her breastband, and bringing it along for the ride. "It's impolite to make a lady say." Her nipple popped free.

Blond Leader tripped over himself, running to the bartender. Rosaleen shot me a *see?*

"What did that prove? Men always buy you drinks, everywhere we go. Me, they ask if I'm lost and looking for my mother."

"I'm not done yet."

We sat back, waiting for the guy to return. He placed two large honey meads on our table.

Rosaleen pouted. "Oh, thanks, I guess. I was hoping you'd buy us some blackberry wine."

My brows rose. Blackberry wine was expensive. They didn't even serve the stuff in Ossian pubs because no one could afford it.

"But if you can't afford it," Rosaleen sighed, "this will do."

Our blond friend puffed up. "Course I can afford it. Two bottles it is."

"Four, please." Smiling, Rosie leaned in close, brushing her lips on his ear. "I like to be nice and drunk when a guy puts it in my ass."

The guy returned with six. He tried to sit with us and Rosaleen held him off with a finger on the chest. "Uh-uh. My friend and I are finishing up a private chat. I'll come to you when we're done."

"Oh, uh..."

"Bye," she said firmly.

He walked off, the portrait of confusion. Rosaleen could not have been more smug.

"That's how it's done. See? Easy, right?"

"Easy?" I hissed. "Are you actually going to let him...?"

"Stick his dick in my ass," she finished helpfully. "No. I never said I would."

"What? But you—"

"I said that I like to be drunk when a guy sticks it in. I never said he'd be that guy. A quick peek and a few words whispered in his ear, and he spent more than I make in a year on us. That's what you have to do to this Dominic.

"The right touch here, the right brush there, a little peek, a soft whisper, *no promises*, and you've got him eating out of the palm of your hands." She grasped my forearms. "You have to try, Ains. Sounds to me like you have more than one good reason to change his feelings toward you. He wants you dead. Make him want something else."

I didn't know what to say. The thought of seducing Dominic Roark was insane. Even if I could get him to believe I didn't want his throne, Reyna choosing me over him was enough for a death sentence. The bond between rider and dragon was strong. Reyna and I had been together for only two moons, and I'd kill anyone who tried to take her from me. Dominic and Reyna had that bond for years.

I'd never admit it to him, but I understood why he hated me.

"Ains? Hey, Ainsley?" she said, pulling me out of my musing. "Do you know those people?"

I turned in my seat, and landed on a waving Ormr and Maili. The smile froze on my face. *What are they doing here?*

They headed straight for us.

"They're recruits," I said quickly. "We have to come up with an explanation for how we know each other."

"Leave it to me."

"Hey, guys," Maili said. "We were going to mind our own business, but you two were looking like you could use some help finishing off that blackberry wine. Can we join you?"

I said yes because no was too suspicious. Every recruit who wasn't me was allowed to leave the citadel and spend their weekends how they wished. Which meant the pubs would be full. Of all the luck, the twins ended up spending their coin in this pub. I thought I was smart choosing a place in the lower city—farthest from the citadel without leaving Golden City.

"I'm Maili. This is my twin, Ormr. How do you and Ainsley know each other?" She glanced at her blue band and flicked off.

"We don't really," Rosaleen said. "She was asking for tips on how to seduce a man. I gave her a demonstration, which resulted in six bottles of blackberry wine. Only seemed right to share."

The twins flicked on my flaming face. *Please, don't ask follow-up questions. Please, don't ask follow-up questions.*

"Who are you trying to seduce?" Maili asked.

"Ormr, of course," I said quickly, cutting off a smirking Rosaleen. "The way you snore so loud and hard, it rattles the bed frame. Can't get enough of it. Want to make sure you keep me up for the rest of our lives."

Ormr howled. "If that's a proposal, I absolutely accept. Who wouldn't marry a future queen?"

"Ha ha." Maili shoved my shoulder. "But seriously, we're friends. You don't have to ask strangers for advice. I would've helped with whoever this guy or girl is. I mean, you know plenty about my sex life with Poet."

"Only because I'm in the bed right next to your sex life."

Grinning, she shrugged—pouring herself a drink. "Not our fault they stick us all in the barracks. I've got needs that have to be met."

This was the philosophy of almost every recruit from what I saw. Every night, I went to sleep with my pillow over my head, drowning out one or more amorous couples. The only one who didn't make his mattress squeak every night was Dominic. But that was not for lack of offers.

Dominic went out most nights, and naturally did not tell anyone where. When he was in the barracks, he ignored everyone while reclining against the bed frame, reading.

"So tell us," Maili said. "Who is it?"

I seized the first name that popped into my head.

"It's Lonan." I made a face. "Sorry, I didn't want to say because I know how Poet feels about Keir and his friends."

"Oh, Mother Zaeah, no," she cried. "Don't feel bad for liking who you like. We've all got that person who pisses us off for all the wrong reasons, but turns us on for all the right ones. Want to know the truth?" Maili dropped her voice. "I shouldn't even be with Poet. If Mother found out, she'd be furious. Part of his appeal."

"What's wrong with Poet? He's such a nice guy. He lets you eat off his plate."

She laughed. "It's stupid. You know the whole ranking thing carries into royals and nobles too. The royals are royalty. Nobles were granted titles by the royal family, or now General Roark, due to exceptional service. The more recently you received a nobility, the lower in rank you are.

"Poet's father was given a title for fighting alongside General Roark, and even saving his life once. But because their title is less than fifty years old, and I'm a royal, he's not fit to be with me."

"Wow. That is stupid."

"No arguments here." She shook her head. "Anyway, the point of telling you that is to say I support you, and all my seduction tips are yours."

"Thanks," I said, and meant it. "But I think I'll just let him come to me. If he's not interested and I make a fool of myself, it'll be more ammunition for Keir to use against me."

"Good point."

Ormr and Rosaleen laughed, drawing our attention. I hadn't noticed them in conversation.

"—tell them to visit The Red Veil and ask for Rosie. You dragon riders work hard," she purred, trailing a finger over theirs. "You deserve to unwind."

"I do get this terrible crick in my neck from sleeping on that mattress," Ormr said. "How's yours?"

"Come over and find out."

"I should get going." I pushed back my chair. "Thanks for your help, Rosemary."

"Rosaleen."

"Oh, right. Of course." We shared a look that said everything, the way only childhood friends could do. "Bye, guys."

I left out of the front entrance and made for the citadel. Ormr and Maili's arrival made for a short visit, but I was glad I got to see her. I wished I'd gotten a chance to ask how Sister Aven and the kids were doing. I wished even more that I could leave the city and find out for myself.

When I arrived at the citadel, I slipped through the kitchens and found my change of clothes behind the goat pen.

Now, I'll do a quick check on the babies, then I'll report early for library duty. Sooner I finish, the sooner my Calthoon weekend starts.

I entered through the back door, mind turning to what Sister Aven and the kids would be able to do for Calthoon with the coin. The table would have meat on it for the first time in a year.

"—strong offspring. We found his mate living among the ice caves in Edjer."

I slowed to a stop.

"We hope to rebuild the species with this pair," said General Roark. "Tizor is certainly proud of their efforts."

"Hmm, yes." Three men in long purple robes gathered around him, listening to him praise Tizor's offspring.

Bang!

The building rattled—shaken under the full weight of Tizor's body. He shared his children's propensity for silence, and as such didn't roar his outrage, but I felt it coming off him in waves. Dragons were a part of our lives. They were to be revered, respected, protected, and loved. No self-respecting Adalindian feared them. As much as I knew this, it meant nothing.

For as long as I lived, Tizor would terrify me.

"He does seem very protective of them," the man finished.

"With good reason," General Roark said. "A father must have a firm and steady hand in their children's lives to lead them down the right path. I have thirty-two children and they are all credits to me and this great nation. Sarcany, Scartha, and Ur will be the same."

The way the general spoke about them, you'd think the young dragons were his thirty-third, thirty-fourth, and thirty-fifth child.

I crept away.

"Ah, Rider Ainsley. There you are." The general and his companions came toward me. "Just the person we've been looking for."

I flicked to the entrance leading to the goat pen and my usual escape route. How long have they been waiting? Had I been found out?

"This is Master Quinlan, Master Peregrin, and Master Liadan." His smile didn't reach his eyes. "They've been most anxious to meet you."

Master Quinlan bowed over my hand. "Princess, it's an honor."

"*Rider* Ainsley," the general corrected. "There is still some question over her parentage."

"We all saw the throne bestow her crown," Master Peregrin said. "There can be no question."

"You say so, but how are we to interpret Rider Ainsley's beginnings? Did not Queen Kisandra, if she is her mother, make her intentions clear when she left her magicless child in the woods to die?"

"It is not our place to guess our queen's intentions," Master Liadan said smoothly. "The throne has chosen. That is all we need know." He was next to bow over my hand, burrowing discomfort further into my bones. "Princess, Mother Zaeah and Father Parthelan bless you. We're most excited for you to lead the Calthoon celebrations tomorrow."

"Excuse me?"

"Calthoon," the general said. "As you know, the new recruits are all invited to the palace tomorrow. It is both a celebration of Calthoon, and your sacrifices."

"But I didn't think I could go to that? You said I wasn't allowed to leave the citadel."

General Roark laughed. "I said no such thing. You must have misunderstood. I suggested that you remain on the grounds where it's safe. You do not have guards or protection. Unsavory characters could take advantage."

"I see. I guess I must've misunderstood. So, to be clear, General Roark, I am free to leave the citadel and Golden City as I wish?" I matched his mirthless smile.

"Of course," he said easily, eyes locked on mine. "With an escort, naturally. For your safety."

"Yes. For my safety."

Bang!

I jumped, nearly falling into the sand nest at Tizor's second attack.

"We will see you tomorrow, Rider Ainsley," the general said, turning away. "We're all looking forward to what you'll do next."

Chapter Ten

I stood in the corner of the ballroom, trying to make myself as small as possible. Poet stood beside me, tearing apart a turkey leg and chattering at me.

"—looking forward to this since Valor and I bonded. A ball in the palace thrown in our honor. Not even my father is allowed in the palace without special invitation from the general."

I tugged him closer, positioning him in front of me. Listening with half an ear, I peered over his shoulder. The ball was incredible.

The throne room was a wonder in the middle of the preparations, but when all was said and done, they transformed the place into a paradise beyond the veil.

Royals and nobles in glittering robes and flowing gowns swayed on the edges of the room, watching the chosen recruits perform their dance. It wasn't an exaggeration to say all eyes were on Dominic and Nuala. Even mine.

Dominic wore the formal rider uniform—black leather, dragon-scale boots, and half a dozen commendations pinned to his chest. He slicked his hair back with something that made it shine in the candlelight—giving all the appearance of a crown. The leather clung to him in the most fortunate of ways, clinging to his sculpted arms and straining to hold on with each dip and spin of his partner.

I drifted off him to the line of men and women standing straight-backed and stiff at the foot of the throne. I couldn't place who they were at first. Their skin tone ranged from umber to fawn. Was this diverse group one of the dragon rider squads? Had they come to welcome their junior recruits soon to join them on the battlefield?

Then I counted them.

Thirty-one.

Dominic made thirty-two. They were General Roark's children.

Ranging from the salty-haired, gently wrinkled smoothness of a dragon bonded who reached their fifties and then stopped aging, to a young girl who looked about six or seven years old—they were all there.

"Are they General Roark's children?" I asked to be certain.

"Oh yeah. They're here because of you, you know." He casually dropped this midchew. "It's a show of strength. All of them against one you."

I didn't have an argument for this. It's exactly what I assumed.

"What should I do?"

"Stop hiding in the corner for one. Don't let anyone make you ashamed of who you are, Ainsley."

I blinked at him. That was the first I had heard Poet speak so seriously.

"You show them they don't intimidate you. You're a dragon rider. Nothing does."

The words sunk in. He was right. This wasn't me—hiding and slinking in corners from men determined to make me feel small. I was the one who danced the silliest and wildest during Calthoon to make my siblings laugh. I was the one who picked the pockets of the filthy louts who shouted nasty things at Rosaleen in the streets. We toasted with mugs of mead they paid for while the bastards were scratching their heads, wondering when and how karma tripped them up so fast.

I kissed his cheek. "Thanks, Poet. You're a good friend."

Stepping to the side, he held out his arm. I took a deep breath and slinked my arm through. A quick peek down confirmed all the crouching and ducking hadn't wrinkled my borrowed dress.

My last-minute invitation hadn't left me time to buy a ballgown, and giving Rosaleen my entire pay ensured I wouldn't be able to either way. I was in the middle of putting on my rider uniform when Maili stopped me—horrified.

That was how I arrived at the palace in a forest-green, shimmering gown with tulip sleeves and a gauzy, tulle skirt. My skirt wasn't as full as those around me. I also had on no jewelry. I had still managed to stand out, which sent me into the corner.

No more.

"Okay, let's— Ah!" Horrific pain ripped through my mind, doubling me over. Bloodlust poured through the open wound in my skull. Raw, violent, and unsettling, my stomach churned as I felt Reyna's satisfaction over her kill.

I loved her, but it'd be a grand day when I learned how to keep these emotions out.

"Are you okay?"

Poet helped me up. I straightened and met the eyes of all the guests now looking at me. The riders had finished their dance just in time to stare at me too. My face heated under Dominic's raised brow.

"My apologies," I said. "I'm still learning to control the bond."

"You have nothing to apologize for, Princess. I know from experience how difficult it is to hold back Reyna." Dominic stepped out of the pack, slipping free of Nuala who tried grabbing his arm. "Are you well now?"

My jaw worked. What the hell was happening? Why was he speaking to me with so much concern after a week of swearing to kill me, stealing my dragon, and keeping me so confiningly close, I had two shadows.

"I am," I finally got out. I felt the weight of dozens of pairs of eyes on us. Including the general who stood on the opposite side of the room with a short, thin woman covered in jewels and fine silks. "Thank you for asking."

"I'd like to thank you," he said, getting on bended knee before me. "For allowing me a dance."

I gaped at him. Now I knew he lost his mind. "A what?"

"A dance," he repeated, smile tightening around the edges. "If you permit me."

"Uhh... No, thank—"

Poet tightened on my arm, swinging my head around. His eyes bulged, spinning back and forth. His message was clear.

"I mean, thank you." I slipped free of Poet and placed my hand in Dominic's. A strange and unwelcome shiver climbed my spine when he immediately laced his fingers through mine.

Everyone parted as he led me under the grand chandelier. They all moved back except for Keir. Snarl on his lips, he advanced on me. I instinctively backed away and fell onto Dominic.

Dominic grasped my waist and swung me around, enticing a gasp.

I couldn't move or think as he draped my arms around his shoulders and leaned in close, holding my waist. Amber pools captured and drowned me. Not even in the deepest, darkest pit would I admit that this was something I respected about him. Dominic didn't speak to your shoes or the spot on the wall behind you. He looked everyone in the eyes.

The music changed. A slow, teasing melody filled the room, as haunting as it was romantic.

"What is going on?" I stated—blunt and nonapologetic. "Why are you dancing with me and pretending to be nice? You hate me."

His smile didn't slip. "In front of all these royals and nobles, I don't."

Irritation chafed under my satin top. "That's the reason? You're putting on a show for people and using me to do it? What a shame, Dominic. I thought you were better than that."

"Did you? I didn't know you had such a high opinion of me."

"I don't," I said quickly. "I have a low opinion and you drove it lower."

He hummed. "I see. So, you would respect me more if I insulted and humiliated you in a room full of strangers like an ill-mannered child?"

"What? No, that's not what I'm saying. Just don't pretend to like me when you don't."

"All I've done is ask you to dance. Hardly a declaration of undying affection. Or do you assume everyone who asks you to dance is in love with you?"

"No," I whisper-screamed. "Stop twisting everything."

He didn't even try holding back his smirk. "I'm not twisting everything. You baffle me, Princess. Just trying to understand you."

My lips parted but nothing came out. I don't know why, but I sensed he wasn't trying to insult me.

Dominic spun me out. Reds, golds, greens, and people blurred in a weird and delightful myriad. We were the sole focus of everyone in the room.

We danced until an unseen cue signaled everyone else to fill the dance floor. Before I knew it, another spin sent me into Poet's arms.

I blew out a breath. "Thank you again, friend."

Chuckling, he winked. "Don't worry. I've got your back. These formal functions can be hard for me too."

I had a feeling I knew why. The stupid ranking of nobles to royals explained why Keir and his friends targeted him for his inferior status and common dragon. I can only imagine what it was like to bend under their disdain for years and years compared to my single week.

Looking up at Golden City, it was easy to imagine their lives were as wonderful as the name. Seemed we all struggle with our place in the world.

Ting, ting, ting.

"Excuse me, everyone." I recognized the prim and polished woman standing before the general's line of children, as the same person from my first visit to the throne room. She oversaw the Royal Riders practicing the Calthoon dance. "I speak on behalf of General Roark when I say it is an honor to celebrate Calthoon with the wise and honorable first families, and the brave and respected young recruits.

"Every year, a chosen recruit stands up and states the collective wish to be asked of Calthoon as you begin this new chapter as defenders of our great nation. We're to welcome Rider Ainsley"—I tripped over my feet—"to usher in a season of strength and fortune."

She looked around for my paling face. "Ah, there you are. Rider Ainsley, if you'll step this way, please."

The guests burst into applause. There was no getting out of this.

"It's all right," Poet whispered in my ear. "Just say we ask Calthoon to bless the wind beneath our dragons' wings, or something like that. Short and simple."

"Okay. Short and simple."

I gave his arm one last squeeze before leaving him behind. *Short and simple. Short and simple. Short and—*

I jerked back—something hard and unyielding snagging my dress. Before I knew what happened, a loud ripping sound split through the applause.

Cool air hit my bare backside.

"Ahh!" Screaming, I covered my ass spinning around. Keir's smile was cold and cruel—standing on the torn remains of my skirt.

"Oops. Sorry, Princess. I thought I was stepping on a dirty pile of rags."

Gasps and smothered laughs echoed in my ears, heating my body with humiliation. I was torn between screaming, crying, or taking another belt and whipping his ass.

Hands grasped my waist. I was snapped back, bouncing off someone's chest. I tipped my head up and a sliver of fear cut through my anger. I'd seen that look on Dominic's face only once before.

The day he swore before Drake, the recruits, and Reyna that he'd end my life.

"Keir, leave," he gritted. "Now."

"What?" His smirk faltered. "Come on, Dom, I was kidding."

"Get out, or you'll be carried out."

I stood trapped between their rising rage. Mostly because Dominic was my shield—holding me firm and steady against him. I tried with everything in me not to think of my bare skin pressed against a firm and unnaturally large bulge.

"Are you serious? You're sticking up for her? You fucking hate her!" He jabbed at me. "No one wants to see this bitch dead more than you!"

"Guards."

Three men posted against the wall came alive. They bore down on Keir fast.

"Don't you dare touch him!" A woman covered in an obscene amount of jewelry burst out of the crowd. She wore layer upon layer of heavy gold, bejeweled necklaces. At least two rings on each finger. Studs going all the way up both ears, and both nostrils pierced with diamonds. Underneath all that, I saw Keir's eyes and the hard set of his lips.

"There's no need for this." A heavyset man wearing shiny gold robes and even more jewels than Keir's mother pushed between Keir and the approaching guards. "The boy tripped and stood on her dress. It was a mistake." He flapped a hand at the guards. "Return to your post."

"That is not for you to decide, Master Stryker. Keir leaves now. No one disrespects our guests in our palace."

"Your palace? Ha!" He whirled on Dominic. "That's a fine thing for the son of a Ghidorian whore to say while he clings to the true princess. I ought to put you over my knee, boy. Teach you proper respect for—"

A hand clamped the man's shoulder. He tensed—eyes bulging out of their sockets. His face reddened. Angry, crimson lines split apart his skin, tearing him at the seams.

I gasped as the seams split and crumbly ash poured from bloodless wounds. The man crumbled to dust before my eyes—robes, jewels, and all.

"My son will not be spoken to in such a manner," General Roark said calmly. "You will leave my palace, and count yourself in my good graces if I let the matter end here."

He killed him. Mother Zaeah, he killed him!

"Father!" Keir launched at General Roark. "You killed him! You—"

The woman clamped a hand over his mouth, hauling him back. "Thank you, General. F-forgive us, General. We'll go."

I could do nothing as the guards physically restrained and dragged Keir away. His mother covered his mouth, muffling his shouted words at the general... then me.

I went cold at the pure incensed hatred in his eyes. This would not be the end to the matter.

Not for me and him.

"Son," General Roark said, dragging me back to reality. I bit back a scream when the general claimed my hand. He trapped my gaze while he pressed the barest kiss to my knuckles. "Help Rider Ainsley find a change of clothes."

"Yes, sir."

Dominic shrugged off his coat and wrapped it around me. I was little more than a doll, held and practically carried out of the throne room.

"He killed him..." I whispered. "He just... killed him."

Dominic's voice was flat. "He does that."

What was there to say? A man was killed right in front of me. By the very man I knew deep down wanted me dead too. Was that my fate? After all I had and still hoped to accomplish, was my destiny to be a pile of ash on a polished floor?

Dominic led me through the winding hallways. Neither of us spoke, although I searched his expression multiple times. He was unreadable.

"In here."

We stopped before a large oak door. It didn't really register that Dominic's hand had been on my back the whole time, helping me keep his coat in place, until he dropped it to let me inside.

I crossed the threshold into a rather plain room by palace standards. A small bed, vanity, a mirror, wardrobe, and couch placed by the window was all it had to say for itself. I fell onto the couch—legs giving away just in time. I didn't pay attention to Dominic's rummaging.

"Why did he do that," I rasped. "He didn't have to kill him."

"Stryker sealed his own fate. Challenging my father's authority. Calling his wife a whore. Disparaging his son. Flaunting his loyalist beliefs. That was going to end no other way."

A bitter, angry part of me wanted to shout that his hard, heartless father cared about only two of those things. And his wife and son were not those two.

But I swallowed it. Dominic wasn't the person I wanted to yell at. For the first time since we met, he was the only person I didn't want to yell at.

"Why did you do that? Help me." I fixed on him. "You were there before Poet even thought to move."

He paused in riffling through the wardrobe. "I did what every decent person was going to do. I was simply faster."

"But why?" I pressed. "Your decency doesn't extend to me. Keir was right. You hate me."

"Why should that make a difference?" He pulled out a gown, shook his head, and shoved it back. "I hate you because you're a lying, duplicitous dragon thief who is after my throne but hides your true nature under a doe-eyed-fawn act. Keir hates you because you're poor and a woman. The latter are not valid reasons, and never will be.

"This half-Ghidorian bastard was raised to respect women." He finally found a gown he approved of and held it up. The breath left my lungs. "I judge my opponents by what's between their ears, not between their legs. I knew from the moment I watched you take those hits from Keir, letting him get full of himself while you quickly and easily loosened his pants—that you're not to be underestimated. The least I can do is show a worthy adversary some respect."

I didn't reply. Dominic threw so many things at me at once, anything I tried to say would've been jumbled and confused. How did a man compliment and declare their hatred for someone all in the same breath?

"I'll be on the other side of the door. Call when you need me."

I didn't know why I'd need him, until I got the gown on. Straining, I half dislocated my arm trying to do up the dozens of tiny buttons going up the dress's spine. I glared at my reflection, asking myself if I was truly going to summon my enemy to help me dress.

How would his help with this be more mortifying than my bare backside pressed against him? No point pretending we can go back now.

"Dominic," I called, cheeks heating. "Can you come in?"

He did. Without a word, he turned me and began doing up my buttons.

"This dress is lovely," I said to break the silence. "Will the owner mind that I'm wearing it?"

"No."

I waited for more, but nothing came. "I didn't steal her. You know I didn't." I said it because I had to. "Why hate me for her choice?"

"Why should I believe it was her choice? You lie as easily as you breathe."

"But you said you know when I'm lying."

"Yes," he said softly, gently tugging my hair free—his fingers brushing my shoulders. "But not when you're telling the truth."

I broke away to leave.

"One last thing." Dominic opened the wardrobe's bottom drawers. I bit my tongue at the collection of rings, necklaces, and expensive bracelets. All of this was collecting dust in a tiny room without a lock? What treasures were hidden in the other rooms?

Shaking my head, I tossed the thief thoughts away. I was a dishonest person making an honest living. I had something to lose now. The last thing I should do was let Dominic Roark read that on my face.

"I'm sure you felt it, and that's why you hid in a corner for most of the night. My dad's supporters are silently looking down on you, while the loyalists are embarrassed by you. You don't look like the princess they want," he said. "You look like a poor little orphan girl surprised by destiny."

Dominic lifted out a gorgeous, diamond-studded choker. He faced me toward the mirror. His hands were soft and sure on my throat.

"If that's true, doesn't it work in your favor?" I asked. "Why help me change their opinion?"

"You have to ask? A poor little orphan girl is an object of pity. When that's true, the cold, disciplined general's son who kills her is the villain in everyone's eyes. No matter how justified." His gaze pinned me through the mirror. "I want everyone to see what I see. The shrewd, calculating thief who beat a man's face in without hesitation, clocks the valuables of everyone who crosses her path, and the rage..."

Dominic brushed the hard, thin line of my lips. He grinned wide at the fire in my eyes.

"I want everyone to see this rage," he whispered. "The world will know the real you, Ainsley No-Name, and when they do, they won't condemn me for killing a sad orphan. They'll praise me for destroying our greatest threat."

"You don't have me nearly as figured out as you think, Roark. You'll find that out too late."

His smirk didn't waver. "Looking forward to it."

We had no more to say to each other as I finished dressing and followed him back to the throne room. No thoughts to voice out loud, though plenty swirled in my head.

I hadn't noticed Dominic watching me as closely as he clearly was. This should've unnerved me. Instead it made me angry at myself. Of course he was watching me closely.

Reyna chose me over him. What would happen if Adalinda did the same? I was his rival in a game I was ill-equipped to play. That was obvious from the fact that I still wasn't taking him seriously. Part of me didn't believe a man who kissed me so passionately, and tried to show me mercy with such a generous marriage contract, would turn around and kill me in cold blood.

Dominic had almost the full measure of me. If I didn't wake up and open my eyes, he'd shut them before I saw it coming.

"Princess."

Dominic opened the door and bowed me in. Stepping over the threshold, I found the dancing was over and a long table had been brought in and set. It was time for the feast, following which everyone would consume their Calthoon drink, and hope to see him on the other side.

It was as though no one had witnessed a man killed right in front of them.

Royals laughed and mingled. Nobles traded stories. General Roark and his children claimed the entire head of the table. And Ormr, Maili, and Poet chatted at the end. They were enraptured with their various conversations.

Until they saw me.

Silence rippled down the table, claiming everyone until it reached General Roark. He stood—peering at me over the heads of the most important people in Adalinda. If I was still in front of a mirror, I'd stare at me too.

The gown Dominic had given me was stunning. Wispy, gauzy material flowed from my waist. The top of my skirt dyed a silvery blue that darkened as it traveled down, becoming almost pitch black as though it was dipped in starlight.

My bodice clung to me in all the right ways. Giving me curves I didn't know I had, and pushing up cleavage that didn't used to be there. Matching the choker, Dominic gifted me teardrop pearl earrings, dainty diamond bracelets for each wrist, and a ring he slid on my finger from bended knee. I blushed at the act. The insufferable jerk smirked. I could tell he was thinking about my kink for men who wanted to kill me.

One such man held my gaze. General Roark had eyes only for me as silence gave way to gasps.

"Princess Ainsley."

"She's beautiful."

"Our queen returned to us."

"No proof."

"When the chit reveals Queen Kisandra's location, then I'll believe her."

I drowned under the mixed reactions. It was impossible to tell how many people believed me to be the princess and wanted me to take the throne, and who believed I was the princess and wanted me to disappear.

"Wow, Ainsley," Ormr cried. "You look incredible. Sit with us. We saved you a seat."

I flicked to them—only for the barest second to acknowledge their compliments with a smile, but when I glanced back, the general wasn't looking at me anymore.

He locked eyes with his son over my head. If I wasn't looking closely, I would've missed the quickest twitch of a smirk... and a nod.

THE BEST MEAL I'D EVER eaten was glue and sawdust in my mouth. I kept eating because it gave my body something to do while my mind whirled.

I played into General Roark's hand, and for the life of me, I couldn't figure out how. Dominic said my looking the part would make the loyalists love me more, and Roark's supporters twice as bitter. I knew how the latter favored him, but why would he want to give hope to the group that wanted to oust him and put the monarchy back in charge?

Regardless, it wasn't possible that he and Dominic planned my change of gown. There was no way they anticipated Keir destroying my dress. There was also no chance that Keir plotted with the two of them. His father was murdered in front of his eyes. No one saw that coming.

So what? My knife scraped the plate, cutting my venison. *Why was the general smiling and nodding at his son while the guests praised me?*

Did it go back to what Dominic said? His desire to strip away the innocent orphan persona so that when he killed me, he couldn't be charged with treason? Not if he was a hero who protected the kingdom from the daughter of a Druk.

I strangled my goblet. There could be no question. If they found out my true parentage, no one would stop him executing me. Loyalist and militarist alike would gather the wood, set it on fire, and toss me to the flames.

The little I knew of Druks said they preferred to put their sons through the change when they were little. The younger you were, the more likely you'd survive the bone-breaking, blood-boiling agony of becoming a Druk. Their bodies were already changing. This was just a little extra.

The same couldn't be said for their daughters. Oddly enough, I did not know why until the general told me about the womb raids. Sister Aven forbade any talk of Druks to protect me. She only shared what I needed to know to survive, and that was that Druks routinely spread their spies and dragon thieves around Adalinda, and they were almost always women. Women had to wait to go through the change, but that didn't make them any less loyal to their dragon-slaying people.

An unchanged Druk was a regular human woman like the rest of them. No one would question her walking about town. No one would blink if she donned a uniform and walked into the Hatchery. No one would spare her if she stole the general's son's dragon, then came for his throne.

Druk spies are executed. No trial. No mercy.

I was a woman and a Druk is my mother. That's all the proof Dominic would need to declare me an enemy spy.

He'll never know. I can protect my secret, but will I ever know his? What was his plan to kill me with the full approval of the nation? How did putting on a dress and jewels play into it?

"Ainsley? Hey, Ainsley?"

I tore myself from Dominic. He was engrossed in a conversation with one of his sisters, and wasn't paying nearly as much attention to me as I was to him. "Wha?" I swallowed my mouthful of meat and tried again. "Yes?"

"Uhh..." Maili looked around. "No offense, but maybe you want to slow down? Everyone is looking at you."

Not everyone. I glared at Dominic. *What was with this guy stalking me one minute, and pretending I don't exist the next?*

"Looking at me why?" I asked.

"You're eating like Cadmus when he catches a cow. And my big guy *loves* cows."

I tore a bite off my bread roll. "I don know wha you wean."

"Never mind," she said, laughing. "Never change, Ainsley."

My brows furrowed. "Oh? Okay."

Poet leaned across the table. "Ainsley, after we travel to the veil, the light mages put on a sky show. Most of the recruits wander off to explore the palace, but I'd like to introduce you to my parents if you don't mind? They're going to watch the show."

"They want to meet me? Aren't they... loyal to the general?"

He shrugged. "We're all loyal to the general. He is our sovereign. But they'd still like to meet Queen Kisandra's heir."

"Sure, I'd love to meet your family."

Ting. Ting. Ting.

"Forgive the interruption, everyone. I hope you enjoyed your meal."

I wondered who this woman was that she was in charge of organizing and leading the Calthoon feast. One of the general's wives?

"Now it is time to journey beyond the veil, and pray Calthoon blesses us. Riders, as you begin this season, let Calthoon open your minds to wisdom, strengthen your hearts to challenges, and guide your path with the sure guidance of those who've come before. This is my wish to Calthoon. It is my wish for you. Blessings."

"Blessings," we murmured back as servants stepped forward to clear the plates and trays of food away. I nodded thank you when a servant replaced my goblet with a clear liquid. There were many names for it, though long ago, we settled on Calthoon wine.

Finally, I had something with a greater claim to my attention than Dominic. This would be my first time enjoying the holiday to the fullest. What did I ask for that wasn't selfish or self-serving? Help to keep my secret? No. Help to literally survive training for the next two weeks? No. My hopes and wishes for Reyna? Was a prayer for my dragon not partly a prayer for myself? To see her hurt or gone would destroy me, so it's still a bit about me?

I drifted to the end of the table, finding the back of Dominic's head. The only thing he'd been giving me since we sat down.

I didn't need to wonder. Looking at him, I knew exactly what I would ask Calthoon.

The general got to his feet. "Friends, family, raise your glasses."

We did, holding them high in the air. Light fractured through my goblet, painting my wrist in rainbows.

"To Calthoon."

"To Calthoon," we chorused.

To the day I sit with my brothers and sisters again. I pray the only pinched faces are from too much food, and laughter flows as I perform another silly dance.

I eyed Dominic's stiff and mostly silent family.

Let there be the happiness and comfort that comes from being surrounded by those who truly love you, and let Dominic know what it is to feel that too.

I drank.

Poet dropped, head falling flat on the table.

"Po—!"

Maili's glass shattered. She was slumped over her seat before I could turn my head to ask if she was okay. Up and down the table, shattered glass and head thumps sent the guests on their way to the veil. The last thing I saw before darkness bled into my vision was Dominic finally turning his head, and smiling into my eyes.

I WOKE IN DARKNESS.

It was impossible to know if my body had made the journey, because I couldn't feel it. All I knew was the vast emptiness and my place in it.

Did I do it wrong after all? Was my prayer too selfish?

I parted my lips to speak, and nothing came out. My thoughts to move evaporated into inaction. This was my answer. Calthoon would not come.

"But I did."

I was in the throne room.

Quicker than a blink, I was transported from the darkness and brought back to where I was, except no one else was there—

I froze on the young man reclined on the throne with his legs kicked over the arm. He munched on a pear as he kicked his legs, the portrait of relaxed while the living gold twisted and writhed around him.

"Lucky you," he said. "You didn't want to waste a trip behind the veil on that old judgmental windbag. I love my brother, but he's an ungodly bore."

"I... Who are you?"

He pouted. "You don't know? How hurtful. I swear, all you humans care about are Parthelan, Zaeah, Tenille, and Calthoon. Only the dragons remember the old gods."

I studied him closer. He appeared to be around my age, although he was shorter. A trickster's grin danced on full lips, and nothing danced in his eyes. Where irises should be was nothing but complete, endless black.

Purple hair— No, red— No, blue hair played with the vines weaving gold through his strands. The color changed every time I blinked, but that wasn't a hint. I had no idea who this man could be.

"Forgive me," I said slowly. "I meant no disrespect. May I know your name?"

"Only if you wish to die slowly and painfully." He laughed. "Silly girl. A human mind cannot contain the knowledge of a god's true name. It breaks like eggshell on the cobblestones. We are known only by the names you've given us, and I never liked mine," he breezed. "I refuse to repeat it but— Oh, better idea. You give me a new one."

"A new name?"

What a strange dream I was having. Obviously, I traveled to the land of sleep instead of the one beyond the veil. I guess this was equally possible after drinking Calthoon wine. That you'd simply fall asleep.

"How about Kai? It means—"

"Fire," he finished. "I like it. Almost as fun as the name I've given you, Shenha."

Shenha. It was hard to remember all the names and words that Sister Aven would mutter in Old Adalindian but I was fairly sure that word meant *troublemaker*.

"Have I done something wrong?" I asked. Why not play along to a silly dream?

"Many things, little thief. That's why I like you. It's why I chose you."

I tipped my head, brows crowding in. "Chose me? I don't understand."

"You don't have to yet. The only thing you need to do is win." Dropping his feet on the floor, he draped his arms over his knees. I flicked away from the changing hair and black-pit eyes. Something in me screamed not to look at him too long.

"Win?" I repeated. "Win what?"

"A bet. Long ago, my brother and I shook on a little wager that I could tear down this world that worships Parthelan and Zaeah above all. It's time you humans paid your respect to the old gods— Well, I mean"—he grinned—"one in particular."

"I don't understand."

"Much of anything it seems." He shrugged. "But it's all right, dragon rider. You'll shed this embarrassing cloak of ignorance soon enough. Because you're finally ready."

"*—you're finally ready.*"

My lids cracked open. Pain swirled in my head—making me almost dizzy. A fog had descended on my mind, the remains of the dream hanging on tight and refusing to let go as consciousness claimed me.

A blurred outline moved in my vision. They were leaning over me and... speaking?

"...little princess... ready now..."

I think I spoke. Called for Calthoon. Mumbled Kai.

The figure leaned in close. Their wide, beaming smile the only thing I saw with perfect clarity. Over their shoulder, they flexed their wings.

"You!" I shot up and toppled out of my chair, crashing into Ormr and taking us both down.

"What the fuck!" they shouted, ripped from the veil. "What happened?"

Above their shouting, I heard the distinct and unmistakable sound of wings flapping.

I gasped—clutching my throat as liquid fire raced through my body. I couldn't breathe. Why couldn't I breathe!?

"Ainsley? Hey, Ainsley, what's wrong?" Ormr shook me.

"Something's wrong." I heard Poet. "Get help— Hey, we need help! Wake up!"

Black bled into my vision. My burning muscles coiled and tightening on themselves—squeezing the air from my body, tightening the cage on my frantic heart.

"Princess? Ainsley!" The voice so familiar in a way not even mine was, called for me.

Dominic had done it. He killed me and I never saw it coming.

My body denied me even a gasp. Fingers loosening, they fell to my sides.

"Ainsley! Tyra, heal her. Now!"

But if this is his victory, why did he sound so...?

"Ainsley!"

Chapter Eleven

I woke in a large, airy room beside an overly large bouquet of flowers. I stared at it as if it'd give me some clue as to where I was, and how I'd gotten there.

"Rider Ainsley?"

I tried to turn toward the voice and my body screamed. I promptly gave up.

"Don't trouble yourself, dear." A woman wearing a long, gray dress and kind smile came into view. "You're going to be sore for a few days, but the worst of it will wear off soon."

"Where am I?" It was hard to describe that string of croaks and rasps as words. "What happened?"

A closer look at my surroundings and the rows of beds like mine, I realized I was in the infirmary.

"What happened is you were poisoned with Ghidorian viper venom. Very deadly and fast-acting. If it wasn't for this young man here"—she smiled at someone over my body—"you wouldn't have made it."

"I am no healer." I tensed and immediately regretted it. "It's my sister who deserves the credit."

"She wouldn't have known how to heal her if you hadn't recognized the signs. You did well."

"Will I be okay?" I asked.

She nodded. "Full recovery. Bondeds heal twice as fast and twice as well. As a result, our potential assassins have to choose fast-acting methods. Once the poison was out of your system, your body did the rest. I plan to discharge you tonight."

"Do they know who did this to me?"

"No, I'm afraid not. Both your glass and food were checked, and no venom was found. Everyone at the table consumed the Calthoon wine, or seemed to," she confessed. "If someone slipped in, or merely pretended to drink the wine, there'd be no way of knowing."

If someone slipped in. Like a Druk, I thought, and a miracle that was.

My head was wrecked from Reyna's fear and concern flooding through the bond. I didn't yet know how to communicate back to her. I just hoped that if she knew when I was in danger, she had the same sense to know I was okay.

"Thank you."

"I told you, I've done very little, my dear. Thank him."

I was quiet as she walked away. Even quieter as Dominic Roark rounded my bed and stood beside me.

The silence spread like spilled tea. Neither of us seemed willing to break it first.

Fuck that. I have questions.

"You saved me." It was both a question and a statement. "If I'm keeping count, that's three times you've come to my rescue. Do I need to tell you what it means to want someone dead?"

The corner of his mouth quirked in the barest hint of amusement. "Let me assure you, Princess, my reasons were entirely selfish."

"You don't have to."

That got a chuckle. "I couldn't let you die. In our palace? At our table? No one would've believed that my father wasn't behind it.

Bold and blatant treason would've thrown Golden City, if not all of Adalinda into civil war between the loyalists and militarists."

I nodded slow, accepting that. In my fevered panic, the first person I thought of was Dominic because he was the last person to wish me dead, but even I knew it benefited his father in no way to kill me in front of all those people. He'd forever lose the tenuous trust of the loyalists, and he wouldn't know if it was for nothing.

Queen Kisandra survived that night and had an heir. Neither he nor I knew if there were more out there. He could kill one and it wouldn't stop a dozen others popping up.

"And that's something you care about?" I asked. "Peace in Adalinda?"

He frowned. "Of course. No one benefits from the opposite."

"Hmm."

"Why do you look skeptical?"

"I'm just wondering how much of this is an act. Shielding me because you respect women. Saving me to save Adalinda from war. Calling me a thief and promising to kill me because of an accident of birth and a dragon who chose me."

I flashed to him laughing and making that sweet little peasant girl giggle.

"You don't get to be both guys, Roark."

"I am one very simple man, Princess," he said, striding away. Seemed my audience with him was over. "I protect what's mine."

"You also protect me."

It was said so low that I'd swear on my life that I misheard, but what I incorrectly heard him reply was—

"Guess that means you're mine too."

He was gone minutes before Maili, Ormr, and Poet rushed in.

"Ainsley, are you okay?" Ormr asked. "I'm so sorry. I can't believe this happened right next to me."

"It's not your fault."

"It's someone's," Maili said, pulling up a chair next to me. "Someone at that party tried to kill you, and it shouldn't have happened. How does a vial of poison get carried in and no one knows? The general employs guards with the kind of magics that sniff assassins out. If he didn't, no one could walk through the palace without tripping over corpses."

I flinched. Not the thought I wanted in my head. Neither was the one it jarred loose.

Him.

In my Calthoon/poison fever dream, I saw my yearly Druk shadow. I heard the sound of wings. Could it truly have been him? Why would he try to kill me? It didn't make sense. He had countless opportunities to kill me, but following my torment, he'd leave me saying I wasn't ready. Wasn't ready to die? Was I to believe he waited twelve years just to put himself at great risk entering the palace to poison me in a room full of people?

No, it simply didn't make sense. I imagined him in the depths of my worst moment because he'd been present for all the others.

"What happened after I was carried out?" I asked. "Did anyone see Calthoon?"

Poet shook his head. "The ball ended quickly after you were brought out. One death and one attempted murder. Party's over. If someone did see Calthoon, they didn't shout about it during their race to the door."

I nodded slow. "Have any of you ever seen Calthoon before?"

"Why?" Ormr asked.

"I was wondering if he..." I hesitated. "If he ever plays tricks. You know, pretends to be someone else."

My friends shared a look.

"Not that I know of," Maili said. "Calthoon isn't a trickster god. Some say Mother Zaeah is. That's why she gave humans strong minds, but weak, breakable bodies. She thought it was funny."

Sighing, I relaxed. "So, it was just a weird dream. After I drank the wine, I saw some kid with changing hair who said he was one of the old gods. But there were no gods before Calthoon, Zaeah, Parthelan, and Tenille. They created everything that is and will be."

"Kid with changing hair?" Poet laughed. "Definitely just a regular old dream."

Ormr got to their feet. "We should go, guys. Let Ainsley get some rest."

They filed out, saying their goodbyes. Poet kissed me on the forehead before he went. "It's funny," he said, "I had a weird dream too. I heard wings flapping, and when I looked up, there was a Druk standing on the rafters above us. Watching."

I lay there in stiff, silent horror long after he left.

I LEFT THE INFIRMARY and made for the front entrance for the first time in a week. The bond had calmed down, which meant Reyna calmed down, but I still needed to see her. If only to fulfill my role as her loving servant and clean her scales and claws the way she liked.

I felt infinitely better than I did that morning, but I had no doubt I would pass out next to her after I was done. That suited me just fine. The worst part of the general's order that I remained confined in the citadel was that I couldn't sleep in the woods with her anymore. Neither Reyna nor I were meant to be indoors.

"Good evening."

I jerked, swinging around. Nuala fell in step with me and I hadn't seen her coming.

I looked around. "Hello. Can I help you?"

"Where are you headed?"

"To the Royal Wood."

"Oh, I'll join you," she said. "I haven't seen Solace since yesterday."

"All right."

I didn't know what else to say, so agreeing was as good as anything. Nuala slept in the bed on the other side of Dominic. We were in the same recruit class, and we got dressed in the same room. That was the end of our interactions.

"How are you feeling?"

We approached the main gates. The guards nodded her through, fixed on me, and... waved me on.

The general had kept his changeable word. I was allowed out.

"I'm feeling much better," I said. "Thanks for asking. But is that really what you want to talk about?"

Nuala cocked her head. She was so pretty, she blinded. "What do you mean?"

"I mean you haven't shown a lick of interest in me all week, and now we're going on a stroll. Was there something in particular you wanted to talk about?"

Her smile didn't falter. "There is actually."

Golden City was new overnight. All the stalls and decorations for Calthoon were taken down, and the pristine, polished streets were as they were again. I wondered if Rosaleen was still in the city.

She'd become popular enough that a few of her callers invited her to spend nights and weekends in their homes. One of them was the Heart Reader that helped us. I'd drop in on him to see if she was there, but not with Nuala on my shadow.

"I was wondering what you were going to ask Calthoon?"

I frowned. I wasn't expecting that question, though it wasn't a secret. "I was going to ask him to protect my dragon, Reyna. With her, everything is possible."

"Aw, sweet." She pushed up her lips. "I didn't know you were one of those."

"One of those?"

"You know. A dragon worshipper. They're so in love with dragons, you'd think they shit gold."

I faced forward. I was losing interest in this conversation fast. "You don't love your dragon?"

She shrugged. "Solace and I are... partners. Comrades. We support each other the way a bonded should in battle, but if she's on a pedestal, it's because she flew up there herself. Not because I put her there."

"Interesting."

"Yes, I don't love her in that way," she continued. "Maybe I would've if I hadn't experienced real love before we bonded. When you've met your soulmate. The person who is your other half and equal in every way. When you've given your bodies to each other and experienced orgasms that make you black out and scream yourself hoarse, you stop thinking a bond with an animal could ever compare."

"I'm happy for you." I started picking up the pace. Woman doesn't acknowledge my existence for a week, then comes up to me talking about blackout orgasms? Time to put some distance between us. "Your love sounds nice."

"He is," she said, easily keeping pace. "That's why I asked Calthoon to bless our love, and open his eyes to the fakes and manipulators around him. When Calthoon came to me from beyond the veil, I asked him to get rid of sad little lying peasants like you."

I stopped so abruptly, she almost went ahead of me. "Excuse me?"

"You heard me." Her sweet smile bled away. "I see through you, Ainsley Whoever-You-Are. You should know that everyone does. The magic that you're so desperate to hide must be a power that can fool the throne, because that's the only way it'd declare a lying impostor like you as Queen Kisandra's heir."

"Am I missing something? Where do you get off saying all of this to me?"

"Ridiculous, isn't it? That I'm wasting my time with the likes of you, but you've given me no choice. I heard Dominic in the mess hall saying he'd draw up a marriage contract for the two of you. I warned his father so he'd put a stop to it, but you still didn't take the hint."

My face screwed up. I couldn't have been more confused than if she got on her hands and knees, and started barking like a dog. "Dominic? This is about Dominic?"

"Don't act stupid. I recognized your cunning. The least you can do is drop the act."

"What act? What are you talking about?" I muddled through all the nonsense she said. "Wait. You told the general about the marriage contract between me and Dominic? Why? Why would you care—?" Understanding dawned. "Ah. He's your great love."

"Yes, he is, and you'll speak of us with respect on your tongue. You're addressing your future sovereign."

"Actually, I'm not." I sidestepped her. "Goodbye."

"Dominic and I signed our marriage contract when we were fourteen years old."

I slowed.

"We're meant to be together. We always have been. Unfortunately"—she pressed her mouth to my ear—"he learned from his father to use marriage to consolidate power. I'll tell you right now, it's not going to happen. I will be Dominic's wife. His *only* wife.

"Don't let some silly little dance, a desperate contract, and his letting you wear his mother's jewels—go to your head. Dominic doesn't give a shit about you. He's just doing whatever it takes to protect his kingdom from a lying troll witch."

"Thank you so much for taking the time to explain all this to me," I pushed through gritted teeth. "Now, if this can be over, I've got to get to the one you're really angry with. She's large, scaly, and the animal your great love was willing to drop you for just to get her back." My clenched mouth twisted into a smile. "No wonder you hate dragon worshippers. Blackout orgasms still don't knock Reyna from the top spot in his heart. I wonder how good the sex is for him if that's the case?"

She lunged at me. I ducked and ran under her swinging arms. Quicker than a breath, my tricky fingers slipped in her pocket and slipped out her coin purse. I ran into the crowd and lost myself while she was shouting for me to come back.

I didn't deal with jealous lovers often. The few men I'd been with refused to tell anyone about me, and we only met in secret. Dominic did not keep our meetings secret. He kissed me in front of everyone. Danced with me in front of everyone. Held my body to him and shielded me from embarrassment before the whole party. Placed his mother's jewels around my neck for everyone to see. Why would he do all of those things if he was in love with Nuala?

Was she right? He was this desperate to keep the kingdom out of my hands?

I thought that, and immediately discarded it. I sensed a lot about Dominic Roark over the last week. But of all things that smirking, confident, threatening man was, I had a feeling desperate was not it.

"GOOD MORNING, RECRUITS."

Commandant Drake addressed us from the head table.

"Now that assessments are out of the way, and your rank is posted, your schedule has changed. Battle readiness, magical accuracy, and teamwork will be held every day, six days a week. Scholarship and special talents are three times a week.

"I know what you're thinking," he said over grumblings. "For some of you, three lessons a week don't seem enough to raise your rank high enough before the first cut." Drake looked directly at me. "To that I say, too bad. This is dragon rider training, not your mommy's living room. You want to survive the first cut, work for it, because crying to me will do you no good.

"Dismissed."

Poet grumbled as he picked up his tray and pushed back. "Nothing like his cheery, inspiring morning briefings to brighten the day ahead."

I snorted. Yes, it was stupid that people looked down on Poet for being the son of a recently made noble. He was so kind and funny. Like my younger brother, Davide, was kind and funny, traits he held on to even while people turned their nose up at his threadbare clothes and avoided him. Seemed people valued all the wrong things in Golden City too.

"Where were you last night?" Ormr asked while we carried our trays to the return. "Was my snoring so bad it sent you out of the room?"

I laughed. "No, it wasn't you. Honestly, I don't sleep that well indoors. I passed out with Reyna in the Royal Wood."

After I used the money I took from Nuala to buy Reyna a new brush and her favorite treat—chickens.

"Weren't you cold?"

I shook my head. "Fire dragon. Her whole body burns just on the right side of uncomfortable. After a night curled up with her, I wake up sweating."

"On the hard, dirty ground," Maili spoke up. "Are you sure you're more comfortable outside? Ormr can take something for the snoring."

"I can," they said. "I don't because it gives me crazy dreams, but I will if it means you can sleep in your bed again. I don't want to drive you out."

"I swear you haven't." I squeezed their shoulder. "Thank you, though. I appreciate it."

I stopped next to the tray return and they kept going. "I've got to speak to Commandant Drake about something."

"Are you sure about that?" Poet asked. "He wasn't kidding about not taking complaints."

"He'll take this one."

"Well, then, it was a pleasure knowing you." Taking my hand, he kissed it and bowed. "Latumire."

"Shut up," I laughed. "See you guys in scholarship."

I waited as the mess hall emptied out. Dominic among the last to approach. Dropping off his tray, he leaned in close. I stiffened as his lips brushed my ear.

"Mmm. You smell good," he whispered. "Like sunshine and rain. Has my dragon finally let you ride her? Or is the only flying you're doing, straight into the ground?"

"I— You— You smell like—" I stumbled over his compliment trying to get to the insult.

Dominic walked away laughing his head off.

"Bastard!"

"Rider Ainsley!"

I snapped to attention. Commandant Drake bore down on me fast.

"You will bear the decorum of your station, or you'll take five demerits next time instead of three."

"Sorry, sir. Thank you." That was the correct and only response. I watched other riders argue their way into twenty demerits and a month of mess hall duty. Commandant Drake was not to be questioned.

"Sir, if I may, I have a question."

He returned his tray and stopped in front of me. I swore I shrunk under his gaze. Something about the cold disproval in his eyes made me feel like he saw through to my every sin.

"Are you about to say something that will get you another month of Hatchery duty, Rider Ainsley? May I suggest you do not."

"I don't think I am, sir. I was just wondering about my rank," I tried. "The ranks are numbers one to forty-eight, and I was given three zeros in the assessments I couldn't complete. Does that mean the zero is just a placeholder?"

"That is exactly what it means."

I took a breath for the first time in a week. Between making lifelong enemies and waking up from a poisoning, it was a relief for one thing to go right.

"You should know you were the topic of heated discussion this weekend, Rider Ainsley."

"I was?"

He dipped his chin. "You were given zeros because you could not complete your assessments, but then came the question of how to proceed. You continue to claim that you're magicless, and every Heart Reader that's tested you reiterated that you're telling the truth. A few instructors argued that it should make no difference. You cannot properly complete training, or indeed defend this nation without magic. As such we should stop the show and cut you now."

"Sir, were you one of the instructors arguing that?"

Amusement lit on one side of his scarred face. "That would be telling."

So yes.

"Unfortunately, all of Adalinda is watching us. They're watching you," he said. "If we treat you unfairly during this trial, it'll be said the general manipulated decisions behind the scenes to have you cut and executed. General Roark is an honest and just ruler. I'll not have such slander so much as darken their minds."

I wasn't sure what that meant for me. I waited.

"Magical accuracy and special talents are removed from your roster. While the other recruits are in those lessons, you'll have library, Hatchery, and mess hall duty. No rider under my charge will sit around idle while others do the work."

"Yes, sir." Truly, that was the best I could hope for. I wouldn't dare argue. "Thank you, sir."

"However."

The single word stopped my retreat.

"You understand this puts you at an advantage that isn't fair to the other recruits. If you're to only do half the required work, Rider Ainsley, it's only right that you do it better than everyone else. You're to be top ten in scholarship, battle readiness, and teamwork by the time these two weeks are over, or you'll be cut."

"But, sir—!"

"Make that top eight," he said, voice hard. "Any more objections?"

I snapped my mouth shut, internally screaming.

"Good. Report to your class, Rider Ainsley, and take another three demerits with you. You're late."

Stiffly, I turned and walked away.

Commandant Drake had killed me. He hadn't used a weapon and it would be two weeks until I died. But the result was the same. With this decision, he killed me.

I DRAGGED TO SCHOLARSHIP in a daze. What was I supposed to do? I ranked well in battle readiness, but that was because I fought dirty and scrappy, catching Keir off guard. Not to mention one-on-one bouts were the least of my worries.

Captain Roan had a grin on his face when he said he was going to put us through every possible trial to prepare us for everything from Golden Guard duty to defending the Dark Border. I didn't have to wonder if my tricky fingers were enough in a fight against a Druk. They never had been before.

As for teamwork, I still couldn't mount Reyna without, like Dominic said, flying straight into the dirt.

Then there was scholarship.

I paused outside the door, and for the first time since I stepped through the gates, I asked myself if I should run. Take Reyna and flee into Nehebkau. Or maybe Hyelong—the last place anyone saw Velez. I could spend my time looking for my lost family, instead of chasing impossible dreams.

There's no running, Ainsley. I'm told what they do to deserters is even worse than the punishment for peasants who bond with a dragon. You're here now.

I grabbed the doorknob.

You have to see this through to the end.

"Ah, Rider Ainsley." Major Sorrel dropped his chalk. "Two demerits for tardiness. Take your seat."

I didn't bother mentioning that Drake already took care of that. I scanned the rows for an empty place.

Ormr sat next to Lonan. Maili and Poet claimed the table in front of them. Nuala and Dominic sat together in the second row.

She made sure I saw her filthy look before she scooted her chair close to Dominic.

The only free seat was next to—

Keir burned me from two tables away. The all-consuming hatred in his eyes prickled my skin, even while sympathy cracked the surface. Those glaring eyes were rimmed with red.

What was Keir doing back in lessons so soon? Surely the instructors allowed time off for those who lost family?

"Rider Ainsley, sit down. I will have none of your disruptions today," said Major Sorrel.

"Yes, sir."

I claimed the seat next to Keir. I felt his eyes bore into my side like a nail through my skull.

"As I was saying," our instructor began. "Each squad is made up of as many different magic types as possible to ensure they can defeat any kind of Druk. A squad of fire mages and fire dragons, going up against a horde of fire-type Druks will have a ferocious fight on their hands. Can anyone tell me why that is?"

Nuala's hand shot into the air. Sorrel nodded at her.

"Because those Druks will have taken on the heat resistance of the dragon they murdered and consumed. Also, the magics of the man he used to be will amplify that resistance and make him immune to even the dragon's hottest flames. Essentially, fire cannot kill them."

My brows shot up. This I did not know.

"With that being the case, which bonded pairs are best to defeat fire Druks?"

Someone else raised their hand and was called on.

"Ice bondeds. Fire Druks have heat resistance, but no cold resistance. If you freeze them out, they'll die of hypothermia."

"Excellent, Rider Taesha. Take a commendation."

Taesha positively preened, and she should. Instructors handed out demerits with twice the readiness that they did commendations.

My skin itched. I kept flicking to Keir out of the corner of my eye. He hadn't stopped staring at me.

"One advantage that we have is Druks don't think like us. Not anymore," Sorrel said. "Becoming a Druk has a cost, and that cost is surrendering to powerful animal instincts. We can diversify our squads. They can't.

"Just think of what would happen if the tiger, the lion, and the panther joined forces. Is there any prey they couldn't catch? Fortunately, they do not behave that way and neither do Druks. They stay with their own and form colonies of only their own kind."

I raised my hand.

"Yes, Rider Ainsley?"

"Is there any way to map the size and location of these colonies?"

"Would that we could, recruit. That is our greatest goal, and the task of every spy we've sent across the Dark Border. None have returned."

I shuddered. Was there a more unsettling phrase than that one?

"Now," he said, moving back to his desk. He flipped through a textbook. "We'll be discussing a ten-year-old battle that riders lost in Edjer. A squad of thirty went up against five ice Druks. They have the same incompatibility to fire bondeds. But even though there were three fire bondeds in the squad, all save one rider was killed. Every dragon was captured and taken across the border."

I raised my hand again. He tipped his head to me.

"Every dragon, sir? Not just the ice- or water-type dragons?"

"I see where you are going with that question, and the answer is yes. Druks will capture any dragon they can get their hands on. They do not fight alongside, or live with Druks of other types, but they do have a sense of cooperation. Each stolen dragon is bartered or sold to the right colony.

"Dragons fled the land beyond the Dark Border long ago. Now, they live in Adalinda. It's the Druks' desire to conquer Adalinda and claim our wealth and dragons for themselves. It serves every individual Druk colony well to help the others grow in number."

I took the information in and filed it away. I didn't yet know what this meant about my birth mother, her connection to the queen, or the Druk who stalked me, but I did know one thing. I was cursed in more ways than one to be born magicless.

If I was a fire mage, then I'd know my mother was a fire Druk. Children inherited their power from their parents. The only reason Dominic wasn't a death mage like the general is because he must've gotten fire magic from his mother.

My mother could be any Druk and anywhere, but I will find her.

A stab of pain bent me over the desk. I bit my lip to stop from crying out. Visions of Druks had been in my head too long. Reyna did not like this topic.

"I will lead the discussion so you get a sense of the kind of analysis I'm looking for in your reports," Sorrel said. "I will tell you the plan that failed. You tell me the plan that would win. These are not just essays. If you do not include maps, battle placements, supply lists, bonded types, and backup plans, then it is your intention to fail."

I sank lower in my seat. Yes, these would be my last two weeks.

"Everyone, open your books to page forty-two and read silently. You'll have twenty minutes to absorb and consider how you'd do things differently. Be ready for my questions."

There was nothing to be heard except quiet coughs and whispering pages. I tried to focus on the words, but it was harder than usual. Keir would not take his eyes off me.

Fah-ah-va-oh— Fa-ah-va-oh-rah-bah-la-e— Faavaoblae kon-di-shons—

The first sentence, and I had already skipped five words I didn't know and couldn't figure out by sounding out.

Felt like an eternity passed sitting there while Keir tried to kill me with his mind. Tenille knew what he was doing when he gifted each person's magic. There was a reason Keir received illusion magic that couldn't physically harm a person.

"All right, let's begin," Sorrel announced.

I was stuck between relief and tears. I hadn't made it through the first paragraph. What was I going to do?

"Rider Dominic, tell me why the attack ultimately failed."

"The squad seemed diverse in power types, but were not. Everyone in the squad specialized in close-range attacks, and only close-range attacks. They had to get close to land a blow. Ice Druks can control the ice within a certain area. They have a nasty habit of cloaking themselves in snow, and then raining a storm of icicles on their enemy with such careful precision, they kill the rider without harming a scale on the dragon.

"The fire mages were so focused on melting the coming icicles, they couldn't melt the snow on the ground to find the Druks. That left the incompatible-type bondeds to search. But as I said, they mastered only close-range attacks. When they finally were close enough to a Druk to strike, it was already too late."

"Excellent, Rider Dominic." Oh, Tenille, was that something akin to happiness in his voice? "Take a commendation for that spot-on analysis. They failed because no one in the squad mastered long-range attacks, and the Druks occupied all the fire bondeds immediately and took them out of the fight.

"It is important— No, it is *vital* that you all understand one thing right now. Druks are not stupid. They know how we and our dragons think. They anticipate our every move, learn from their mistakes, and make sure they never repeat them again. That is why we have this class," he said. "Out there, you learn how to fight. In here, you learn how to think. A Druk enters a battle with fifty backup plans in case something goes wrong. A dragon rider has fifty-one."

I found myself nodding along. I didn't doubt the vitalness of this class. Tenille knew there was nothing more genuine than my desire to learn. But desire and reality were rarely bedfellows.

"Rider Maili, how would you have used your earth magic to find the Druks where they hid?"

"Um, well, ice and winter aren't compatible with my vines. Everything is dead."

"Ah," he replied, "so your plan would've been to lie down, expose your belly, and wait?"

She flushed. "No, sir. Of course not, sir. I guess I wouldn't be able to do much, but Cadmus could. He loves to burrow. With him disturbing the earth, all the Druks would fly out of their hiding places."

"Good answer."

Maili visibly relaxed. We were all in competition with each other for our lives and our dragons. We didn't have the luxury of bad answers.

"Maili was correct in that when her strengths fall short, she relies on her bonded. You are a team. If there are no civilians nearby, let your dragon free to wield their full abilities."

Movement on the edge of my vision turned my head. Eight little eyes locked on to mine.

"Ah!" Shrieking, I flung myself out of the chair, throwing out all my limbs.

I crashed into Keir and we both toppled over. He came down on top of me, punching the air out of my lungs. I tried to get up.

His arm clamped around my throat.

My eyes bugged from my skull. Legs flailing, nails clawing his arm, Keir squeezed tighter.

"This is for my father."

"He— He—" *Help! HELP!*

"What's going on over—? Tenille bless us!"

Shrieks and shouts filled the classroom. I heard the sound of people abandoning their seats and running... but not toward me.

"Spiders? Where did they come from!"

I thrashed on the floor, kicking the table leg. No one could see what he was doing from the angle of our position, and the objects blocking our way. Keir made a plan to kill me in a room full of people, and it was working.

Keir tightened his grip ever more. The full weight of his body pressed down on me, pinning me in place. I wasn't going anywhere.

Gasping for breath, black bled into my vision.

Then he was gone.

I sucked in deep lungfuls and scrambled up. A silent Keir was secure in Ormr's hold. All around us, people fled, screamed, or ducked the swarming horde of large hairy spiders. Half the class was already out the door, never to be seen again.

"It's okay, everyone," Ormr said. "Just Keir playing another one of his hilarious pranks. He did the same thing during junior cadet training. We all woke up thinking there were snakes in our bed."

"Hilarious? Hilarious!" Major Sorrel's voice reached octaves that didn't exist. "There is nothing funny about this. I will not have these juvenile pranks in my class. Leave, Rider Keir, and take ten demerits with you."

Keir didn't even argue. Throwing Ormr off, he snatched up his things and turned to leave. "Next time I'll get the job done..."

I swallowed through my ruined throat. I thought the cackling, smirking jerk was hard to deal with. I was wrong. This silent, calculating assassin was much more terrifying.

"I thought he would try something," Ormr said softly. "Sorry I wasn't faster."

"You don't have to apologize," I rasped. "You were fast enough."

"Everyone, collect yourselves."

The spiders vanished as quickly as they appeared.

"There's nothing to worry about now," Sorrel continued. "Now sit and let us finish the lesson. Your first report is due Watersday. No exceptions or excuses."

It took some time for us to settle down and return to work. Best I could, I pushed Keir out of my mind. He wanted me dead. Dominic wanted me dead. And Drake would have me dead if I didn't find a way to make top eight in scholarship in two weeks. I could only focus on one of those things at the moment.

I spent the rest of class asking myself what Major Sorrel would do if I told him the truth. I can't read.

Such was the natural result of outlawing education for commoners. Most peasants resort to teaching their children at home, which Sister Aven tried to do for me. But she had so many children to take care of by herself—at one time, our orphanage swelled to sixty after Druks slaughtered a nearby village—she didn't have the time.

Sister Aven told Velez, my smart and clever borrowed brother, to teach me. Instead of sitting me down with books and scales, Velez taught me to fight, climb trees, pick the good plants from the poisonous ones, and how to steal. He'd say people like us didn't need to know how to read. We needed to know how to survive.

I loved spending time with him too much to rat to Sister Aven that he wasn't teaching me words and math like he promised. Sooner or later, regret always finds us.

"—all for today," Sorrel called. "Your first report is on the Battle of Blood. A thirty-day-long fight in Nehebkau's capital that ended in the slaughter of the regent and her family. What went wrong, why, and what would you have done if you were leading the squad?

"These are not group projects, so I expect forty-eight different battle plans. Dismissed."

At that second, I made up my mind.

Waving my friends on, I crossed the row and stopped in front of Dominic's table. "Roark, do you have a minute? I need to talk to you alone."

"No," Nuala snapped. "Go away."

I hummed. "That's funny. I heard a reply, but I didn't see your mouth move, Roark. Did you learn how to talk out of your ass?" I goggled at Nuala. "Oh, look! There's the ass."

"Bitch!" Nuala launched at me.

Dominic held her back. "It's all right, Nu. Give us a second."

"Why would you want to talk to her?"

"I'm curious."

Sniffing, Nuala gathered her things and followed our class out. "I'll be waiting outside." She said it like a warning. I was almost certain it was.

"What?"

"One second."

I waited for Major Sorrel to leave. Finally, we were the only ones in the room.

"First," I began, "what's up with you and Nuala? Are you really getting married?"

"This is what you wanted to ask?"

"Am I not allowed? You asked me to marry you a week ago. I'm curious if you give out marriage contracts like candy, or if you really love Nuala and were prepared to betray her."

He rose to his feet. "I don't see how that's any of your business."

"You said you respect women." He paused, half turned to leave. "The answer to that question will tell me if you really do, or if it's just something you tell yourself while you tramp on other people on the path to power."

Dominic eyed me for a long time. Long enough to make me thoroughly uncomfortable.

"Nuala is a close friend," he said. "We grew up together in Azura. Then, her father plotted a rebellion. He and his rebel group attacked the Royal Riders and almost gained control of the city. When they lost, the coward fled and abandoned his wife and four daughters.

"The general decided not to let them bear the weight of their father's sins. Instead, he drew up marriage contracts for Nuala, her sisters, me, and three of my brothers. I had no say in that contract, and I likely won't have a say in the ones to come. Nuala remains a close friend of mine, but there was no betrayal in drawing up a contract for me and you. We're not in love with each other."

Does she know that?

"Any more questions?" he asked. The heavy sarcasm in that response told me there better not be.

"No, not a question."

"You have more than one good reason to change his feelings toward you. He wants you dead. Make him want something else."

Rosaleen's words rang in my ear. If Dominic and Nuala truly weren't together in that way, I'd lost my last excuse. I had to be top eight in scholarship, and that would never happen if I had any part in these reports. My best friend was right. If I can steal to save my life, then I can seduce for it too.

"The right touch here, the right brush there, a little peek, a soft whisper, no promises, and you've got him eating out of the palm of your hands."

"So..." I laid my hand on his chest. "About these reports..."

Dominic looked down at the appendage like he'd never seen one before. "What about them?"

"They're pretty hard."

"For you, I'm sure."

I gritted my teeth. Ass.

Focus, Ainsley. Don't let him get to you. Remember what Rosaleen said to do.

"It'd be great if someone could—" *Soft whisper, soft whisper!* "If someone could do them for me."

"What? I didn't catch that."

I sidled closer, peering at him through my lashes. "I was hoping you'd help me."

"With what?"

"The reports."

He threw me big eyes. "What the fuck about them?"

"It's impolite to make a lady say."

To say the man was confused was putting it lightly.

I winked at him, trying for the flirty smile that Rosaleen wielded to make men walk into the side of buildings, and empty their entire coin purse in her hand.

"What the hell are you doing with your face?"

"I just need you to do this one little thing for me," I purred, burrowing into his side. "If you do, I'll—" *No promises!*

"Nothing!" I blurted, making him jump. "I'm not making any promises."

"Okay." Dominic grasped my shoulder and firmly moved me away. "I've got battle readiness. Good luck with... whatever this is, Princess."

No, no, no! my mind shouted at me. *You can't let him go. Your life depends on this in so many more ways than one.*

I had no choice. Rosaleen left me one last instruction. It was this, or die.

"Wait!"

I scrabbled at my shirt. Dominic turned and I snapped my hem up, exposing my breasts.

His brows blew up his forehead, jaw slackening. I'd never seen this look on this face before. I'd bet three hundred ryus that no one had.

"Do my reports." My hands were shaking so hard, I kept bumping them against my chin. "I like my reports done when a guy put—puts it in my ass."

He blinked at me. I wasn't sure if understanding was finally dawning, because it couldn't be seen behind round-eyed shock.

"This… is a first for me, Princess," he said slowly. "I have to tell you that I was wrong and apologize for what I said the night of Calthoon.

"I don't have you figured out at all."

Nuala burst in. "Dom, what is taking so—? What the fuck is this!"

I ran.

Shooting past a shouting Nuala, I bolted down the hallway and ran till my lungs gave out, then I ran faster.

I didn't stop until I was outside, crashing through the trees in the Royal Wood.

That's it. I was out of this place. Let them hunt me down as a deserter. I couldn't show my face in that citadel again. My seduction plan succeeded in changing Dominic's opinion of me.

I went from conniving, sneaky dragon thief to a small-breasted lunatic all in the space of one monumental lapse in judgment.

Goodbye, Dominic. Goodbye, General. Goodbye, Golden City.

You'll never see the princess-that-could've-been again.

Chapter Twelve

I trudged through the barracks that night, chin as high as it'd go.
My escape attempt fell short when Reyna threw me off her back. Afterward, I poured out the whole sorry story to her and she comforted me the best she could. She was kind enough to not let her amusement through the bond.

Poet, Maili, and Ormr huddled around my bunk. I focused on them so I didn't have to look at the silent, reading figure on the bed next to mine.

"There you are, Ainsley." Maili hugged me. "Where were you?"

"I had to get away for a bit." I felt Dominic's eyes on the back of my head. "Clear my head."

"We're about to head to the B Barrack," Poet added. "The second-year riders snuck in whiskey and targets. We're going to see how good our aim is drunk. Want to join? The drinking part," he added. "Not the target practice."

"No, thanks. I'm tired. I'm going to get some sleep."

"All right. See you in the morning."

I waved them out, then kept my back to Dominic while I changed for bed. Climbing in, I flipped for a brief second to get something out of my bedside drawer and our eyes connected.

Dominic had dropped his book. The sweetest, most warm smile brightened his full lips as he looked at me. My heart picked up speed, hammering my rib cage loud enough to wake a dorm drifting to sleep.

Had it worked? My clumsy, embarrassing attempt to seduce him? Was Dominic seeing me in a new light? Would that beautiful, heart-fluttering smile always be for me?

He snorted.

Clapping his hand over his mouth, Dominic couldn't hold it back anymore. He burst out laughing—guffaws echoing off the walls.

"No!" Shrieking, I threw the covers over my head, praying they'd swallow me whole.

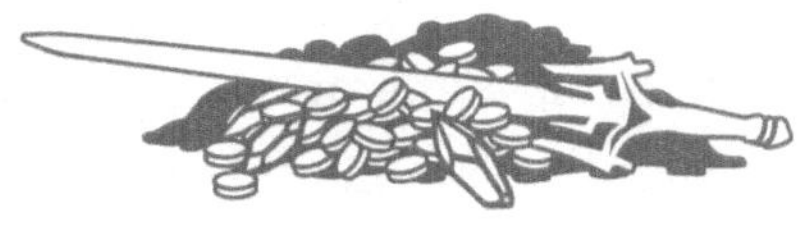

THE NEXT DAY, WE HEADED outside for battle readiness.

"Fall in."

On cue, we formed three lines. I was careful not to get anywhere near Keir or Dominic.

"Morning, recruits," Captain Roan began. "For the benefit of yesterday's absent rider—five demerits, Rider Ainsley—I'll explain how class will be structured from here on.

"Start of every lesson begins with a sparring match. Hand-to-hand combat is your last line of defense when your dragon is dead and your fire attacks are doing nothing against the fire Druk flying at you. As such, you will sharpen and hone your skills until you can take me down." He grinned. "Your final test to ensure you don't have to retake this class next year."

There was no doubt in my mind that every single first-year that had Captain Roan, saw him again the following year.

"These sparring matches are important. Too many of you pompous, pampered silver-spoon babies have skated by on your superior magic ability. Your powers were strong before you bonded, and they're ten times as strong now. You feel invincible."

A few people nodded.

"You're fools," he barked. "*Invincible* riders die every day. They fall before an enemy they've only ever heard about, but never seen. They run screaming when their superior powers run dry and they can't summon a flame to light a candle.

"Want to know who does impress me? Commoners."

I raised my head. *Commoners?*

"It's them that face the Druk threat on a daily basis. Druks abduct their women, and slaughter their men. They lurk around their homes, hunting for wild dragons. They purposely attack them to force the riders into traps. Commoners, on average, have low magical ability, and they don't have bondeds. Still, they fight back.

"Commoners don't lie down and give up when all the odds are against them. They strike, they win, or they die trying. That is the entire goal of this class—teaching you to fight like a commoner."

I could see on a few faces that they did not love the comparison. Royals and nobles lived in a world that favored and praised them every minute of every day. Now this man was telling them that in a fight, he'd put his money on the poor, low-magic peasant any day.

"Here is how it'll work. Every morning, those ranked forty-eight to twenty-two must choose a sparring partner from ranks twenty-one to seven. Only by facing stronger opponents will you improve. Literally," he said. "If rank forty-six beats rank eight in a match, they trade ranks."

Excited, and angry, whispers broke out. Seemed Captain Roan hadn't explained all of the details the day before.

"As for ranks six through one, at your level, there's little benefit in your fighting a weaker opponent. As such, you will face off with each other, but with different handicaps. One day you'll spar with a broken leg. The next you'll fight five on one. The next day I might tie both hands behind your back. The point is, when I'm done with you, you'll be ready for anything."

I raised my hand.

"Question, Rider Ainsley?"

"Will our rank be assessed in the same way?" I asked. "If I win against Ormr, will I be rank two?"

He shook his head. "At your level, I expect more than a lucky win because your opponent wasn't expecting you to pull down their pants and stomp their testicles."

Titters broke out.

"Druks are highly trained warriors. You will need technique, speed, quick thinking, and resourcefulness to move up a rank. You'll need to consistently fail at the above to move down."

Nodding, I accepted this easily. It wasn't about if we could beat each other. At the end of the day, the only thing that matters is if we could beat a Druk. I had the unique and unwanted experience of fighting a particular Druk yearly. I had yet to lay a scratch on him.

"After sparring matches, if you're still conscious, we'll train in weapons, first aid, surviving different terrain, and whatever else takes my fancy. Any questions?"

No one spoke.

"Excellent. Top six, step out of line and pair up. Bottom rank, choose your opponent."

The top six were me, Dominic, Nuala, Ormr, Keir, and Maili. I'd just begun to turn toward Maili and Ormr's direction when an arm slung around my waist.

"Team," Dominic called.

"Yes," Roan said before I could get a word out.

Dominic whisked me away to one of the practice mats. My feet weren't touching the ground.

"What are you doing?" I tried to wriggle free. "We are not sparring."

"Would you rather face Nuala or Keir?"

That was an immediate no. The look Nuala gave me as Dominic carried me off would've peeled my head like a grape if she had the power.

"I'd rather spar with one of my friends."

"Terrible idea. Roan favors the ruthless. How long will your friendship last after Ormr breaks your nose, and Maili stomps you all the way to the bottom rank? Better to fight someone who won't blatantly try to kill you, or drop you as a friend if you beat them."

The logic in that reply was impossible to break. Keir tried to choke the life out of me in scholarship. What would he do when he had a perfect and legitimate reason to put his hands on me?

"Whatever. It's not like I have a choice."

Dominic set me down on the mat. He faced me, bouncing on the balls of his feet. "Have you recovered from yesterday's breakdown, Princess?"

My face heated. "We never speak of it again," I hissed. "Never. As far as you're concerned, all of yesterday is a black hole where the memory should be."

He chuckled. "Are you sure? Seemed like you had something really, *really* important to ask me. Please, ask me again. I'll pay close attention this time." Slowly, Dominic peeled his shirt over his head. "Very close attention."

What was wrong with me that my heart thumped extra hard at his firm, chiseled, scarred body? I was discovering a few new kinks. I didn't think I was the type of girl who liked scars on a man, but the story they told of blood, battle, fire, and a refusal to give up and accept the cushy pampered life, was a story I wanted told beneath my curious fingers.

"Even closer than you're looking."

I snapped out of it. "I'm not looking at anything! Your mind games don't work on me, Roark. This won't go how you want."

"Everything goes how I want. You'll find that out too late."

I glanced around to avoid his piercing gaze. Ormr paired off with Keir. Maili with Nuala. That left the bottom-ranked to choose their partners and find a mat. When they were done, Captain Roan headed in our direction.

"Recruits, assessment rules apply. You're not done until your opponent is pinned or unconscious. Anything goes short of murder. Understood?"

"Yes, sir," we shouted back.

"I said you'll be fighting with a handicap. I drew straws before the start of class," he said, grinning away. "Broken leg won."

"How do we fake a broken leg?" Nuala asked. "Do you want us to limp or—?"

Roan waved a hand.

An audible snap echoed in my ears. I dropped to the mat screaming.

Vicious, soul-wrenching agony ripped through my leg. I had broken bones before, but nothing like this. What had he done to me?!

I screamed loud and unrestrained, and I still wasn't as loud as Maili, Keir, Ormr, or Nuala.

Dominic dropped to one knee—pale, sweaty, and shaking. He didn't let out a sound, and his face was purpling with the effort. "What did you do?" he hissed.

Roan shrugged. "When you're bonded, your pain receptors are dampened and healing is sped up. I temporarily suspended both abilities for you. Actually, I heightened your pain receptors. You're welcome."

"Why!" Maili half shrieked, half sobbed.

"As explained, if your dragon goes down in battle, you'll have no such abilities to rely on. If you can fight and win in the unbearable agony you're suffering now, when the real thing happens during a fight with a Druk, you'll defeat them with no effort.

"You don't train with puppies before you fight a wolf. You train with lions."

"But, sir—!"

"That's a demerit, Rider Ormr." Never in my days had a man displayed such cold indifference to the torture he caused. "Enough whining at me. If you want the pain to stop, fight and win. Begin."

I gasped—chest heaving and bouncing me up and down on the mat. I couldn't move. I couldn't think past the blinding pain and how to make it stop. I clutched my useless, floppy leg to my chest, sobbing wretchedly.

The bond stirred. Reyna picked up on my distress, and therefore added more to it. Screams leaked through my teeth as that familiar spike drove through my skull.

Weight pressed down on me. Crying, I lashed out.

"Relax," Dominic grunted, voice laced with pain.

For the barest moment, it made me feel better that he was just as mortal as me. He wasn't an untouchable god.

"We're ending this now. I'm going to pin you," he gritted. "I'll be gentle."

Dominic was. Carefully, he flipped me over, and secured my arms behind my back.

I didn't have the presence of mind to stop him. Was my leg still attached to me? This kind of pain could only exist if it'd been sawed off at the knee with a blunt, rusty sword.

"Done," Dominic shouted.

I heard a scoff. "Nice try, Rider Dominic. Do you think a Druk will sweetly pat you on the head, and let you on your way to heal up? Get your asses up and fight for real. Or you'll face me instead.

"Same to you, Nuala and Maili! Get up!"

Roan was a monster. A beast! He could shout about training us to fight Druks all he wanted, but making a broken bone hurt ten thousand times more than it ever could was torture. It was inhumanely cruel, and he did it with a smile.

"Get up, Princess."

"No," I cried, "leave me. Hit me, kick me, whatever he wants! Just beat me so this can be over."

"I'm not doing that. Come on, you're stronger than this. Get up, Ainsley."

He tried to lift me, and jostled my legs. Swinging out, I screamed.

A roar sounded in the distance, bellowing through the Royal Wood. But not as loud as in my head. Reyna's fear for me smashed into my mind.

I blacked out.

Next thing I knew, Dominic was shouting and shaking me. I blinked up into his swirling amber eyes.

"—Princess! Hold her back," he cried. "Roan will hurt her too if Reyna attacks! He'll have to."

That got my attention. Roan would not put Reyna through this pain for trying to help me.

"I c-can't hold her... back," I gasped. "Can't control bond."

"You don't control it." He held my face in his hands, his body hard and warm on mine. To anyone watching, we were lovers in an embrace. "You can't. You don't stop the tide, Princess, you put obstacles in its way."

I sobbed loud and pathetic. "I can't."

"Yes, you can. Think of your favorite place. Where you're safe and nothing can hurt you. Imagine you're there right now," he whispered. "Build it up around you. Cloak yourself in so many good memories, the pain can't find you."

Despite myself, I tried.

I pictured the orphanage. All my brothers and sisters around the table as they were every night, laughing and joking about a silly thing one of us did. Sister Aven went around the table, setting down our meager dinner offerings. Disappointed faces were chased away quickly as she tickle-attacked the littles and smooched them when they tried to wiggle away. This was happy.

This was home.

The pain from Reyna began to fade, leaving behind the searing torture from my ruined leg.

"See? You can do this," he said. "On your—"

"Time's up."

Dominic's presence ripped away.

Through frozen shock, I watched Captain Roan toss Dominic on his feet. His leg gave out immediately, forcing him on one knee.

Roan kicked him dead in the face.

Dominic's head snapped back, blood spurting from his mouth. Roan reeled back and punched.

Rebounding fast, Dominic caught his wrist and twisted, wrenching a strange noise from Roan's throat.

Was he... laughing?

Loud, bellowing guffaws smothered the noise from wrestling cadets. What the fuck was this man?

Roan threw himself at Dominic, catching him off guard. He tried throwing his hands up to block, but it was too late. Over two hundred pounds of muscles and mayhem dropped on top of him, putting unbearable pressure on his leg.

"Argh!"

Roan smashed his fist in his face, cutting off his shout. Dominic was done.

My heart jumped in my throat when he turned to me. My peaceful place obliterated.

"Sir, no. No!"

He snatched me by the collar, hauling me to my feet. I could do nothing but put up a weak, trembling hand.

That hand was driven into my own face. The last thing I heard as my knuckles cut on my teeth, was Roan laughing.

"GET UP."

My eyes fluttered.

"Wake up, you fools."

I peeled a lid open. Roan stood over me—hands crossed in front of him and arms flexed. He had the calm and stillness of a Hyelongan monk. You'd never have known he just finished savaging a couple of twenty-year-olds.

I sat up and was surprised I could. "The pain..."

"Gone," he said. "Phiala complained about me sending you to the next lesson all battered up. So I fixed your boo-boos this time, and only this time. Because this I know, you all won't dare repeat this lousy performance a second time. Dismissed."

Captain Roan walked off, taking his disgust with him. I stared after him in disbelief.

"Evil, miserable bastard," Dominic muttered, sitting up.

"I have never agreed with anyone more. What the fuck is with that guy?"

Ormr, Maili, Keir, and Nuala were in no better condition. They were all groaning and peeling themselves off the mat.

"My guess," Dominic said. "It's the same thing that's wrong with all the instructors. I've had thirteen brothers and sisters go through this training. They weren't half this hard on them."

"They weren't?" I turned that over in my mind. "Is it because of me? Testing the princess to make sure she's worthy?"

He shook his head. "My father warned me things were changing long before you showed up."

Part of me recognized this was the longest, civil conversation we had. "What does that mean, Roark? There were rumors about the Druks. That they're changing. Getting stronger. Were those true?"

"I don't know. I'm a recruit too, Princess, and military secrets are military secrets. Details are only released decades after the battle, and that's during lessons like scholarship. No one is going around, shouting in the streets that our greatest enemy is growing even stronger. The panic would turn Adalinda upside down."

It was hard to question that truth. The idea that Druks were becoming more fearsome shattered any idea of a happy, comforting place in my mind. If this was true, nowhere was safe.

"Don't go anywhere," Dominic said, climbing to his feet. "You and I have something to discuss."

Confused, I watched him walk off and help Nuala to her feet. They fell into a deep heated conversation. I couldn't tell if what he was saying was pissing her off, since she didn't take her hand off his arm the whole time.

"Ainsley, you okay?" Poet jogged over. "That was... hard to watch."

"What? You mean the part where we screamed in soul-destroying agony, crying out for Tenille to strike us dead and save us from misery?"

"Yes," he deadpanned. "That part."

"Oh, yeah. That was pretty bad."

He laughed. "You're one of a kind. Only you can crack jokes after being tortured by a madman."

"Maybe not so mad," I replied, drifting across the field to Captain Roan. "Poet, the rumors about the Druks. I think they're—"

"Leave."

"See you later, Ainsley."

Poet was up and gone so fast, my lips hadn't parted yet for the bye.

"You don't have to do that," I told Dominic. He crouched in front of me, his commanding presence and disturbingly alluring scarred chest throwing me off. "You could be nice to people. Say excuse me, instead of tossing them around. Or—"

"Calthoon, bless me, you worry about the most insignificant things," he said, shaking his head. "My answer is yes, Princess."

"Yes? Yes to what?"

"Yes to what you tried to ask me yesterday—"

"Yesterday didn't happen," I gritted. "There was no yesterday for you."

He cracked a grin. "Does that mean you don't want me to write your reports for you?"

I stilled. "What?"

"You heard me. I'll do it. Already started actually. You'll have it first thing tomorrow morning."

I glanced around. No one was near or looking at us. No one would make it in time to stop whatever trap he was about to spring.

"I don't understand," I said slowly. "Why would you do this for me?"

"Why did you bother seducing me if you didn't think I would?"

"I've fallen out of a lot of trees. Hit my head more times than I can count. That's the only explanation for why."

Another grin. "That guy's right. You are funny. I assume humor was how you got through growing up poor."

My face shuttered closed. "I didn't grow up poor. But I bet you think everyone who didn't grow up in a palace with a thousand servants is poor."

"No, but I do think people who don't know how to read did."

"I never said I don't know how to read."

Dominic gave me a flat look. "We don't have to do this dance, Ainsley."

I tensed. I hated when he said my name. Hated the way he rolled it around his tongue and growled it like he was about to punish me. Hated even more what that thought did to my lower belly.

"That uniform is your size and you're still swimming in it. You eat like someone who's never had enough. And, the biggest hint, you were willing to let me put it in your ass to get out of all the reading and writing required to do these projects."

"I didn't make any promises," I blurted stupidly. Like that was the point. "None of that means I can't read. Maybe I just like anal sex more than silly busywork."

What the hell is wrong with me? Why can't I learn to stop talking?

"Maybe, or maybe we can drop this line of conversation since you obviously don't want to talk about it, and I'll still do your reports for you."

I gave him a long look. "Why? You're not doing this for sex, and you're definitely not doing it because you were so bewitched by the kumquats hiding in my breastband."

"I have my reasons."

I leaned in. Our lips were a hairbreadth apart. "That's not good enough. You're going to sabotage the reports, aren't you? Reveal I cheated and then get me cut."

"Revealing you cheated would be revealing I cheated. We'd both be cut."

He had a point there.

"So then why? Tell me."

Reaching into his pocket, Dominic pulled out a small pad and pen. He wrote something down, ripped out the page, and showed it to me. "This is why." He smiled over the paper. "Since you can read, you won't need to ask any more questions."

"Nope," I said lightly. I understood a grand total of three words. "No more questions. I got it."

"Good. Meet me outside the Hatchery tomorrow morning."

"Okay."

I got up as Dominic did. We collided—my head bumping his chin and him instinctively circling my waist to catch me.

"Sorry," I said. I slipped the note out of his pocket. "You first."

Dominic untangled from me and left. I waited until he was gone, then chased down Poet, Ormr, and Maili on the way to magical accuracy.

"Ormr, read this for me, please." I shoved the note in their hand.

Their brows shot up as they read it. "Um, are you sure?"

"Yes."

"Okay. It says, 'I'm definitely doing it for the sex. I'll be coming for your muguru juice, and that is a promise.'"

"I see," I forced out. "And what is muguru juice?"

"I don't know. I think it's lemon, lime, and kumquats."

I WAITED FOR DOMINIC in the spot we agreed. All night I tossed and turned, trying to figure out Dominic's goal. He helped me at the party and his father was pleased. He came to my rescue and offered to do my share of the work, just because I asked in the most humiliating way possible.

Then the day before, he gave me the first helpful advice I'd gotten in almost three moons for how to control the bond. When I wasn't obsessing about his motives, I spent the night practicing. I can't hold back the tide, but I can put obstacles in its way.

When her fear and worry became pain, I became calm and hopeful. Damn him, it was working. That morning, I woke up with a dull ache in my head instead of the usual pounding.

This is all a part of his plot to kill me, but I can't figure out how. Commandant Drake made his life easier by forcing me to remain in the top eight. All Dominic has to do is refuse to help me, I'll fail scholarship, and his father's wish comes true. The impostor princess is no more.

"Princess."

Dominic strode down the hallway, carrying something for me in his right hand. He looked more handsome than usual that morning. Our standard uniform was traded in for a tight, sleeveless black shirt, and his hair was slicked back from a shower.

He came in close and a sweet honey scent washed over me.

"As promised."

I took the report from him and flipped through it. I couldn't read it of course, and that didn't stop me being impressed. Three maps, diagrams, and an expertly drawn sketch of a battlefield and the riders' place on it.

"You're really giving this to me?" I asked. "Just like that."

He nodded.

"What happened to killing me? You've given up?"

"Look, if you don't want it—"

Dominic reached for it and I lurched back, snapping it to my chest. Without this report, I was dead too. Drake wasn't the type to bluff.

"I want it," I said, "and I'll play your game until I figure out why you're doing this. Here." I reached in my pocket and pulled out something for him.

Dominic raised a brow at the small bottle. "What's this?"

"Payment in full. Muguru juice."

Dominic's laugh followed me down the hall.

MAJOR SORREL STOPPED me on the way out of class.

"Rider Ainsley, I need to speak to you."

I halted, swallowing hard. Dominic brushed past and continued on without a glance back.

I knew he had done something to sabotage me, and I went along with it. *Cut today or cut in two weeks, I chose wrong.*

Slowly, I turned and walked down the stairs. The major's expression gave nothing away as I approached.

"Rider Ainsley."

"Yes, sir?" I rasped.

He slid my report across the desk.

"I... I can explain—"

"Excellent work."

What did he say?

"Truly impressive," he said, a pleased half smile breaking on his face. "I could not find fault with a single conclusion, or your plans of attack. I thought you were going to be my biggest problem, Rider Ainsley. Your comments about the uselessness of this class left much to be desired."

I gritted my teeth. *Damn Keir for dirtying my name before I walked through the door.*

"I see now that you said those things because there's nothing more I can teach you. You have a superior strategic mind."

"No, sir," I blurted. "I don't think that at all. I know I have a lot to learn from you."

He laughed heartily. "You're good to say so. But there's no shame in being confident when you're this good." Sorrel patted my shoulder. "I look forward to your next report. We're covering a battle lost at the Dark Border, and I'm very much looking forward to your take."

"Thank you, sir," I said forcing a smile. "I will... do my best to meet your standard in the future."

"I have no doubt that you will."

I left as quickly as I could.

Dominic didn't sabotage me. The report was so good, Major Sorrel praised me. I should be celebrating. I might still get cut, but it won't be because decades ago, a selfish, peasant-hating man made it illegal for me to go to school.

This was a good thing, if only it wasn't a trick. Somehow, some way, Dominic was playing me. But what could I do about it?

My recruit class was headed to special talents. I had my library duty moved up to that time.

For weeks I dusted shelves, swept, mopped, and moved carts around. Reshelving books wasn't possible since I couldn't read the titles. Not that I told the attendant that. I said there was a problem with my eyesight, and the dim lighting in the library made it hard for me to pick out titles. They said they didn't care and to stop bothering them.

I walked straight up to my apathetic companion. "I won't be sweeping, mopping, or pushing carts anymore. Neither will you while I'm here. From now on, you're teaching me how to read."

The short, freckled guy glared at me. "Why the hell would I do that?"

"Because if you do, I won't tell Drake you've been stealing, and likely selling, the rare books from this library and replacing them with impressive fakes. Seriously impressive," I said, grinning at his wide-eyed shock. "What kind of power is that? Earth magic for the paper? Or is it a kind of illusion magic?"

"I—I—I—didn't steal anything!"

I winked. "From one thief to another, you need to lie way better than this if you get caught. But don't worry, you won't get caught because of me"—I held out my hand—"since we have a deal..."

His throat bobbed. Broden flicked from my eyes to my hand, a thousand emotions flitting across his face. "Deal."

We shook.

I WALKED TO TEAMWORK feeling slightly better. My first reading lesson was rocky, and Broden yelled a lot when I told him he had to start at the alphabet, but at least I was taking my life into my hands.

Leaving my fate to Dominic Roark was a mistake I didn't need to learn the hard way.

It was one thing when delusion and desperation convinced me I could make him fall in lust with me. That plan failed and he was still helping me. Despite that note, it wasn't for my ass or my kumquats.

"Ainsley? Hey, Ainsley?"

I blinked to attention. I rejoined Ormr, Maili, and Poet while they crossed the citadel to get from one field to the next.

"Did you hear what we said?" Ormr asked. "A couple of us are sneaking out to the Royal Wood tonight. You coming?"

"Sneaking out to do what?"

Maili shrugged. "Drink, dance, swim, fuck. The usual."

"It'll be fun," Poet said. "If there's one thing we all rank first in, it's having a good time."

I fell back a bit, hiding a smile. So this is what it was like. There was no drinking and partying in the orphanage with my underage, borrowed siblings. The closest I got to this kind of life was watching a drunken brawl break out in the pub. They were usually fighting over Rosaleen.

Poet stopped when he noticed I wasn't with them. "Hey, you okay?"

"I'm okay. Just excited. Can't wait for tonight."

We reached the staircase leading down to the field. A hard hit connected with my ankle. I pitched forward.

"Ahhh!"

I flew over the steps, crashing into a group of recruits at the bottom. My face smashed into someone's shoulder blade. I bit down on my lip, a small shriek of pain muffled against them. Blood filled my mouth.

"Keir," someone hissed. "What the fuck are you trying to do, man?"

"Doesn't matter." A boot stomped on my hand. "Didn't work."

I cried out. My bones crunched under the unforgiving pain, but I couldn't stop him crushed under two people.

"Get off!"

Suddenly the boot was gone.

"You're a fucking psychopath, Keir!"

Strong hands lifted me dazed out of the pile of recruits. My vision cleared on a shouting Maili.

"It's not her fault the general killed your father. Stop taking it out on her!"

"It is her fault! My father died defending that useless piece of trash. He was loyal to the crown. He was loyal to her. And what does she do? She fucking stands there and says nothing while he's murdered in front of everyone!"

"He wasn't defending her, Keir. He was defending you." Not a trace of the happy, smiling Maili remained. "Protecting you after you acted like a childish bully. Again. If you're mad at anyone, it should be yourself."

Keir reeled back like she hit him, then his fist balled like he was going to hit back.

"Hey!"

"Don't you fucking dare!"

Ormr and Poet shouted at once.

"No," Maili said. Vines bled through the walls, rushed down the stairs, and shot in through the open door. They gathered around her like writhing snakes—waiting. "Let him try it."

Lips peeled back, he flicked from the vines to me. I didn't shrink at the naked hatred.

No... it was the deep and haunting pain in his eyes that made me step back.

Keir shoved through the onlookers, stomping off in the opposite direction of the field. Lessons were over for him.

"Thanks, Maili," I said softly, "but you didn't have to say that to him. It wasn't his fault his father was killed. The blame belongs to the general."

"I know," she whispered, "but you don't say anything like that where people can hear. Generals don't stand for insubordination."

"What? Are you saying he has the recruits reporting to him or something?"

She gave me a look I'd never seen on her before. "I'm saying there's a reason there's never been an attack on Golden City, or the general. Not since the usurper. People with powers that are almost impossible to believe even with magic, work in the palace. Those who wish the general ill always seem to get found out.

"Keep those thoughts here." She tapped my head. "And even then they might not be safe."

There was nothing to say after such a chilling statement.

We headed out to the dragon field, called that because the ground was reinforced to stop their claws tearing it up every time they landed. But because the ground was harder than normal—

It hurts way fucking more when Reyna tosses me off her back.

Narrowed eyes followed Dominic across the field. Those who could mount their dragons were practicing flying. Those who could fly with their dragons were practicing coordinated attacks with a still target. The next step was practicing with a moving target. Then the final skill before we were allowed to move up to second-years was to fight as a team, taking out multiple targets with our fellow riders without killing ourselves, or hitting a rider in the cross fire.

I understood why things were done this way, and how they structured the lessons to build on top of each other. Scholarship taught us to think strategically in battle. Battle readiness prepared us for the harsh realities of losing our dragon or running low on magic in a fight.

Magical accuracy helped us—them—control the explosive, heightened abilities bonding gave them. Teamwork helped put it all together. And special talents, from what I was told, worked with every rider individually to perfect a unique attack that only they could do, and no Druk would see coming. Like Dominic's scatter-shot—blasting a hole through dozens of enemies at the same time.

All of the lessons prepared us for the fight ahead, but none of them got me ready for a brash, unapologetic jerk who ran me out of the way, and jumped on Reyna's back every time I summoned her.

Colonel Kinryu wasn't prepared either. Maybe that's why he didn't know if he could, or should, punish him. It didn't help that

Reyna happily took off at his order. And I wouldn't admit how it felt that Dominic and Reyna together were already at the second to last stage—attacking moving targets together. They were just waiting for the rest of us to catch up.

"Stay away from her," I said in his ear. "We're going to fly today. Don't get in our way."

"I don't have to," he breezed. "I just have to wait until you're lying on the ground unconscious."

"You—"

He strode off. I glared after him, steamed. I didn't have a reply for that. What would I do about it while I was being hauled off to the infirmary, and Reyna was sticking around to let another man ride her?

Poet came up behind and bumped my arm. "Maybe I can help. Since Kinryu isn't punishing Dominic for riding another dragon, he can't punish you for it either. I don't mind if you mount my guy. I'm sure he won't either."

I smiled gratefully. "Thank you, Poet, that's really sweet, but I have to figure this out with her. I can't ride your dragon into a real fight."

"What are you going to do? She obviously doesn't mind being ridden, or she'd throw Dom too. She just doesn't like..." Poet trailed off.

"Doesn't like being ridden by me," I finished, blowing out a breath. "It might help if I saw how you do it. Then, I can see where I'm going wrong."

"No problem. Let's go over there."

Poet and his fire dragon were in the "learning how to fly together" group. No dragon at all, anywhere, would allow a human to put a saddle on their back. As such, riders had to make do by holding on to their natural horns and bony ridges. And if they fall off midair, they pray to Tenille their dragon catches them before they hit the ground.

"The riders that can fly without their dragons are lucky. The number of times they plummeted to the ground screaming and shitting their pants is zero. I'm up to four."

I snorted, holding back a laugh. "Your scream is very... high-pitched."

"Kinryu said I sounded like my balls were sawed off with a rusty spoon, and if I kept it up, he would."

"Ouch." I winced. "Didn't have to be that harsh. Your reaction to impending death is completely normal. Was everyone in Golden City raised to be a warrior? Is that why Roan snapped our legs in half, then expected us to brush it off like it's nothing?"

Poet nodded, gazing up into the sky. The sound of wings cresting through the air broke the morning's peace. The dragons were coming.

"Training starts long before bonding. The best riders retire with regencies, money, glory, power. That's all anyone cares about, except my father," he confessed. "Father wanted me to have a real childhood, not a military one. Some days I'm thankful for that. Other days I'm not."

Valor dropped out of the sky and landed next to us. Fire dragons looked similar due to sharing the same burnished, color-changing scales. Where Valor differed from Reyna was a longer, more pointed snout, and a row of pronounced bony ridges going down his spine.

"Okay, first what you do is—"

"What's this?" Kinryu advanced on us so fast, I jumped back. "What are you doing over here, Rider Ainsley? You should be summoning your dragon."

"Yes, sir. Poet was just giving me tips to—"

"Tips?" He turned raised brows on Poet. "It's your job to give out tips, is it? You're the instructor now?"

"No, sir. But Ainsley needed help, and it's not against the rules."

"Isn't it?" he shot back, voice hard. "Well then, by all means continue to hold Rider Ainsley's hand through training. As a matter of fact, while you're telling me what the rules are in my class, you go ahead and tell everyone, Rider Poet. I'm sure they're all anxious to hear your *tips*."

Poet straightened his back, standing to attention. "No, sir."

"No? Why not? I thought you were more qualified to teach Rider Ainsley than me?"

"No, sir. I apologize, sir."

"Laps," he barked. "You stop when you throw up."

Poet took off running without a word.

"Seriously? You make Poet run laps because he tried to help me. But when Dominic steals my dragon, you've got nothing to say. Maybe Poet should be teaching the class. No one needs an instructor that plays favorites."

My retort was out of my mouth before I could stop myself. Either way, I wouldn't have if I could.

I had a lifetime watching people, those I cared about, treated as less than for the stupidest of reasons. So many treated Poet like trash because he was the son of a recent noble. Kinryu deserved to be yelled at by a subordinate for piling on the nicest guy I knew.

I braced myself as he bore over me, refusing to break eye contact.

"You are worthy of the title you possess, Rider Ainsley."

I blinked. What?

"But I will not be questioned by someone little older than a child. It is up to you to figure out why your dragon rejects you. If you're not willing to put in the effort, your feet don't deserve to get higher than the ground. Do not dishonor yourself by looking for a shortcut again. Do I make myself clear?"

"I... Yes, sir."

I stood next to Valor, confused by how I let that get turned around on me. A few tips on how to properly mount a dragon seemed like innocent advice, but was he right? Was it just me looking for another shortcut because like so many times in my life, the main path was blocked and I was done fighting my way through.

I hadn't realized I summoned Reyna until she touched down before me. Or maybe she sensed I needed her amidst my musing.

For a moment, I studied her. She was very interested in Valor—sniffing him and butting his head. I used her distraction to walk around and study her.

It didn't feel right to say she was rejecting me. I felt Reyna's affection for me. I knew she felt my respect for her. Every night, I scrubbed her scales pristine. I did not, nor would I ever reduce her to a pack animal.

But even with the mutual respect we had for each other, she throws me off her back and happily takes off with Dominic.

What is he doing that I'm not?

Reyna's wings were down and lay stretched on the ground. I got in close and looked at the place where I usually hopped on. Reyna had horns where Valor had hard, bumpy ridges. At her age, the horns were blunt, but I knew from working in the Hatchery, she would instinctively sharpen them after laying her first egg, to become even more lethal.

She had no feeling in those horns, or that process would hurt like hell. So my grabbing and using them to climb on her back shouldn't bother her at all.

Am I too heavy?

I dismissed that thought immediately. Dominic was twice my size, and they flipped and soared through the air like a couple of swans.

Is it her scales?

I trailed a finger along her side, and she turned her head to see what I was doing. They were definitely sensitive enough to feel my light touch, but the brushes I used to clean her were rough. She delighted under the scrubbing. Her scales can't be it.

I stepped back, picturing an imaginary me hopping on Reyna's back. I'd jump, grab her horn, then put my foot—

I flicked to her wing. My foot.

Reyna was too tall for me to climb her with a jump, so I used her wing to boost myself the rest of the way up.

Carefully, I brushed the lightest touch on her wing.

She snatched it up, almost taking my head off. I flew back and dropped hard on my butt.

"Now you're getting it." I hadn't noticed Dominic standing close by. "Took you long enough."

"Her wings are sensitive," I said, mostly to myself. "Kinryu was right. It's my fault for not taking the time to learn these things about her."

I went up and hugged her snout. "I'm sorry, my beauty. I didn't know I was hurting you. I won't do it again."

She nudged me. Affection flowed through the bond.

"Let's try this again."

Backing up a ways, I sorted out in my head exactly what I needed to do. Jump, grab horn, push off her foreleg, swing myself over. I took off.

Jump, horn, leg, swing.

Wind blew my hair back as I settled on Reyna. It tickled my cheeks, cooling the feverish joy that rushed through me. I did it. I finally did it.

"We did it, Reyna." I flashed Dominic a triumphant smile. "Now, let's fly. Ka—!"

She roared, blowing my eardrums out. Bucking, Reyna violently tossed me over her head. Valor saw me heading for him and reacted.

I screamed as he wielded his head like a club, and smacked me out of the air.

Something snapped.

I skidded, flopped, and beat up the ground—coming to a painful, battered halt face-first in the dirt. The pain in my mangled arm told me what happened. I didn't need to see for myself.

A low whistle penetrated my haze.

"That was brutal." I made out a blurry figure standing over me. "Shame you figured out the wing problem, but not the other one. I have a feeling Reyna's going to really lose her patience if you don't get the hint soon. Ever seen a dragon eat their own rider? I have." Gentle fingers wiped the blood from my cheek. "Maybe I will again."

"W-w-wait..."

Before my eyes, Dominic climbed on Reyna's back. He shot me the same cocky smile as they took off.

Chapter Thirteen

"Are you sure you're okay?" Ormr helped me over a fallen log. "Valor and Reyna were not gentle."

"Sorry again about that," Poet said.

"I'm fine. Still sore, but this dragon-bonded-speed-healing is amazing."

The four of us trampled through the Royal Wood, making for the lights and noise in the distance.

"Even though Kinryu lost his mind over it, I've got to tell you that I saw you, and you're not doing anything wrong," Poet said. "I don't know why your dragon keeps throwing you, but it's not because you're mounting her wrong."

"I'll figure out what it is. I have to. I won't make it into the top eight by limping off the field with a mouthful of grass every day."

"I know what you need," Maili said. "To get drunk."

I laughed. "Agreed."

We broke through the trees, I stopped—wide eyes barely taking everything in.

I had no expectations for what a party with dragon riders would be like, and still they were blown out of the water.

Floating balls of warm, multicolored lights hung over the clearing. The alcohol was flowing. As in, literally flowing. Jets of liquid spurted from jugs placed around the clearing. Each was surrounded by recruits holding out their mugs to get filled up.

Seated under a large oak tree, a young band plucked, strummed, and blew a catchy melody for half- and fully naked dancers. Their state of undress easily explained by the river they were dipping in and out of.

It was amazing. Displays of magic I'd never hope to see in Ossian.

One guy juggled balls of fire. Another summoned sultry water sprites from the river, who slinked and danced under the moonlight. A group of guys played dice and sat on stones too flat and formed to be natural. The same stone magic provided a table for the feast the likes of which rivaled the mess hall's offerings.

We took a step and a wall of ice appeared in front of us.

"Uh-uh." Rider Alannah peered around the wall, winking. "Tax for entry. Either a bottle of wine or two articles of clothing."

My friends started stripping without question, leaving me the only red-faced one with clothes on while they skipped off in nothing but breastbands and underclothes, and Maili quickly ditched the breastband too as she and Poet beat it for the water.

"Problem, Princess?" Alannah asked, smirking.

Zaeah knew I spent most of my days running barely clothed through Ossian Forest, and swimming naked in the river. Thing was, I was always alone. The only one who'd seen my naked body outside of my handful of lovers was Dominic.

Oh, well. I'm living a new life now.

"Nope," I replied, smiling. "No problem at all."

I peeled off my top and pants, and chased my friends into the water. A laugh turned my head, skidding me to a stop.

Dominic stretched out between tree roots, laughing loud and unrestrained, with a full mug in his hand. His shirt and boots were nowhere to be seen, wreaking havoc on my new and confusing attraction for scarred, muscled men.

He basked under a blue glow light next to Nuala, Benen, and a couple of guys from our recruit class. Nuala draped in the middle of them naked as the day she was born. Even if everyone vanished, I'd never be that free and comfortable in my bare skin.

I assumed that's the kind of confidence one gets when they're impossibly gorgeous and their ribs don't show.

One of the water sprites broke off and snuggled next to Dominic. It lost its form and a gallon of river water soaked him. He jumped up and whipped a snaking fireball through the crowd. Ten feet away, someone yelped.

"Hey! Fighting back with fire isn't fair!"

Dominic and his group burst out laughing.

Beautiful. The word floated through my mind, taking irrational anger with it. What was wrong with me? Why couldn't I look at this man and see the monster he very clearly said he was?

Nuala flicked to me and screamed. I half jumped out of my skin.

"Oh, Zaeah, I'm sorry," she said, clutching her chest—and pushing up her bosom. "Forgive me, Ainsley, but when did you get over there? You were sitting next to us the whole time."

I didn't know what she was talking about, until she picked up a stick.

Benen howled. The asshole fell back, carrying on and giving everyone an unwelcome full-frontal view of his testicles.

I gritted my teeth. *Nice job, lightning mage. You struck the insecurity bull's-eye dead-on.*

"No, I'm sorry, Nuala. I traded places with my body double to take a break from your constant need for attention."

Her smirk tightened around the edges.

"I'm back now," I sang, skipping over. Staring her straight in the face, I curled up next to Dominic and draped his arm around me.

I trapped her gaze as I tickled my lips on his ear and whispered, "Touch my dragon again and I'll cut off your favorite appendage."

Dominic chuckled like I knew he would. The man did not take me seriously. But Nuala and the fury on her face was.

"You're going to cut off my hand?" Dominic palmed my backside. "Because that's my favorite appendage right now."

My cheeks caught on fire. Regret was a swift, bitter mistress. Rosaleen's words roared in my ears. Dominic's been playing the game of sex, power, and status much longer than I have. This opponent had me hopelessly outmatched.

Don't back down. If I keep acting like sex intimidates me, he'll start calling me Virgin Princess next.

"No," I purred, fingers skittering down his chest. "I meant this one—" I slipped beneath his waistband.

Blinding, white-hot pain ripped through my hand.

"Ahh!" I screamed, ripping away from him. Clutching my hand, an angry welt was quickly swelling to twice my size.

"Oops," Nuala said flatly. "I missed. I was aiming for your head."

The bitch struck me with lightning. I whirled on her, fist flying.

"Enough of this shit," Benen snapped.

Something white, fluffy, and soft appeared beneath me. I didn't have a chance to react as it lifted me off the ground and carried me out over the water.

"Wait—!"

The cotton disappeared, dumping me into the river. I sputtered to the surface to raucous laughter so loud, it drowned out the music.

Poet swam over. "That was hard to watch. You okay?"

"No." I held up my hand. My fingers were spasming out of control, and each uncontrollable movement was agony through my nerves. "This hurts like a bitch. Or I should say it hurts like Nuala."

"Come on." He put his arm around me and helped me out of the water. "There's got to be a healer around here. They'll fix you up."

There was a healer. Rider Fiona was passed out in the dirt, cuddling an empty bottle of wine. It took a lot of shouting and shaking to wake her, and she hit Poet over the head with the bottle for the trouble. Eventually, she spread cooling, healing magic through my fingertips.

The welt shrunk as my spasming fingers stilled. Within seconds, there wasn't a trace of my wound.

"Wow," I whispered. "Magic is amazing."

I let Poet go back to his swim and drifted to the food. Growing up, there was never enough money for pastries or sweets. When we did have coin, Sister Aven focused on filling us up on healthy food. Whenever I stole food, I went for sturdy stuff that would survive a mad sprint through the market. Crumbly pastries didn't fit the bill. It was when Velez started sending us his pay, that I ate a cookie for the first time.

Now I was standing before a table with twelve different kinds of cookies. Sadness washed over me, picking up a chocolate treat. What I wouldn't give to bring the entire feast to my brothers and sisters. It would never feel right for me to have so much when they had so little.

"Princess."

I turned—mouth stuffed with three cookies. "Wha?"

Saying nothing, Dominic ran his fingers down my arm, taking my healed hand in his and checking it over.

I swallowed. "I'm fine. Despite your girlfriend's best attempt."

"She's not my girlfriend."

"Oh, right. She's your fiancée," I snapped back.

A half smile hung on his lips, easily surviving in the face of my irritation. "So what did you want?"

"What do you mean?"

Dominic was still holding my hand. "You're developing a habit of attempting to seduce me when you want something. Let's hear it."

"No, I'm not!" *Tenille, why in your revenge, did you curse us with this asshole!* "What I'm developing is a habit of giving you as good as I get. You try to use sex to mess with my head, I'll fuck yours right the hell up too."

Dominic's brows shot up his forehead. "Really? Damn, Princess, you're saying that like it's a threat." He tugged me to his chest, wrapping his arms around me. "Please, please, please, use sex to fuck with my head."

My hands flew to his chest—to push him away, I wasn't sure. Despite myself, the feel of him warm and strong beneath my hands gave me pause. I traced the bumpy, healed ridges of a scar across his chest. "Okay." I leaned in, slipping my leg between his. The barest pressure against his middle and his cock rose to attention. "I will."

Dominic's grip tightened on my waist. He bent as I rose, closing the distance between us. Our lips connected—

—to the chocolate cookie I stuffed between us.

I smirked at his dazed confusion, munching on my treat. "If you're good," I finished, spinning away.

Walking off, I left him standing there blinking, and swore right then that I'd kiss Rosaleen's feet the next time I saw her. She was right about everything. Never again would I question her methods.

I was heading back to the water and my friends when a burst of laughter drew my attention. Awnan, the guy I tried to share a textbook with, gathered under a tree with three guys and another girl. They cracked up while looking at something up in the branches.

"Hey, Awnan. Something going on up there?"

Awnan saw me and snapped upright. "Princess? We were— We were just messing around. I'm sorry."

I giggled. "Why? You didn't do anything. And you don't have to call me princess."

"I'm sorry."

Smiling, I poked his shoulder. "Stop apologizing. But really, what are you guys looking at?" I strained to see.

"It's me," Awnan said. He still managed to sound apologetic. "My magic. We're playing a game to see who can catch my golems the quickest."

"Your gol—" A tiny, mashed-up face poked out of the leaves, startling me into dropping my cookie. It jumped off the branch and landed in my arms. "Ah!"

"Sorry," he said again. "They're mischievous."

The creature skittered around my neck and climbed my head. Everyone ignored my flailing and sputtering.

"Before I bonded with Fiernan, my mud magic didn't form. Now I can make these golems, but they have minds of their own." Awnan plucked the creature off me. "I'm working on control."

It was a stubby, grumpy-looking thing the size of a baby, and as Awnan said, entirely made of mud.

"Until then, chasing after them makes for fun target practice," said one of his friends.

"Isn't that mean?" I asked.

"It doesn't hurt them." Awnan snapped off the creature's arm. Its black, empty eyes didn't even blink. "And I'm making a lot of money."

My ears quirked up. "How do you play?"

His friends introduced themselves to me as Carlow, Flynn, Kane, and Keely. Awnan set the golem down and waved his hand. Its arm grew back.

"It's easy," he said. "We each give the little guy twenty ryus. If you can't catch him, but you get a hit, we split half the take. If you catch him, it's all yours. If no one can get him before he climbs to the top of the tree, I win." Awnan shrugged. "For some reason, they shoot for the nearest tree to get out of trouble. I've won every game, so I'm not complaining."

"Aw, I want to play, but I don't have twenty ryus."

He waved that away. "I'll cover you."

"You don't have to do that."

"Trust us, Ainsley," Carlow said. Full lips smirked, wrinkling his freckled nose. "He wants to cover you."

"Shut up," Awnan hissed. He avoided my eye. "Let's just do this."

All of them pulled out their coin purses and handed them to the golem. The creature happily took and stuffed them in his stomach. Picking him up, Awnan carried him a ways to the edge of the clearing, farther from the party.

"Everybody ready?"

"I've got him this time." Keely crouched low. She was a slender Ghidorian with a long, black braid going down to her knees. "Our next round at the Yellow Tail is on me, boys."

"Generous," Kane crowed. He was cute with round glasses perched on his nose and an easy grin. "When I win, I'm not buying any of you shit."

"Good." Carlow bumped him from behind. "We don't want shit. You're full of enough of it."

I smothered a laugh. I could tell they'd been friends for a long time.

"Okay... go!" Awnan released the golem.

Carlow, Kane, Keely, Flynn took off like the veil opened up beneath their feet.

Carlow ran ahead of the group. Throwing himself down, he whipped his head and a rope shot out of his mouth, flying straight for the golem.

No, not a rope.

My eyes rounded. Carlow's tongue stretched five—ten—fifteen feet and lassoed around the creature.

The golem leaped into the air. Landing flat on its coin-heavy stomach, it scuttled across the dirt so fast, I cracked my neck trying to follow it.

"My turn." Kane made a fist and whipped it back.

Dog-sized mushrooms forced out of the ground, penning the little guy in.

We froze.

"Did you do it?" I breathed. "Is he—?"

Golem burst through the fungus. Little, stubby legs had never moved so fast. Too fast for Kane with the trail of popping mushrooms in his wake, fighting to get ahead of him. Golem jumped and zigzagged—expertly dodging tongues and mushrooms.

"Now!" Keely shouted.

She spread her fingers and something thin and long flowed from her hands, snagging the branches, stumps, and roots. Flynn rushed in and my vision went white.

Blinking, I stared in awe as a heavy, dense fog rolled over the grass, surrounding Golem. Floating through the fog, we heard the sound of coins clinking—getting louder and more frantic as the creature struggled.

Silently, I backed away until my back hit the tree.

"Ha," Keely said. "We win."

"Not fair," Kane cried. "You can't pair up."

"It's not against the rules."

"The rules we made up while drunk and naked. It's in the rules now."

"Nope. Too late." Keely could rival Dominic for smug. "We'll take our winnings now."

"Uh, guys?" Awnan called. "You might want to check your trap."

"What?"

The fog cleared. Spiderwebbing threads claimed half the clearing, and nothing trapped between them.

"Are you kidding?" Flynn cried. "Where the fuck did it go?"

The tree branch next to me rustled. I climbed a little higher, wedging myself between two and standing lightly on my perch. Golem poked his head out of the leaves.

"Hey, baby," I cooed.

Golem paused. I felt his iris-less eyes look back at me.

"It's okay, sweetie. Don't be scared. Come to me."

I held out my hands—slow so not to spook him.

"You can come to me. I won't hurt you."

Golem crept closer on the branch, hesitant.

"Who's a cute little mud baby? Come to me. I'll take care of you," I trilled. "No one is going to mess with you anymore."

Golem jumped in my arms. I rocked back and quickly grabbed a branch as he burrowed into my neck. Holding him, I climbed out of the tree and dropped before five gaping recruits.

"No," I sang. "I win."

"But... how?" Awnan asked.

I laughed. "I figured him out pretty quick to be honest. When he first saw me, he jumped out of the tree into my arms. Why would he do that if he's afraid of people? He wanted me to protect him, and he runs... because you keep chasing him." I bounced Golem, holding him close. It was hard to tell, but his jagged mouth looked like it was twisted into a smile. "You say you're struggling to control your golems, Awnan? I don't know much about magic, but I have a feeling they'll obey you much easier when you stop using them for target practice."

"Well... fuck," Awnan dropped, scratching the back of his head. "Why didn't I think of that?"

"You were too close to the problem." I playfully shoved his shoulder. "You would've gotten there eventually."

"I don't think I would've." He grasped my hand, and didn't let go. "Being nice to a pile of mud didn't cross my mind. Shows how sweet and kind you are, Princess. You'll make a great queen."

My body heated. Suddenly, I was highly aware of the fact that I never got a chance to buy new underclothes since starting training. My tatty old breastband and underclothes were not up to facing the tender look Awnan was giving me.

"I'm not that great— I mean, it was just a guess."

"You are that great," Keely said. "You're not just kind to mud. You're kind to us. The only reason we're over here playing with walking dirt is because the rest of the recruits don't want anything to do with us. But you actually stopped to talk to us."

My forehead crumpled. "No one wants anything to do with you? Why? Don't tell me it's some stupidness about you being new nobles?"

"Nah," Carlow said. "Worse. It's our magic. It's the wrong kind."

"The wrong kind..."

"It's too weird," Kane admitted. "I've got fungus magic. Carlow has body magic. Mist magic for Flynn. Mud magic for Awnan. And thread magic for Keely. It's not like fire, water, earth, or lightning magic that can tear apart a Druk all on its own.

"We're useless in a battle." Kane stated like it was simple fact. "What good is having a long tongue or growing big mushrooms when a Druk is charging at you? We're a liability on the field. That's why we're headed to the fodder battalion."

"What's the fodder battalion?"

"It's what everyone calls the battalion that is never deployed to the Dark Border, isn't assigned to the Golden Guards, but is always assigned to handle peasant uprisings. And we do it without our dragons."

Keely dropped her gaze. "They say it's because peasants have weak magic, so we don't need dragons, but the real reason is—"

"—to keep your dragon out of harm's way, and increase your odds of dying so that your dragon goes to someone worthy," I finished. A chill climbed my spine. Only a fortnight in this world, and I was already starting to understand the minds of coldhearted, ruthless generals. "That's awful. I can't believe this. Why would anyone say your magic is useless? It's amazing."

Carlow tossed his head. "You don't have to say that."

"I mean it. Keely, Kane, that trap you made for Golem was genius. A Druk would walk right into it. And, Kane, lots of mushrooms are poisonous. Grow one of those fuckers in a Druk's throat, and they're dead."

I was on a roll and couldn't stop myself. "Awnan, once you get a huge, obedient army of golems on your side, you'll be unstoppable. An army of mud creatures that can't get hurt, hungry, or die? How would anyone think that's useless?

"Carlow, if you can change and stretch your entire body like that, then you're a secret fucking weapon. We can't follow a Druk into the air without our dragons." A fact my Druk tormentor used to his advantage many times. "They'll think they're safe, flying out of reach, until your hands go flying after them and tear their wings off."

I scoffed. "Mother Zaeah, bless me. I've been around you guys for all of thirty minutes, and I can think of a hundred uses for each of your powers. What is wrong with the Royal Riders that they can't?"

The five of them stared at me, wide-eyed.

"You..." Awnan gently took Golem from me. "You really think that we can go up against Druks?"

"Yes," I said, and meant it. "Absolutely."

"Thanks." Kane shuffled his feet. "Does that mean when you're queen, you'll change things? Make it better for mages like us?"

I froze.

Why did I say all of that? What am I supposed to say now?

"Yeah, *Princess*."

I whirled around. I hadn't noticed until that moment that it wasn't just Awnan and his friends who were listening to me.

Half the party was staring, having listened to my rant. Including Nuala, Dominic, and their group.

"Well?" Benen continued. "What's the answer?"

Straightening, I said clearly, "Yes. When I'm queen, that's exactly what I'm going to do."

Benen's grin turned nasty. He fixed on a silent Dominic. "What do you say to that, Dom? Princess Ainsley thinks she can run this country better than the general. I guess the decades that we've lived in peace don't meet her high standards."

The band stopped playing. Recruits stopped their laughing, drinking, and dancing. The only sounds were splashing and hushed moans from the bushes.

"I say..." Dominic erased the distance between us, getting so close our chests bumped. "Ainsley is right."

Roaring sounded in my ears. What did he say?

"The system is wrong if it dismisses magic like theirs just because it's different," he said, smiling over my head at Awnan and the others. "Different is what we need for every reason Ainsley said. Druks aren't expecting different. When I rule Adalinda, there'll be no such thing as a fucking fodder battalion. Your dragons deemed you worthy to fight for this country. That's all I need to know."

He sidestepped me like I wasn't even there. "Tell me more about your magics. And your dragons. If you've got body magic, Carlow, what type is your dragon?"

"Nuri's a blood dragon, but she's incredible. She can shapeshift..."

The five of them went off with Dominic, gushing in his ear.

"Isn't he amazing?" Nuala's voice pinned me through. "He'll make a great leader."

"He's great."

"Thank Tenille for Dom."

How did he do that? I don't know what I expected him to say or do in response, but it wasn't that. Somehow, I improved people's opinion of Dominic, and lowered my own.

"Sex, power, status—it's all a game. Roark has been playing his whole life."

"Come on, friend." Ormr, Maili, and Poet dripped a trail out of the river. They put their arms around me, leading me away.

"Ainsley, wait."

Awnan jogged up to me. He placed all the coin purses in my hand. "For you. You won fair and square."

My arm dipped with the weight of them. One hundred and twenty gold ryus. It was more coin than I'd seen in my entire life combined.

"I can't take this," I blurted. "It's too much."

He cocked his head. "Too much? This is nothing. We've bet more than this on drinking games to see who'd vomit first."

I couldn't conceive of that.

"I wanted you to know I liked what you said earlier. I could tell you meant it, unlike..." Awnan trailed off gazing over his shoulder.

Dominic was deep in conversation with his friends. He suddenly turned and locked on me as if he felt my eyes on him.

"You don't think he means it?" I asked, unable to look away.

"It's hard to know what Dom thinks. He's not like other royals, and he could be. Son of the general, he could order us all to lie down on a rainy day, and walk across our backs so his boots don't get muddy.

"But he doesn't. Don't get me wrong, he's not afraid to shove aside anyone in his way, but it's not because he thinks you don't belong there. It's because he belongs everywhere." Sheepish, he dipped his head. "That doesn't make any sense. Sorry, I'm babbling because I'm nervous."

I broke from Dominic and smiled at him. "In a weird way, it does make sense. But not why you're nervous." I swatted his arm, and lingered. "You're not freaked out by me, are you? A princess is still a normal person."

He shrugged. "I'm sure other princesses are normal, because they're not as kind, funny, or beautiful as you."

I bit my lip, insides warming pleasantly. The direct approach was new, but I very much liked it.

It'd been a long time since I tumbled anyone. Two years to be exact. Times got hard in Ossian, and I got skinner, dirtier, and more desperate for coin to feed the kids. The rare times I thought about sex and headed in a guy's direction, he saw a dirty beggar peasant coming at him, and ran.

"I'm really not that much of either of those things."

"Are you kidding?" Awnan placed his hand on my hip. "You're not like anyone I know. You're special, Ainsley."

"You know just what to say, don't you."

"I never know what to say," Awnan returned. "That's why the only people who hang around me are made of mud. Or those assholes."

Laughing, I sidled closer. It might be impolite to make a lady say it, but I'd tell him in every way I could.

"Your friends are pretty great. I'd like to take you all out for drinks sometime after the two of us go."

"If the two of us go"—Awnan flicked over my shoulder—"I'd be the one taking you. I hope."

"I'd like that."

"Yeah, okay," he said somewhat distractedly. His hand disappeared from my waist. "Let's uh—go to—"

I turned to see what he was looking at, and jerked back.

Dominic glared at us so fiercely, I thought a Druk appeared and perched on my shoulder.

"Ignore him," I said, tugging him behind the tree. "About that drink...?"

"Um, sure." Awnan shook himself. "We usually go to this pub called the Yellow Tail. It's kind of the go-to place for mages like us. They hold the same kind of competitions beneath the club, but it's all good fun."

Footfalls sounded behind me.

"Everywhere else we go, our magic is met with eyerolls, disgust, pity, or no interest. It's nice to hear cheers when we win."

"Sounds great." A presence loomed over me. "I'd love to go." I felt behind me and landed on a hard, chiseled chest. I hated that I knew by touch alone who it belonged to. "We can go now if you like."

I shoved on him, trying to get him to go away. Dominic was immovable.

"S-sure." Awnan bounced from me to Dominic. "Let's do it. I'll just... tell my friends we're going."

"No."

That did not come from me.

"Yes," I forced through gritted teeth, pushing harder on Dominic. "I've been dying to leave this party anyway. Bit of a bad crowd."

"Okay." Awnan reached for my hand. "I can't wait to—"

Dominic shot out and seized his neck.

"You must not have heard me. You're not going anywhere with her."

Eyes bugging, Awnan pounded his arm. Creatures grew out of the mead-soaked dirt—a small army of golems racing to help their creator.

"Cute."

Dominic slashed the air. The golems ignited, collapsing into squirming flaming piles in the dirt.

I swear I heard their screams.

"Touch her again— You fucking *think* about her again, and they won't find your ashes."

Dominic tossed him across the clearing. Awnan stumbled trying to right himself. Feet tangling, he plunged in the river.

"Awnan, are you okay!" I chased after him.

Awnan broke the surface sputtering. He saw me coming and shouted, "No!" Whipping around, he swam to the other side of the river—far from me.

I whirled on Dominic. "What the fuck was that!"

Dominic looked at me, and walked off. Fury set my soul on fire.

"Hey! Come back here." I chased him down, pulling him up short. "Why did you do that? What I do and who I do it with are none of your business, Roark."

"Not with him."

"Excuse me?" I shot in his path when he tried to sidestep me. "You don't get to tell me—"

"Not with him!" he shouted, blowing me back. "Anyone else, Princess, but not him."

Dominic stormed off. I made to follow.

"Whoa."

Maili, Poet, and Ormr ran over and stopped me.

"Better not," Poet said. "That fight won't end well."

"It didn't start well," I returned. "Where did all that come from? Is there something about Awnan that I should know?"

They shrugged.

"We don't know anything about him," Ormr said. "He grew up in Edjer and didn't move to Golden City until last year. We shared a few trainers, but he fell in with mages like him and stuck to that group."

"Did you really like him?" Maili asked. "I thought you wanted Lonan?"

"I do," I said, covering with my lie. "But that's not happening anytime soon, and I haven't had sex in two years."

"Two years?" Maili cried. "Fuck, girl, no wonder. You should've told me. I would've pointed you in the direction of the best easy lays. Rafa, over there, already has his pants off before you ask."

"I have a better idea," Ormr said. "Let's dream."

The three of them traded grins and winks that I didn't understand. "Dream?"

"This way," Ormr said. "Phelan said they're through these trees."

I didn't know what was happening until they tugged me through a bush, and I tripped over a body.

Poet caught me, helping me back up. It was his arms around me that prevented me from running away.

"What the hell is going on here?"

Half-naked recruits sprawled on the grass, fast asleep.

"It's him," Poet said softly, pointing to a guy sleeping in the middle. "Want to meet another unique mage? That's Darvin. He's a dream mage."

Ormr answered the question on my face. "It's amazing, Ainsley. When he sleeps, he pulls all the sleeping consciousnesses around him into a dreamworld where he's in control. When you're inside, he can see all your hopes, fears, and desires."

"And he can kill," Maili added. "Well, not so much a true death. If you die in his world, you never wake up. It's a sleeping death that takes hold of you until you eventually slip away."

"Useless in the fight against Druks," Poet admitted. "But during a party, he's everyone's favorite person."

"Why?"

"He'll create the perfect world for you. If your deepest wish is to be locked in a room full of sweets, and eat your way out—"

"—get fucking ready because that dream's about to come true," Maili said. "And no regrets in the morning."

I nodded slow. "So if I go into his dreamworld, he'll know how long it's been and... fulfill my needs?"

"Isn't it great? He once put me in a dream with three guys and a girl who spent what felt like hours giving me orgasm after orgasm while I stuffed myself with my favorite wine and blueberry marachs." She skipped over sleeping bodies and found herself a spot on the ground. "I'm hoping for five guys and two girls this time."

"No orgies for me," Poet said. "You gave me an idea with the blueberry marachs. Let my place be made of that. I fuck sure want to eat my way out."

"Ormr?" I asked.

They winked. "Secret."

"Come on, Ainsley," Maili said. "You get sleepy just being near Darvin. Quicker than you can believe, you'll wake up in a perfect world."

The three of them got comfortable. Felt like seconds passed before they were asleep, sinking into their deepest fantasies. I wasn't quite so quick to join them.

A fun and sexy tumble where I didn't have to worry about awkwardness the next morning sounded fun but what if that's not the dream he gave me? I had a lot of wishes.

To live in a grand house with Sister Aven and my brothers and sisters. To never go hungry, or watch those I love cry over empty bellies again. To wield the magic I see around me every day, but never got to experience myself.

Those were all my wishes, and to have them for just one night only to wake up and in my regular old life, didn't sound like a dream.

Why bother? Just turn around and find that Rafa guy.

"There you are, Dom."

Voices floated through the bushes.

"Are you okay?"

"I'm fine, Nu."

"You're not fine. You're letting that useless, no-magic bitch get to you. Baby, trust me, she'll never have our kingdom. The queen deemed her worthless the day she was born, and the rest of the nation will too."

My chest tightened for so many more reasons than one. I held my breath listening for Dominic's reply.

"It's not that simple anymore."

"It is that simple. She's nothing," she crooned. Sounds of kissing reached my ears. "Less than nothing. I could kill her now, and what could she do about it? She's a stupid, weak nobody that no one wants—"

I dove for the ground. The only thing I wanted less than listening to Nuala badmouth me, was listening to her put that mouth on Dominic.

Curling up next to a fallen branch, I closed my eyes, silently sending a wish to Darvin to fulfill all my sex fantasies. The others could wait until they became reality.

GOLD SLIPPERS.

That was the first thing my eyes saw.

Gold slippers adorned my feet—soft and heeled, they looked as silly as the shoes I saw in the shops I passed through Golden City. So silly, I never let myself admit they were beautiful.

I pushed myself up. A cool, marble floor stretched out beneath me, leading down a long, empty hallway. My soft breaths were the only echoing sound as I took stock of myself.

A gold, sheer dress wrapped around my body. Much like the ones Rosaleen wore, they gave a perfect view to my weaving tattoos and brand-new, not-threadbare breastband and underclothes. My outfit left nothing to the imagination, but it didn't need to. I was alone.

Disappointment ran heavy in my bones, surprising me. It all felt real. The fabric against my skin. The breath filling my lungs. The faint chill in the air. Nothing of this world felt different from the one I knew, and even so, its wrongness hung in the air.

I was in a dream, but it sure wasn't my fantasy. What did Darvin see in me that he thought my deepest desire was to stand in an empty hallway, wearing see-through clothes?

Noise drew my attention to the right. Curious, and a tiny bit hopeful, I set off in its direction.

My silly, pretty shoes *click, click, clicked* on the marble, trumpeting a steady tune to match my pounding heart. I couldn't help my growing excitement. Chain orgasms while gorging on all the amazing foods I could only have if I stole them? I was eager for my fantasy to come true.

The closer I got, the easier it was to make out the sound. I turned the corner, and walked into the women's bath.

There was no other place I could be, barring the unfamiliar hallway.

Marble steps led down to a sloped basin mimicking a river-bank. My path would guide me to a large bathing pool fed by a waterfall. After a long, grueling day, the female recruits gathered in the pool—laughing, splashing, soaking up the hot water. A dozen small alcoves overhead held sweetly smelling candles, scenting the air with jasmine, pine, and vanilla.

The bath was paradise compared to the freezing cold river baths I'd taken my whole life, but it was not my deepest fantasy. Why would my fantasy be to bathe in a bath I had access to every day?

"Excuse me, Darvin," I whispered. "I don't want to question you, but I'm pretty sure I'm in the wrong place. If you could point me—"

"...fuck..."

I stopped. Who was that?

Stepping down, I tiptoed along the short wall that concealed the bathers from the casual looker sticking their heads in. Peering around the wall, I discovered I wasn't in the women's bath, and why my subconscious offered up this fantasy.

Dominic stood in the pool, water to his thighs and no higher as he furiously stroked his cock.

My feet glued to the floor. I couldn't move. I couldn't look away.

To say Dominic was a handsome man was to insult him. He was more than handsome. His perfect, sculpted form, and teasing grin tightened my lower belly just thinking of him. The word to describe his beauty hadn't been discovered yet, and even that word became inadequate as I gazed at him.

Scarred chest glistening with greedy, clinging droplets—the waterfall beat on his shoulders, stealing his whispered grunts as he strangled his length. Thick, but not too thick. Long, but not so long he wouldn't fit like a glove. In these warm scented waters, the dangerous, sexy man who tempted and kissed me within an inch of my life, basked in his sinfulness while he stroked a cock that I sensed on sight would both fit and stretch me in all the delicious ways.

I had fallen into my deepest desire, and I hated myself for it.

No. My fist curled, nails scraping the wall. *I don't think about sex with him because he's nice, or kind, or the only gorgeous jerk I'd met.*

I wanted Dominic Roark because he did the worst thing to me that he could ever do. He kissed me in front of everyone, told me I was beautiful, and almost handed me my every other desire in a single contract.

No one in my life who wasn't Sister Aven or Rosaleen told me I was beautiful. It was worse that he meant it.

That was my secret shame fantasy that embarrassed even me. Every lover looked at me as a pair of holes to satisfy them until they were done with me. They hid me out of embarrassment, and didn't acknowledge me when we passed on the street.

All those times I lay on the forest ground, sweating under some frantically pumping man and eking out the tiniest bit of pleasure to brighten my hopeless life, I'd imagine I was with someone who respected me. Who told me I was beautiful and cupped my cheek as he kissed me.

Like Dominic did.

My secret desire molded with the only person who'd given it to me, and now there he was, ready for the taking.

Don't, I thought. *I can't have sex with Dominic. Not even in a dreamworld.*

Why not? a teasing voice echoed in my mind. I couldn't tell if it belonged to me. *It's not real. You've always wanted to be with someone who saw the real you, despite his many flaws, there he is.*

I willed my feet to move. Take me away. Arrive in another fantasy.

They didn't move.

Why was it a big deal? I didn't want to dream of palaces, wealth, and lives I'd never have. It was too cruel to wake up without those again. But waking up without Dominic was hardly a misfortune.

The real him chased away a nice, sweet guy who could've ended my two years of no tumbling. Why shouldn't the fake him do something about it? Everything felt real from the cool stone against my palm, to the pinchy shoes. I had no doubt that massive cock between my legs would feel plenty real too.

Stop trying to convince yourself this is okay. Despite Dominic's delusions, you don't have a kink for men who want you dead.

I turned to go.

"Fuck, yes, Ainsley."

Everything stopped.

"Zaeah, bless that fucking tasty pussy."

My body exploded with heat, weakening my knees and nearly sending me to the floor. "Fuck you, Darvin," I hissed. If there was any chance of me walking away before, that was incinerated to the other side of the veil.

Clinging to the wall, I peered around again. Dominic thrusted in his hand, so seductively beautiful, it was cruel. He was imagining it was me. Or I was imagining that he was imagining it was me. Or Darvin was imagining that I imagined Dominic was thinking of me.

Whatever was happening, it was my name on his full lips.

My hand crept down, sliding over my spiraling tattoos. He didn't know I was there. It could stay that way. Just watching him was enough to—

I caught my lip on a moan, teasing the sound as my fingers slid past my folds. My scandalous outfit left nothing to the imagination, least of all my nipples pebbling beneath a breastband that was little more than string and gauze.

Chancing another look, Dominic tossed his head back, waterfall taking his rising groans. I picked up the pace as he did, palm slapping against the bundle of nerves between my legs and sending spasming shockwaves through my body. *Please, don't finish yet. Please, not yet.*

My name floated over the rushing water, and I contracted around my fingers so hard, my lip bled keeping me from crying out. I had given myself pleasure too many times to count, and not one time did it feel as good as this.

Was it the magic of the dream heightening my senses? Or was it the thrill of watching this man want me?

I tugged the string and gauze away. My modest mounds were topped with disproportionately large nipples—according to my appreciative, grabby former lovers. I pictured that mouth around them then, rolling his tongue over his captive, sucking, nipping, biting—

"Ah," I moaned, feverishly tugging and fingering, and still not matching Dominic's pace.

Would he be that rough and determined with me? Pounding my pussy while my screams echoed in this sound basin.

I nearly came on the spot.

Dominic bent back, balancing on one hand and thrusting like I was riding him. I'd never found a man's business attractive. Honestly, cocks were so very aggressive in their unattractiveness, I wondered every time why my body responded while my mind rebelled.

I did not have such wonderings then. It was suddenly so clear to me why I closed my eyes while sucking those dicks.

They did not belong to Dominic Roark.

There wasn't an inch of him that wasn't strong, powerful, and sexy. Other men had saggy, wrinkled, weak sacs that cowered between their legs. Dominic's were as big and bold as the pillar he strangled. I would not look away while that fucked my mouth. To do so would be a crime.

My lips parted imagining he was parting them. My finger slicked with my arousal, melting a burning pleasure that made me unsteady on my feet. I didn't need to have sex with him to enjoy our little interlude more than any experience I had with any other lover. And what a shocking truth that was.

"Fuck, yeah, Princess. Ride that cock. Shit, that pussy's so sweet." His voice strained.

I sensed his climax coming as quick as mine, and I would not miss a second of it. I stuck my hand out farther, and slipped.

I hit the ground hard—body smacking the marble and bouncing my cry off the walls.

Dominic shot up and our eyes connected.

I ran.

Scrambling to my feet, I bolted up the stairs—heart leaping into my throat over the sound of hurried splashing.

The beginnings of my climax clung to me, tightening my lower belly, and weighing me down with pressure between my legs. My heel slipped on the middle step and sent me flying.

"Ah!"

I dropped face-first on the stairs, only saved by my hands coming out at the last second, saving me a pile of broken teeth on the marble.

I knew these fucking shoes were a waste of money! Were they invented to stop women from running away?

A shadow fell over me.

"Princess."

"Wait—"

"No." Dominic flipped me over. Grasping my wrists, he pinned them down on either side of my head. "Did you enjoy the show?"

He raked me up and down, seeing everything. My askew breastband. Hardened nipple quivering a bull's-eye for his attention. Flimsy underclothes. Glistening fingers.

Dominic narrowed on my left hand. Flames licked my cheeks seeing his brows pop. He knew exactly why they were wet.

"I'll take that as a yes."

"That's not what you think," I blurted. "There are puddles all over this place. I slipped in one and got wet."

"Very wet," he said, that smirk stretching his lips. "By the looks of it."

"I told you, it's not what you think."

"Hmm. Let's find out."

Dominic took my hand, and before the hushed squeak could escape me, wrapped his lips around my finger.

My jaw worked but nothing came out. Dominic sucked me in to the knuckle, licking every drop of my juices clean.

Smirking, he sang, "Liar."

"I—I— You can't... do that..."

"Then, stop me."

Dominic took my middle finger between his lips, scraping it between his teeth. The wanton moan that echoed off the walls was downright embarrassing. The man hadn't done anything to me yet, and I was so turned on, I'd come if he blew on me. Rosaleen said going so long without sex would have disastrous consequences. Why was she always right?

"Fuck, you taste even sweeter than I knew you would." He placed the lightest kiss on my neck, popping goose bumps on my heated flesh. "How did these fingers get so wet? What were you doing while you watched me stroke my cock?

"Show me."

I blinked. He wasn't saying what I thought he was saying.

This is your fantasy. You're in control.

"You don't get to tell me what to do. You show—"

A firm swat landed on my backside. I choked on a shocked gasp that was more a moan.

"Tenille, why in your wisdom did you make this beautiful, sexy woman so damn stubborn? You're not going to fight your way out of the numerous cross-eyed orgasms I'm about to give you. Tell me how much of a problem you're going to be tonight, baby"—he kissed me hard and thorough—"so I can start breaking you now."

Time to go. Get up and find yourself another fantasy. These kisses are too real. His hands on my body will linger long after I wake up. I can't do this even in a dream.

"I'm going to be a problem," I rasped, slamming and locking the door on common sense. "I'm going to be a *big, fat* problem. What are you going to do about it?"

Another smack tightened my backside, making me moan. This was new, and very, very welcome.

"I'm not doing anything."

"What?" I cried, snapping up. "Why?"

"Not until you show me what you did while you watched." Dominic rocked back, palming his cock. "Say my name. Tell me how much you want it."

Heart racing, I felt dizzy. These games were new to me. All I knew of sex was rapid pumping, rough tugs on my breast, and trying not to gag when a man pounded my throat.

My hand was trembling sliding down my body. "I... I grabbed my breast like this," I whispered, squeezing the sensitive mound. "And I slipped two fingers in my pussy like this."

"I think you did three."

Zaeah, have mercy on me.

"It was three," I rasped, pushing the third digit in. My stretched hole wept. "Definitely three."

I lay bare and wanton on the marble steps, no part of me hidden before him. Leaning on one arm, I started slowly, awakening my body to the new, full sensation. "Ah," I breathed. "That feels so good."

"That feels so good..."

My face was bright red if it was anything. The words came to my tongue, pouring out much easier than they should. "That feels incredible, Dom. Fuck me."

He started stroking—his long, powerful cock pliable in his hands. "I will."

I clenched on my fingers. He wasn't even touching me, and I wanted him so bad, I couldn't see straight. "I want you to—to fill me with your cum. I can't get pregnant in a dream, so you better not fucking hold back."

"That's a promise."

The cart had taken off down the hill. There was no stopping it now.

"I want to sit on your face. Put that smirking mouth under my mercy, and ride your tongue till I drown you."

"No one's gonna fucking stop you."

Darvin, I will never question you again.

My hand picked up speed. I wasn't sure who was bringing me to my pinnacle. Me, or Dominic's intense, smoldering stare.

"I want you to taste this pussy for real. Steal every last drop."

"How badly do you want that?" he asked, smacking my ass again.

"Ah! I want you so bad. I'll do anything you ask. Suck anything you ask. Let you fuck. Anything. You. Ask."

"Give me another taste."

My hand trembled reaching out to him. He ducked it and buried between my legs.

Dominic draped my legs over his shoulders, and had his way. Head bobbing, his tongue plunged my folds—warm, insistent, and thorough. How could this be a dream? It didn't just feel real. It felt like heaven.

My legs trembled, struggling to hold me up as Dominic undid every fiber of my being. Pressure built in my middle. *Yes, final—*

He pulled back so abruptly, I screamed. "What are you doing?"

No one had ever been more unrepentant with a cock harder than steel and juices on their lips. "Take all that shit off. Although, you look amazing in it, and should wear it every day. When I'm not fucking you."

"Finish first." I grasped the back of his neck. "I want to come on your tongue, baby."

"Take your clothes off and I'll come on yours."

I took my clothes off.

Capturing his gaze, I peeled off my scant layers.

"Fucking hell, you're gorgeous."

I was not gorgeous. I was too thin, too big-nosed, and too short. But what it did to me to hear him say it...

My final piece, my breastband, I threw on him. Dominic claimed and laid it between my legs. Grasping both ends, he ended my confusion with rough and glorious tugs—rubbing the fabric against my clit.

I spasmed, feet nearly coming off the bottom step.

Heat burned in his eyes. True, burning heat that steamed the water off his skin. He was losing control of his magic. That was the effect I had on him.

I came hard, screaming without shame or restraint. "More."

"Beg."

"Make me."

He grasped the back of my head, tugging me onto my knees. I grabbed his thighs, my digging nails telling the tale of my eagerness.

Dominic bent my head back. Rough, breathy pants escaped me as he painted my lips with the beaded pearls on his crown.

"Beg."

"I want you in my mouth," I whispered, licking the tip. "Please, Dom. I need you."

"Hmm." Raven locks dangled before burning eyes. He was hotter than a person should be, but I liked the burn. Made touching him even more dangerous. "Do you? I don't know if I believe it."

I launched at him.

"What the— Fuck!"

We went down. Dominic fell flat on his backside—hard. Shimmying down his chest, I descended on his cock and swallowed it to the hilt. I was done playing games. I wanted him inside me—now. His noise turned to ragged groans fast.

"Fuck's sake, they don't make them like you, Ainsley. Damn my father for destroying the contract."

I bobbed between his legs, sucking hard to cave my cheeks. I imagined his cock filling my mouth more times than in just this dream, and this was better than it all.

He slid in and out of my mouth like butter, warm on my tongue—filling to burst me.

"You're perfect," he gruffed, tangling in my hair. "I'd burn all of Adalinda for this mouth."

I felt a silly blush stain my cheeks. This was usually the part of the tumbling where the guy pushed down hard on my head and called me a dirty slut, whore, and that my filthy cunt was next.

Not Dominic. He caressed my head and told me I was perfect. *This is definitely a dream. Men like him don't exist. At least they don't for me.*

"Turn."

I didn't know what he meant until he pressed his back on the ground.

I swung my legs around, positioning his head between my legs. His fingers found something to do immediately.

"Uh, yes," I breathed, tugging on him almost frantically. His palm *slap, slap, slapped* against me, making sounds as delicious as it felt. I lowered my ass, and didn't need to say anything else. Dominic's tongue flicked my clit. Cries teased out of me I didn't know I could make.

I swallowed him again, letting my moans rumble and vibrate his cock. His grunts and clenched thighs were the praise I needed.

Our moans filled the room, competing with the waterfall. The feel of him fingering my pussy, sucking my clit, rubbing my legs, and filling my mouth breathed life into my barely living body. My skin tingled all over like a thousand lightning strikes within my nerves.

I wanted to be in that moment with him forever. The Dominic that saw the real me, and not the threat I never wanted to be.

I felt him tighten beneath me, and knew what was coming. Lifting my head, I stroked faster—strangling his cock without mercy. Dominic bucked. Hot ropes of cum burst from him, painting my face and tongue.

Dominic yelled hoarsely, delighting my ego while I milked every last drop.

"Shit, woman. Marry me."

Giggling, I rocked back on my heels. "Okay. If you're good."

"I sure as fuck won't be good." He swatted my left cheek. "Sit on my face."

"Ah, yes, Dom." I obeyed happy and quick. How had I gone my whole life without knowing I liked to be spanked? No— How had I gone my whole life without knowing I liked to be spanked by Dominic? Oh, the perfectly satisfying sex I could've been having if I met him sooner, and he wasn't such an ass.

"Smother me," he ordered. "If I'm not drowning, you don't stop."

"Well, if you insist. Who am I to disobey?" I dropped down on him, wiggling my ass on his face. Dominic let out a low, rumbling growl—spurring me on. "Stick out your tongue."

I rocked on my new favorite seat, grinding my pussy on his tongue. Dominic traveled up my thighs, skating over my stomach, and covering my breasts. Squeezing, pinching, rolling my sensitive nubs over his calluses. Bursts of electricity spread through me, making me shudder with each tweak. "Harder," I gasped. "Don't be gentle with me."

I laid my hands over his. Inexplicably, he laced his fingers through mine, holding me as tightly.

His tongue probed me, finding the loveliest spot to explore. My body moved on its own. Balancing on my toes, I bounced on his face, impaling my pussy on his tongue.

Up, down, up, down—cries and moans came from me that I didn't know someone could make. Primal, dangerous grunts that shed the last of my inhibitions.

I came so hard, I bucked off his face and landed flat on the floor, shaking and shuddering as wave after wave of pleasure washed over me—each more mind-bending than the last.

Dominic lifted me up. I was sweaty and weak from the aftershocks of my orgasm, helpless to stop him. I didn't come to until hot, rushing water tickled my feet.

He carried me through the waterfall. Dizzy, a shadowed, secret world came into focus. In the real shower room, the nooks and crannies in the rock wall were for washcloths and shower items. In our room, they were filled with a million candles.

Flames flickered off the wall, lighting the tiny specks of silver in the rock, and glittering like stars. Before us, a curtain of water protected us—concealed us. We were not the princess or the general's son. We were just Ainsley and Dominic.

"It's beautiful," I whispered.

"It is. It's where I'm going to fuck the shit out of you."

I laughed. "So romantic."

Grinning, he said, "We can do romance…" Dominic tipped my chin, and captured my lips. Nipping my bottom lip, I melted as he tangled with my tongue.

Dominic kissed me slow and deep, scrambling my mind and all sense of self. I broke away gasping.

"Or," he finished, "I can fuck you like a wild animal trying to break your pussy and ass."

My heart jumped out of my chest. "The second one, please."

Dominic squeezed my cheeks. "Hold on, what's this?" he asked, frowning.

"What?"

"Feels like an ass that needs to be spanked."

I cracked up. Only this guy could make me laugh and turn me on at the same time. Is this what sex was supposed to be like?

Fun.

"It's an ass that needs to be pounded too."

His brow shot up his forehead. "Are you saying—?"

"You know what I'm saying. I told you, Roark." I kissed him, holding his gaze firm. "Don't be gentle with me."

"Oh, there's no chance of that. Do we need a word to end the fun?"

"Nope." Turning around, I grabbed the wall, wiggling my ass for his invitation. "I've got a pussy, Roark. Doesn't mean I am one."

"Fuck's sake," he growled. "Marry me now."

I winked at him over my shoulder. "Yes."

"I like that word on your lips." *Thwack.* "Say it again."

My body rocked at the firm slap to my right cheek. The water was barely thigh-high, giving him all the access he needed. "Yes, Dom. More."

Thwack.

Thwack.

"Ah! Fuck yes!"

"Who do you belong to?"

"You, Dom," I said without hesitation. It didn't occur to me to say anything else. "I'm yours."

Thwack.

"Fuck me, please." I begged loud and without shame. "Please, Dom, I need you inside me—"

Dominic pushed in, catching my plea on a choked cry. No time to prepare or adjust, Dominic started pumping—pounding my middle and slamming his against my red cheeks.

My eyes rolled up in my head. Stretching me, fucking me, dominating me. It felt so good it hurt. Maybe it actually did hurt. Pain mixed with pleasure to rack my body with back-bending, toe-curling, screaming shudders.

He fucked me hard and dirty, lifting my feet off the stone. Only water and his unyielding grip held me up, refusing to surrender me to mercy.

"Shit, you're so tight. Strangle my dick, baby. If it doesn't live for you, it doesn't want to live."

"M-more," I gasped. "Tenille, forgive me, fuck me h-harder."

I don't even know how he obliged. Was it the power of a dream? Dominic went from fast to inhuman, cracking my jaw in a silent scream.

Holding tight, I glanced back at him. That same majestic glow of ecstasy twisted his lips in an almost feral snarl. His shoulder caught fire, startling me. As I watched, a flicker of flame claimed his chest.

His magic was out of control. The most powerful mage I knew, and all it took was me to shatter his concentration. Why was that as sexy as everything he did to me?

Dominic hit that spot, and I came so hard I slipped off the wall and drowned. My scream ripped through the water, and it came right back—filling my nose and mouth.

I think I blacked out, because I came to in his arms. He held me chest to back, my head draped over his shoulder. Something small and broken inside me healed when I felt the soft, tender kisses he dropped on my cheek, nose, and lips.

"Wow," I said softly. "Sex can't be like that for everyone, or no one would ever get anything done."

"Believe me. No one has ever had sex like this."

I flipped over, wrapping my legs and arms around him. "Let's do it this way this time. I want you to suck my breasts while you fuck me."

"Holy veil, woman," he cried. "If you can recover this fast from that orgasm, I didn't do it right."

I shivered. Dominic did it every kind of right, and I needed more. He awakened something in me I didn't know existed, and we weren't stopping until I couldn't move.

"Don't hold back." I brushed my lips over his. "Every single filthy thing you've ever even thought about doing. We're gonna do it twice."

"Shit, I'm in love. So this is what it feels like."

My giggles turned to squeals as we sank under the surface.

Chapter Fourteen

Dominic fucked me in every hole twice, and two of them four times. I came so many times, I stopped counting.

Hours, days, or years passed. I lost sense of time lying in his arms, the water only high enough to tickle our feet on the edge of the basin.

Soft, caressing fingers traced the golden tattoo on my left arm. For a while that's all we did, lie there in a comfortable silence.

"Like them?" I asked, voice soft. Too loud and I might break the spell.

"I do. Is it strange to say they suit you?"

"Spiraling, golden tattoos that cover every inch of my body? No," I said, gazing at my fingers. "That's not strange. I like them too." I traced a line down his chest, following the path of a scar. "How did you get this?"

He looked down. "I could tell you the truth, but a lie would go down easier."

"Well, now you have to tell me the real story."

"This scar..." Dominic laid his hand over mine. "My brother tried to kill me."

I stilled. "He what?"

"Roderick and I were inseparable growing up, because my father was never around."

"But." I thought back. "Your father said he had a steady hand in each of his children's lives."

"After we bonded with a dragon and could begin training—yes. Before then, I did not lay eyes on my father's face before I was nine and my brother was ten."

"Nine," I whispered. "That's awful."

"I thought it was... until he moved in."

I waited for more, but none came. Stroking his chest, I propped on my chin, smiling softly. "You can tell me. I know a little something about absent parents."

He chuckled. "I guess you do. Why not? It's all a dream." Dominic flipped over, facing me. He pressed his nose to mine and held me close. "That steady hand my father spoke of. All of us received it after bonding. The ones who didn't aren't allowed in his presence."

"The ones who didn't? But all thirty-two of you were at the Calthoon feast?"

"Not the ones who are unworthy. Or dead."

"Then, how many children did your father have?"

"Fifty-six."

My eyes widened. Twenty-four? The general had two dozen children he doesn't speak of? How could that be?

"I got most of these scars during the two years he lived with us in Azura. Every year, we were brought to the Hatchery. I bonded with Reyna, but no dragon chose Roderick. It wasn't a surprise, though.

"Roderick inherited my father's kind of magic."

"Death magic?"

"Death magic is just a general term for magic whose only purpose is to maim or kill. Poison magic, curse magic, and Roderick's acid," he said. "Dragons prefer riders with the same type of magic. Doesn't have to be the same specifically, but sea dragons choose an ice mage over an earth mage every time.

"Despite my father's hope that a dragon would make an exception, none chose Roderick, and Tizor was the only other death dragon we knew. Until we found his mate, Father feared Tizor was the last of his kind."

"So because he couldn't bond for reasons out of his control, your father declared Roderick unworthy?"

"The opposite, actually. Everyone believed all the death dragons had gone—fled beyond the Dark Border for new lands an ocean away from Adalinda. Then, Tizor came to him," Dominic said. "My father believed Roderick would be similarly chosen and honored once he was strong enough. So when I, the youngest of our mother's children, finally bonded, training began for both of us.

"It was brutal. We woke up before the sun rose, and weren't allowed to sleep until long after it set. In the first month, he went through our rooms and threw out every toy, book, portrait—everything. All we were allowed was a cot and wash basin. We were soldiers now. Soldiers didn't sit around all day with their heads in a book."

My heart squeezed. Tenille knew I grew up without all those things, but not by choice. If Sister Aven could've, she would've showered us in clothes, toys, and books. Here was a parent who could give their children everything, and instead took it away.

"My mother did her best to help us. But she's one hundred and eighty. Older than the general," he confessed. "She was born to Old Ghidorah—the kingdom that existed before the end of everything. She wasn't fluent in Adalindian, and couldn't read the marriage contract she signed."

"Oh no," I breathed, a heavy sick feeling settling in my gut. "What did he make her agree to?"

"That she would bear him as many children as he desired, and not interfere in his raising of them. We went from happy days playing with her and my cousins in the fields, reading books together under the lemon tree, and clinging to her leg while she showed us how to make Old Ghidorian dishes, to one-hour visits once a week."

I asked for the truth, but I didn't think the story would be heartbreaking. "You were allowed to see your mother for an hour, once a week? For what possible reason?"

"We were soldiers now," he said like someone who heard it many times. "Soldiers don't cling to their mama's apron strings."

My eyes closed. I didn't want Dominic to see my pain. How desperately I wished to meet my mother. To touch her. Know her face. All that time, Dominic's mother was right there, and he wasn't allowed to be with her. Somehow that was just as terrible.

"It was terrible," he said as if he read my mind. "But Mother didn't let us be sad. She rescued as much as she could from the things our father threw out. Two of my favorite books, and Roderick's best wooden carvings. We'd read, and play, and laugh during that stolen hour, then hurriedly put everything away and return to different sides of the room when my father came in.

"For the first year, we survived like this, then I turned ten."

"What happened when you turned ten?"

Dominic gazed at me unseeingly. "That day, my birthday, the general woke us up and said we'd be doing things differently from now on. Instead of fighting targets, we'd be fighting each other."

I didn't have to say anything. Dominic read it all over my face.

"Roderick didn't have a dragon to boost his power. And although my father tried to force it, Reyna wouldn't let him on her back. Even at ten, my magical ability was unheard of. After bonding, I brought seasoned fire mages to their knees. The only way for his favored heir to improve was for him to fight me, and the only way for both of us to improve was for us to fight him.

"I got this scar from my father," he said, pointing to a long, jagged one above his left thigh. "And this one. And this. And this."

I felt sick. None of these scars were like the nicks I got from running through the forest and falling out of trees. They were horrid, brutal wounds.

"He'd have you burn and spray each other with acid?"

"Worse," he said quietly. "I was his opponent for physical training only. Roderick was his favorite, but we were both promising heirs. If I was carelessly killed, there'd be no one to help Roderick complete his training. Acid magic isn't made for a sparring match, so magical training was against riders of the fodder battalion.

"We were expected to fight like our lives depended on it. Any holding back, and the other brother was beaten for their weakness. My choice was between hurting a nameless rider, or my brother.

"I killed five men before my eleventh birthday."

"Oh, Dom..." I trailed off, not knowing what to say.

"I didn't want to, Ainsley," he rasped. "Even with the threat against Roderick, I held back as much as I could, but my magic was too strong and I was still learning to control it. They died, my flames eating them alive. I... still hear them scream."

I pressed his forehead to mine, trying to send him waves of comfort. He was ten. Still a baby. How could his own father do this to him?

"Months of this, and Father wore us down to nothing," he said. "That hour a week was no longer spent laughing and sneaking cookies. We'd sit in silence, our mother begging us to talk, but unable to look at each other or tell her what horrible thing our father ordered us to do that day."

"Poor baby." I peppered kisses on his cheeks, nose, jaw, and lips. "I'm sure your mother wanted nothing more than to snatch you both and run away."

"I wish every day that she did, but the three of us still had hope by that point. The two years were almost over. The general had many children and a kingdom to rule—he couldn't stay indefinitely. That was our saving grace. Everything would go back to how it was when he was finally gone.

"Maybe he knew that." His voice was ragged. "The general knew the second he left, the books, toys, fluffy beds, and afternoons under the lemon tree would return. The sons he spent months molding into the perfect warriors would become pampered pets tied by their mother's apron strings. He wouldn't let that happen."

I regretted the words as they came out of my mouth. "What did he do?"

"The general woke us up that final day, and said Roderick and I would have one last match... to the death."

Horrified, I tore away to that scar on his chest. It didn't look like the others, which is why I asked about it. Then, it was all too clear. It didn't look like a normal scar because it wasn't one. It was a burn.

Acid burn.

"We didn't want to do it." He squeezed his eyes shut. "We fought, begged, and screamed. Roderick attacked him, but the general put him on his ass. We were told that either we fought and one of us died, or he killed us both. We spoke at once, and said *both*."

"But if you were both willing to die—"

"We both were," he gently broke in, "until he ordered a servant to bring my mother."

My hand clapped over my mouth. General Roark was a beast. A monster! They were children. *His* children. How could he do this to them?

"We didn't have a choice. We fought, and Roderick won."

"He won?"

Dominic nodded. He took my hand and brushed my fingers over the burn. "Hit me square in the chest. The acid was eating through to my heart. It was over. I lay there, writhing on the ground while my father clapped for Roderick. He didn't so much as acknowledge me—dying in the dirt."

"But... you lived." The question in my words was clear.

"I was terrified. In pain. Panicking. I lashed out, and the next thing I knew, Roderick was dead."

"Oh, Dom, I'm so sorry." I held him tight, tipping his head to kiss his forehead. "I can't believe he did this to you both. He's responsible for your brother's death, and I hope you know that. The general is a monster. I just don't understand how you can stand to be around him. How do you not hate him—?"

"I do hate him!"

I blew back.

"I despise that rotted sack of shit in a skin mask! He praised me, Ainsley. *Praised me* for having the logical indifference needed to defeat an enemy. Roderick wasn't an enemy. He was my brother! And that bastard called his death logical.

"I hate that man with every ounce of bile that's corrupted my soul. Ever since that day, he named me his favored heir and kept me close to his side. I was forced to help him train my other siblings under the same brutal rules. Nine," he croaked, clutching his chest. "I've killed nine of my brothers and sisters. The road behind me is riddled with my own blood!"

"It wasn't you," I cried, grasping his head. "He made you do these things. You would've made a different choice if you could."

"What does it matter the choices I would've made? All that matters is the one I did make. My mother was destroyed, Ainsley. When she found out her youngest son killed her eldest, her mind broke. The general's idea of care was to move her into that pitiful room in the palace.

"Barring the servants, I was the only one to visit her, sit with her, and the whole time my mother looked right through me." His lips curled. "Then, he found out about the visits. I was showing my weakness again. Clinging to my mother like a child, so he sent her away, and to this day I don't know where. I don't even know if she's still alive."

"Dominic..." I dropped my head on his chest—hiding my tears.

"My idea of a father died ten years ago. A vile bastard remains in his place. I want nothing more than to stick a blade through his heart and light him on fire. For years I plotted to do just that."

My eyes widened, but I didn't speak.

"But then I realized I was thinking too small. Too short-term. I wasn't going to kill the man. I was going to let him hand me his throne. The general fooled himself into thinking he fashioned the perfect warrior heir. Once Adalinda is in my hands, every one of his laws will be repealed.

"The walls come down around Golden City. The commoners will be allowed to live their lives and send their children to school without fear. Dragons will bond with who they deem worthy, not who the throne deems worthy. Edjer, Nehebkau, Ghidorah, and Hyelong will return to independent nation-states. The Royal Riders will be open to anyone who wishes to defend their home. Not just the noble and wealthy.

"My father's legacy will be destroyed. My brother will be honored. And my mother will come home."

He stroked my cheek. "That's why I can't let anyone get in my way. Not even you."

I didn't want to stand in his way. Everything he planned was everything I wanted. If Dominic wasn't on his father's side, he was on mine.

"Dom, you need to know—"

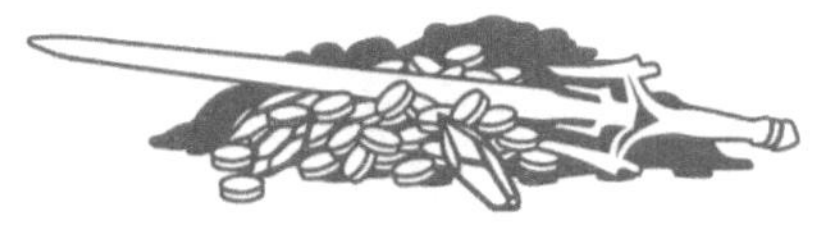

I WAS STANDING IN A forest.

One minute I was by Dominic's side, and the next I wasn't. It happened faster than a blink.

Unnaturally bright-green grass tickled my bare feet. I wasn't wearing my sheer dress anymore.

Tight leather pants and a vest lined with steel covered my body. I looked like I was going to war.

Confusion chased away my lingering contentment. What was Dervin doing? Was this another dream fantasy? Why would he put me in another one when I wasn't ready to leave the first?

"Dervin?" I called. "Dervin, bring me back to Dominic—"

"Afraid not, Shenha."

I snapped my head up. Color-changing hair and a cocked brow reclined on a tree branch, one leg bent and resting on the other. "Kai?"

"You need to ask? How many gods do you know?"

I gaped at him. "What is this? Why would Dervin imagine you? Bring me here?"

"Don't be ridiculous. That dreamminder has nothing to do with me," he said, sitting up. "I plucked you out of your little fantasy world. You don't have time to dream."

"What does that mean? If you have something to tell me, say it."

"I... can't." A flash of irritation twisted his handsome features. "Not in a direct way. The consequences would be worse for you than me."

"Worse for me? I don't understand. What are you trying to say?"

"I can't tell you what I'm trying to say. Even gods answer to a higher authority."

I quieted, studying him. "Is this real? Are you... real?"

"I am."

"You're a god?"

"Yes."

"One of the old gods?"

"Technically, I've existed as long as the gods you know. Your people have simply forgotten about me, and the others."

Approaching the tree, I took that in. "What do you want with me?"

"I can't say."

"What can you say!"

He chuckled. "You have a short fuse. Good. You can't be meek for what we're about to do." Kai suddenly twisted around, growling. "Shit. They found me faster than I was expecting.

"Listen, girl, because I've risked much to tell you this. You're barreling toward a huge mistake. You don't understand what you are, but it is so much more than you ever thought possible. Something is coming," he hissed. "A decision that will change everything, and you must do the opposite of what you know is right. Do you understand? The opposite!"

He shot up. "I have to go."

"But— Wait! I don't understand—"

The world started fading around me. Too-green grass faded to black. His tree warped in my vision.

"Wait!" I cried. "What am I? What am I!"

"You're a thief." His words whispered through the gloom. "Start acting like one."

I WOKE UP.

Blinking, my vision cleared on swaying trees and a star-dusted sky. A rock dug into my leg, breaking the skin as I sat up. Drowsy riders and recruits stirred next to me.

Maili whipped around on Darvin. "What the hell, Darvin? My dream was just getting good."

"Sorry, guys," he said, pushing his glasses up his nose. "I was woken up... by him."

"Who—?"

"Recruits." Commandant Drake broke free of the bushes. "You have ten minutes to collect your clothes, retrieve your garbage, and return to the barracks before I bring down so many demerits on your head, you'll all be cut!"

No one moved.

"Now!"

We tripped over each other, racing out of the Royal Wood. Running, jumping, darting through trees, I left the party behind like the experienced forest child I was, but it wasn't demerits on my mind.

All I could think of was Dominic.

There was no familiar and lovely ache between my legs. I didn't feel his kiss lingering on my lips. His smell clinging to my skin.

It felt like we were in there for hours, exploring each other's bodies. The only memory my body held was of dirt and scratches.

Truly, it was all a dream. Dominic and I didn't have sex. We didn't have a moment that changed the way we saw each other forever. The fantasy was over.

The enemies live on.

THE NEXT MORNING, I piled my plate high with meat and pastries, preparing for another day of training. We were supposed to have the day off. Commandant Drake took care of that.

"This is cruel." Poet trudged to our usual table. "I'm too wine sick for this. Two minutes into sparring, I'll be actual sick."

Ormr and Maili grunted similar.

I felt for my friends. Between getting tossed in the river, chasing after mud, and enjoying a dream, I didn't have time to get drunk. By the groans, slumped shoulders, and massaged temples, no one else could say the same.

Dominic brushed past me with a grunt behind him, carrying his tray. He looked as fresh and clear as he did every morning.

I chose a seat that gave me direct view of him, and stared.

It wasn't real, I accepted that. But it also didn't follow that everything was fake. Darvin created that world for me with a Dream Dominic that looked and acted very much like the real one. The scars were the same and in the right places. His smirk was the same.

The Dream Master saw through to my deepest wishes and insecurities, and gave me everything I wanted. Wasn't it possible he saw through to Dominic's motivations, and everything he told me about Roderick and hating his father was true—even if it didn't come from his lips.

But wasn't it also possible that the dream spun a fairy story to humanize Dominic, and sate my guilt about lusting after a monster? The dick slides in easier when it's attached to a misunderstood, secretly good person.

I flicked to Nuala. *"Don't let some silly little dance, a desperate contract, and his letting you wear his mother's jewels—go to your head."*

Dominic brought me to that tiny room during the Calthoon feast and placed his mother's jewels around my neck. Nuala told me so herself. If the little room his heartbroken mother was kept in is true, then doesn't that mean the reason for her heartbreak was true as well?

This could change everything. Dominic didn't trust me because he knew I was hiding something, and he hated me for stealing Reyna. I also didn't help myself by announcing to all the recruits that I would make life better for unique mages if I were queen. A heat-of-the-moment comment, that I meant.

Life was terrible in Adalinda for so many people, and I wanted to see it change. Seemed like Dominic did too.

A poor, illiterate, magicless orphan couldn't rule a country, but Dominic—the Dominic who held me in a dream—could.

I had to ask if the story of Roderick and the siblings he was forced to slaughter was true. If it was, I'd convince him to end the war between us. He could not have Reyna, but could have all of Adalinda, secure in the knowledge that I wasn't secretly planning a coup.

I pushed back from the table. No time like the present.

Dominic tracked my approach. I sat down next to him even though Nuala's expression was screaming "go away" over his shoulder.

"Roark, can we talk?"

He reclined in his seat, tearing a bite from his apple. He didn't respond until he slowly chewed and swallowed. "About?"

"It's private," I said clearly. "We should go outside."

"Oh? Will you be... messing with my head?"

His implication, and the smirk behind it, sped up my pulse. The sex wasn't real, but it sure as fuck felt real when he was pounding me into the marble floor. Visions of the things we did together while that same smirk smiled down at me, floated through my head.

"No."

"Hmm. Then, no," he said. "You'll have to ask your favors of someone else."

"This isn't a favor, and it's important."

"Not interested."

My temper flared. "What is your problem? It'll take two minutes. Get off your ass."

He took another bite of his apple—chewing slow and relaxed. He wasn't going anywhere.

"What if I said I was going to mess with your head?"

"Moment passed. Again, not interested."

Leaning over him, I pressed my nose to his. "You will be."

I returned to my table. I wouldn't get anywhere arguing with him, and it didn't feel right to shout his childhood tragedy for the entire mess hall to hear. I'd corner him later.

DOMINIC IGNORED ME all day.

He sidestepped me in scholarship. Pretended he didn't hear me calling him on the way to magical accuracy, and chose Ormr as his sparring partner in battle readiness.

Keir headed in my direction.

"Team," Nuala called. She linked her arm through mine before I could think Maili's name. "Team, sir."

"Yes," Roan said. "No mats. Take a practice sword."

I'd been wondering why crates of wooden swords were waiting for us when we stepped out onto the field. Part of me wanted to ask for another partner, but I didn't see Roan granting that request. More likely, he'd make me partner with her every day for a month for daring to ask.

A hard hit struck me from behind, sending me flying into the crates. I pitched into the bucket and tipped it over. A cascade of shaped wood rained down on my face—one smacking me in the eye.

Keir gazed down at me entirely unrepentant. He snatched up a sword and stormed off like he hadn't assaulted me.

At least Nuala is better than Keir.

"Ah!" A boot crunched my hand, digging in as Nuala took a sword and pretended she didn't hear me screaming.

"Get off the ground," she tossed over her shoulder. "Someone will think you're a piece of trash."

I pushed myself up, clenching my teeth. Cursing her out wouldn't give much satisfaction. Beating her in front of everyone would.

I got my own sword and faced her across the grass. I broke from her grin only long enough to watch Captain Roan approach. What hellish nightmare would he put us through that day in the name of training?

"Every rider is issued a sword, two daggers, and a vial of poison to kill yourself and your dragon with in case of capture." Roan stated this with no inflection. "Whatever other weapons you pick up along the way are your business. But those four you're to have on you at all times, and will be replaced at no cost if they're lost for any reason.

"As such, we'll begin weapons training. After the second cut, these swords will be real. Any questions?"

No one spoke. Across the field, the bottom-ranked recruits tackled and pounded each other during their daily sparring match. These wooden swords were only for us.

"The circumstances are these. Your dragon is dead. You were thrown and injured in the fall, and the Druk that killed your dragon is heading straight for you.

"The average Druk doesn't need weapons. Their claws suffice. I cannot replicate Druk claws, but I will increase the muscle and power in your nondominant arm. That will replicate a Druk strike as you fight back against your opponent.

"Your dominant arm will fight back with the sword. You're not finished until your opponent is disarmed and on the ground. Any questions?"

We shook our heads.

"Begin."

It happened so quickly. Standing there, I was whole and healthy. With a flick of his hand, dozens of cuts open on my skin—bleeding and staining my uniform. Mottled bruises covered my arm, but that wasn't why I was gawping at it.

My left arm doubled in size. Muscles bulged and rippled down to my fingertips.

Nuala swung at my head.

Snapping to, I ducked, spun, and struck her back as she lost balance. The hit sent her to the ground. She glared up at me. A glare tinged with surprise. She wasn't expecting that any more than I was.

Was Captain Roan's brutal and borderline evil training getting through to me? I've had a Druk's fist fly at me many times, and I was never fast enough to duck.

"Lucky hit." She rose to her feet. "Hope you enjoyed it because you won't get another one."

"We don't have to be enemies, you know." I took my stance, raising my sword. "I don't want Dominic, or his throne. Why doesn't anyone believe that?"

"Shut up!"

She forward-charged and struck. I barely blocked in time. "No one believes your little innocent act. Neither do you. You announced to the entire party that you'd destroy our traditions if you were queen. Unfortunate for you, Dominic was ready to counter your bullshit with his charm. That's why he was born to be king general."

She swung again, driving me to my knees. I dropped and rolled, forcing Nuala to chase me. Her foot came down within my reach and I smacked the shaped edge of my sword across her ankle. She swore, scurrying back.

Couldn't say if Roan's insane methods were working, but I was learning. All these rich recruits were gifted seasoned instructors growing up who taught them how to fight *the right way*. They never had three bullies pin them to the ground, with one sitting on your chest, while you kicked, bit, scratched, and hit anything within reach.

They never had to jump on someone's back and smash their head into a wall to stop them trying to kidnap your little borrowed orphaned sister, that they thought no one would miss. They knew how to fight to win.

They didn't know how to fight to live.

Nuala didn't charge me right away. I sensed her opinion of me shifting in her shrewd eyes. A thought occurred to me too.

"Nuala is a close friend. We grew up together in Azura."

Nuala must've known Roderick.

"Why does he want to be king general?" We circled each other. "Did he mean it when he said he'd change things for unique mages? Do better than condemning them to the fodder battalion?"

"What the fuck are you on about? Fight!" She ran at me and brought the sword down.

I snapped up to block, and the punch came from the side.

Blood spurted from my mouth, spraying the liquid in a horrible arc as I spun and went down. Nuala kicked my back. Reacting fast, I tossed the sword over my shoulder.

Thud!

"Ow!" I flopped over as she stumbled back, clutching her bleeding nose. "Sir! She's not taking this seriously again."

"I say she is. Throwing your weapon away is a solid battle move," Roan said flatly. "Especially when you don't miss."

"Fine." Nuala grabbed my weapon in her overpowered hand, and snapped it in two. "Then, so am I."

I clambered up and danced away from her. I wasn't worried yet. I've been underfed my whole life. The same could not be said for my bullies. I was used to fighting people bigger and stronger than me.

"You hate me, yes?"

"What was your first clue?" she snapped.

Nuala moved as I did—maintaining our distance. Out of the corner of my eye, I saw Roan turn his back to watch Dominic and Ormr fight. This was my chance.

"Because you think I'm after Dominic, the throne, or both. What if I tell you that I'll back off all of the above if you answer a question correctly?"

She halted. "What? What are you talking about?"

"I don't want the throne. No point saying that since no one believes me, but I'll say it anyway. I don't know the first thing about leading a country with many nations, all in the midst of war. Adalinda would be ashes in a week.

"But..." I hesitated. Time to be honest. "Even without the Druks, things aren't good in this country for a lot of people. If I can do something about it, I understand that it's my duty to."

"Again, what the fuck are you talking about?"

"All you have to do is tell me Dominic will be a good king general, and he... and you... will get everything you want," I said. "Adalinda."

Her eyes narrowed to slits... but she didn't argue.

"Answer a question for me," I continued. "Did Dominic have an older brother named Roderick?"

She frowned. "Dominic has many brothers. None are named Roderick. Are we done with this foolishness—?"

"Not his living brothers," I broke in, a touch impatient. "They shared the same mother and father, and Roderick died when Dominic was ten. You grew up with them. You must know him."

Nuala's scowl deepened. "I'm telling you, Dominic never had a brother named Roderick—dead or alive. Dominic's mother and the general had four children—him and three sisters. No Roderick," she repeated. "Are we done?"

I bit my tongue, swallowing my disappointment. "Yeah, we're done."

"Good." Nuala switched her sword to her powered hand. She threw it at me full force.

I had enough time to scream before pain erupted in my face. I fell into darkness.

Chapter Fifteen

Slowly, I approached, carrying the dead opossum in gloved hands.

Sarcany, Scartha, and Ur watched me unblinkingly—calm, still babies among a mess of snapping, violent monsters.

After I woke up in the dirt with a massive, throbbing lump on my forehead, Roan sent me and Nuala off with "adequate jobs" for both of us. Apparently, my unconventional style of fighting provided a new challenge to the recruits. A good thing.

What wasn't good, according to him, was that I failed to realize highly trained warriors become highly trained warriors by learning to adapt. Eventually, Nuala, Keir, Dominic, and the others would learn to fight fire with fire, and I'd wind up on the ground with a goose egg on my head.

The way Captain Roan instructed left a lot to be desired, but I couldn't deny that he was rarely wrong. Nuala wasn't expecting me to throw my sword at her. Unfortunately, I wasn't expecting her to do it back.

I mulled over my loss while sweeping and mopping the Hatchery floors. The first cut was next week, and if things continued how they were, I'd be executed.

Securing the top rank in scholarship was a given thanks to Dominic. It was battle readiness and teamwork I had to worry about. Reyna regularly tossed me off like a bug on her back. I'd get nowhere near top eight as long as that continued. As for battle readiness, Roan acknowledged when we did right, and shouted when we did wrong. What he didn't do was give a hint about our rankings, and if they were going to change.

All I knew was I couldn't wait to find out. I had to do something to ensure my rank. *Today.*

"It's okay, guys," I crooned. "Got a little treat for you before I head out. Least I can do since you keep my secret so well, and don't let anyone know that I sneak out to see Reyna."

Dragons were highly intelligent creatures. Even as babies. Tizor's offspring knew what I was saying. They just weren't reacting to it, or anything I said or did ever.

"That's okay," I whispered, setting down their food, then backing up a healthy amount. "I don't think you're scary or strange. You can't help the power you were born with, any more than I can help being born without. One day, you're going to bond with a rider, and you'll have adventures all over Adalinda."

Bang!

"In the meantime," I said, peeking up. Tizor hooked his claws through the grating, straining to rip the entire dome off. "You have a devoted father. Must be nice."

Their green eyes stared at me—neither one moving to eat their treat.

"As always, it's been lovely chatting with you."

I left out of the side entrance and made for the goat pen. Lengths of rope tied to a post beside it. I claimed one, picked a goat at random, and tied it around their neck.

"I'm sorry," I said. "I'm truly sorry."

Together, we set off into the Royal Wood.

The deeper we traveled, the more the goat screeched and tugged on the rope. I couldn't blame him. I knew the predators in these woods.

"I'm sorry." I lifted the thrashing creature over a log. "Reyna won't let me on her back. I'm desperate at this point. I have to do whatever it takes, including bribes. I'm really, really sorry."

I apologized to the animal the whole way to our clearing. It was a long shot, but maybe distracting Reyna with eating was the key to her getting used to a different rider on her back.

We broke through the trees.

"Reyna. Hello, my beaut—"

Dominic and I locked eyes.

"Hmm. You don't usually come during the day." Leaning against Reyna's stomach, he looked as relaxed as she was—lying on the grass reading a book.

"What the fuck? What are you—? You can't be here!"

"And yet, I am."

Reyna lifted her head, focusing in on us. I felt that familiar bloodlust coming through.

"Baaa! Baaa!" The goat choked itself trying to run away.

"Hold on." Dominic got up. "What are you doing with that?"

"What?" I quickly tugged him behind my back. "Nothing. What?"

His eyes narrowed to slits. "Is this what you do? Spoil her? Reyna isn't a fat, pampered housecat. She hunts her own kills. They aren't brought to her on a platter."

"This is none of your business. If I want to bring her goats, I'll bring her goats."

"The fuck it isn't. I'll not have you spoil her with bad habits. She'll be expecting this shit from me when I get her back, and it's not happening," he said to Reyna.

Snapping, she huffed. Dragons were intelligent as I said. She knew he was sending her goat away.

"You aren't getting her back," I said. "Get out of here, Roark. I can't believe you'd come here and mess around with someone else's dragon."

He wasn't listening to a word I said.

"Is this why you left me?" he demanded. "You wanted a pretty little pet who'd scrub your scales and bring your kills to you? That's bullshit, Reyna, and you know it."

I don't know what pissed me off more. That he thought I was Reyna's pet, or that a small, stupid part of me thrilled when he called me pretty.

Stop it. The dream was exactly that. The fun I had with Dream Dominic means nothing to the man glaring at me now.

"This isn't what you think," I said, "but I don't have to explain myself to you either way. Go away, and *stay away*. Leave my dragon alone."

Reyna came toward me, narrowing in on the bleating, terrified goat.

Dominic moved so fast, I didn't know what was happening until light glinted off the dagger.

"Hey!"

He sliced the rope. My goat captive went tearing through the bushes. I wasn't sure his hoofs touched the ground.

Reyna roared, snapping at Dominic. He spun and growled right back—a rough, heady sound too similar to the noises Dream Dominic made when he was drilling me into the marble.

Irritation came through the bond with a tinge of resignation. Growling, she left us both behind and dove into the water.

We stared each other down.

"What is your problem?" I gritted. "Despite your delusions, we are not sharing her. She's my dragon. She has nothing to do with you anymore. I'm not going to ask how long you've been seeing her behind my back, because I don't care. It ends today!"

"What's wrong, Princess? You sound more pissed at me than you need to be." He wandered back to his book.

I was hot on his heels. "I'm just the right amount of pissed at you. You ignore me all day. I find you snuggled up with my dragon. And, you freed the fucking goat, so now I have to go back, get another one, and hope the handlers don't notice."

"Last part is easy," he said, dropping down by the tree. "Don't get another goat. Reyna's a predator. The minute you stop seeing her that way, you're both dead."

"I know what she is. You're the one who doesn't know anything. The goat was just to distract her. You got in the way for no reason."

He picked up his book. "Why do you need to distract her?"

"No. We're not doing this." Visions of kissing him under the waterfall assaulted me. I was only too aware that we were mere feet away from another one. "We're not going to sit down and have a chat about my dragon. I want you gone. Go."

"Obviously, I'm not going anywhere. But you're welcome to try and make me. Should be fun to see."

I jumped on him.

Stifling a curse, Dominic lost his book, because I snatched and threw it. "What the hell are you doing!"

I scrabbled at his clothes—tearing and ripping at his shirt with half an idea in my head, and rage all over. How could he be this awful, when I wanted him to be so wonderful? My deepest wish was that the man who called me beautiful, offered me a fair marriage contract, and gave me the first step to controlling my bond, was also the man I could feel safe leaving the throne.

We wrestled, rolling over the dirt. Dominic defended my flailing, uncoordinated attacks.

"Ainsley!"

I slid down his body, grabbing at his belt. He flipped over, hooked his leg around, and twisted back—ensnaring me between his leg and the ground.

"Calm down," he ordered. "Don't—"

"Argh!" I snagged his leg and rolled like I wanted to rip it free. His boot popped off in my grip. "Go fetch this!" I flung the boot through the trees with all my might. "Don't be surprised if we're not here when you get back."

"What the fuck is your problem! You're such a child."

"I'm a child?" My voice reached octaves I didn't know possible. "You're the one who makes bitter enemies of anyone who dares to have something you want. I bet you were that little brat who bit other kids for looking at your toys."

"Nah, I just threw a tantrum and tossed them into the woods so no one could touch them. Like a fucking child." Bronze cheeks stained red. Rage burned his eyes. So much for the cold and unaffected prince.

"Well, I'm sure you don't want to be in the presence of a fucking child any longer." I smiled wide, sweeping out my hand. "Please, be on your way."

"I'm not going anywhere, but you are." He erased the distance between us, knocking our foreheads together. "Go get my boot, and my book while you're at it. Now."

"Oooh, I'd love to see you make me."

That familiar, dangerous growl leaked through clenched teeth. He raised his hands—brow-singeing balls of fire erupted from his palms. "Go get my fucking boot, Princess. You won't like what happens if I ask again."

"I'm not scared of you, Roark," I said—voice just as low and dangerous. "Fate itself has been my bully since I was born. I've survived things a pampered little prince like you wouldn't believe. Your little magic trick is nothing."

"You don't know what I've survived. And you don't know that I don't bluff." He pushed back on my forehead, snarling. "Take the first hit. Please. Make everything I do afterward justified."

"With pleasure!"

I reared back—fist flying at his head.

A blast of water blew us off our feet. We hit the ground in a tangle of limbs, sputtering and hacking. I sensed another emotion from Reyna as pain twisted my body—satisfaction.

"Reyna," I cried. "What was that for?"

A series of growls and huffs followed that. She snapped at us one more time, then dove underwater.

"I'll translate," Dominic said dryly. "Mother doesn't like it when the kids fight."

"You started it." I forced myself up and grimaced down at my clothes. The water she spat at us mingled with a heavy amount of dragon spit. Being a fire dragon, Reyna's spit was both hot and acidic. The fabric was decaying before my eyes.

I began stripping it off.

"What are you doing?"

"What's it look like I'm doing?" I tugged my shirt off, getting it away before the spit touched my breastband. "Don't stand there all cool like dragon spit doesn't affect you. Take your clothes off."

"Been waiting a long time to say that to me."

"Don't flatter yourself." I kicked off my pants. "I've been cured of any and all attraction to you. I no longer have that kink."

"Why?" he tossed over his shoulder. Dominic went to pick up his book, shedding his clothes as he went. "Because I freed your goat?"

"Because fantasy isn't reality."

"What's that supposed to mean?"

I didn't answer. I took a running start, and dove into the water.

Reyna's presence heated the pool a few pleasant degrees—not too cold or too hot. Below me, she cut through the water, ridding her scales of dirt. I felt him splash in beside me, but paid it no mind.

I swam farther out. The water wanted to carry me, so I let it. I floated on my back, basking in the sunlight.

"What did you mean?" His words broke through my peace. "Because fantasy isn't reality."

"Answer me first. Why are you in this battle over Reyna when you could bond with another dragon any time?"

"I can't, and you know it." Inexplicably, he stopped and floated beside me. "Dragons choose the rider, not the other way around."

"The Hatchery is half a mile that way. There are more fire dragons in there than any other kind. We both know more than a few would bond with you on sight."

"Yes, and they'd be a hatchling. Years away from leaving their mother. More years away from being mature enough to carry a rider or go into battle. I can't wait years," he said, devoid of sarcasm or indifference. "I must lead my people now. I must join the war now."

"Why?"

He threw me an irritated look.

"No, I mean it," I said. "Why? Tell me."

Dominic seemed to find something in my expression because his brows smoothed out. "My scattershot. It took me years to perfect. Daily training for hours and hours. Now it's the ultimate weapon. As I am, I can take out an entire Druk clan in seconds on my own, as long as they're not fire Druks.

"Good, but not good," he confessed. "Just like fire dragons are most common. Fire Druks are as well. They outnumber the others ten to one. But with Reyna boosting my power..."

"You can kill fire Druks?"

"With one hit."

I gaped at him, shock stealing my reply. There was powerful, and then there was this man. Suddenly, I knew. Dominic Roark was destined to be legend.

It was also then that I understood why it had to be Reyna. No other dragon type would bond with him. The only other fire dragons around were babies or rearing babies, and if he abandoned training to go in search of mature, unbonded dragons to bond, he'd be labeled a deserter and the Royal Renders would chase him down and execute him.

His options were to stay confined in Golden City and hope the right dragon just came along one day... or get his old one back.

Dread traveled through my bones. It wasn't until that moment that it truly hit me, I should be afraid of this man.

"So, no matter what I say or do, you're going to kill me to get her back."

"Did I not promise you just that?"

Words failed me. Of course he had. He said he'd kill me many times, but every day that passed without him harming me, the words began to weigh less and less.

"But no," he breezed. "That isn't my only option. There is also the chance she leaves you and comes back to me. Which is why I spend every day with her. Waiting for her to come to her senses."

I relaxed a fraction. He didn't want to kill me if he was holding out for the alternative. One that was still terrible for me, but proved that for at least that time as we floated together, he wasn't rushing to turn me into a burning corpse.

"You don't like to see life taken needlessly, do you." It sounded like a question, but wasn't. Slowly, a portrait of the true Dominic was beginning to form. "That's why you joined the academy even though you weren't bonded. You won't waste another minute when your power is needed on the battlefield. So many lives, so many riders, will be saved by your scattershot."

He said nothing, and he didn't have to. I knew as I said it, I was right.

"I'm not in your way, Dominic. Not to the throne, or to you leading the army. I wish you would see that."

"I see nothing but your telltale giveaway every time you lie," he said, tone low and smooth. "I saw it just then. Lying when you say you don't want the throne."

I swallowed hard, jaw clenched tight. I had a giveaway when I lied.

That would be a problem.

"Okay." I matched his tone. "I admit, there is a part of me that wants to be queen. Every single person in this kingdom wants the same. But I know I can't have it. I don't have the magic, experience, or education. Adalinda would not survive under my rule, and I don't waste time telling myself otherwise. When you grow up as I have, you learn not to dwell on silly daydreams.

"I want the throne," I said clearly. "But I won't take it."

I pierced his gaze. "Am I lying?"

"Yes," he rebounded. "Every time you drop these cryptic clues about your past, but refuse to explain. How did you grow up, Ainsley? Why not name the woman who found and raised you? Why not admit you were poor? It'd cost you nothing to tell the truth."

"The truth costs everything! Anyone who says otherwise only has to wait."

He frowned at my explosion. I expected another accusation or sarcastic reply.

"You're right."

I blinked. "What?"

"The truth is deadly in the wrong hands, and these hands"—he held his up—"are wrong. Don't tell me your secrets, Ainsley." He smiled in a way that terrified and thrilled me. "They're not safe with me."

"Goodness, the things you say. Like you're trying to keep me off-balance at all times."

"I don't have to try. You make it easy. A little kiss and you take out half the classroom and drop a bookcase on a man."

"Ass," I muttered.

He laughed. "How about this? I'll tell you my secrets because there is nothing those hands can do to me. Well, there are a few things I *want* them to do to me, but you're not attracted to me anymore." He grinned. "That's why you're not blushing."

Tenille, help me, I thought, knowing damn well I was blushing. *I hate this guy.*

"It's true. I'm no fan of needless killing," he said, growing serious. "If we're going to go around killing each other, why not let the Druks run loose? There's no difference."

"I... agree with you." It shocked me as much to say it as it did for him to hear it. "We're one people. We should protect and support each other. Not ground the lowly down so far, they'd rather be killed by a Druk than live another day."

We fell silent, those words hanging in the air between us.

"What else?"

"What?" I asked.

"What else do you want to know?"

I kicked lazily in the water, searching him. "I can ask anything?"

"Yes."

"And you'll tell me the truth?"

"I will."

"Your father and mother. How many children did they have together?" I blurted. What question did I need answered more than that one?

"How many children? What does that matter?"

"Just tell me."

Confusion furrowed his brow. "Four. Me and my sisters, Nisha, Drisana, and Tanay."

Confirmed from his own lips. *A dream is just a dream.*

"Oh. Okay." I thought of something else. "Who was that little girl who gave you a Calthoon treat on your birthday? The commoner girl?"

"You saw that? Fuck's sake, woman. How long have you been following me?"

"I haven't been following you," I snapped, face hot. "Just answer the question. You said you would."

He shrugged even while floating. "She's no one really. Orla, the girl, got separated from her mother one day and ended up lost and crying in the lower city. I crossed her path and wound up bringing her back. On the way, she told me her mother makes the best jamun kalkans in the world.

"It's a Ghidorian pastry that's difficult to make. You can only get them in special shops in Ghidorah, and I haven't had one since I was a kid. After that day, I visited her mother's stall often and..." He trailed off with another shrug.

I nodded, accepting this. I'd never seen a noble or royal show kindness to a commoner, but I guess Dominic had no reason to disdain a lost child, or the woman who made him treats from home. "But why did you give her a book and promise to teach her to read?"

"How close were you listening? And you say you don't stalk me." He shook his head. "It was more than an offer. We had our first lesson over the weekend, before the party."

"Why risk yourself?" I pushed. "It's against the law to educate commoners. The richest merchants only get around that through bribes."

"And? Irene and her children are Ghidorian. The father of their household is dead. In Ghidorah, when a parent is lost, it's the duty of others in their community to help. To not do so is to blacken the name of everyone who knows them and looks the other way. They became my responsibility when I found Orla crying in the street," he said.

"As my responsibility, I've decided Orla and the children will be educated. As I'm sure you know but won't admit, the only jobs for low-magic commoners who can't read are housekeeper or tumbler. She wants more. I'll see she has it."

"Wow," I said softly. "Ghidorah sounds like... a much different place than here."

"It was, but it's changing. People are forgetting the old ways. It's all about money and station now."

I resisted saying he could blame his father for that.

Reyna surfaced. She left the water, curled up on our clothes, and got busy drying under the sun.

"Can I ask another question?"

He waved me on.

"Why were you so generous with that marriage contract? A regency? A stipend? No children or contact required? Why give so much to the woman you thought stole your dragon?"

"If I hadn't, no one would believe you signed it of your own free will. It'd look to the world that I forced the true princess into a terrible marriage to claim the throne. The loyalists would make ruling a nightmare for the rest of what would likely be a short life."

I smiled.

"What? What's that face? You're going to show me the kumquats again, aren't you? Because if you are, please proceed."

"Shut up," I said, laughing. "I'm smiling because you're lying. You didn't believe I was the princess when you had that contract drawn up, so that can't be the reason. You did it because you thought I was lying.

"A desperate commoner who stole a dragon, and made up a royal bloodline to save herself. You also knew what your father does to everyone who claims to be the queen's heir. You were trying to both get your dragon back, and save my life."

He scoffed. "If you say so."

My grin widened. I hit that target spot-on.

"Ghidorian culture demands a lot of chivalry from a selfish ass like you," I teased, bumping him to take away the sting. "How can you stand it?"

"I assure you, the rewards I receive for treating women well are... substantial."

Grin vanished. "You're only decent for sex? I'm much less impressed."

"People do worse for sex," he breezed. We floated closer to the waterfall. "You were about to tumble that slimy mud man just because he tossed a few lazy compliments your way. That guy isn't worthy of breathing your air, let alone touching you."

"There you go again. Saying confusing things. If he isn't worthy of me, who is?"

"I could tell you, but it's a short list." He stared into my eyes. "Only has one name."

Alarm bells sounded, warning away from this road. Whether he was being honest or teasing, either option had the power to destroy. I wouldn't give him the chance.

"Don't tell me that. Tell me what you're going to do if Reyna doesn't come back to you." I dropped my feet, treading water to face him down. "When training is over, Reyna is still with me, and you have to make a choice. What will it be?"

"You want me to tell you... again?"

I splashed him, enjoying his shock and coughing. He flipped and faced me too.

"You're not going to kill me, Dominic. If it was in you to commit cold-blooded murder, you'd have done it already. Reyna isn't coming back to you, but that's okay. You will bond with the right fire dragon, and I know it will be sooner rather than later. You're too powerful for anything else to happen."

"Glad you have it all figured out, Princess." He cocked his head, smile playing at his lips. "Guess this means we're not enemies now."

I nodded. "I guess it does."

"Shake on it?" He held out his hand. "No more stealing my boots, dragons, or kingdoms?"

"I can make that promise." I reached out, then snapped my hand back. "If you answer one last question."

"Say it?"

"Why the fuck won't Reyna let me ride her? What am I doing wrong?"

He chuckled. "I was wondering when you were going to get to that one. Here it is. It's nothing you're doing wrong. Reyna was injured as a hatchling. Her nestmate broke her back. No one thought she would live," he admitted. "But she did, because that's what my girl does.

"Even so, it didn't heal properly. She can't stand a hundred-pound weight on the old injury. You hurt her every time you try—"

"—so she throws me," I finished. "Of course she does. My poor beauty. I had no idea I was hurting her. But you did, which is why I'm once again tempted to call you a selfish ass."

His smile didn't twitch. "What can I say? I was hoping she'd get fed up and come back to me. But I said I'd be honest, and I keep my word."

"Keep being honest and tell me what to do. If she can't handle my weight, how do I ride her? How do you?"

"Simple. I don't sit on her back."

My brows snapped together. "But that's impossible."

"Is it?"

"Yes." I cast back to the many times Dominic hopped on Reyna and left me wheezing in the dirt. Did I ever actually see him drop his weight on her? "You had to. This is a trick, isn't it? You can't ride a dragon without riding a dragon. Their scales are too slippery for you to grip and stay upright."

"Yes, they are. That's why I had special boots made." His eyes slid sideways. "The one you threw into the forest."

"Special boots? How do they work?"

"I commissioned them from a unique mage. I don't know what they called their power, but they knew how to make things"—he smacked his palms together—"stick."

"Stick to dragon scales," I said slowly.

"Exactly. Once they stick on, they're immovable. No slipping or sliding. No letting go as she's turning and flipping through the air. As long as you lock your knees and hold on to her horn, she won't throw you."

I looked to Reyna. "How do I get a pair?"

"You ask nicely."

"Really? You'll give them to me."

"Why not? I had three dozen made. I still have a few pairs from when my feet were smaller. They're yours," he stated. "I have no use for them."

I didn't know what to say. Just like that, my problem was solved. I'd be able to ride Reyna. Fly with her.

We'd fly right into the top eight. I was saved.

"Thank you, Roark. There is goodness in you."

"I'm not the guy you think I am." He winced. "Or the guy I've been. You're right, Ainsley. I've been a selfish ass, but there's something I want to tell you."

A hand slipped around my waist, surprising me. My breath trapped in my chest as he drew me closer.

"Ainsley Boreen, you…" he whispered, lips closing the distance, "…are the most…"

"Yes," I breathed.

Water assaulted my face, invading my mouth, eyes, and nose.

"…gullible person I've ever met." Dominic howled, swimming away fast.

"Ass!"

I swam quick on his tail. Leaping out of the water, I jumped on his back. We wrestled beneath the surface—smacking, pushing, tickling. I wasn't sure what we were doing. I just knew I was laughing so hard, I was in danger of drowning myself.

We broke through, cracking up.

"Why are you like this?" I asked, sides splitting.

"No one knows. The healers have all given up."

I giggled, trying and failing not to be charmed. Dominic was funny. Why had I never realized he was funny?

"Well, I'll finish that sentence for you. Ainsley Boreen is the most beautiful, smart, talented, kindest woman you know," I sang. "You're in constant awe of me. You dream of one day becoming my equal."

A soft smile played on his lips. "Yeah, that's what I meant to say."

I dropped fast, hiding my face in the depths. It wouldn't do for him to see me blush. *Stop flirting with this guy. A cease-fire won't protect your heart from the regular old stomping every lover has put it through.*

Dominic appeared in front of me. Smiling, he pointed up, telling me to rise.

"About the party," he began. "I watched you with those mages. They were running around, flinging magic like spaghetti, while you sat back, observed, and won."

"Yes, I did. Why?"

His grin showed all his teeth. "You were playing against fools who fatally underestimated you. Want to bet against a guy who won't?"

My brows climbed my forehead. "I'm listening."

"My sisters and I were bored a fair amount growing up, so we challenged each other to do random things. Steal a Watcher's hat without them noticing. Run from our home to the dock, buy the biggest fish, and run back with it. Stuff like that.

"You set the challenge. Bet however much you want," he said. "Either way, I'll win."

"I want you to remember this moment, and your utter confidence. It'll be even more embarrassing when I win."

Thus began the most fun day I had since entering Golden City.

I bet Dominic I could climb the tallest tree higher and faster than him. I bet I could beat him in an all-out sprint over the forest terrain. We even played search and find for different dragon types in the Royal Wood. Whoever found the dragon we were looking for, they had to claim one of their discarded scales, then race out of there before the creature took exception.

I lost as many challenges as I won. We were tied before we finally called it a day, and headed back to the city.

Dominic broke off before the Hatchery. "You're not so bad, Princess."

"Ainsley," I said. "Just Ainsley."

"Ainsley."

My name on his tongue did all the funny things to me that it usually did. Dominic may have been honest with me, but I wasn't honest with him.

My attraction for him had gone nowhere. After that day, it burrowed deep in my heart where it'd never get free.

"GET THAT IN YOUR HANDS," I crowed, dropping the coin purse on the table. "Feel the weight of one hundred and twenty gold ryus."

"By the gods!" Rosaleen snatched it off the table, whipping her head around.

She didn't have to worry. I purposely asked for a private table behind a curtain. There was a reason I asked her to meet me in a snake charmer den. Walking in, I weaved through a smoky room under watch of writhing, sultry dancers on their platforms.

Those dancers weren't allowed to strip nude or provide sexual services within Golden City by law, but if something happened behind the curtain, no one knew.

"What did you do to get this money?" she hissed.

"I chased mud up a tree."

"What?"

Laughing, I said, "I made a bet with a couple of mages. I won."

She shook her head, eyes blown. "One hundred and twenty gold ryus. I can't believe I'm holding this in my hands right now. Even my most besotted callers only tip me a silver here and there. Sister Aven is going to fall over when I give her this. All this coin will feed the children for a year. Easily."

"Half a year," I corrected. "Half is for you."

"No," she said immediately.

"Yes." My voice was firm. "It's okay, Rosie. I'll make more. If not by betting, then with my normal salary. The children will be taken care of, and we'll get you out of your contract."

"Ains, it... it doesn't feel right," she said softly. "When you made that promise, I was never going to hold you to it, but I knew you would because you're a big sister. Doesn't matter all your siblings are borrowed. You see someone who needs you, and you sacrifice everything to protect them.

"I love that about you." She took my hands. "But I don't want to be another person you have to save. I make my own way in this world, and I always have. I don't need to be rescued."

"All right. You don't have to take the money, and I won't bring it up again—"

"Good—"

"—if you answer one thing." I squeezed her tight. "If the roles were reversed and your rancid aunt wasn't taking every single coin you made, would you not have done all you could to save me from stealing and eating food out of the garbage heap? Because that kinda sounds like rescuing to me too."

Lips pressed tight, she looked away, eyes shining. "Fine."

I smiled at the faint croak in her voice.

"I will take thirty ryus, and *no more*," she stated when I opened my mouth. "I'll use twenty to buy toys and clothes for the kids, and say they're from you. The rest goes to Sister Aven."

"Very fair."

"*But* this changes nothing. I still believe coin shouldn't be at the center of a friendship."

"Absolutely."

"*And* I'm paying you back every cent. No arguments."

I made a face. "Why should you pay me back money you shouldn't owe in the first place?"

"I said no arguments."

"But there's no difference in owing me three hundred ryus than it is to owe her."

"Ainsley," she said, smile tugging at her lips. "You've never met a fight you won't pick."

I harrumphed, folding my arms. "Well, it's true. Transferring your contract from her to me isn't good for a friendship either."

"The difference is you won't force me to fuck strangers to pay you back. You also won't charge me for room rent, clothes, food, makeup, breathing, and whatever takes your fancy, all to make sure I never get ahead of the debt.

"We agree it's a loan, or I'll give it all to Sister Aven like I did the last time."

Blowing out a breath, I weighed my options of giving in, or fighting her. "Okay. It's a loan. But take sixty, not thirty."

"Still arguing," she cried, laughing. "What am I going to do with you?"

"Eat with me." I dug out my other coin purse with that week's pay. "Dinner's on me. Want to go to a proper pub?"

"No, these Golden City dens usually have decent food to make up for no breasts, cocks, or sex." She tugged back the curtain and waved someone over. "Also, we're splitting it."

"And you say I'm contrary."

Despite us both being stubborn wenches, we had a delicious meal of mutton stew, barley bread slathered in butter, cheese, and a mug of honey ale. It was only a dim hope that she'd be there when I dropped in on her Heart Reader, but chance turned into a fun evening.

We hugged, kissed, and said goodbye in the den. Stepping into the cool night, I turned my face to the stars, basking in moonlight and the rush of people. Golden City never slept.

I set off up the cobblestone lane, making my way out of the lower city. Sister Aven and the kids were only a few miles away. Oh, how I longed to see them.

I could only imagine the questions and worries they had about where I was, and how I was able to send them so much coin. I wanted to tell them everything—the good, bad, and wonderful. I wanted to see Jon-Jon's face when Rosaleen gifted him the new teddy bear, or Sarsi, my self-taught reader, when she carried in a stack of new books.

I wanted to hold them, and kiss them, and say the things we heard all our lives but never believed.

"Everything would be all right."

Halting, I frowned. There was something... I didn't know what.

A feeling that... I whipped around, alighting on a cloaked figure before he dashed into an alleyway. *I'm being watched.*

"Hey!" I took off without a thought.

Pushing through jeweled nobles and shouting royals, I skidded around the corner into the alley. "Who are—?"

No one.

I stood in the empty alleyway, getting familiar with musty crates and old chamber pots. No one else.

"How? I could've sworn..." I went farther in, scanning every inch of the one-way prison.

Shaking my head, I left the alley behind, returning to the dorm.

Chapter Sixteen

My new boots sunk in the ground. Amazingly, they fit me perfectly.

Dominic said all I had to do was ask, and that morning, there they were. Waiting at the foot of my bed.

I walked a ways from the recruits, planting my feet on my own patch of grass. *Today is the day.*

Sinking into the bond, I summoned Reyna.

Today, we fly.

"Rider Ainsley." Colonel Kinryu approached from my rear. "I expect to see progress from you today. Need I remind you of what's coming?"

"Will you tell me what's coming?" I asked. "What do I need to do to rank top eight?"

"Most recruits here haven't bonded long. Magic or no magic, you're on equal footing in terms of learning to fly for the first time," he said. "To be frank, the only one ranking numbers one through eight is Dominic Roark.

"He has mastered all lessons save one—fighting as a team—and that's because you all fall so short of him." Kinryu was a blunt man. He didn't sugarcoat when a jab to the gut worked just as well. "Hitting a still target will guarantee you rank two. None of these other fools can do so."

Part of me was surprised he answered me directly. Kinryu wasn't the warmest of instructors. He went around barking orders and harshly calling out mistakes. Calmly telling us what we needed to do to succeed wasn't his style.

"Thank you, sir. I can do this. I'm ready."

He inclined his head. "Of that I have no doubt."

Reyna dropped down beside me. Her scales were resplendent in the noonday sun, shining like a million rubies dipped in gold.

I drew closer to her, wondering if she sensed my anxiety.

"This is it, my beauty. Are you ready?"

A feeling I couldn't place came through the bond. I decided it meant she was ready.

Taking a deep breath, I circled her wing and took my place in a familiar spot. This was it. Either the boots worked, or I'd take another flying dive headfirst into the dirt.

I jumped. Not thinking, not hesitating. I grabbed Reyna's horn, swung my leg over, and locked knees.

"Tenille, bless me..."

My legs didn't move.

Eyes huge, I twisted, gazing down at the boots sticking like iron welded to steel. I tugged a bit to test it, and the boots didn't so much as slide. It was as if I was standing on a level platform. Nothing easier in the world than to stand upright.

"Reyna?" I wasn't touching her back... and she wasn't throwing me. "Are you okay?"

She swung her head up. A large, reptilian gray-green eye beheld me. I got the feeling she was wondering how I did this.

"Dominic," I answered. "You trained him well, beauty. He realized nothing matters but you."

Satisfaction poured through the bond. She agreed with that sentiment deeply.

"What do you think about us flying? We've got five days to master it. On top of hitting a still target with magic I don't have."

She huffed.

"One problem at a time." I patted her horn. "So... with the blessings of Tenille, Calthoon, Parthelan, and Zaeah upon me... Kaja!"

Reyna shot into the air. My scream trapped behind my teeth—pinned inside like my flattened ears and blown eyelids.

She was fast. Reyna was faster than fast. She flew like she was playing tag with the wind itself—chasing after the clouds.

Hold on. Don't let go. Don't sit down! Those words shouted in my head on a loop. It was one thing for Reyna to throw me while I was a few feet off the ground. If she threw me high in the air while I was stuck to her by magic boots, she'd drop down and greet the entire recruit class with my body impaled on her horns.

Don't sit down!

I couldn't make out sights, shapes, or sounds. Everything whirled by so fast. Wind roared in my ears, blocking out the world. Were we still over the citadel? We must've traveled miles—tens of miles. Golden City was a speck in my memory.

"R-R-Reyna! P-p-p-p—" *Please, slow down!*

Her wings snapped up, catching the wind as her plaything. I almost bounced on her horn. Her hard bank stopped everything, and we glided.

Eyes round, I tried and failed to take in all the wonderment before me.

Golden City stretched out beneath my feet. People moved through the city like ants in a maze. All so rich and larger-than-life in my eyes, but up there, I couldn't tell the commoners from the nobles. They were all just people.

I looked out over the horizon, seeing past to the Ossian border and beyond. Rosaleen, Sister Aven, and my family were down there. Playing with the toys Rosie bought. Planning a new future. Looking forward to the first night of restful sleep knowing the children would be taken care of.

There was hope up there in the skies. The realization that none of my problems were as big as I thought they were, and I wasn't too insignificant, useless, or worthless to solve them.

I was a dragon rider.

"Reyna!" I was crying, or laughing, or maybe both. "This is amazing! Why didn't you tell me?"

A mix of happiness and amusement filled me. Reyna's, but also my own.

I patted her side, simply basking in the sun. While she was careening and zipping through the air, my life and impeding death flashed before my eyes. Now that she was lazily zipping through the air, staying upright couldn't have been easier.

It was like I was standing on a ship's deck. Reyna rolled and moved beneath me, but as long as I stood firm, I was safe from the sea.

"Okay," I called. "We've got the flying down. Now we've got to figure out how I'm supposed to shoot a still target from the air with no magic, or weapons experience. Any ideas?"

I got nothing back—through the bond or otherwise.

"That's okay. We'll figure it out later. Right now," I said, throwing my head back to the sun. "Let's fly."

POET, ORMR, MAILI, and I walked to battle readiness in good spirits.

"How did you do it, Ainsley? Last week, Reyna was tossing you into the infirmary?" Poet asked.

"I realized I wasn't mounting her properly, on top of touching her wings—which she doesn't like. But Kinryu said I've got to hit a target while in the air to have any chance of making it into the top eight."

"That sounds so easy, but it's not. Not even close," Ormr said. "I won't lie, I was plenty full of myself before starting training. You have to be twenty or older to join the Royal Riders, so for those of us who bond young, we've got years of training on everyone else. Kenna and I have practiced hitting still targets, but no one told me Kinryu's were the size of a walnut."

"Wait, what?" I said. "They are?"

Maili cringed. "Also found that out the hard way, and yes, they are. Kinryu said training has to be as close to battlefield conditions, or it's useless. It's unrealistic enough that a Druk will stand there like a statue during an attack, but if they are still, it's because they're trapped or using someone as a human shield."

"If they are trapped," Poet continued, "they're protecting themselves with their wings. Druks' wings are deceptively strong and magic-resistant. If they're using someone as a shield. You have to strike without killing the hostage. In both cases—"

"You'll only have a tiny window to strike," I finished. "That's why it doesn't make sense to send us after big, open targets. Druks would never give us that chance. Makes sense. It also makes everything harder."

"By the final year of training, only a quarter of the starting recruit class remains," Ormr said. "Rider training is the hardest thing anyone can do. It's not made for us to survive. It's made to strip the weak from the strong."

The good spirits quickly evaporated.

I fell into my thoughts for the rest of the trek through the citadel, thinking of any way I could possibly hit that target and save myself from the cut.

"Recruits," Roan barked. "You know what to do by now. See to—"

"Team!"

The shout knocked me sideways. Literally, he startled me into tripping over my feet.

Keir ran over and grabbed my arm—grip like iron. "We're a team, sir."

"Fine."

"No," I cried, yanking away. "We're not a team."

Roan flicked from me to him. "Yes, you are. You haven't fought Rider Keir since the assessment. Both of you have improved since then. Or maybe you haven't. We'll find out today."

"But, sir—"

"That's a demerit, Rider Ainsley. Another word and it's ten."

I clenched my teeth, penning a frustrated scream. How could Roan not see the seething hatred in Keir's eyes? Was he truly blind to Keir's murderous intent?

Unless he's not. I bet this is another test. Every Druk I go up against will want to kill me. It's the instructor's job to put us through battlefield conditions. I narrowed on Roan's smirk. *The bastard.*

Keir half dragged me to a practice mat.

"Let go of me!" I yanked free. "I've been walking unassisted since my second year. I do not need your help."

Ormr and Maili met my eyes. I could tell what they were thinking as I stepped onto the practice mat. This would not go well.

"I've been watching you." Keir's deep hiss of a voice brought me back. "Roan was right the first time. You have no talent, experience, or skill. You just pull enough dirty tricks until you get lucky. It won't work this time." Keir lifted his uniform shirt. Suspenders secured his pants. "In the name of my father, and for all of Adalinda, I will correct the mistake of your birth right here, right now."

"I'm very sorry for the death of your father," I said, voice steady. "But whatever it is you think you're going to do to me, won't change a thing. He'll still be gone, and you'll still be angry."

"Maybe, but you'll be dead."

Seemed Keir was also not one to beat around the bush.

"And we'll all be better for it."

"How's that? The person who actually killed your father will still be living and in charge. That's the outcome you want? Hmm. Are you actually a militarist, Keir? Did you make such a scene at the ball so that your parents would step in and give the general a reason to kill them?" The words were pouring out of my mouth too fast for me to stop them.

"You're the head of your family now, right? Maybe you staged the events of the ball so that your father would die, you'd take over, then you'd have a handy excuse to murder the person who threatens your way of life? It's as clever as it is cold—"

"Ahhh!" Keir tackled me.

I landed hard on my back. My head fell off the mat and slammed on the ground, ricocheting pain through my skull.

Keir pinned me down and slammed his fist in my face again, and again, and again.

People were screaming. I think it was him. I think it was me.

I couldn't lift my hands to block him. I tried, but strained against an unknowable force. What was wrong with me? Why couldn't I move? Why was no one stopping this!

"Argh!"

Suddenly, Keir was gone. Through blood-soaked, swollen eyes, I saw him fly off me—screeching to make my eyes bleed.

"That's enough." I sensed rather than saw Captain Roan tower over me. "You want to beat someone's face in, Rider Keir, you do it after I clear you to engage. Is that understood?"

"S-s-sir— Please—" he shrieked. "My arm— Please!"

I blinked, clearing the blood away enough to see Keir's arm... bent in a direction it was never meant to go.

"I said..." Roan spoke slowly like he had all the time in the world. "Am I understood?"

"Yes! I understand— I'm sorry!"

Keir's mangled arm snapped back into place. Roan hauled me up and put me on my feet. The moment his hand left my shoulder, the pain was gone.

Tentatively, I touched my face.

No blood.

No matter how many times I saw or experienced Captain Roan's bone magic, it never ceased to stun me. The man could break a person apart and put them back together again all with a wave of his hand. He had to be devastating in the fight against Druks.

What kind of mages made up the Ryuku squads that they could afford for this man to leave the battlefield and become an instructor?

"Face your opponent," Roan ordered. "Get into position."

It made no sense to me that Roan still kept us partnered after having to torture Keir to get him off me.

This is rider training. There is one goal, and one goal only—for the weak to die.

Keir bore a hole in my head. His eyes were red and brows furrowed from the ghost pain of his injury. He was coming for me, and this time, there'd be no mistakes.

"Begin."

He flew at me. I was expecting it and spun out of the way, dodging his grasping hands.

"What is everyone staring at?" Roan bellowed, walking off. "On your mats. Take your places. Everyone!"

I almost screamed for him to come back. With his back turned, there was nothing holding Keir back.

"How dare you say I wanted my father dead."

I shuddered, stepping back. That couldn't have come from Keir. The menace and hatred in that voice must've come from beyond the veil itself.

"He was a great man. Worth a hundred times a useless slut like you—" He lunged before he finished the sentence.

I darted to the side, and something hooked my ankle. Yelling, I dropped hard on the mat. Keir was on me in a blink.

Thinking fast, I flipped to stop him pummeling my face. My first mistake.

An arm wrapped around my throat and squeezed to pop my eyes from their sockets.

Gasping, I punched and clawed at him—desperately thrashing to get free.

It was no use. Keir was too heavy. He pinned me to the mat with his weight alone, and the two-arm headlock kept me right where he wanted me... on the brink of death.

I heard no shouts from Roan. He wouldn't step in. Keir was allowed to render me unconscious. If he went too far and *accidentally* choked me to death, that was too bad for me.

Black spots danced in my vision.

This was it. After all the lying, stealing, and bribing to get this far, I'd die gasping in the dirt at the hands of an enraged rival and my smartass, runaway tongue. Rosaleen once said it'd be the death of me. I guess she was right.

Goodbye, my beauty, my borrowed family, and my one true friend. Find another thief to take care of you when I'm gone.

"Die, bitch." Keir squeezed tighter still. "Die!"

He bent my body like a bowstring, pulling back on my head and lifting me half off the mat. I kicked up.

A blind, and desperate kick... that connected.

Keir cried out. The momentary break in concentration loosened his grip. I got my hands between him and my neck, then shoved him away.

He scrambled to get hold of me again. I was too quick.

I crawled out from under him, flipped, and kicked him in the face. Keir snapped back, head flying. I tried to keep the element of surprise and jump on top of him like he did me, but my head was still pained and woozy.

I jumped but went wide, landing beside him. Keir punched me in the face and broke my nose.

Blood gushed down my chin, choking me as I cried out.

Pain. My whole world was pain.

Keep your head, Ainsley. You're in a fight for your life! Whatever you do, don't let him get on top of you again.

I rolled over and pushed onto my feet. Keir stood up and tackled me.

I was expecting it. He grabbed around my waist, intending to lift and slam me down. Quicker than light, I yanked his uniform up and grabbed his suspenders. Keir wisely looped them through his belt, but that suited me just fine.

I pulled them up and over his head. Looping them around his neck, I pulled.

Keir gagged. He released me and flew to my hands—pulling and straining to rip them off, which only pulled the straps tighter. I smashed my knee into his face, threw him up, then kicked him in the chest.

Keir went flying. The bastard dropped like a sack of rocks, nose gushing to match mine. I chased after him, and stomped on his crotch.

"Arrghh!" He bent in half, clutching his middle.

Keir thought he was smart not wearing a belt. He forgot about mine.

The position of his hands gave me the perfect opening. Moving fast, I wrapped my belt around his wrists and pulled tight.

"Hey! What are you—?"

My boot came down on his throat. "Yield."

"Fu— Fu—"

I pressed down harder. "Yield!"

Burning, hate-filled eyes scorched me. I saw his answer clear as day. Not even death would make him yield.

I didn't blame him. I'd respect Keir even less if he did.

"Suit yourself." I stomped on his face.

Keir's head flopped to the side. He was out cold.

"Calthoon, save me..."

My eyes snapped up, and landed on my audience. Everyone had stopped their sparring to watch the outcome of our fight.

Roan pushed through, storming up on me fast. "Rider Ainsley!"

I backed up a step. "Sir?"

"After all this time, you still have no technique. No form. No coordination. You fight like a peasant."

"Yes, sir." I wiped the blood from my chin, feeling my top six ranking sliding down.

"Good to see one of you recruits knows how to listen."

What did he say?

"All of you! You're still fighting like you're sparring with a friend before you skip off to play hit-the-target using your limitless magic ability. Neither of those things are true. The person opposite is not a friend, they're a Druk. And your magic is not limitless. Even the deepest well runs dry.

"Killer instinct!" Four people in his vicinity jumped. "The will to win at any cost even if it means throwing away the rulebook. You children are too afraid to get a boo-boo. A little cut on your cheek sends you running to Mommy. If I don't see more blood and broken bones. If I don't see recruits who want to *live*... then I'll assume you want to die," he dropped.

"Any recruit with no killer instinct will be cut, no matter what you rank. Am I understood?"

"But, sir!"

The blowback was loud and immediate. He was understood, that was the problem.

"You can't do that!"

"What do you want from us! You won't be happy until we're killing each other!"

"You're insane!"

My eyes blew. I didn't know Poet had it in him to call an instructor insane.

Roan turned his back on the ranting recruits like their noise was a babbling creek. "Excellent, Rider Ainsley. Take a commendation."

I almost smiled. Roan never gave out commendations. I believe he said it was ridiculous to reward someone when they did what they were supposed to do. Did we also want pats on the head for using the toilet without missing?

"Thank you, sir."

"Yes," he said, nodding. "You'll be paired with Keir from now on and until I say otherwise. I like what you two bring out in each other." Roan laughed. "I'm certain he'll be even more motivated to beat you after this loss. Keep your wits about you, Rider Ainsley. Summon that killer instinct. The same tricks won't work twice."

Roan walked off, leaving me staring after him. Poet was right.

The man was insane.

"WHY IS IT WHENEVER you win in Roan's class, we all lose?"

Maili eased herself into her chair. With the help of Ormr, they lifted her braced leg onto the chair beside me. Nuala broke it clean in two without hesitation. She found her killer instinct all too fast.

"I'm pretty sure I lost too," I said. "Roan says Keir is my permanent partner. He'll get another chance to kill me tomorrow, and every day until he gets it right."

"What? I keep saying the man is insane," Poet cried. "Why is he allowed to teach us? He's obviously trying to save the instructors the trouble of cutting us by making us do it ourselves."

"He refused to heal my leg," Maili said. "Told me to stop whining, it'd heal on its own soon, and let the pain be a lesson to me. Are we sure the man doesn't plain hate us?"

I didn't say anymore as they got out a healthy amount of bitching. It wasn't that I disagreed with them. Roan was taking it to the extreme, but not everything he said was wrong. I knew all about fighting a Druk. That Druk wasn't trying to kill me, but I was trying to kill him.

It wasn't enough.

My hardest punches, fiercest kicks, and desperate pummeling wasn't enough to scratch a creature that was playing with me. Roan was going about it an interesting way, but the recruits did need to understand that if they walked into battle with less than the need to win and live at any cost, they were already dead.

Someone dropped in the seat next to me.

"Dom? Dom, what are you doing? We're sitting over there."

My seatmate didn't react to Nuala. Dominic threw his hand over the back of my chair, casually setting my skin on fire with an absent stroke of his thumb.

"Hey," Dominic said. "What are we talking about?"

Maili, Ormr, and Poet stared at him with their mouths open. My reaction with a side effect of internal screaming.

"Dom…" Poet looked around. "You're sitting with us?"

"Yes. Why not? Am I not allowed to sit with you guys?"

"What? No! That's not what— I didn't mean it like—"

"Course you can sit with us," Maili sliced in, saving Poet. "We were talking about Roan and his crusade to kill us. The man takes it too far."

"You think he goes too far? I don't think he goes far enough. He should have us beat each other to bloody pulps. Fight to near death." He shrugged. "Roan has the power to knit us back together. As long as he does, there's no excuse for going easy on each other."

The others stared at him in open-mouthed silence. I think Ormr pushed their chair back.

"Kidding." Dominic beamed a wide, mischievous smile that made my stomach flip, and Maili blush. "Roan's a sadistic bastard who is most assuredly getting off on our pain."

"That's what I said," Poet remarked over our laughter. "He even comes after you, and you're the best fighter by far. If he doesn't think you're good enough, we might as well lie down and die right now."

"Druks are worse," I blurted.

I kicked myself when they all turned to me.

"I mean, Druks will make Roan look like a harmless puppy. They want to murder us and rip our dragons' hearts from their chests. Now there're rumors that Druks are getting stronger? You ever worry that he isn't pushing us hard enough?"

Silence descended on the table.

"Yes," came a quiet reply.

We flicked to Ormr.

"Because they're not just rumors." Looking around, Ormr dropped their voice and leaned in. "Two more Ryuku squads were slaughtered. One squad, and the squad sent to rescue them when they didn't report back in. All of them gone and their dragons taken."

Dominic sat up straight. "How do you know this?"

"I shouldn't," they admitted. "But the Watchers had to inform the families that they weren't coming back. The widows put it together. Everyone in those squads is gone."

"But then how did you find out?" I asked.

"A friend of mine from Nehebkau is one of those widows. I got a letter from her yesterday. Her letters to the Royal Rider High Command are going unanswered. She needs them to send his remains for the burial ceremony.

"It's a ritual that preserves the soul for seven years, and prevents it from crossing through the veil. She's afraid if they don't do the ceremony in time, he'll be gone from this world in every way," Ormr said. "She was hoping I'd speak to the king general for her. She knows I'm allowed to enter the palace, but doesn't know the king general has no reason to give me an audience and never has."

I looked at Dominic. "Could you—?"

"No. I'm sorry." He truly sounded it. "The High Command knows about this tradition, and they respect it. They always do everything they can to bring the remains home for burial. If they're not doing it this time, it means..."

He trailed off because he didn't need to continue.

"There's nothing of them left," I rasped. "But how could that happen? Why after hundreds of years, are they getting stronger now? What's changed?"

No one had an answer for me.

"Roark, I understand the military keeps its secrets, but shouldn't we of all people know?" I asked. "What use is it keeping the recruits in the dark? We're going to find out soon enough anyway."

"What use is it telling recruits who might not make it through training? We'll know all when we prove ourselves. Before then, consider us another fodder battalion."

"Wow, this is a depressing conversation," Maili said. "All I ever wanted to be was a dragon rider. I'd go to sleep every night dreaming of the dragon that'd one day choose me. No one tells a little girl that this isn't a dream. It's war."

"Is it a war we can win?" Poet spoke to the table, shoulders tight. "Think about it. I mean, really think about it. Druks were people. They were just like us before they made the choice to slaughter a dragon for power.

"We keep hunting down Druks like they're the problem, but the truth is that they're the symptom. The real problem is that there are people so soulless and desperate, they believe becoming a Druk is the best way to escape their horrible lives. There'll always be people who feel that way. Something tells me that this won't stop... till all the dragons are gone."

"Dominic!"

I jerked, banging my arm against the table.

Nuala planted herself in front of us. "Dom, there's something I need to talk to you about. In private." She narrowed on the hand grasping my shoulder. "It's important."

"Sure." Dominic stood up, his hand gliding along my shoulder, skating up my neck. I smothered a small, involuntary noise as he drew a tiny circle on my shivering skin, then tugged sudden and firm on my hair.

It was so intimate and out of nowhere, there was no chance to hide my stained cheeks.

"Bye, Princess. I'll see you tonight."

I think I squeaked something in response.

"Tonight? Why are you seeing her tonight?" Nuala demanded, following him out. "Dominic? Dominic!"

I STOOD SHOULDER TO paw with Reyna, watching Ormr and Kenna soar through the air. At the start of the week, the "fools" were nowhere near mastering hitting a still target, and second rank was mine to claim.

That was the start of the week.

Something unseen struck the fist-size target, slicing it in two. Ormr whooped in the air.

"Yes, Ormr!" Maili jumped up and down for her twin. "Ainsley, did you see that? Ormr was still perfecting their wind slicer in special talents yesterday. I can't believe they did it!"

"Amazing," I said, and meant it. "An attack that no Druk will see coming? They should promote them to a Ryuku squad now."

Ormr's success made them the sixth recruit to master hitting a still target from the air.

Six plus Dominic. All top seven ranks were claimed. That only left one for me.

I went around and stroked Reyna's snout, feeling her calm through the bond. We spent every lesson getting the hang of flying while I thought of how I'd hit the target from the air without magic.

Nothing.

This task was impossible for me. Even though Commandant Drake dropped all my classes that required magic, my accident of birth found a way to write my death sentence in the end.

Kinryu did tell me I was allowed to use a weapon where everyone else was not. A bow and arrow, specifically. He appeared on the field with a new and beautiful ash bow, and handed it to me with no preamble.

I loved it. I dreamed of the day I'd use it in battle, perfecting my long-range attack. But that day was not today.

I'd never used a bow and arrow in my life. I couldn't even bend the string. To go from novice to lethal enough to hit that small target from that distance within the coming few minutes, wasn't happening.

"Rider Ainsley."

"Yes, sir?"

"You're up."

Nodding, I moved back behind her paw, the boots snug and fitted on my feet. I had one shot at this. One shot to claim the last rank, and save myself from the cut.

"Are you ready?" Maili asked.

"I'm ready."

Climbing onto Reyna's back, I locked my knees and whispered for her to take off slowly. I learned my lesson about shouting Dominic's Ghidorian commands at her without knowing what they meant.

Her wings pushed the air down and us up. That familiar euphoria filled me as we touched the sky. Reyna stopped at the required distance of one hundred feet. Below, we watched Kinryu place a new target. All eyes were on us.

"Are you ready for this, my beauty?" I patted the base of her horn. "There's no point winging around, shooting arrows that'll miss, and delaying what I have to do. This will work or it won't."

I was saying this more for my benefit than for hers. I didn't sense a shred of nerves from Reyna. I wondered if dragons ever got nervous, unsure, or had regrets. I certainly hadn't felt either come through the bond.

"Maybe because I've got enough for the two of us," I muttered. "Could we get a little closer? Make it as easy for me as possible."

Reyna glided over the target, circling it like prey.

I don't know why I looked for him. Sweeping the staring crowd, I landed on Dominic's upturned face—handsome and impassive as always. He helped me fly, but the rest I had to do myself. My lack of magic would be my burden to overcome for the rest of my life. Neither Dominic nor anyone else could waste their time covering my weaknesses in battle.

I had to find my own strength.

"Hurry up," someone shouted. "We don't have all day, Princess."

I didn't bother looking to see who that was. My focus was on that too-small target and nothing else.

"Do you know what to do, Reyna? Can you handle this?"

Irritation flared up in me like my own. They say after about a hundred years, the bond matures to the point you know your dragon's mind as well as your own. I didn't need to wait that long to know Reyna's thought, "*How dare you question me?*"

"Forgive me, my beauty. I haven't forgotten who's the better half in this pair."

She snorted, bobbing her head.

"Well, if I don't do it now, I never will." I broke the boots' stick, swung my leg over, and jumped.

"What the—!"

"Fuck!"

"Do something!"

Panicked shouts reached me as fast as the ground. Wind attacked my face—smothering my open-mouthed screams and watering my eyes. I could barely see the target. *Fucking hell, where was the target!*

There—

No. A white, fluffy material appeared on the ground beneath me. In a split second, I remembered the cotton mage. Nuala's friend who dumped me in a river, was trying to save me.

More magic sprag up beneath me. Mud, plants, thread, snow. All of it swirling around the target, and showing me exactly where it was.

"Argh!" I thrust the blade like a lance— No, an arrow. My body the shaft, and my weapon the tip. Screaming past the rock in my throat, I aimed right at the heart of the target like the head of a Druk—my dagger going straight through his smirking mouth.

"Ainsley!"

A shadow fell over me.

Reyna's claw snapped around me, snatching me out of the air, with a makeshift rescue that may or may not have saved me.

I heaved—heart hammering my rib cage and breaths coming so hard and fast, I couldn't suck air in before my body forced it out again. My fingers were numb. The way I was squished in her grip, I couldn't turn my head to see them. Where was the dagger? Was I holding it? What happened?

"Reyna, put—put me down."

Dropping down, she lowered her paw and carefully released me—sliding her lethal claws out from under me. Even with her caution, my uniform sliced open in three places.

I clambered to my feet and searched for the targets. Shouts and cries were coming at me all at once. None of it mattered. All I need-ed to know was if—

I fixed on the target.

There, only slightly off-center to the bull's-eye, was my dagger. Target hit.

Druk dead.

"Yeah!"

The bubble burst, and the noise flooded in. They were cheering.

"That was fucking insane!"

"Mother Zaeah, you've got balls, Boreen. That was the craziest thing I've ever seen."

Maili, Ormr, Poet, Carlow, Flynn, and Keely rushed me. I fell shrieking laughing to their pile-on.

"You did it," Maili screamed, shaking me. "Who the fuck says you need magic to be a rider? Not Ainsley."

"You're fearless." Poet squeezed the stuffing out of me. "That was amazing. I can't believe—"

"Of all the stupid, braindead, asinine things to do! All of you, fall back, now!"

My cheering squad disappeared. Running around a charging Colonel Kinryu, they formed neat, straight-backed lines behind him. All of them against me.

"You're proud of that performance, girl?"

"Sir, I—"

"Stand up!"

I stood in the face of his fury. I'd never seen him this angry. Kinryu's long, dark ponytail whipped and snapped in the wind, appearing as alive with anger as his blazing eyes and desert-sand skin bleeding red.

"What were you thinking?"

Balling my fists, I lifted my chin. "I was thinking that I had no other way of hitting the target. I knew Reyna would catch me."

"You knew that, did you? You knew she wouldn't miss in that split second and *skewer* you on her claws! You knew she'd react fast enough to catch you from five feet off the ground? Because it looked to me that you were being reckless and stupid, and gambled your life on the million-to-one shot that she wouldn't miss!"

My jaw opened and shut trying to get a word in.

"Do you think this is a game, Rider Ainsley? That you're here to show off who has the biggest death wish to your friends!"

"No, sir."

"Then what was the point of that idiotic display? Do you truly believe flinging yourself off your dragon is an effective strategy in battle?"

"No, sir," I said quieter.

"That was stupid and dangerous and you're never to do it again!"

"Yes, sir." The wind stole my whisper before it reached his ears.

"I gave you a bow and arrow. Why didn't you use it?" he demanded.

"I don't know how, sir. But I will," I added quickly, seeing his darkening expression. "I'll train every day."

"Yes, you will." He swung his arm out, pointing behind him. "Get out of my sight."

I did so as quickly as possible without running away. Maili, Poet, and my friends tossed me sympathetic looks on my way past.

I wanted to be mad at Kinryu. I did exactly what he asked me to. But I couldn't. I knew what I'd done was no use in battle. There were an infinite number of reasons why it wasn't a good idea to jump off my dragon's back onto a Druk's head. I had to learn a real way to fight on my dragon's back, and that wasn't it.

I knew all of that, and that's why I did it. I wouldn't get the chance to learn to fight on my dragon's back if I didn't live to next week.

And now I won't. I trudged inside. The truth of what was coming settled in my bones. *Kinryu won't let me anywhere near the top ranks after that. After everything I've done, it ends here.*

Chapter Seventeen

Rider Ainsley
      Rank Two
Rank Five
Rank Eight

I read it twice, three, five, nine times and didn't comprehend.

I knew my name and my numbers. The recognition told me I was reading the rank board correctly, but it could not be true.

"Poet," I breathed. "Could you read this for me? I think there's been a mistake."

"No mistake, Ains. Two in scholarship. Five in battle readiness, and eight in teamwork. You did it," he cried, shaking me. "Holy shit, I thought you were done after Kinryu chewed you up and spat you out."

"I didn't want to say it, but me too," Maili said. "I was so scared, I was one bad rank away from tunneling under the citadel and sneaking you out.

"We'd have done well on the run," she mused. "Your savvy and my looks. We could have started our own kingdom."

I laughed—a light, free sound that I didn't know I could make. I'd done it. True, it was with Dominic's help. I wouldn't have made it without him doing my reports for me, or giving me the final clue to riding Reyna. But battle readiness—that was all me.

Me—the useless, magicless orphan who wasn't worth educating—beat out dozens of trained nobles and royals to top five in battle readiness. I'd done it. I accomplished something on my own without magic. Next, I'd learn how to read and master the bow. I would move up to second-year on my own merit, and with my abilities. Not good enough for society, but good enough to be a rider.

"Recruits, your attention."

Commandant Drake took to the podium. Trailing behind him were Kinryu, Roan, Phiala, and Sorrel.

"Well done to those who've survived the first cut. It's an accomplishment you should be proud of," Drake said. "This season, we started all new recruits at the level of a third-year."

Mutters broke out. It was one thing to whisper about, and another to have it confirmed that they were going harder on us than any other new recruit.

"I assure you, this change was necessary. Many of you struggled, but even more rose to the occasion as the pride of Adalinda. A celebration will be held in your honor tonight. Once again, well done."

Applause and whoops broke out, from me and my friends loudest of all. Drake was throwing us a celebration? We must've truly impressed him. I was still waiting to see the man smile.

"Settle down," he barked, ending the noise instantly. "Now, I'm sure most of you are wondering why we displayed the ranks only for the top twenty. This is not because the rest of you have been cut."

A few tense, silent figures visibly relaxed.

"We purposely do this because we found if we don't conceal who has been cut until the last moment, those disgraced riders will try to flee, or attack." Drake smiled. "We can't have that now, can we?"

No one spoke. The grins and achievement on everyone's faces disappeared.

"Phiala."

The lieutenant colonel broke from the line and handed Drake a scroll.

Here? In front of all of us, after we celebrated, they were going to tell us which one of our new friends has to die?

"Take your seats."

I did, and I knew why. Drake wanted everyone farther from the doors.

"If I call your name, you're cut. Do not try to run. The consequences for cowardice won't be pleasant."

Poet took my hand under the table. He ranked in the top twenty for every class except special talents. That wasn't enough to get him cut, but the same couldn't be said for his other friends. Almost everyone knew each other. Royals and nobles, it was a tight circle.

Something told me the celebration tonight would be a bleak affair.

"Mazi Kobina," he announced. "You're—"

Crash!

A chair toppled over behind me. I twisted as Mazi bolted. He flailed and flung his hands around, wildly shooting icicles.

"Ahh!" I screamed, grabbing and shoving both Poet and me down when one came our way.

Over the table, I saw Roan wave his hand. Bloodcurdling screams shredded my ears.

I couldn't bring myself to look at what Roan had done to him.

"Take him away," Drake ordered.

Felt like an eternity before Mazi's screams faded down the hall. Drake moved on to the next name without an ounce of sympathy in his good eye.

"Ashwin Koum."

No running or attacks that time. Ashwin simply burst into tears.

"Ivo Camoi.

"Larkin Oran."

Drake rattled off the list of names—much longer than I anticipated. Fifteen riders, all determined unworthy of continuing on, and unworthy of their dragons.

There were shouts, screams, and tears. Three more riders tried to run, and one blasted flames at Roan. They nearly got him too.

Despite this, they were all taken down and dragged out one by one. Tenille, bless me, let me never find out where they were taken. What's the final sight a rider lays their eyes on before they're snuffed out forever?

"That completes the first cut," Drake said. "As promised, your celebration begins now."

The doors opened, and a short, stocky woman in a third-year uniform made for the head table.

"The kitchen staff will be serving mead. Limit of two mugs per person. No exceptions. Buffet will remain out for another hour, and curfew is extended. Begin."

Maili rubbed her temples, ever-present smile gone. "Two mugs of mead and cold food are his idea of a party after fifteen recruits were dragged out to their deaths?"

"I'm kind of glad it's so depressing," Poet said softly. "Doesn't feel right to celebrate."

Not one of us could argue with that.

"Excuse me," Drake said, drawing our attention back to the head table. "Seems we have another recruit to add to the list."

Oh no. Not again. This is so cruel. Why are they—?

"Ainsley Boreen." That rare smile that showed itself more in the last hour than I'd seen in two weeks, twisted his lips. "You're cut."

"I DON'T UNDERSTAND why. Tell me why!"

Two blank-faced riders dragged me down the steps. The tips of my boots skimmed the marble, making an odd *shhh*ing sound that echoed in the narrow staircase.

"This is a mistake!" I thrashed in their iron grip. "I ranked top eight in every lesson. I did what was asked."

They didn't even look at me. Seemed they didn't see the point in speaking to a dead woman.

"Help!" I shrieked. "Help! Help me!"

The stairs opened up into a bare, cinderblock room with a chair sitting ominously in the middle. The two wrestled me down, each pinning my hands to the chair arms. Shackles snapped into place, securing my wrists and ankles.

"You can't do this! I did nothing wrong. This is murder! Treason!"

"Don't try it, *Princess*," said the woman who gave Drake my name. "You know exactly what you did. You're a disgrace. We honor the throne by keeping you off it."

"What are you talking about? All I've done is what was asked of me."

"All you've done is cheat."

I quieted, every muscle in my body going rigid.

"That's right," she crowed. "Thought you were so clever, and no one would notice."

The reports. They knew about the reports. How? Did Sorrel finally notice the similarities between my reports and Dominic's?

No, that doesn't make sense. If he knew we cheated, Dominic would be down here with me.

"Thought I was clever about what?" I asked, keeping my voice steady. "What is it you think I did? Why won't you tell me plainly?"

"Because the proof is on your feet."

Confused, I strained to see what they were talking about. "What the fuck is on my feet? Stop talking in riddles!"

"The innocent act doesn't become you." Her companion stood a foot taller. She had long, brown curls wrangled into a hair tie, and a cold look that tried to fill me with shame. "It reads clear and plain in the Royal Rider handbook that any recruit found to be using magicked items or curses to give them an unfair advantage, will be cut. No exceptions. What do you call magic stick shoes that keep you on your dragon's back?"

A faint buzzing sounded in my ear. Low and growing louder, drowning everything out.

"...get away with it..."

"...shame on the House of Boreen—"

"But I didn't know," I rasped. "I didn't know the boots weren't allowed. I wouldn't have used them if I didn't have to. Reyna wouldn't let me on her back otherwise."

Stocky scoffed. "Save your sob story for the commandant. He'll be down to finish this shortly."

They turned to leave.

"No, wait! You don't understand. This is a mistake." I shouted after them as their footsteps faded up the stairs. A slammed door was my only reply.

My mind spun. How did this happen? I'd never seen that recruit before. Why did she know anything about me, or my boots? None of this made any sense.

I heard noise upstairs. Footfalls sounded in the small, desolate room. It was the commandant.

All I have to do is explain Reyna's back injury. I wasn't trying to cheat or give myself an edge over the other recruits. I just didn't want my dragon to be in pain.

He had to understand that. If any exceptions would be made, it should be for Reyna, not me. Killing me wouldn't get her to choose a better rider. The same one wouldn't be able to ride her.

"Sir?" I called. "Sir! I can explain everything. I never intended to cheat. I only used those boots because Reyna hurt her back. This is all a mistake."

"There was a mistake." He stepped off the last step. "But don't bring Reyna into it. I can't have Drake examining my boots when I get her back."

That wide, beaming, beautiful smile punched me in the gut. "You are beautiful, Princess, but you in shackles"—he whistled—"I fucking love you like this. It's your best look."

"I..." My voice was a raspy croak. "...don't understand..."

"You don't, do you?" Shaking his head, he clicked his tongue. "How can that be when I told you? Told you so many times, you could've carved it on my heart as my gods' given mission. I said I was going to kill you," Dominic said, grinning away. "Promised to get my dragon back, and protect my throne at any cost. I also promised you wouldn't see it coming.

"How easily you took those boots."

I swallowed through knives in my throat. "You knew the boots would get me cut."

"Course I did. But you didn't, because you can't read. I admit, I didn't know how I was going to do it," he said, ambling in. "Killing you in a way that wouldn't come back on me. I had a feeling my best way in was your inability to ride Reyna, but if I suddenly gave you the boots out of nowhere, you'd be suspicious. Then, you adorably tried to seduce me.

"You accepted my help to cheat in one lesson. There was no reason you wouldn't accept my help in teamwork. All I had to do was wait for you to ask the question first."

My stomach heaved. I was going to be sick. "Why would you do this? We put our differences aside. You said you wouldn't do this. Fuck's sake, you can bond with any other fire dragon any time you want!" I screamed. "What the fuck is wrong with you! Who goes this far over one dragon!"

Dominic blinked lazily in the face of my rage. "That's where you've gotten it wrong, Princess. That's where I let everyone get it wrong. Reyna isn't just another fire dragon, and I'm not just another fire mage. Reyna is irreplaceable. I could search the far reaches of Adalinda... and never find another death dragon like her."

My lips parted, but nothing came out.

"Shock. Gasp. Awe," he cried, mocking me. "Yes, it's true. My father's relentless mission to impregnate every woman he laid eyes on, was successful in producing the heir he truly wanted. Another death mage." He twisted his hand and a small, flickering ball of fire appeared, illuminating a wickedness in his eyes I saw far too late. "Beautiful, isn't it? Looks like regular fire."

He blew on it—light and whispering, he sent the flame floating to me. "Hellfire," he whispered. "Unlike anything you've ever seen. It burns hotter. Can't be doused by water. Won't be extinguished by wind. The smallest flame grows until it consumes everything in its path. Unstoppable. Unforgiving. It's the power of a god.

"No," he breathed. "It becomes the power of a god with Reyna by my side. I still remember the first time I saw her—growling over the torn, savaged remains of her nestmates. For years, the Ghidorian Hatchery mistook her, her mother, and her nestmates as fire dragons. Father prepared me to wait years—decades to find another death dragon. They're just too rare in Adalinda, and no one can cross the Dark Border to find more.

"But there she was—meant to be mine. Not just a death dragon, but a hellfire dragon. The rarest of them all." His expression changed. "Then, you stole her."

"No," I forced through numb lips. "Hellfire doesn't exist. It's not real. You made that up in your crazy, twisted, power-hungry mind!"

"Everything I say to you is true, Princess. You wouldn't be here right now if you believed it." Shrugging, he extinguished the fire with a snap. "It's a shame because I like you. You're odd, funny, and fearless. You take to nature like a forest child, and have a sadistic streak in you that's"—he hummed, licking his lips—"so very sexy."

"I'm not sadistic!"

"No? So it's necessary for you to keep stomping Keir's balls when you've already got him down and beaten?" Grasping my shackled wrists, tender fingers stroked my pimpled flesh as he leaned over me. "Admit it. There's the tiniest part of you that enjoys it. Making your enemy feel the maximum amount of pain on your random whims. Just because you can. Just because his screams fill you with power—"

I smashed my forehead in his face.

"Ahh! Fuck!" Dominic snapped back, clutching his bleeding nose. He burst out laughing. "See what I mean? Damn, you're amazing. More than once I've wished the marriage contract could've worked out. With me the only one able to pass down my magic, all our children would be death mages, and..." He winked even as blood ran down his face. "We'd have so much fun making them."

"Let me out of here, Dominic. Tell Drake what you've done."

"Nope."

Rage exploded into a fever pitch. I screamed, thrashing in the chair's hold. "What is wrong with you? This isn't you, Dominic. You're not this much of a cold-blooded bastard!"

If anything, his grin widened. "So you did like my performance? What was your favorite part? Was it how I acted like your rival, but kept kissing and flirting with you? If I was too all over you, it would've freaked you out. But if I was too hostile, you wouldn't have trusted me enough to take the boots." Nodding, he blew out a breath. "It's a fine line fucking people over."

"How can you just stand there laughing like this is some kind of joke? They're going to kill me," I gritted. "Your games put me in this chair, and that's funny to you?"

He cocked his head. "Are you trying to appeal to my sense of shame? It's not personal, Princess. I told you, I've got an embarrassing, pants-tenting thing for you." Even in the midst of his lunacy, he could make me blush. "I've wanted you since that first kiss, but after everything that's happened, it can't be.

"Even if you undid the forbidden magics that bound Reyna to you—"

"I didn't do any forbidden magic!" I was so frustrated, my scream reached new octaves.

Dominic waved it away. "Of course you did. Reyna is a death dragon. You're not a death mage. Dragons only bond with their own type. Period. Madame Sela has spent the last couple weeks searching for the kind of magic that can bond a dragon to a magicless person. Once she finds it, my father will have all the proof he needs to order your execution. The loyalists can't stop him.

"Oh, yeah," he said, seeing my expression. "Did I forget to mention that? Let's suppose I was willing to let Reyna go, the general was never going to allow you to live. Even if you mean it when you say you don't want the throne, you and your heirs will always have a claim to it. What good is your willingness to step aside, if twenty years in the future your son steals the throne from his?

"So, you see? It was going to end like this either way. It was simply better that I got it over with now," he breezed, "before I fell any harder for you than I have."

I shook in the seat—fingers twitching from terror and anger. "I'm going to kill you, Roark," I hissed low and dangerous. "I'm going to rend your head from your shoulders, and mount it on Reyna's horn like a pike. Then, I'll take your precious throne, and shove it so far up your ass, your ugly little heirs will shit gold for ten generations!"

"Oooh, dirty talk. I like it." He leaned over me again, out of head range. "More."

I strained, snarling and snapping at him. Heat welled beneath my skin—burning hot with fury. *I'll kill him!* The evil, lying, manipulative, rotting cow dung. I'd never forgive him for this.

"It never had to be this way. We could've been friends. We could've been—" I choked on the word coming out. "There's a good man underneath... whatever the fuck I'm looking at! You can be that guy, Dominic. Not what your father expects of you."

Something flashed in his eyes—too fast for me to be sure.

The door opened upstairs.

Dominic grabbed the hem of my shirt, and ripped it. I cried out, which was what he wanted. Quickly, he stuffed the strip of cloth in my mouth and gagged me.

No one would hear my story of sticky boots, hellfire dragons, and revenge.

He was straight-backed and off to the side when Roan and Drake stepped down.

"Rider Dominic," Drake said. "What are you doing here?"

"My father will want confirmation of her death, sir."

He nodded, accepting that all too easily.

"Let's not waste time, then. It's unpleasant business to cut a recruit for not measuring up." He bore over me. "It's a tragedy when one as promising as you is cut for cheating. You embarrassed me, Rider Ainsley. You embarrassed yourself, your dragon, and every rider in this academy. How dare you presume yourself above the rules?"

I shouted at him through the gag, telling a story he wasn't hearing.

"Should we let her speak in her defense?" Roan asked.

Dominic stepped forward.

"No," Drake said. "I'll not hear her excuses and justifications. The boots were found in her possession. Kinryu confirms she went from being thrown to riding her dragon flawlessly overnight. That's all I need to know. Do it."

"Hmmmphf!"

Roan took his place. "I'm sorry it's come to this, Rider Ainsley. You were promising. I'd have liked to see what you were going to accomplish. But this is how it must be." He raised a hand. "This will be quick."

My muffled shouts grew louder and more desperate. *Take out the gag. Listen to me!*

Heat raged under my skin—burning to blister. I thrashed, growing hotter by the second. Roan was boiling my blood. Burning me alive! What kind of barbaric monsters were they!

"Hmm—"

My head wrenched to the side. Something snapped.

I screamed through the gag, head lolling.

"Zaeah, forgive me," Roan hissed. "Doesn't always work the first time."

Dominic, for all his smirking and bluster, looked away. He wasn't smiling anymore.

"Do it again," Drake snapped. "Do it right. Put the poor child out of her suffering."

Agony. My whole world was pain. This was how it ended. In a dim, dank room underground without my friends or one last goodbye to my family.

Tears leaked from hazy eyes. Wisps of smoke blurred my vision. Hallucinations?

No. Steam.

I was burning. My nerve endings lit aflame. He was cooking me from the inside out.

My head lifted through power not my own. Roan ripped the air with both hands, mimicking the magical grip wrapping around my neck. He ripped his hands apart, twisting. My chin snapped to the side, and I fell into darkness.

PAIN. BLOOD. FEAR.

Nestmates attack. Nestmates die.

Mother. Where is Mother? Mother, come. Mother, help me.

A smell invaded my nostrils. The wretched stink of humans. Humans always coming. Always looking and pointing at me. *Where is Mother?*

Shadow fell over me. Small one. Small human. Mother's milk still on his mouth.

What do they call—? Boy. It's a boy. What does boy want? Why is boy here? Back hurts. Mother! Mother, help me!

Shadow moved, and I swung my head, snapping. *Leave, boy!* His wrong-way eyes met mine.

Boy... My boy.

DOMINIC AND HIS NESTMATE were fighting again. Always fighting. Always bleeding.

Dominic must defeat nestmate. Sire has terrible plans for him if he doesn't. A low growl leaked through my teeth. *I have plans for him if he tries.*

Elder Tizor bit my neck, scolding me for threatening his human.

I will kill Elder and Sire.

He bit harder.

My boy fell down. He screamed as acid ate through his chest. The nestmate stood over him and covered his eyes before he's dead. I growled and thrashed in Elder's hold. *Must save boy. My Dominic.*

"Well done, Roderick. You're read—"

Hellfire soared through the air.

The nestmate's screams replaced my boy's.

DOMINIC WASHED FRANTICALLY in the river, its waters running red.

He is a good human. He washes his pink, fleshy coating often as he should. Bearing the victory of your kill is not worth the unappetizing smell of human blood.

"Dom!"

I raised my head above the surface as my boy's nestmate broke from the trees. I watched his face change. The big and un-dragonlike emotions pouring through the bond evaporated. My boy disappeared, and Sire's Dominic rose in his place.

"Calida," he called, grinning. "Problem?"

"How could you!" She shoved him. "You killed him. Your own brother. You didn't even hesitate, you fucking monster. What's wrong with you!"

"Not a thing. We fought. He lost. That's how it is."

She shoved him again. "You're like a—a copy of him! A cold, lifeless beast that doesn't love anyone or anything. How are you not fucking ashamed to look at yourself in the mirror? You're disgusting, Dom! You're even worse than him."

She ran at him, fist high. Dominic caught, spun, and trapped her in his hold.

"I am disgusting," he whispered.

I knew his words because they reached me loud and clear through the bond.

"Everything he touches is. But you're safe, Cali. A plant mage isn't worth his time, and you're better off for it."

"Let go of me!" She threw herself back and forth. "I'll kill you for this. You and *him*! If it's the last thing I do. You'll both regret this day."

"You won't remember this day."

A figure broke through the trees. My growl disturbed the water, rippling the surface as I stalked closer.

This human was wrong. Cursed with unnatural magic. She had never bonded and never would. No dragon could do what she should not be able to do.

"It'll be like Irad never existed," Dominic said softly.

I perched behind my boy, ready to separate her head from her shoulders if the cursed mage touched him. She dragged the nestmate away screaming.

"But I'll remember."

GOLDEN CITY ROSE IN the distance, beckoning me to my new home.

I did not care for it. Too loud. Too noisy. Too smelly. Too dirty.

I longed for the peace of the Ghidorian firepits. When my boy claimed the throne, I prayed to the mother of dragons that he sent half the inhabitants away. Humans baffled in their need to be penned in together like cattle.

Noise turned my head, drawing my eye to the forest floor. Four humans. One of them screaming.

"Help! Someone, help me, please!"

"Oh, do keep screaming. That's my favorite part."

Years learning the ways, habits, and tricks of humans, I knew all too well what it meant when half-naked males descended on a screaming female.

"Don't do this! Help!"

I dove.

Chapter Eighteen

I was on fire.

Flames covered my body, crackling and roaring on my skin. I felt nothing.

My head lifted on its own power—raising my chin above my lap, holding still as broken neck bones knit themselves together. My heart restarted with a hard thump against my rib cage.

Drake and Roan were shouting. Waving and flinging their hands at me as I broke free of the melted shackles.

Silver lances appeared in the air. Beautiful, lethal, magical—they flew through the space and skewered me in a dozen different places.

I stepped off my death's throne, not slowing for a moment as the lances melted into nothing.

"How is she doing this? She has no magic!"

"Roan, stop her! Break her legs!"

Faint pain tickled my shins. Enough to sting, but not enough to do much else.

Then, I saw it.

Clear as a setting sun, I saw Commandant Drake. Saw the blood rushing through translucent veins. His heart a wildly fluttering bird in a cage. His bones white sticks waiting to be broken.

I slashed the air. Drake fell howling.

The pain attacked my arms, chest, head, neck. Roan was trying to murder me by any means—suffering included.

I thrust my chest and silver lances burst forth. They pinned his arms, legs, and chest to the wall. His head slumped over. *Gone.*

Movement snapped my head around. Dominic was flinging fireballs at me. The magic hit and absorbed in the parade of flames covering my body.

I made a fist—lazy and slow, and Dominic crumpled like a used handkerchief.

"Ahh! Ahh!"

His screams were terrible. To be fair, it couldn't feel great to have every bone in your body broken.

I took my time approaching him. I was calm in a way I'd never been before. For the first time in my life, I knew exactly what to do.

Dropping down, I straddled him. Beads of sweat drenched his forehead. He wasn't screaming, and the effort of holding it back popped angry red veins on his face.

"H-how... are you doing... this?"

"I have no idea," I said honestly. "It's like all your magic is somehow mine too. Too bad for you three."

I kissed him.

Soft and sweet, I tasted the pain on his tongue, and replaced it. Roan's magic flowed out of me, pouring into his body.

"There," I sang. "I dulled your nerves, but didn't heal the bones. If you try to move, you'll do serious damage, but this way we can talk. But just in case you unwisely take the risk..."

I formed the silver dagger in my mind's eye, then there it was hovering before me. Magic was amazing.

Dominic leaned back with nowhere to go as I held the blade a mere centimeter from his left eye.

"Understood?"

His throat bobbed. "We... understand each other perfectly, Princess. What did you want to talk about?"

"You tell me, lover. When did you know Darvin put us in the same dream?"

Amazing. Even riddled with pain, Dominic's eyes gave away nothing. "When did you?"

"Something you said while we were in Darvin's world. *Why not? It's all a dream.* Why would my ideal Dominic ruin the moment by telling me he wasn't real? He wouldn't. But the real Dominic would say that if he thought I wasn't the real me."

A faint smile danced on pale lips. "Gods, you're clever. You make it impossible to resist you."

"You can save the flirting for later. Every second word out of your mouth is a lie, so I'm going to do the talking now, and you're going to listen.

"I know everything, Dominic."

The smile twitched. "What do you think you know?"

"I know everything you told me in the dream was true. You did once have a brother named Roderick, and he died in a death match forced by your father. Like many of your other siblings died by your hands while the general looked on approvingly.

"Something else. I was told this, but I didn't think about what it meant. The world looks down on unique mages, but the general doesn't. He surrounds himself with never-before-seen powers and the mages who wield them. Unnatural mages that couldn't bond with a dragon alive. Like the memory mage that wiped Roderick and your other siblings from the minds of those who knew them."

Something in his eyes flickered.

"Because it wouldn't do for people to know the truth about the king general," I rasped. "That he's a twisted, evil, barbaric monster who doesn't value the lives of his own children, let alone anyone else's. My only question is why didn't your father have her wipe me from everyone's memory too?"

"Because." His whisper slipped low and calm through his lips. "She died first."

My grip tightened on the dagger. His meaning came through loud and clear.

"That's the thing about aberrant mages, as my father calls them. They tend to be one of a kind. Once the piece is moved off his board, he can't play them again."

"You've been moving pieces off his board. You hate your father with every drop of your soul. This isn't the Adalinda you want, but the only way you can change it and undo what he's done is to play the part of the perfect heir. No matter what it costs you."

He blinked lazily, lashes brushing the tip. "Is there a point to this speech?"

"Patience, lover. We're getting to the good part."

Dominic raked me up and down. "I hope so."

Only this man could lie broken on the ground under threat of half-blindness, and still make me feel helpless to his power.

"I do love that you find me so irresistible, because the war between me and you is over. Reyna is mine. You're not getting her back. You're also going to undo what you've done, and get me off the cut list."

"Both of those things are impossible. You've killed Drake and Roan. Your execution is set in stone," he said. "As for Reyna, I told you there was no giving her up even if I wanted to. She's the only other death dragon in Adalinda that isn't bonded or a hatchling."

"She's not."

"Wait, what?"

"And they're not dead," I said irritatedly. "It's Roan's power. Lets me see into a body like a marketplace map. I know where everything is. I know where to strike, and where not to. I'll wake them up when we're done here, but—"

"Fuck them," he snapped. "What were you saying about the death dragons?"

"Uhh, them." I grinned. "I don't know how but when I was..." I couldn't bring myself to say dead. "When I blacked out, I saw into Reyna's mind. I think in the same way she looks into mine.

"Dragons are incredible," I breathed. "The bond they have with their riders, it's the same bond they have with each other. This amazing, interwoven hive mind that connects every dragon as one.

"I was in her mind the day she saved me. She was thinking about the firepits of Ghidorah, where her mother lives."

His gaze sharpened. "Reyna's mother? She died."

"No, she left. After she returned to the Hatchery, found her babies dead and Reyna gone, she abandoned humans and fled deep into the firepits. She gave birth to her next two broods there."

"Two? How many hatchlings?"

"Reyna's mind is connected to five of her nestmates. That's right," I said, seeing the look in his eyes. "Not just five death dragons. But five hellfire dragons, and they're only a few years younger than Reyna."

"Where are they?" he demanded. "They'd have left their mother's side a long time ago. Why have I never seen or heard of them?"

"Why would you have? Dragons love their mothers, but they couldn't give a shit about their siblings. It's not like any of her nestmates had a reason to visit Reyna in Ghidorah. Plus, they look like an average fire dragon. If they were spotted, no one would've known who they were looking at.

"All I know is Tanis and Tanwen are in Nehebkau. Jiyong is in Hyelong. Libelle is in Edjer, and Nada is somewhere across the Dark Border. I don't know where or how. I just know she's alive."

"Across the— No," he said. "This is impossible. What you're saying is impossible."

"It's not impossible. There are other hellfire dragons, Dominic. Losing Reyna killed you. I... I understand that now." I softened my voice. "I felt how much she loved you. How much she still loves you. She didn't break from you because she thought you were no longer worthy. She only did it to save me. Because she knew what it was to be alone, broken, and helpless, until a little boy helped her.

"Nursed her back to health. Stole chickens to feed her. Fell asleep with her so she wouldn't be alone. She is only so kind because you taught her how to be. That is why I know this guy isn't you. The man that held me in that dream is."

He ground his jaw. "What does it matter if I am or not? I don't have time to trek through Edjer's ice mountains to find wild hellfire dragons. Not when you admit Reyna didn't want to break the bond in the first place."

"She didn't. As embarrassing as it is to admit," I forced through my teeth, "Reyna sees me as a helpless little chick who needs her. She can't leave me until I'm ready to be on my own. She made a choice of her own free will, and you're fucking going to respect it, because what I'll give you in return is worth it."

"What? The location of the others? What good would that do me?" he barked. "There's no guarantee any of them will bond with me."

"That's your own problem. No, what I'm going to do is sign the marriage contract and become your wife. Once it's drawn up, signed, and witnessed by the High Council, loyalists, and militarists, I'll abdicate the throne."

Dominic went still. Strange to say when he already wasn't moving, but with Roan's stolen magic filling me, I sensed everything from his tightened muscles to his trapped breath.

"What did you say?"

"You heard me, and I heard you. I'll always be a threat to your father, because— How did you put it? What did it matter if I step aside as long as my son has the power to take the throne from his?

"So, I'll give it up. My claim, and the claim of my heirs—abdicated. Unless your father really is a crazed monster who kills just to kill, this will end his seeing me as a threat."

"But why the marriage contract?"

I smiled wide. "You didn't think you'd get something for nothing, did you? If I'm to give up all of Adalinda, I'll want a few things in return."

"Of course you do." His smile matched mine. "Name them."

"Everything promised to me in the original contract, except I want a twenty-thousand-ryu stipend."

"Naturally."

"And not only will I bear you children..." I took a deep breath and said the rest. "I'm the only one who will bear you legitimate heirs. Once we sign our marriage contract, all others will be void. I'm to be your only wife."

If he had a reaction to that, he didn't let it show on his face. "Why?"

"Because I can't be queen. I've never been to school. I can't read. I've seen little of Adalinda. As we speak, the borrowed magic is fading, and I'll return to being magicless. I know nothing about running a kingdom or leading a war. I'm not right for the throne, but neither is your father.

"I pass the throne to him—for now. Because I know you're working to unseat him and change Adalinda for the better," I said. "But if that turns out to be another lie, or you change your mind, my children will do what you don't.

"I'll raise them to love the people—poor or noble. Nehebkan or Ghidorian. Rider or commoner. They'll undo the harm he's done, with the support of loyalists and militarists. The true heirs to both. And yes," I hissed, "I'll put in the contract that you're not allowed any contact with them if that's what it takes. I won't make the same mistake your mother did."

"Ouch, Princess. Right for the jugular. So you're telling me in exchange for a possible new bond and the throne, I'll have to spend the rest of my life with a scheming, distrustful wife who is willing to raise my children against me?"

"Yes."

"But what about Nuala? She is noble by name, not by riches. After her father betrayed the general, he took everything from them. She's relying on our marriage to restore their good name, and take care of her family."

I cocked a brow. "And?"

Dominic burst out laughing, then immediately cringed. "Shit, this fucking erection hurts so much, but damned if it isn't worth it."

I almost blushed to see he wasn't lying.

"You're ruthless, clever, and clearly have a power no one can comprehend. Our children will be legend, and our marriage bed will be cinders." He nodded to himself, bumping the knife's edge. "We'll kill my father together. Rule... together."

I hesitated for the space of time it took me to recall Reyna's memories of the true General Roark. No memory mage could erase from her mind all the brutal, cruel things he'd done to the sweet, innocent boy she loved.

"Yes."

ROAN AND DRAKE AWOKE with shouts.

"What? How— You!" Drake shoved to his feet.

Dominic pushed me behind him as a dozen silver lances appeared in the air.

"No need for that, sir. She used all the magic she took healing you both."

"How did you do this? What are you!"

"I don't know, sir," I said from over his shoulder. "I didn't know I could do any of that. It just... happened."

"It just happened!" Drake's shouts echoed even louder in the small room. "How does magic theft, insubordination, and attacking a commanding officer just happen!"

"I didn't really steal it," I tried. "It's like you were giving it to me."

Roan stepped forward—cautiously. "What nonsense are you saying, girl?"

"I felt it when you were attacking me. It was like my body was absorbing it. The more you threw at me, the more I had."

"If you didn't try to kill her, none of this would've happened," Dominic said. "But it's my fault you did. Ainsley didn't know she wasn't allowed to use those boots. I tricked her to get her cut."

Drake's scarred face hardened. "Excuse me? Do you understand what you're saying, boy?"

"I do. I'll take the punishment I'm owed, but Ainsley is not to be cut, or punished in any way. Not even a demerit," he said. "Captain Roan, she had your magic. I'm sure you know that if she wanted to kill you both, she could've done so easily."

Roan looked to Drake. He nodded.

"You're both unharmed. You were stopped from doing a terrible thing. Most importantly, you told Ainsley she had to rank top eight in the hardest trials any first-year recruit has been put through, and she did it. You can't deny that she belongs in rider training," he said, "or that you're not eager to see what a rider who can take and wield multiple magic types can do in the battle against Druks. She'll be unstoppable."

I blinked at the back of his head. While we talked about what he would say to stop Drake from trying to kill me a second time, he didn't mention this would be a part of his speech. Even worse, it sounded like he believed it.

Will this be the rest of my life? Him saying wonderful things, and me not knowing if he means them?

Drake fixed on me. A hard, piercing, unrelenting stare that made me shrink in my boots—which I'm certain was his intention.

"Very well," he said, making my knees nearly give out. "Welcome back to the Royal Rider Academy, Rider Ainsley."

"To that end," Dominic slid in, "let's forget about any boots she may or may not have. She's working hard for Adalindian victory. There's no need to monitor her footwear."

"What interest have I in her footwear?" Drake replied smoothly. "Rider Ainsley and I will be too busy with her extra training sessions. We will discover exactly what her magic is, its limits, and its use in battle, or she'll die trying."

That didn't sound good either. I'm sure that was his intention too.

"Can I go, sir?" I asked, voice small.

"There's no need for you to go anywhere. Master Whelan will come to you."

I expected this. Didn't mean I was happy about it. "Of course, sir."

"Sit."

I sat.

Roan left and took Dominic with him, despite heavy protest. I sat there under Drake's unwavering gaze, mind spinning.

There wasn't time to think about it while everything was happening. I woke up on fire and under attack. I had a clear and simple plan, and Reyna gave it to me. It was impossible to describe but it was like I... borrowed her mind.

Reyna's wisdom, calm, ferocity, and hellfire. It all poured into me, and when I woke, I knew exactly what to do.

Surprise of my life that Reyna had thought about my situation with Dominic and the general more than once. It was obvious to her that I should abdicate, then marry Dominic. Apparently, she smelled the arousal on both of us whenever we were close to the other. It was obvious we were destined to mate, and she thought it was incredibly stupid that we hadn't done so already.

Yes, being in her mind was embarrassing in a number of ways. Not just for the fact that she practically saw me as a hatchling.

But how was I supposed to do it again? I don't know how I did it the first time.

I sat there, mind spinning about my upcoming interrogation with Master Whelan, while everything I was taught for fooling a Heart Reader went out of my mind.

Voices at the top of the staircase brought me back to the present.

I had to calm down—slow my breathing. I wasn't a fool. Everything I said and did in this room would be reported to the king general. Dominic let Roan drag him out of the room so that he could get to him first.

Tell him the marriage would go ahead, but that I'd abdicate, and he'd find and bond with one of Reyna's siblings. Nothing about our plan should offend or give him reason to question. He'd get everything he wanted... until we took it away from him.

"Princess Ainsley," Whelan greeted. "We meet again."

"Hello, Master Whelan."

"I was told quite an interesting tale on the way here. Is it true you stole the magics of Captain Roan and Commandant Drake, then used it against them?"

"Yes."

"I didn't quite steal it."

Drake and I spoke at the same time.

"I felt it," Drake gritted. "My magic was *pulled* out of me. I grew weaker while she wielded my silver with mastery. It took me five years to form my lances. She did it in five seconds. How is this possible?"

"How indeed," Whelan murmured.

"You've never heard of such magic?"

"Never." They carried on like I wasn't there. "But more and more aberrant mages appear every day. You have twelve in this season's recruits alone. It's no longer the case that children inherit one parent's magic type. Your mud mage has an earth mage father and water mage mother."

"Earth and water. Mud."

"Yes, but they're not all that straightforward. The thread mage has two fire mages for parents, and yes," he added, "I checked that they are indeed both her parents."

My eyes widened. They did that much research into us? How hard were they trying to dig up information on me?

"And the boy with the body magic who can change, lengthen, or shrink any part of his anatomy. One parent has fire magic and the other wind magic. Tenille knows how he developed such an ability."

"But isn't it like your magic, sir?" Gods, what possessed me to speak? I regretted it the second they both turned to me. "I mean... you sense what goes on in the body. Captain Roan can break and mend the body. Isn't changing the body just like that?"

"Our bodies are made up of mostly water," Whelan said, not unkindly. "Roan and I manipulate that water in different ways. Specific ways, but still, we are water mages. This *body magic* isn't the same. He can change his hair, cartilage, muscle, and flesh. He can shrink and grow. Nothing like that has been seen before." He faced me fully. "Nothing like you either. Is that why you lied and said you were magicless? More to the point, how did you lie to me? I'm not easily fooled."

"I didn't lie," I cried. "I didn't know I could do that. I've never—"

"*You don't understand what you are, but it is so much more than you ever thought possible.*"

Kai's words ripped through my mind.

"Oh my gods," I whispered. *He told me. Kai told me exactly what I was.*

"What?" Drake gruffed, voice sharp. "Explain yourself."

"I'm a thief." As I said it, the rightness burrowed into my skin. "I did steal the magic. Captain Roan's magic to heal myself. The commandant's magic to defend myself. And Reyna's mind and fire to free myself.

"I was in danger, so I took what I needed to survive. Like... a thief."

"I don't know that I would use that term," Whelan said, snapping me out of the memory with Kai. "But I guess a kind of aberrant borrowing magic could exist. If there's magic that can take a person's life, why not a type that takes their magic?" He rubbed his chin, sweeping me up and down. I assumed he was using his magic on me then.

I could only assume because I couldn't feel it anymore. Not like I did when Roan was trying and failing to break my bones.

"Is your magic returned, Commandant?"

He inclined his head. "I am at my full ability."

"Then, whatever she took, she did not, or could not keep. Forbidden magic is not nearly so kind. Yes," he said, nodding to himself. "We can be fairly certain we're in the presence of our thirteenth aberrant mage."

I was beginning to understand why Awnan and his friends preferred unique. Aberrant mage made me feel like a pus-filled boil they found on the backside of Adalinda.

"You assumed you were magicless, because you are. You don't have any magic of your own, but it seems in a life-threatening situation, you borrow the magic close to you."

"Shouldn't you be questioning her instead of feeding her the story she'll spread?" Drake asked.

"I don't need to question her," Whelan replied. "Her rapid pulse and fluttering heart tells me she's feeling many things—confusion, hope, relief, fear. But nothing approaching deception. She's learning about this at the same time we are, Commandant."

"We must be sure. The general will expect a full report." He glared at me. "You say there's no forbidden magic afoot, but never in my eighty years have I heard of a mage that can wield multiple magics at once."

"Neither have I. It may have something to do with her being naturally magicless. She's an empty vessel. Pour milk, mead, and ale—it will hold it all. Try to pour mead in a mug already filled to the brim with ale, and it overflows." He seemed to be speaking to himself, putting the mystery of me together in his mind. "This is all speculation of course. No aberrant mage I've spoken to can explain why their magic manifested in that form. It's like asking someone why they have a long middle toe. She is this way... because she is this way."

"That will not satisfy the general."

"I suppose not." Whelan gestured toward the stairs. "After you, Rider Ainsley. We'll continue this conversation in my office."

I felt Drake's eyes on me the whole way up. Why couldn't he decide if he saw me as an asset or threat? Although my true worry was how the general saw me. Would he accept the marriage contract and my willingness to abdicate? Or would he continue patiently waiting for his chance to get rid of me?

I STUMBLED OUT OF WHELAN'S office so late that night, it was almost day. Hours into the circular interrogation, one of the palace's Heart Readers joined in.

Over and over they asked me how I stole the magic, did I dabble in curses or the forbidden, who were my parents, what else was I lying about... on and on.

My head spun from hunger and the strain of remembering everything Rosaleen's Heart Reader told me. By the end, I was too exhausted and starved to keep anything straight. No doubt their intention. Either way, they finally let me go without a word to if they believed my story.

Poet fell out of bed when I walked in.

He was in the middle of having sex with Maili on the top bunk. I flinched when he hit the ground.

"Ahh! Fuck!"

"Shut up."

"Assholes."

"We're trying to sleep!"

"I see you guys moved on from my death quickly." A glance at Dominic's bunk showed he wasn't there. It was possible he was still with his father, convincing him that I should be his one and only wife.

"Are you kidding?" Maili jumped off the bed, fully naked, and blew past a groaning Poet. I grunted when she threw herself in my arms. "I was a fucking wreck. Poet was making me feel better." She squeezed me of breath. "How are you here right now? You were cut. Gone. Did they realize it was all a mistake?"

"It wasn't a mistake. It was sabotage. Once I got Drake to listen, he accepted the truth and let me free."

"I can't believe this. You're here. You're really here."

I rested my head on her shoulder, melting into her hug. "Should we help Poet now?"

"Yes, please," came a pained groan.

We flew apart and rushed to our friend, and his dislocated shoulder. I helped him pop it back in and his fast healing did the rest.

After they dressed, we left for the Royal Wood. Or more like, I left to see Reyna and they followed because they weren't letting me out of their sight.

"You stole Drake's magic?" Poet hissed. "And he let you live?"

"No one is more surprised by both of those things than me."

"But how?" Maili slowed to climb over a log. "What kind of magic lets you take magic from someone else? Earth, fire, water, air. Our magics are a gift of harmony with Tenille of the earth and heavens. A magic that only lets you steal magic when your life is under threat kind of sounds like a curse."

"Maili." Poet threw her big eyes.

"What? No! I don't mean it like that. I'm not saying you're cursed," she rushed out. "I just mean, think of all the things you've gone through. I'm sure it hasn't been easy believing you were magicless all these years. I know people haven't been kind."

I looked away.

"Not to mention training," she continued. "Roan snapped our legs. Keir attacked you multiple times. Reyna threw you. All those times you could've used magic, even borrowed magic, to help you and nothing happened. Only having power when someone breaks your neck doesn't sound very pleasant, or useful."

I wanted to argue with a single thing she said, but couldn't. There were many times in my life it would've been helpful to take the magic of the person hurting me. Just as helpful to tell those people who denied me work, service, or kindness that I wasn't the useless orphan they knew.

A power that only appeared when you were standing before the veil, was a curse.

"I fear what's to come more than I mourn what was." The trees opened on the clearing. "Drake promises to bring my magic out of me. By any means necessary."

Reyna raised her head, beholding me. I froze.

The only reason I didn't go straight to Reyna's side was because I was covered in blood and charred uniform remains. A smell I knew she hated from my sudden and intrusive poke around her mind and memories while I drained her hellfire. Did she hate me? Was she going to knock me into the pool and take off in search of a mage who wasn't cursed?

She bounded over to me. I cried out as she smacked my back, sending me flying into her foreleg. I almost cried feeling her huge and warm head resting against me.

"I love you too," I whispered. "I'm so sorry. I didn't know I could do those things, but I sensed it. I took more from you than the others. Drake said it was like being drained. I hate that I did that to you."

If she was angry, it wasn't coming through the bond. Nothing but love and relief flowed from Reyna.

I laughed. "I guess if you can forgive me, I forgive you for thinking I'm a helpless hatchling that needs looking after."

"You humans take two decades to mature, and sometimes not even then. You do need looking after. I apologize for nothing."

Reeling back, my feet tangled and I fell on my ass. Barely felt the pain in my shock. "Reyna, did—did you just—?" I wheezed.

"Guys, did you hear that? Did you hear her? She spoke! She spoke to me!"

"*Wait. You understood me?*"

"She did what?"

Maili and Poet ran over.

"She spoke to you?"

"How is that possible?"

"What did she say?"

They rapid-fired questions at me one after the other. All I could do was gape at Reyna. Was this because of what I did? Taking her thoughts and mind into mine? Did I change our bond, or could every rider do this if they knew how?

"*Every rider could, but the dragonkin don't allow it,*" Reyna answered easily. "*We must protect our secrets from the abominations.*" Reyna poked and sniffed my stunned body with her snout. "*How are you doing this?*"

"Is she speaking to you right now?" Maili asked. "What's she saying? Will Cadmus speak to me one day too?"

I started and stopped multiple times trying to reply. I came back from the dead, wielded stolen magic, pledged to marry my enemy, was interrogated for hours, but Reyna speaking to me was the most shocking thing to happen in the last day.

"She said that," I croaked out, "every rider could hear their dragon speaking, but they don't allow it. Dragonkin must protect their secrets from the Druks."

Maili and Poet visibly deflated.

"Protect their secrets?" Poet repeated. "What secrets? What does that mean?"

I didn't have to ask her. One peek into her mind, and I became a part of the dragonkin hive. A beautiful, ever-flowing fountain of shared knowledge, history, and thoughts. More than that, I discovered the location of six rare hellfire dragons in an instant.

That information was dangerous in the hands of someone seeking to become a Druk. Why be a common fire Druk, when you could wield flames that can't be put out by water, wind, or will?

"Don't they trust us?" Maili asked.

"They do," I replied, repeating the words Reyna poured into my head. "But the decision isn't hers, Cadmus's, or Valor's. The Elders have decreed the bond remain one-way. All of dragonkin must obey."

"Elders? Who are the Elders?"

"*We cannot say.*"

"She can't say."

"But this is amazing," Poet said. "Even if she can't tell you dragon secrets, there're so many other things she could tell you. Stuff we've wondered for hundreds of years. How do dragons choose their bonded? What reasons make them break a bond?"

I looked to Reyna. "She says it's not really a choice. They look at their human and know they're the one."

Maili clapped. "Aww, it's like love at first sight."

I winced. "Reyna says love is silly human nonsense. Choosing a bonded is about obeying the voice of Mother Zaeah."

"So why do they break a bond?"

Reyna shook her head. I didn't need to translate that.

"I thought you'd be here."

I looked up as Dominic stepped into the clearing. He pointed at Maili and Poet. "Leave."

"Excuse me?" Maili planted her hands on her hips. "Just because you're the general's son, doesn't mean you get to order us around."

"That's exactly what it means. Go."

Fireballs appeared. Swirling through the air, they attacked Poet's and Maili's backsides, sending them yelping and running away.

"Guys! Guys, are you okay!" I rounded on him. "Roark, what is wrong with you? You can't treat people like this."

"That's exactly how I have to treat people. What do you think my father would do if rumors spread that I'm kind and agreeable? I told you what he did because I visited my ill and grieving mother too often. The general doesn't stand for weakness."

Damn him. There was no room for argument in that reply. Dominic made a good, and sadly very true point. Everyone saw him as hard, cold, and arrogant. I'm certain that's exactly what the general wanted of his favored heir.

"Does he at least give you word of her?" I asked, tone softening. "Let you know that she's okay?"

He shook his head. "I dare not ask."

"I'm sorry." I truly was. It pained me to be apart from a mother I never met. I couldn't imagine being separated from one who knew and loved me. "I want to help you find her. Even if helping means to bring down your father. He's done too much that can't be forgiven."

"Well, today he's done one thing right." Dominic tipped my chin, popping my brows. "He said yes, Ainsley. To our marriage, to the terms, and to your abdication. He didn't question a single thing except to ask how I tricked you into this. Tonight, we celebrate."

"I can't believe it." My mind spun. "He said yes."

"Are you okay?" I couldn't stop him grasping my waist and pulling me close. Or the heat that filled my body when he did. "I thought this was what you wanted."

"It is. I guess I expected more. Things don't usually come this easy for me. What about the magic I stole from Drake and Roan? Is he going to bring me before Madame Sela again?"

"He doesn't see the need. Drake is loyal to him. He trusts he'll discover the extent of your magic, and put you down if needed. His words," Dominic explained, "not mine."

"That's it? Again, why would he give in so easily? He destroyed the first contract, accused me of forbidden magic, and tried to kill me during our first meeting. Now we intend to get married and he has no questions?"

"He believes I manipulated or threatened you. In anyone else's eyes, this is a bad deal. You're giving up all of Adalinda for the regency of one small province. Trading in a kingdom's coffers for a mere twenty thousand ryu a year. He's not questioning it because he's praising it."

That did make sense. Me abdicating and giving him the throne of my own free will was beyond the comprehension of a man like him. Blood and pain were how he solved every problem. Compromise and negotiation were foreign to him, and if they weren't, they were a weakness.

"Okay," I murmured. "When does it happen? How will it work?"

"Father's already begun telling his advisors and the High Council the news. Ending the contract with Nuala won't be easy," he confessed. "It's worthless parchment before it's signed, but afterward it's binding. Women can't back out without risk of jail or execution. Men have to pay their former fiancée a one-hundred-thousand-gold-ryu fine. Most people do not back out."

I caught my tongue, holding back what I thought of those unequal punishments. "Will the general pay the fine?"

"Happily."

"Wow. This is really happening."

"As soon as possible. My father won't allow you time to change your mind."

I nodded, chewing my lip.

"What is it?" My breath caught as he cupped the back of my neck. He touched me so casually—as if he'd been holding me all his life. "We don't have to do this, Ainsley. Only I thought you wanted to."

"I do want to. I meant everything I said yesterday. I can't rule Adalinda. No part of me is ready for that responsibility, and as long as you're that guy I spent that dream with, I want to marry you. But I don't understand why you want to marry me!"

It was out and I couldn't take it back.

"We've done nothing but argue, bicker, promise to kill each other, and succeed in killing each other since we met. I don't understand why *you* are saying yes. Is it just because you want the throne and locations of the hellfire dragons?"

"I want both of those things," he said, killing my heart. "I also want you."

"Me? You want the dragon thief? The throne thief? Or the magic thief? Which one of those flaws said lifelong partner to you?"

He laughed. "All three, and also neither. I want you because you're different, Ainsley. You're set apart from every woman I've ever known."

"Because I... can't read?"

"No," he replied, holding back amusement. "Because you know me. The real me. Other than her"—he glanced at Reyna—"you're the only one who does. That sounds like the basis of a lifelong partnership, doesn't it?"

"Damn you again." My voice shook. "You always have a good answer."

"I have something for you."

Dominic dropped to his knees. I watched curiously as he drew something from his pocket. "A body chain." Dominic held out a delicate golden chain dripping with tiny ruby teardrops. "This was once my mother's. In Ghidorah, secret lovers give each other chains like these to hide under their clothes.

"My mother wore this every day since I could remember. The first time she parted with it is when I found it in her empty room in the palace." Dominic lifted my shirt, exposing the tight, goose-pimpled flesh to his gaze. "I used to wish this man, whoever he was, was my real father, and that one day he'd come and rescue me. I see now that I wasn't waiting for him."

Calloused, gentle fingers traced the jewels along my belly button. "I was waiting for you."

I bit my lip hard, anchoring myself on the pain. The thing about Dominic Roark was... he always knew the right thing to say.

"Is this real?" I asked softly. "Are you just saying all the things I want to hear because of the very reasons you gave? I made a bad deal. Willingly chose the wrong end of the stick, and you have to make sure I don't back out before you get everything you want."

"This is real, Ainsley. You're going to have to trust me."

"Until you ruin me with another betrayal I should've seen coming."

His smile didn't waver. "I promise I'll make you wait a long, long time for that betrayal. So long I'll likely forget."

"I won't." I tugged him onto his feet. "That's why you can tell the general not to rush himself. I won't sign any marriage contract or abdication letter until I can read it."

"A fair request."

"And you're going to teach me."

The slightest twitch of his brow. "If that's what you want."

"And," I continued, "we look only to the future. All the digging into my past by Madame Sela, Drake, or anyone else stops now."

"Because you plan to tell me the truth yourself?"

I lifted my chin. "Because there's nothing to tell. It doesn't matter who I was or where I came from. All that matters is who I will be."

"My wife," he finished. "So you'll know everything about me. Even the things I wanted no one to know. But I'll lie next to a stranger for the rest of my life?"

"There's nothing in my past that you need to know. If I'm to trust you, then you can trust me."

"I will trust you," he said, giving me a long look. "And how long do you plan to make me wait for your betrayal?"

"Until the day after you."

He backed away, a humorless smile on his lips. "You have it backwards, Princess."

Princess.

"If I'm to trust you, then *you* have to trust me." He stalked off. "I'll leave you to your secrets."

"*See?*"

I jumped at the sudden voice in my head.

"*You and my boy will never mate at the foolish, stubborn rate you're going. This is why I must take you both under wing.*"

"What am I supposed to do? I can't tell him what my mother is." I dropped to my knees. I was suddenly so tired, I couldn't stand. "You know this. Telling him that truth will not make him trust me."

"*I kept you despite your vile and despicable parentage. My boy will do the same. I order it.*"

This talking-to-my-dragon thing might not be so great after all.

"*Now leave me, fetch your brush and bucket, then return. There is still blood on my claws from the day's hunt. While on your journey, consider how you'll regain the favor of your future mate.*

"*You humans like to shed your wrappings, and beat your genitals together until you smell terrible, but pleased. You will do that to Dominic.*" She nodded. "*Yes, I will allow it.*"

I amended *might* to *absolutely*. This talking-to-Reyna thing would absolutely not be great after all.

Chapter Nineteen

I stepped on the special talents field for the first time. I don't know what I expected of the area Commandant Drake claimed for himself and his lessons, but an almost bare field with a few Druk-shaped targets scattered around wasn't worth the wondering.

Ormr, Maili, and Poet followed behind, pouring information and tips in my ear.

"Keep your head down, focus on training, and don't draw Drake's attention," Ormr said. "That's how you survive."

"What happens if I draw his attention?"

"Doesn't matter what we're doing, or how hard we're pushing, if his eye lands on us, he finds something wrong." They turned and directed me at a particular target on the far side of the field. "I finally perfected my wind slicer, and was working on my aim, when he came out of nowhere and bellowed at me for slacking.

"Claimed a child could throw a single wind scythe. A true weapon against a Druk is multiple invisible wind scythes coming at them in a barrage. He then unleased such a barrage of silver lances at me, and told me to knock them out of the sky all at once. That's how I got this, and this, and this."

Ormr lifted their shirt and showed me the wicked, jagged cuts on their torso. I tried not to react, but the terrible cringe and shocked noise that came out of me ruined that.

"He also gave me five demerits. Just to drive the failure home."

"Okay," I drew out, "so what you're saying is I should train behind that wall."

"That's exactly what we're saying," Maili replied. "I'm so glad you understood."

We broke apart—Poet planting himself before the Druk, Maili and Ormr facing each other, and me going off behind my wall. Despite everything, I stopped and watched them.

Drake hadn't arrived yet, but that didn't slow the recruits down. They began training immediately, and it was a spectacle to behold.

Maili's vines shot from the ground and swallowed her—climbing her legs, wrapping around her arms, tangling in her hair, growing, growing, and growing. She was Golem. Golem if he was ten feet tall and covered in writhing vines, but Golem nonetheless. Towering over her twin, she attacked.

A vine-powered fist flew at Ormr, pummeling them from the top, while individual vines jabbed and attacked from all sides. Ormr didn't stand and take it. They drew double swords, slicing the coming vines in a blurred flurry that dropped my jaw. The fists coming from above didn't land. Somehow, they were striking and glancing off an invisible shield.

Ormr didn't just perfect their wind slicer. They created a wind barrier.

I flicked to Poet. His flames weren't like Dominic's—this I knew from before I learned the existence of hellfire.

I'd never seen Dominic's fire in any shape other than fireballs. I'd certainly never seen them grow and lengthen into a rope.

I smothered a happy cry when Poet flung his fire lasso at the Druk, wrapped around its neck, and ripped it off in one clean stroke. If that was not a secret weapon, what was?

Everywhere I looked, recruits did things with their magic I didn't know was possible.

Awnan commanded his golem army. Three were crawling all over him like excited pups, but the rest attacked the fake Druk.

But the sight to watch was Keir.

Druks surrounded him. Ice Druks, fire Druks, kaminari Druks, earth Druks—flying, diving, slashing, attacking. The horrific detail and ferocity of his illusions almost made me want to look away, but it was Keir's ferocity that kept me glued.

His sword blurred—cleaving heads, severing wings, and stabbing Druks in a symphony of blood and mimicked pain. He didn't have to make his illusions scream or writhe in agony. He didn't have to drench himself in the fake blood.

He didn't have to show us the true and gory horrors of battle.

But I need to see it.

It doesn't make sense to be worried about being cut from training, and not worried about a Druk slicing me to ribbons. They were putting more on our shoulders because they wanted us to survive. I either rose to that challenge now, or died later.

Breathing deep, I turned away and planted my feet—preparing myself.

I had the full training schedule, and all the expectations that went with it. I had no doubt Drake would cut me if I tried the "I don't have magic" reply again. I had to make what I had work for me—aberrant magic or not.

"Reyna?"

"*Yes?*"

I shivered. That would never not be strange. "I've thought about this all night. Somehow, whatever I did downstairs in that dungeon room changed our bond. Opened it, or altered it, or something," I said. "I was thinking that it's possible I don't have to *take* your fire from here on. You could give it to me."

"*Give you my fire? What nonsense do you speak?*"

"I don't know if I'm making sense. I'm not sure how this works. I was thinking maybe if you focused your flames down the bond, like you would send me pain, I could use it to fight."

"I did not send you pain, my bond. A dragon's mind contains all of dragonkin. It is too big for a human mind. It hurts you until it doesn't hurt you anymore."

"Huh. That explains a lot actually." I shook myself. "Well, if neither of us knows how to do this, then we'll just have to practice."

"You took it from me as you said. Left me weakened and tired. You will have to take it again. I know not what it is to share."

"Are you sure? I don't want to hurt you."

"It is for me to look after you, youngling. I will be fine. Get on with your practicing."

I mumbled something, then walked farther away from the group. Wasn't thrilled about being a youngling, but there was something nice about a motherless mite like me finding two loving mothers on life's path.

I sat cross-legged on the ground and fell into my mind. I didn't remember what I did or felt when I summoned Reyna's fire. There was pain, screaming, darkness, then I woke up on fire. That was more reason to believe I could do this. I borrowed magic subconsciously, surely I could do it consciously.

Reyna was my bonded. We shared minds. If I focused on that bond and thought of what Dominic told me...

A marketplace unfolded in my mind's eye. A blacksmith manned a stall with the finest Nehebkan steel tools and weapons. Ruby-dipped sheaths and diamond-crusted hilts glinted in the noonday sun. Two stalls down, a silks merchant laid out the day's prizes.

People bustled about—laughing and shouting across to friends with pockets weighted down by coin purses. I watched it all from the shadow of the bell tower like I'd done so many times before.

Dominic taught me the key to keeping out the pain of the bond was to retreat to a place where I was happiest and safe. What if the key to opening the bond was the opposite?

This was the place where I was unsafe. Where I risked my literal fingers to feed myself and the children. Heart-racing, blood-pumping, breath-stealing adrenaline was my companion through the pressing crowd. To tap into the power of a thief, I had to hunt with that companion again.

I slipped between two people, searching the faces and behind veils for my prey.

There.

A woman in reddish-gold robes stained black at the hem, parted the square. She was coldly beautiful. Regal without a crown. Rich without coin. Deadly without a weapon. A pointed nose lifted over full lips set in a haughty twist even while mischief danced in her eyes.

Reyna.

"*No.*"

My eyes popped open. "What?"

"*I am not haughty, a human woman, nor does the mischief dance in me. Make me as I am.*"

"But, my beauty, she's not supposed to be you. She's just a representation of you."

"*No.*"

"It's to help me practice," I argued. "Don't you want me to practice?"

"*You have made me fleshy, weak, ugly, and smelly—*"

"She doesn't smell!"

"*Make me as I am.*"

I bit back a groan. "Reyna, please. It doesn't make sense for a twelve-foot-tall dragon to be strolling the marketplace. Pretend she's someone else if that helps."

Displeasure rolled through the bond heavy and sigh-inducing. I tried to put it out of my mind and sink into that place again.

Once more, I was a shadow in the square, watching my prey—

"*I am no one's prey!*"

I was a shadow in the square, watching my beautiful, strong, and deadly companion part the crowd as she moved. I sensed more than knew a heavy coin purse tucked away in the folds of her robe.

I rarely pickpocketed women. Why fuss around with their mountainous skirts or tricky robes when men carried their coin in back pockets ripe for the taking?

Stealing from this woman would be no easy feat. I risked more than my fingers to try.

Reyna stopped at a flower stall and bent to smell a rose.

Memory mixed with fantasy. The steady warm heat of Reyna's flames enveloping me came to the forefront. The flames were hot, but not burning. Bright, but not blinding.

They were small, but not too small. Round and hard, the coins that were her flames bulged against her hip. I'd steal them, make them mine to have and use. This was a thief's domain where the only magic I'd ever known reigned.

I approached, closing the distance. Lifting my hand, I reached for—

"*Your clumsy, obvious stalking would not fool me. This smelly human is not me. Make me as I am.*"

"That's it," I cried, throwing up my hands. "I give up. My beauty, if you'd be so kind, would you fly to me? We'll have to do this another way."

I didn't receive a reply. I hoped that meant she was on her way.

Using Dominic's meditation was just one thought I had for tapping into Reyna's fire. Blocking her out in my mind held back the pain of the bond. Maybe stealing from her in the bond would make something happen too. It was a long shot that wasn't going to work out.

I had another plan that was ten times riskier and a hundred times more stupid. I should've known that was meant to be plan *A*.

A shiny spark rose in the distance, coming fast. Reyna shook the earth when she fell out of the sky.

"Let's try this again," I said. "Maili made a good point about only having power when someone breaks my neck. It gave me an idea that the trigger is my life being in danger. It has to be because I've never been able to steal magic, minds, or hellfire before. I've also never died before."

I held out my hands. "Burn me, Reyna. Dominic said even the smallest flickering flame of hellfire blazes out of control until it consumes everything. You unleash your fire, and just a little bit of it, and my power should take over before it kills me. That'll give me a chance to learn what it feels like when my power takes over."

She eyed me. *"Are you certain of this, youngling? I am not like my boy. He can control his fire. I cannot."*

I swallowed hard. I figured such a thing was true, but it was frightening to hear it. "I'm sure."

"Bring Dominic here. He will protect his mate."

Another thing I would never get used to. Dominic being called my mate.

"Strange to say, but it's too risky. If he's there to stop it, I'll know I'm not truly in danger, and my power might not work," I said. "I have magic now. Powerful, mind-boggling magic. I need to be able to use it when I choose, or I'll be another rider sent to the fodder battalion. If I survive training that is."

"As you say, youngling." She sat back on her haunches. *"Prepare yourself."*

I planted my feet, shaking from hair to toe. How did one prepare themself to be set on fire?

"Okay. Read—"

Reyna expelled a puff of fire. More smoke than flame, the smallest embers landed on my uniform.

It caught fire.

Flames erupted on my body, consuming the material and eating through to my skin.

I screamed.

White-hot, blistering agony devoured my body, turning my skin, nerves, bones, everything to cinders.

My shrieks shredded my burning ears, louder than Reyna's roar could ever be. This was it. I would die a fool's death. For the next twelve decades, recruits would gather around the place of my death, laughing at the marker telling the tale of the girl who told her dragon to set her on fire.

I screamed and screamed, then stopped.

The pain vanished as quickly as it came. Chest heaving, my tear-laced vision fought to make sense of what I was seeing.

Charred, ravaged skin healed before my eyes. My ruined throat knit itself together. Muscles and skin regrew over bones. Hair sprung anew from my scalp. The fire faded, absorbing into my body. I couldn't tell how I knew this. I simply felt it... become me.

Shaking, I stumbled to Reyna, feeling her shock as keenly as my own.

"It worked," I gasped. "It really worked."

Reyna sniffed me all over, knocking me around.

I choked back vomit—the smell of my burning flesh clung to my nose. "I never want to do that again."

"My fire is in you. I feel it."

"Do— Do—?" I shook myself. Taking a deep breath, I let it out slow. "Do you feel drained and tired like before?"

"No. You only have the fire that burned you. We shared."

That was something at least. Reyna and I had to fight as one in battle. It'd be wrong for me to fight by draining the life out of her. We solved one problem. Next was figuring out how to do it without setting me ablaze.

"Okay, I have it. Now I learn how to use it."

"I eagerly await your attempt. We all do."

Jerking, I spun and came face to face with Commandant Drake. Behind him, half my recruit class openly stared at me.

"Sir, I was just—"

"You were just recklessly playing around with things you don't understand," he said, stepping forward. "Did it occur to you that the people most qualified to teach you to use your newfound abilities are the instructors who've trained their magic for decades?"

"Of course, sir. I only wanted to make sure I could do it again—"

"—and you were willing to die trying," he finished, voice flat.

"Um…" Sweat beaded on my unnaturally hot skin, but Reyna's borrowed fire wasn't the reason. "Yes. What difference does it make if I die during training or during a battle? Dead is dead. Slacking off and not giving my best now will only give me regrets later. I have to master this power, because one day it could save my squad and innocent people. I have to do it, sir, or die trying."

He gave me a long, unreadable look.

"Well said, Rider Ainsley."

Excuse me?

"Let those words ring in all of your ears," he bellowed, rounding on the watchers. "You do yourself and your squad a disservice when you do not give better than your best. Your goal is to survive battle, not survive training. Druks don't care about your rank.

"Rider Ainsley," he barked, startling me again. "With me."

"Oh. I thought maybe I should practice on my own today, sir, because—"

"No. And send your dragon away. You're never to summon her without my permission again."

Reyna growled. "*I will bite the small, loud man.*"

I smothered a noise. I'd bet my week's pay no one had referred to the six-foot-tall commandant as small in a long time.

"No, it's okay," I said softly. "I can feel that you're hungry. Go hunt. I'll be fine."

Drake stalked off. I ran to catch up with him.

"—train with me every day."

All the warnings to avoid Drake's attention died on my ears.

"We will craft this aberrant power into a deadly weapon that turns the tide for your future squad, and brings them all home."

"Yes, sir."

"You also have a month of Hatchery duty."

"What? Why?"

"I believe I already spoke of your recklessness. You did not come to the citadel to train yourself," he said, stopping fast and sharply pulling me up short. "You came to learn to be a rider."

"Yes, sir."

Drake pointed to the lone Druk target before us. "Attack."

I gazed down at my hands. I felt Reyna's fire humming beneath my fingertips. The last time, I didn't use it to attack because deep down, I wasn't trying to kill Drake, Roan, or Dominic. Even in the midst of my fury, I knew hellfire was nothing to mess around with.

It was like Dominic said. Magic like this had one purpose and one purpose only: to kill.

But how does Dominic wield his hellfire? He's so concentrated and controlled. No shouting, or running around, or waving his hands. It's like he thinks a simple command, and his fire obeys.

Curious, I raised my palms to the Druk. "Attack."

Flames erupted from my body, blowing me off my feet. I skidded across the ground, leaving behind bits of skin and remains of
my tattered uniform.

I ached all over, and the pain did nothing to hold back the
smile on my face. The spot where the Druk existed was nothing but
a hole in the ground.

"Hmm," Drake sounded. "Adequate. Do it again."

Wincing, I pushed onto my feet. "I don't know if I can. I think
I used it all up."

"Then we need to work on precision and control as well as tapping into this magic at will. Pay attention to the inner workings of
your mind and body when the magic is absorbed."

"Okay. Should I summon Rey—?"

Silver lances pierced the air. Five stuck through my
chest—shredding my lungs and filling it with blood. I dropped like
a sack of potatoes.

"No need."

Chapter Twenty

"That was the most horrific thing I've seen in my entire life," Maili said. "You died, Ainsley. I watched you die five times, then spring back up like Poet's erection when it's time for round two."

Ormr took my arm and tugged me aside. We gathered in an alcove, letting the dirty and weary recruits trudge to their next lesson.

"Does this mean you can't die?" they whispered. "Because that goes beyond magic, Ainsley. We are blessed by nature, but also bound by nature. An immortal mage is unheard of."

"I'm not immortal," I said, glancing over Poet's shoulder.

Keir stood at the opposite end of the hall, openly watching us. Almost every recruit gave up any semblance of politeness and gathered to watch after Drake *killed* me for the third time. They didn't stop even after he ordered them away.

"I think the true explanation is that the magic can't kill me after it becomes mine. Poet, does your fire burn you?"

He shook his head.

"That must be it, right? Your fire burns everything else, but you're protected from it. When I steal the power, the damage is healed and I'm protected too. But I can die," I rasped. "I have no doubt starvation, strangling, poison, or a normal steel blade to the heart would kill me just fine."

"But it's still amazing magic," Poet said. "Anyone tries to kill you, and you take their ability for yourself."

"How can such magic exist?" Ormr asked.

"*You're a thief. Start acting like one.*"

"In a way," I said, "it's the only magic that makes sense for me."

I wriggled through Ormr and Poet. "I have to go. I have Hatchery duty."

"Hatchery duty? But our punishment is finally over," Maili said.

"Not for me. Drake gave me another month for going off to train alone. Meet up after?"

"Oh yes," Poet called. "We're getting drunk in Barrack *B* again. You need that more than anyone. We're not letting you miss out."

I just waved bye, running off. With my magic being what it was, walking into a room with a bunch of recruits doing target practice sounded like a great way for me to become the target.

I slowed down as the sound of recruits faded, sinking into my thoughts. Were days like that day what I had to look forward to for the next four years? In spite of Drake's bellows and disappointed glares, I didn't feel anything when my borrowing magic took over. All I knew is one moment I was in pain, and the next I was filling with power.

If I couldn't figure out how to do this without nearly dying, then there was no hope of me truly controlling it.

"—has to be this way."

"Why?"

I slowed down.

I stood at the crossways of the hall, gazing down the right and the entrance to the Hatchery. Voices filtered from the left. Familiar voices.

I made to continue on but my feet didn't move. *It's none of your business, Ainsley. Keep going. We can't be late.*

"—the marriage contract."

My feet moved... away from the Hatchery.

Pressing my back to the wall, I peered around the corner—heart squeezing as my eyes confirmed worse than my ears.

Dominic and Nuala stood close together. Too close.

She glued to his chest—fingers grasping his collar while his hand squeezed her waist. Why was he touching her waist?

"I don't understand. How could you do this? End our marriage contract." Her eyes shone bright with unshed tears. "Is your father making you do this? I told you we can fight him together, Dom. I'm on your side always. I love you always."

I rocked back, flinching like the confession was a physical blow. Nuala said the words so easily, and not as if it was the first time.

"Nu, I'm sorry. Things have changed. Neither of us can fight this."

Fight this? Why did he say it like that? Dominic didn't want to fight our marriage... did he?

"You'll be taken care of," he said. "I promise. Your family name will be restored. Your sisters will be taken care of."

"I don't give a fuck about my family name!"

"Nu," he whispered, tugging her farther down the hall.

I almost jumped out and followed them.

"This is..."

Their voices faded the farther they went, making hearing them impossible. But I still saw. The hand on her waist. The true pain and regret in his eyes. The pleading on her lips.

"I was waiting for you."

His promise so sweet and reassuring as he gazed up from his knees.

His lips so fervent as he spoke to Nuala.

"This is real, Ainsley. You're going to have to trust me."

I wanted to protect my heart from the man who smiled mischievously and kissed me like he didn't want it to be the last time. The man who made all my dreams come true without knowing he was my dream.

"*I promise I'll make you wait a long, long time for that betrayal. So long I'll likely forget.*"

He kissed her.

I stumbled back, heart punched out of my chest.

Lies. All of it lies, and I fell for it again. I fell for *him* again! I was so stupid. Of course Dominic wasn't madly in love with the illiterate, gullible fool that fell out of the sky and tried to take everything important to him. I handed it all back on a silver platter, and he poured sweet nothings in my ear to make sure I didn't change my mind.

Eyes shining brighter than Nuala's, I peered around the corner—driving the knife deeper one final time.

They were gone.

Running off to finish what they started in private, and me left standing alone as I always was and will be.

I TRUDGED THROUGH THE Hatchery in a daze, sweeping around the periphery to stay out of the way. The keepers were arguing and shouting about something, but I didn't pretend to pay attention.

Didn't matter how many times I forced myself to think about my newly discovered magic, and the horrible things I had to do to make it surface, my thoughts returned to Dominic and that kiss.

Was every word out of his mouth a lie? Did he truly hate his father, or was I dancing on the puppet strings of two master manipulators?

No. I saw Reyna's memories for myself. That hatred is real and deserved.

But just because he doesn't love his father, doesn't mean he loves me.

I dropped the broom and walked out. I couldn't deal with this. I couldn't think.

I was spending the rest of my Hatchery shift hiding in the goat pen. Purring mother dragons with their happy chirping babies was not the sweet sight it usually was. My mood was better suited to cowering creatures waiting for the slaughter.

I'll cheer them up with a few treats, I thought, digging through the fruit bin and pulling out a bunch of brown bananas.

I carried them out to the pen, already seeing them come alive as they carefully trotted out of the corner and sniffed the air for treats. I would ask again for the pen to be moved farther away from the Hatchery. It wasn't right to live your whole life in terror of a horrible ending. The least they could do is let the cute little trotters live out their short days in peace.

"Hey, guys. How are you—?"

The bananas slipped through numb fingers.

Ur rested on a mound of hay—a still, silent ship in a sea of death.

I clapped my hands over my mouth, eyes bugging. They were all dead. Every single goat in the pen lay unmoving. You could almost believe they were sleeping for their closed eyes and unbroken skin.

Ur hadn't eaten any, but she didn't need to in order to slaughter them.

"Oh, Ur, no," I cried. "How did you get out here?"

She popped up, making me shoot back. To my surprise, she started chirping and happily bouncing up and down.

"Wow. Who knew carnage was what it took to brighten your day?" I eased closer, looking for something that would help me get her back inside without touching her. "What's got you so happy, baby? Is it nice to be outside and—?"

Boom!

The ground rumbled, popping me off my feet. I hit my knees hard and grabbed the pen gate to stop me from falling on my face. Hissing in pain, a deep, heated growl sounded from behind me.

"No," I whispered. "Please, no."

I flipped over, coming face to face with Tizor. Anger so lit his eyes, they tinged red.

Every muscle in my body went rigid while a happy Ur greeted her father.

What was Tizor thinking? What would he do? I'd been a part of the dragonkin hive mind and all its glory. I knew the intelligence and understanding that lived in Tizor.

He could see I wasn't harming his baby, and likely knew I had no reason to put her in a goat pen. But he also knew I was one of the keepers who ignored his obvious rage at being separated from his mate and offspring. Was he thinking he had to stop me before I brought her back in and out of his reach again?

"No, Tizor," I said, keeping my tone soft and soothing. "I mean no harm to you or Ur."

He stalked closer, lowering his head the way I'd only seen Reyna do when she was narrowing in on a kill. Green, vibrant grass browned and withered away under his paws.

I clenched my teeth, scream bleeding through. My back pressed into wooden splinters. I had nowhere to go.

"Please, stop! I'll leave, okay? I won't take her. She's your baby. I'm sorry we kept you apart, but she's with you now. She'll stay with you!"

"Arggh!"

Screaming, I clutched my ears, heart leaping into my throat and choking me. I didn't know Tizor could roar. In the times he tried to break into the Hatchery, he didn't utter a sound. What did it mean for me that he was finally sounding the war cry?

"No, no, no. Tizor, stop!"

It didn't matter if I was likely to survive his death touch. Tizor's magic was the least frightening of his abilities. His claws and razor teeth would easily deliver death in his magic's place.

"Ur," I shouted. "Go to your sire, Ur. Ur, hurry!"

The little dragon clawed at the gate behind me, scrabbling to obey, and climb up and over to her father.

Tizor's growls grew more menacing. I was in the way.

I smacked the gate blindly feeling for the latch. Grabbing it, I yanked it free and opened—

Tizor reared back. Five-foot-long razor-tipped claws slashed the air, coming for me.

I froze to my spot, throwing my hands over my eyes. There was nowhere to run or another plea to scream. This was it.

"Ains!"

A hard force slammed into me. I tumbled over the ground, escaping a rain of jagged, wooden remains as Tizor tore the pen apart, freeing his excited babe.

My knee struck the earth hard. Something broke, ripping a howl from my throat, then a gurgle when a shoulder slammed into it.

We came to a blessed, tangled, painful halt fifteen feet away from Tizor and Ur.

Vision spinning, I strained to see the face of my rescuer. Memories of a small scar cutting through his beard tormented me. It couldn't be him. Why did my mind insist on torturing me with phantoms from my past?

"Mother Zaeah, thank you for—" My sight cleared. "Velez?"

That bright, perfect, all-too-him smile split his face. "Yeah, it's me, Pain-in-the-Ains. You get yourself in a lot of messes, but pissing off a death dragon? That deserves the *biggest of all fuckups* award."

"Ahh!" I screamed, shock taking away any kind of normal greeting.

It was him. Velez was here. On top of me. Smiling at me. Saving me. Teasing me.

Following me.

"You!"

He shrugged. "Me."

"But— But— I saw you. I saw you outside the kitchens and in the street. I knew it was you!"

"You shouldn't've but I told them you were too good. Eyes in the back of your head, you. That's why you're the best thief I know."

"If only I fucking knew you!" I shoved him and immediately regretted it. Pain racked my ruined knee.

I rocked back, clutching my leg and breathing through the pain. "I don't understand this," I tried again. "Where have you been? Why haven't you come to see us in all this time? Why have you been stalking me like a freak?"

"I can't explain it all right now, Ains. You're figuring out what your magic is, that's good. I won't let you die before you do."

"That's not a good answer. What do you know about my plums?"

"What?"

"You tell the king I'm shitting in his outhouse. He can have a bucket of cantaloupes for dinner."

"Ainsley, what the fuck are you talking about?"

My head lolled—black spots danced around his face.

I fell over.

"Ainsley? Ainsley?!"

His voice reached me from far away and got farther still.

"Ains— Oh no. You've got a cut on your arm. The beast got you... do something... going to be..."

I fell and kept falling, sinking into darkness.

Chapter Twenty-One

"Rider Ainsley? Ainsley?"

I peeled an eyelid open, making out the blurry outline of a figure. *Velez?*

"Ainsley, I need you to get up now. It's important."

"Wha...?" Cotton stuffed my mouth. "Was's going on?"

"Recruit, there was a terrible mistake and one of the babies escaped the Hatchery. You were attacked by—"

"Tizor!"

I flew up, hand swinging to brace myself.

"Be careful!" Healer Elora sprung away, surprising me. "I'm sorry. I didn't mean to react so harshly."

"What's wrong?" I looked myself all over, not missing the bandage on my forearm. "Did something happen to me?"

"Tizor infected you with his death power. The tiniest scratch or it would've killed you instantly. Or not," she said, eyeing me. "The staff have been informed of your newly discovered magics. If you've recovered because you made his magic yours, then it is inside you now." The healer pointed. "I will need you to pick up that plant. You do not leave here until I'm sure your touch doesn't spell death."

"But I..."

The only thing on my mind was Velez. Where did he go? Was he close by? Watching me? Why was he watching me in the first place? Where had he been all this time?

"But what?"

I shook myself. "But I don't feel anything. I don't have any death magic in me."

"Touch the plant."

Sighing, I reached over and touched the delicate orchid petals. Nothing happened.

"See?"

Her lips thinned. "We will check every hour on the hour until I'm satisfied. Get some rest."

I watched her go—confused. Was it me or did her presence leave a distinct chill in the air? All the other times we met, Healer Elora had been nothing but kind. Did I do something to offend her?

"Ainsley." Dominic rushed in, hurrying to my side.

My face, eyes, and feelings shut down. Suddenly I remembered that being attacked by Tizor was not the worst thing that happened to me that day.

"Are you okay? I just got word of what happened." The mattress dipped under his weight. "How? A hatchling has never gotten out before."

I shrugged, inching away as far as I could go without falling off the bed. "Who knows? Maybe someone got tired of him attacking the Hatchery every day, and let one of his babies out to see him. The rule to keep them separate is stupid to begin with, but fitting for Golden City. In this place, you hurt others just because you can."

"The reason the rule was made was to stop you ending up in this bed. Dragon fathers are too protective and territorial. Unlike the mothers, they'll attack unprovoked. This should not have happened, Ainsley." He laid his hand over mine. "I'm sorry it did."

Visions of him kissing Nuala invaded my mind. I pulled away. "Why are you here? I'm fine."

"I came to make sure of that," he said, treating me to that smile. "Also to say I thought about what you said. You're right, Ainsley. The past is the past."

His smile faded, replaced with a deep, mournful gaze. "If I hadn't thought you were a dream, I would not have told you all those things about Roderick and my mother. At least not as much as I did. It's painful, embarrassing, and humiliating to have lived through it, let alone see the pity in people's eyes when I share it.

"I have no doubt that your life was difficult. Maybe you did things you weren't proud of. Stuff you simply want to forget. I more than anyone should understand that." He bent, pressing the lightest kiss to my lips. "Tell me when you're ready. Or don't. Your past doesn't matter to me. As long as I have your future."

I clapped. Slow, then picking up the pace as his brows furrowed. "Nice. Well done, Roark. Stellar performance as always."

"What? What are you talking about?"

"I'm talking about that load of cow dung that fell out of your mouth."

He half rose from the bed. "Ainsley, I—"

"No," I snapped, holding up a hand. "You had your turn. Now you listen. I'm done with the pretty lies you spin to keep me stupid and off-balance. What is wrong with you that you're incapable of being honest?"

"I am being honest." I had to give it to him. He faked confusion remarkably well. "I'm giving you what you asked for. Why are you upset?"

"Because you're not giving me what I asked for. You're telling me what I want to hear so that nothing stops me from signing that marriage contract. A contract you don't even want!" Suddenly, I was shouting. "You don't truly want to marry me. You're only doing it to get the throne. Fine. But why lie! Why say all those sweet, sexy things when you can't stand me?"

Dominic threw out his hands. "I have no idea what you're talking about! True, I'm not all that fond of you right now, but by now, I find your constant unpredictable mood swings kind of cute when they're not fucking irritating! I haven't lied to you, Ainsley! Why won't you believe it?"

"Because lying is all you know how to do, Roark. You're a fake. A wooden doll filled with magic and pointed at the throne, you stomp over anyone and anything that gets in your way."

"Why are you saying this to me? Where is this coming from?"

"Think back to what you did today and who you did it with. Then try to play innocent."

His face didn't change. "I didn't do anything with anyone, Ainsley. I have no idea what you're talking about."

"You didn't betray me today?" I wasn't truly asking.

"No."

I balled my fists, shaking from more than the aftereffects of Tizor's scratch. "Come clean, Dominic. Do it on your own, and I'll forgive you. We can move on into the future like we promised."

"Ainsley," he said, leaning over the bed. "Hear me clearly. Whatever you think, or whatever someone told you is the lie. I did not betray you. I did nothing wrong. You couldn't trust me before. You can now.

"I promise."

I searched his eyes. "Get out."

"What? Ainsley—"

"I don't want to hear it," I cried, forcing him back. "I don't want to see you. I don't want to talk to you! Go back to your father and tell him to draw up the contract that says after we make an heir, we'll have nothing to do with each other. We won't even live in the same province."

"Why are you saying this! I don't want that. Neither do you!"

"No, what I don't want is you!"

Dominic reeled back. In the split of a second, something else broke through his surprise.

Pain.

Don't fall for it, a voice scolded. *He says and does anything to reel you in and keep you dancing to his tune. He dares to act like you're the one hurting him when hours ago he was kissing another woman, and wishing he could be with her.*

"Get away from m-me, Dominic." I prayed he didn't hear my voice crack. "Before I back out of the whole plan. You and I are nothing to each other from now on. No... we were always nothing to each other."

Dominic backed away. "Fine. You know what? Fuck this. It's my fault for trying to turn a dream into reality."

Dominic shook the building slamming the doors. I burst into tears the second he was gone.

He said he'd wait so long to betray me, he'd forget. I guess his memory only lasted a day.

"I'M SORRY, AINSLEY. Rosaleen hasn't been by."

"But doesn't she always come to see you on this day?"

"She does unless her aunt is causing trouble," said Mathias, Rosaleen's Heart Reader. "She tries to force me to choose another girl by pulling stunts like this—forcing Rosaleen not to show up on our days."

"That does sound like her," I muttered. "Thanks anyway. I'll try again tomorrow."

Mathias closed the door without a goodbye. Not surprising since he only talked to and tolerated me because Rosaleen willed it. Even in her absence, Mathias obeyed her wishes and treated the peasant with respect because he refused to do anything that'd upset her.

What did I have to do to inspire such devotion? Were my skills in bed to blame? I didn't have much experience with men. I thought Dominic enjoyed our time together in the dream, but maybe my clumsy moves showed him a future of dissatisfaction. He stole away for one last time with Nuala to get him through the coming tumblings with me.

The reason doesn't matter. All that matters is I was right all along. I can't trust him.

I wandered through the city streets, taking my time. Ending any hope of a happy, loving marriage with Dominic hurt more than I imagined it would. I don't know when it happened, but I started to feel something for him after pinning his broken body to the floor, demanding what I wanted from him, and Dominic praising me for it. I wanted it for a lifetime—this man telling me how wonderful, strong, and fierce I was simply for existing.

I wanted his pretty words to be real, and like a fool, I convinced myself they were enough to fall for him. Again.

I stopped outside a tavern and waited, hoping Velez might appear. I had so much I needed to tell him, and he had so much advice to give me.

Minutes bled into hours while I waited. Eventually, I gave up and returned back to the barracks.

Maili, Ormr, and Poet weren't there. Good guess was they were in Barrack *B*, getting drunk, remembering the recruits who were cut, and practicing to make sure they weren't next.

Dominic propped up on his bed, reading as usual. He didn't lift his head or acknowledge my existence in any way.

"Look who's returned." Keir wandered over from his bed. The other side of the room wasn't far enough away from him. "Where is it you go every night, Boreen? Is it the place where you practice forbidden magics? Or the place where you bed the guy that does it for you?"

"You will not give that rumor life." I couldn't help a glance at Dominic. You would've thought he was alone in the room for all the attention he paid the gathering crowd. "If Drake or the king general suspected me of dabbling in forbidden magic, I wouldn't be here."

"No one believes this story of sudden, mystery magic that you knew nothing about. One second you're magicless, the next you're wielding power no one has ever heard of," he said, eyes narrowing. "Something stinks like shit, and it's you."

"You're confused. It's you and your jealousy that stinks like shit. You came in here thinking you were special with your illusion magic and shadow dragon, but no one cares. You can't stand that someone is getting all the attention you thought you deserved. It's pathetic to be honest."

"How dare you speak to me like that, bitch?" he spat. "Being another one of these unnatural magic freaks doesn't make you special. If we were in the right place, you'd be hauled away and studied. If we were in a better place, you'd be killed for the curse you are. You—"

"Enough!" Dominic barked. "All of you shut up and go to bed. I'm trying to read."

The others dispersed quickly. Only Keir hung back, a look on his face like he wasn't close to done.

"Got something you need to say, Stryker?"

"No," Keir said, suddenly straightening with a smile. "Enjoy your book, Dom. Die in your sleep, bitch."

"Charming," I gritted at his back.

I dropped on my bed, casting a glance over Dominic. He had returned to his book.

"You didn't have to step in," I said. "I can take care of myself."

"Nothing to do with you." Dominic didn't look up.

I flicked past him to Nuala. She was climbing into her bed with nothing but her breastband and underclothes on. Her eyes were clear and she hummed a merry-sounding tune. She didn't look like someone whose heart was broken only hours before.

My fists balled. "About our lessons, I'm asking someone else to teach me."

"Good idea," he said, snapping his book shut. He swung his legs off the bed and reached in his bedside drawer. "You'll want to learn from someone you trust. Here."

I jumped when he tossed something on my bed.

"See if your new instructor wants that. Or throw it out," he said, walking off. "I've got no use for it."

Confused, I picked up the black leather folio and flipped through it. The pages wrinkled in my grip.

It was the alphabet.

At the top of each page a character, drawn examples of things starting with that character, short words, and lines for me to practice. I slid off the bed, sinking onto the floor as I traced a beautiful and familiar design. On my hip the swirling golden tattoos formed a particular design that could've been a flower or a dancing lady.

Dominic and I argued/giggled over it while we were in the dream, holding each other in the sweet-scented pool.

He remembered it so well after only seeing it once?

If I'd gotten this that morning, I'd have made a joke about his stalking me. Holding it then made me want to cry.

"Ainsley?"

I looked up as Keely came to join me.

"Hey. Are you okay?"

My hand flew to my eyes. Was I crying already? "I'm fine. Why?"

She scoffed. "That fucking asshole Keir. I can't believe he said all those awful things to you. What's wrong with that guy?"

"I have no idea. I want to say it's grief, but he hated me long before his father was killed."

"I hope he didn't scare you with that stuff about what they do to unique mages."

"None of it is true, is it?"

Keely dropped her gaze. "No… and yes. It's not like it was. Fire, water, air, earth. All magics are descended from the elements, and that's what everyone knew. When the first few unique mages appeared, it was assumed they were either cursed or performed forbidden magics. They simply didn't know how to make sense of a mage who could control time or speak to the dead. So they experimented on or killed them."

She shook her head. "That's not allowed these days. More and more unique mages are born every year—royal, commoner, and noble alike. It's only in certain parts of the kingdom that you hear about… things being done to them."

Or them being sought out and bound to a king general determined to use their unique magics to stay in power.

"But we don't have to worry about that anymore. Thanks to you."

My brows snapped together. "Thanks to me?"

"Yeah," she said, dropping her voice but not her excitement. "It was amazing enough having a queen who's magicless, but a unique mage for a queen? You'll change everything. Free us from the fodder battalions, and in those backward awful places, you'll save lives." She squeezed my arm. "Adalinda is changing, Ainsley. It needs new leaders to take us to the place we're meant to go. Stuffy, one-hundred-year-old royals who think new is another name for hemorrhoid, aren't the ones to do it. You are."

I would've laughed at her joke, if not for the way it ended. "Keely, about that. There's something you need to know—"

"Ooh, what's this?" She plucked the folio from me. "Wow."

"It's nothing," I blurted.

"It's not nothing. I didn't know you were an artist too. Pretty, talented, and a way with mud. You're everyone's dream."

"Stop it," I said, bumping her shoulder. "I'm not that great. For one because I didn't draw this. I just— It was on Ormr's bed. I'm going to put it back."

"Oh, okay." She kept flipping through, making my chest tighten. I couldn't explain it, but I wanted it back. Needed her to stop pawing the delicate parchment with indelicate fingers. "Whoever did this must really like Ormr."

I stiffened. "Why would you say that?"

"These drawings took a long time. Weeks."

"No, not weeks." I ordered Dominic to teach me to read the other day. "Only a couple days or so."

She arched a brow. "Ah, no. Trust me. My younger brother likes to draw too, and just one of these pages would take him all day to get right— Goodness, look at this one," she said, pointing to the same depiction of the golden tattoo. "Beautiful."

"It is beautiful," I said softly. "The perfect gift."

"I don't know about that. Looks like a children's reading workbook. It's a weird gift for a grown person, but still, great drawings." She rose up and dropped my folio on their bed. "Anyway, do you want to grab something to eat from the mess hall? My aunt works in the kitchens and always makes and saves me dessert, even though Drake banned it and everything that makes us happy."

"You had me at eat."

I took off after her, then stopped. "Oops, I forgot something. I'll meet you outside."

Jogging back, I waited until the door closed, then snatched my gift back. I tucked it safely under my mattress, feeling that urge to cry come back even as I shook my head.

This folio wasn't a labor of love by a guy who secretly liked me and always did. Over the last few weeks while he was working on it, he was also working on bringing about my death. Dominic clearly drew the folio for Orla.

But what would it have done to my silly, unloved heart if I hadn't seen him with Nuala, and he presented me with this gift during our first lesson?

I would've been so touched. My chest filled to bursting with how much he cared about me.

Everything with Dominic Roark was a lie or manipulation. I would keep the folio so I never forgot that.

I PICKED AT MY BREAKFAST, barely listening to my friends' conversation.

Nuala whispered in Dominic's ear. He burst out laughing. Not a polite chuckle. But a belly-bouncing, raucous laugh that he had to smother.

Slipping her arm through his, she dropped her head on his shoulder—and kept it there.

"Ainsley? Ainsley, are you okay?"

"What?" I forced away from Nuala and Dominic. "I'm okay. Why wouldn't I be okay?"

"Because," Maili said, looking down. "There's food in front of you and you're not eating it. There's not only something wrong with you, but I think you might be dying."

"Ha ha." I pried my fingers off my fork. The painful lines on my palm showed how hard I strangled it. "I was thinking about special talents. There has to be a less gruesome violent and traumatic way for me to use my power, but Drake doesn't seem all that committed to helping me find it."

"The man is disturbingly comfortable shooting you with silver arrows," Poet muttered. "I wonder why he won't let you work with Reyna. You channeled her fire from a distance before. If you keep working on it, I bet you can do it again."

"Why do you need to train at all?" Maili asked. "We know by now that your magic always works to save your life. When a Druk attacks you, they'll strike the death blow and then you'll turn their magic on them and rip their black, scaly heart from their chest. You can and will kill Druks. Isn't that all that matters?"

"Maili does have a point," Ormr put in. "He wants to train you to use it at will. Whenever you want to, or always when you need to. Both are equally good."

"You should tell him you're not going along with his type of *training* anymore," Maili said. "You just learned you have this magic. You need time to learn more about it and how it works. Getting killed five times a day isn't how to do it."

I inclined my head. "I was thinking—"

Another bout of laughter cut me off. Nuala clung to Dominic—the two of them cracking up like someone made a joke about fate bringing the two most terrible people in the world together.

Is that why her tears have dried up? Dominic told her that she couldn't be his wife, but the position was open to be his mistress.

I shot up. I didn't have control of my body or I would've stopped myself ripping Nuala off him and hauling Dominic out of the chair.

"Hey!"

"Shut up! I don't have anything to say to you, Nuala. You don't want that to change."

Dominic glanced lazily at my grip strangling his collar. "Problem, Princess?"

"What the fuck do you think? Or are you playing innocent again?"

I dragged him to the far wall. He didn't fight me.

"Why is it so impossible for you to tell me the truth?" It was difficult not to scream. "First you don't love Nuala, then you do. You're giving me body chains and saying you were waiting for me, then you're practically humping Nuala on the breakfast table! Make up your fucking mind!"

He shrugged. "I have no idea what you're talking about."

"Don't give me that. I sat there and watched you—"

"—do nothing. I was doing absolutely nothing, but you didn't let that stop you from inventing a reason to hate me. You know, this is getting boring, Princess," he hissed, putting his face in mine. "The marriage contract. The abdication. None of it was my idea. It was yours. I gave you what you asked for, and you've been punishing me for it ever since. Fuck me if I know why. You and I were doing just fine as enemies."

I rocked back. "Just fine as enemies." My voice was a croak. "Really? So what are you saying, Dominic? You wish you succeeded the other day... and killed me?"

"I—"

"What is this?" spoke the very last voice I wanted to hear. "Why does it look like you two are fighting?"

"Nuala," Dominic said sharply. "Not now."

"Why not now? Because the great and terrifying Ainsley Boreen might have something to say to me? Oooh, so scary." Laughter went up around the mess hall. She was not speaking quietly. "What does she have to be angry about in the first place? She's the one dangling the promise of giving up the throne in exchange for money and exclusive rights to your cock. There are womb-raiding Druks with more honor than you!"

"Give up the throne?" Maili rose from her seat. "What are you talking about?"

"Didn't she tell you?" Nuala laughed—it wasn't a pleasant sound. "Of course she didn't. Wouldn't do for the loyalists to find out their precious heir is only in it for herself. Not before the ink dries on the marriage contract."

"Nuala," Dominic barked.

She wouldn't be stopped. "Ainsley is abdicating the throne for her and the entire Boreen line. All so she can marry Dominic and have him to herself. All of you pathetic little aberrants who thought she flew in to save you from your sad, cursed lives"—she looked right at Keely—"should take a look at the real Ainsley.

"The only thing she wants is Dominic. From stealing his dragon to force her way into rider training, then blackmailing him with the throne. She's nothing but an obsessed freak who'll stop at nothing, and betray everyone, to get what she wants.

"Right, Dominic?"

Every eye in the room turned to him. Including mine.

He couldn't let her get away with twisting the truth into her own evil version of events. I couldn't let myself think of why Dominic told her the truth about everything when we agreed to keep silent until the contract was witnessed and signed.

Wide, filling eyes beseeched him. My stomach did flips, pushing bile up my throat that choked me. *Say something. Tell them she's lying, Dominic. We, the both of us, agreed to this because it's what's best for Adalinda. We both want a better future for our people, and I'm giving up everything so that I don't lose what's important on the way.*

"I have no idea what you're talking about, Nu."

My heart soared.

"Abdication? Marriage contract?" He laughed. "You think I'm going to marry her? Don't be ridiculous."

Dominic sidestepped me, and walked away.

Rage lit in my soul. "Don't leave without this, Roark!" I ripped the body chain off and threw it at the back of his head.

He didn't so much as slow his stride.

I watched him go—humiliation leadening my bones. Profound silence pounded my eardrums

Stiffly, I turned tail, and ran. A figure crossed my path and I slammed into a hard body.

"Whoa. Ainsley? I'm sorry, I didn't mean to get in your way."

Apologizing when he'd done nothing wrong. "Awnan."

"Are you okay?" he asked, setting me back on my feet.

"I'm okay. I just need to get out of here."

"Let me help you."

Awnan grasped my waist and helped me out past the stares and snickers. I couldn't begin to guess what people were thinking. Nuala announced to the entire recruit class that I wanted Dominic Roark by any means necessary. And he replied that he wanted anyone but me.

Humiliating wasn't close to the right word to describe the burning, chest-crushing shame I felt. Did I imagine all the sweet things he said and did to me in the dream? Was him getting down on his knees and giving me that chain just a game? How besotted could he make this girl with the love-men-who-want-me-dead kink?

"I'm assuming you're not up for Phiala yelling and calling you a shithead right now."

"You assume right."

Awnan led me in the opposite direction of magical accuracy. "I'm so sorry that happened. Why would Nuala make up those lies?"

"A lot of liars around here," I replied flatly. "Lies are your first language. Adalindian is the second."

"Not mine. I'd never lie to you."

"Or talk to me," I snapped. I was feeling bitter and he was the only one around. "You haven't said two words to me since the party. Why are you helping me now?"

"I'm sorry. I wanted to, but Dominic kicked my ass for trying to court you. I couldn't risk his wrath because... it wasn't worth it when you'd never be with a guy like me anyway."

"What? Why would you say that?"

"Are you kidding? You're you, and I'm me. I was amazed you spoke to me and my friends that night, so I fooled myself into thinking I had a chance. Dominic was kind enough to wake me up from that dream."

Speaking of dreams and that night made my jaw clench. "I don't know why Dominic had that break from reality and tricked himself into thinking he decides who courts me, but I promise you nothing he said or did reflected how I felt. I did want to go with you that night."

"If you mean it, then come with us to the Yellow Tail Firesday night." He smiled sweet and nervous. "You're a unique mage like us. You should meet the others in the city." Awnan must've seen the hesitation on my face. "I promise it'll be fun. We'll drink, we'll bet, we'll play, we'll relax. No pressure, and no courting if you're not ready."

We walked into the barracks, ending Dominic and Nuala's conversation midsentence. Dominic stepped back from her, as if that half-a-foot distance made a difference to how close together they were standing.

Fists balling, I said out and clear, "I am ready, Awnan. I'd love to go out with you."

Chapter Twenty-Two

Firesday arrived, bringing an end to the longest week of my life. Dominic and I didn't speak one word to each other since that fateful day in the mess hall. He ignored me, and I ignored him. Honestly, there was no time to think about the lying cheat with how busy our instructors kept me.

Roan kept to his word and made me spar with Keir every day. With rage blinding his movements and unpredictability leading mine, I lost as many matches as I won, but with both motives coming head-to-head, I walked away limping, bleeding, or needing a trip to the hospital wing every time.

Dominic stopped doing my reports for me. I practiced with the folio he gave me every day, but one didn't learn to read and write an entire language in a couple weeks. I had no choice but to get my unwilling instructor, Broden, to help me complete them. Needless to say, the quality dropped so much, Major Sorrel pulled me aside to ask if I was sick, and needed rest.

It wasn't much better in teamwork. Kinryu granted me the top eight rank because I technically fulfilled the requirement, but he made it clear if I ever did anything so reckless again, he'd make me run around the city barrier; every day; rain, shine, or snow; lap after lap until I vomited. I wasn't interested in testing him, so I spent every lesson practicing with my bow and arrow. I had the burning and bleeding blisters to prove it.

But none of that compared to my magic lessons. Phiala's determination to punish me for lying about being magicless resulted in her following Drake's lead, and *killing* me as often as suited her.

While Drake had moved on from slinging lances at me, and paired me up against other recruits—sometimes four against one. He wanted to know if what I did in that basement room was a fluke, or if I was naturally able to wield others' magic with mastery—even multiple magics at one time. It was beginning to feel less like training, and more like I was being... experimented on.

Suggesting such a thing wasn't wise though, because I said as much to Commandant Drake, and he gave me twenty demerits on the spot for questioning his integrity. His only goal was to train elite warriors who'd turn the tide in the war against Druks. If I wasn't prepared to be one of them, I only had to say and he'd cut me.

By the grace of Tenille, Calthoon, Parthelan, Mother Zaeah, and all the deities I begged to help me get through the week, I somehow made it to Firesday.

Carlow, Kane, Keely, Flynn, and Awnan waited for me inside the gate. Together we left for the tavern.

"I'm excited you're joining us tonight." Keely wrapped around my arm. "The Yellow Tail is the best place in the world for mages like us."

"We can eat, drink, fuck, and use our magic without judgment," Carlow threw in. "The place was started by a prophetic mage."

"Prophetic?"

"Has visions of the future."

My eyes bugged. "You're kidding. Such magic can't be real."

"You're gonna be saying that a lot tonight," Kane teased. "Believe us, her powers are real. Lemomi's from a small town in Hyelong. She made her coin from card games and betting. Knowing the outcome of every hand goes a long way."

"She made enough to buy an old tavern in Golden City, and turned it into a sanctuary for unique mages," Keely finished. "I promise you'll love it."

"I know I will. Sounds amazing."

By chance we passed by Mathias's home. I'd gone back to ask after Rosaleen every night, flouting the rule that recruits could only leave the citadel on off days. Each time, Mathias told me she hadn't been by.

I wondered at the twisted games her aunt was playing now. It was ridiculous to me that she dared to resent Rosaleen for burdening her all those years. The woman was the furthest thing from a mother figure, and did less than the bare minimum to care for her. Most days, Rosaleen was in the orphanage right next to me—begging food and clothes off Sister Aven because her aunt had disappeared for weeks with another married beau.

What chore or punishment has she thought up now that's keeping you away from Golden City, and your wealthiest companion? For someone who claims you're a burden, she does everything in her power to keep you under her thumb.

I forced myself to continue walking. I'd come back after the pub, and check to see if she was there. If she wasn't, I'd break our rule and go to see her in Ossian.

Rosaleen warned me about revealing any details about my life before the Royal Riders. For what I was going to do and the enemies I would make, the last thing I should do is lead the king general to the people I cared about most. After discovering the kind of man he truly was, I accepted that as the best and wisest advice she ever gave me.

But things were different now. Despite everything that happened between me and Dominic, I still planned to abdicate and marry him. King General Roark was close to securing his place on the throne for good, he had no reason to go after Rosaleen or my borrowed family.

The promise of that lifted my spirits during the hellish week. Finally, I would see the little ones with their new clothes, toys, and shoes. I'd get to hear Sister Aven's many fears about where I'd gone, and tell her the true and better story. Best of all, I'd tell them to pack their things because we were moving to Nithe Palace—where we'd worry for nothing for the rest of our days. Rosaleen's aunt would get the same special greeting, albeit with more profanity and slights to her shitty character.

I smothered a laugh, imagining dear Aunt Uma's face when I called her a saggy-titted troll with a rotted soul and clinging stench from her dead teeth. It'd be just as satisfying as making her watch while Rosaleen packed her bags, and set off to Nithe with me.

"What's so funny?" Kane asked.

I grinned. "Revenge."

"Against Keir?" Keely cringed. "That guy really has it in for you. I swear he's not training. He's trying to kill you."

"Why is it you can see it, but Roan does not?" I shook my head. "It's even worse that I'm fairly sure if Keir kills me without using magic, I'll stay dead. Every day, he tries to finish the job."

Keely shivered. "He frightens me. No one should be filled with that much hate."

"Ainsley, look." Flynn stuck his head through us and threw his arms around our shoulders. "We're here."

I don't know what I expected of the place they basically described as unique mage paradise, but a normal-looking pub built out of clover-green-painted wood, an askew sign, and blacked-out windows wasn't it.

A rush of breeze tickled my neck, and I turned my head, searching the passing mages. I was looking for Velez. Where had he gone?

Why did he disappear, reappear whole and healthy, then vanish again? Why was my life nothing but unanswered questions and mysteries?

Sighing, I ducked through the curtain, stepping inside the famous Yellow Tail. A low whistle escaped my lips and was swallowed by the noise.

I walked into a case of "better on the inside than on the outside." Actually as I thought about it, it made perfect sense that the owner didn't go out of her way to make the Yellow Tail too inviting. The pub was for unique mages only, and there were so many more of them than I anticipated.

Flickering lanterns cast down on crowded tables and occupied stools. Plastered all over the walls were faded wanted posters and hooks for hanging plants. Those plants reached their vines and stems through the room, picking up trash, refilling mugs, and carrying drinks to their tables. In the midst of their work, the reason for the pushed-back tables skipped and threw themselves around the makeshift dance floor—merry and free the way you only were among friends.

It was perfect. Not the intimidating exclusive place that I imagined, but a fun pub where magic flowed as freely as the drinks.

Flynn towed us to the stone bar top and waved down a woman in a low-cut sheer top and short brown leather skirt.

"Flynn, baby. Who'd you bring me?"

"Lemomi, this is Ainsley. Ainsley, this is Lemomi."

Lemomi wasn't what I was expecting either. Fawn skin paled from working nights and sleeping through the day. Black locks streaked with gray shorn close to her scalp, and she had the smooth, unblemished skin of someone who didn't spend their life riding dragons or fighting Druks. A pleasant and pretty face gifted us an equally pleasant smile. But none of that is what shocked me.

Lemomi was covered in tattoos. A strange thing for someone also covered in tattoos to notice, but her revealing outfit gave me the chance to get a closer look, and none of hers made sense.

One was a mutt with dragon wings. She had a tattoo on her shoulder of a broom. That was it. A plain and normal broom. Riding her cleavage she chose the face of a man midsneeze. Crawling up her elbow was a lizard wearing boots. Ranging from the bizarre to the painfully normal, I wondered what about these depictions screamed "ink on my body for life."

"Looking at my tattoos?"

"Yes," I said easily. "Why do you have an empty ale mug under your ear? If you don't mind me asking."

"I don't mind at all." Lemomi poured a drink and set it on the bar top. A flower-tipped vine appeared out of nowhere and carried it away. "I see into the future, but my visions are confusing. Sometimes it's a quick flash of a mug of ale tipping over before a man in black attacks me." She held out her hands. "These are all hints and reminders of futures that haven't come true yet."

Lemomi pointed to the booted lizard. "This one I pray never does."

"Wow. I can't imagine such amazing magic."

"Not amazing." She winked. "Unique. What's yours?"

"It's... thief magic. When I'm in trouble, I steal the magic around me and use it to get out of trouble."

Lemomi howled. "Thief magic? Now that's a new one. I love it." She slapped the bar. "Now, what can I get you, loves?"

"Two bottles of blackberry wine, Mimi," Awnan said, "and keep them coming. We're going to show Ainsley around."

"Don't include me in that *we*. I'm going downstairs," Carlow said with a wink. "See you down there."

Keely and Awnan led me off, but Kane and Flynn hung back.

"Ahh," Flynn said, exchanging a look with Kane. "We're gonna go with Carlow."

Keely rolled her eyes. "Guys, we came to introduce Ainsley to other mages like her, not to get your dicks wet."

"Who says we can't do both?" Flynn returned, grinning away. The two sped off with the kind of rush men only summoned when headed for sex.

"Do I want to know what goes on downstairs?"

"It *all* goes down downstairs," Keely replied.

Strangely, that was all the explanation I needed.

The three of us sat down in a booth under the staircase. Flickering candles lining the top of the booth, smothered us in a sweet, flowery scent. It wasn't that Lemomi did anything special to the pub, it was that the little she did made the Yellow Tail warm, cozy, and inviting. It felt like the kind of space a family came home to, not a tavern.

I clapped as weaving tendrils brought our bottles and three glasses. Awnan poured us both wine and we toasted.

"Sooo...." I drew out. "Don't keep me in suspense."

Awnan laughed. "How about this? You like a game, so let's play one. You think of the wildest, most impossible magic, and if someone in this room has it, we drink. If you're wrong, you drink. Deal?"

"Put money on that and you damn sure got a deal."

"I like the way you think."

We cracked up. This was what I liked about Awnan. It was so easy with him. From the first time I walked up to him and his friends playing with the golems, we fell into fun and conversation without barbs, doublespeak, tricks, or lies. Why couldn't it be like that with—?

I abruptly cut the thought off. It didn't matter because Dominic and I never built something worth losing. We'd endure training together, then it'd be separate squads, separate provinces, and separate lives. This was best for everyone, so I might as well enjoy my night, because I knew Dominic was off with Nuala enjoying his.

"Okay," I began, rubbing my hands. "If we're doing this, we need cheap, gutter wine—none of this fancy stuff."

Keely popped up and bowed. "Cheap, gutter wine coming right up."

"And the coin," I said, dropping my purse on the table. "We bet five silver ryus each. I've got three right guesses to win it. Three wrong to lose it for good. Then another five."

We slapped palms and shook. Thus began the most fun and strange night of my life.

"Wrong! Drink, drink, drink, drink!"

I laughed as the entire pub took up the chant. Pouring myself another tipple, I drank it down along with any hope there was a unique mage around who could see into the past.

"I like the way she plays," Lemomi called. "Naming opposite magics of the ones she knows. Clever."

"Hnot cleverer... enough," Awnan slurred, smacking the table. "Alright, Princess. Two more ta lose it fa good!"

I threw out my hands. "Okay, okay, okay..." My tongue was too big for my mouth, but the room wasn't spinning. I was doing good. "Magic that lets you lift this"—I knocked a candle over pointing at it—"with your mind."

"Telekinesis," Keely belted. "Telekinesis, anyone? Step up now."

"Show us, show us, show us." Another chant went up.

I had thirty-five ryus in my corner. Keely and Awnan both had thirty. I was holding my own impressively well, or I should say I was surrounded by the impressive. I'd name a power so outlandish and be forced to give up my coin and drink. Then I'd name another outlandish power and win.

I was beginning to see why King General Roark hunted down and employed unique mages. The ignorant and frightened saw unnatural powers they couldn't explain, and assumed they violated the laws of Tenille. General Roark saw men and women who could erase memories, negate magic, speak to the dead, sense and control the emotions of others, walk through walls, and stop time... and he realized they were his key to staying in power.

Fire mages were a dime a dozen. Earth mages were as common as the rocks you picked up in your shoes. I grew up with half a dozen air mages in the orphanage alone. But someone who could mess with memories, there was no one like that except for the person who once stood by the general's side.

The candle wobbled, dropping a hush over the pub. Suddenly it shot up and flew into a raised palm. "Telekinetic mage," a short girl with long hair and a button nose sang. "At your service."

"Yeah!"

Everyone cheered louder than they needed to, but I was louder still as Keely and Awnan drank. Under the table, Awnan laced his fingers through mine.

"I—I—" I stumbled over my next guess.

Of course. I agreed to come out that night knowing what Awnan expected. Holding my hand was the least of which. It wasn't a big deal to let him. Dominic Roark was no more than a sideshow in my life, and he didn't control what I did, or who I did it with. If I wanted to tumble a cute guy who made me laugh, it'd be no worse than what he was doing with Nuala.

I withdrew my hand, reaching for my mug. I didn't make eye contact with him while I sipped.

"Next guess," I announced, firmly holding on to my glass. "Magic that lets you understand all languages."

"Oooh, that would come in handy. Anyone?" Keely asked. "Anyone?"

I looked around, and received a symphony of headshakes and "nuh-uhs."

"You know what that means…" Keely grinned. "Wrong!"

I accepted my penalty and drank. "Okay—"

"Wait," Awnan cut in. "Why don't we change up the game a little? How about I guess magics that I know are or aren't in this room, and you guess if I'm right or wrong?"

"Sure." I burst into a giggle fit. "Why not?"

"But first." Awnan dug in his pocket. "Keely, could you give this to Kane for me? I know the idiot spent all his coin by now."

Keely claimed another heavy coin purse, and staggered off. Within the foggy depths of my brain, it occurred to me that we were losing the buffer that prevented this from being a courting. I bit my tongue to stop myself from calling her back.

I liked Awnan, but Dervin showed me who my dream man was. Despite him being a great, thumping asshole, Dominic made my pulse race with his grin, and my heart melt with his sweet words.

Awnan didn't.

What I needed was time to smother my feelings for Dominic under cold reality until they died. I didn't need another lover.

I'll tell him so before the night is over.

Awnan signaled the plants for another drink. They carried cool, blessed water to our table.

"Ready?"

I tried for a smile that could've been a grimace. I stopped feeling my face an hour before. "Ready."

"I bet someone in this pub can send their thoughts into people's minds like dragons do through the bond."

"Hmm. No."

"Final answer?" he teased.

"Final answer."

"Is she right, everyone?"

"Yes, no, yes, no," they belted. "Yes!"

"Yes," Awnan cheered. "You're right. I might as well give you all my coin now. You're too good at this."

"I can't believe I'm good at this. Your magics are all so amazing."

I gulped a healthy swig of water. My head began to clear. "Next?"

Sitting up straight, I nodded sharply and nearly knocked off-balance. "Next."

"I bet someone in this pub can secrete a liquid that makes people tell the truth."

"No," I said easily. "Even the thought of that is crazy, and a bit gross. No one is going to drink their rancid truth sweat."

I choked, eyes bugging. Why did I say that? I didn't mean to say it that way.

Awnan smiled. "Wrong. There is someone who makes *rancid truth sweat*. Dazai, introduce yourself."

A dark, curly-haired guy with an impish smile stuck his head through two women. "Hello, Princess. By the way, it's not rancid. I'm told it tastes just like water."

My gaze slid to the glass before me—condensation sliding innocently down the rim and pooling on the surface. It was then I finally noticed, Awnan wasn't slurring anymore. "What the fuck did you do?"

"I'm sorry, Princess, but if you don't mind, I'll be asking the questions." He jerked his head at the crowd. "Fuck off."

Laughing, drunken merriment disappeared from their faces like a candle going out. Most of them melted away, leaving me alone with Awnan, Lemomi, Dazai, and three other people I didn't know, but had hung by our table all night.

"What is this?" I stood up and was shoved back down. "What are you doing!"

"Awnan, hurry up," Dazai hissed. "She didn't drink enough for it to last long."

"Let me out of here!" I rammed the human wall again. "Let me go—!"

"Is it true you're abdicating the throne?"

"Yes, it's true." The words were tumbling out of my mouth and wouldn't be stopped. "I have to. I won't risk my life and the lives of the people I love for a throne I'm not fit to sit on."

Shut up! Stop talking, Ainsley!

"Why aren't you fit to sit on the throne?"

"Because I'm a worthless, orphan peasant who can't read and barely learned to count. Someone who can't spell 'ruling a country' shouldn't do it."

My eyes widened in time with Awnan. *No. Please, no.*

"You're a peasant?" he cried.

"Yes!" I threw myself at them again, and Dazai wrestled me down—pinning me to the seat.

Quicker than anyone could stop me, I grabbed the glasses of truth sweat and flung them across the room.

"Fuck's sake," Awnan belted. "What part of hold her down do you not understand?"

"They understand," I said instantly, "they're just not strong enough to do it."

The look he gave me chilled me to the core. "Are you actually the heir to the House of Boreen, or not?"

"I—I—I..." I bit hard on my lip. Forces I couldn't control pried it up. "I am."

"Is your mother really Queen Kisandra? Where is she?"

"My mother is a—" I clapped my hands over my mouth, smothering the answer into my palm.

"What? What did she say?" Awnan yanked on my wrists. "Help me!"

"She's starting to fight it," Dazai grunted, struggling with my arms. "Hurry up and ask what you need to ask."

"Fuck's sake. Ainsley, do you have a marriage contract with Dominic Roark?"

"Not yet. I will—" I smashed my head on Dazai's nose. He flew back shouting, spurting blood. "—sign it as soon as I can read it," I gritted.

"Oh, there's no need for that." Awnan removed his glasses, and tossed them over his shoulder like nothing. Wetting his hand, he slicked his hair back—replacing the cute, dopey guy I knew with a smirking, darkly handsome stranger. I didn't want to know why he suddenly reminded me of Keir.

"I'm sorry, Princess," he said mockingly, "but we won't wait around for you to learn to read. A wife doesn't need to know how to do so anyway. Now, what were you going to say about your mother?"

My lips didn't move. I realized it a second after Awnan did.

I grabbed a mug, smashed it against the edge, and leaped over the table.

"Rutendo!"

I crashed on the surface—jagged handle skittering out of my hand. A deep, peaceful calm enveloped my mind.

"Why couldn't you have done that earlier!"

"I told you. Two types of magic putting stress on her mind would break it. Do you want us all to be executed for torturing the crown heir?"

Their fighting went in my ear, stirred no reaction or emotion, then filtered out. I lay on the table—content to rest there forever.

"Sit her up."

Hands grasped under my arms and sat me back in the booth. I stared at Awnan unblinkingly.

Irritation wrecked his handsome face. "Can you make her answer my questions? I want to know what she was going to say about Queen Kisandra."

A tall, Nehebkan man with long dreadlocks and a long scar going down his neck, shook his head. He kept tight hold of my hand. "I have control over the body, not the mind. I can only make her repeat the words I say. That won't help you."

Reyna? Can you hear me? Tell me you can hear me!

Awnan cursed. "Fine. This will have to do for now. We've got plenty of time to get the truth out of her." He turned dark, glittering eyes on me. "Hey, Princess, I bet there's someone in this bar who can control others' bodies.

"Yes." He helped himself to half my coin. "Princess, I bet there's someone here who can move people great distances in the blink of an eye.

"Yes." He plucked more off the pile.

"Princess, I bet there are people here who've been waiting for a better life. One where they're not hunted, experimented on, feared, or thrown into the fodder battalion just because their magic is a little different.

"I bet there's someone in here who would do whatever it takes for them to have that life and more." Awnan took it all.

I didn't move. I didn't reply. Deep in my mind, I screamed for help.

"Blink," Rutendo ordered.

I blinked.

"Let's hurry up and do this while Kane and Flynn are keeping Keely busy downstairs."

Lemomi left and returned with parchment and a quill.

"Celebrate, my princess," Awnan said, "for the wedding will be a formality. Upon signing this contract, today will be the day we become husband and wife."

What? What the fuck was this lunatic talking about? Help! I screamed at the pubgoers. *Stop standing there. Do something. Help me!*

"Reyna? My beauty, where are you?"

"Is this really going to work?" asked one of the three that didn't name themselves. "Noble and royal contracts have to be approved by the High Council so that this very thing doesn't happen to those of important birth."

"It will work. There is a member of the council who owes a large debt to my father. That debt is wiped clean with their signature on this paper," Awnan replied. "He will not refuse."

"Truly? Wow, then this is real." Their faces brightened. "We can really do this."

"We are doing it."

"Blink," Rutendo said.

I blinked.

It amazed that I breathed without his command. My body was not interested in doing anything without his say-so.

Awnan began writing, and writing, and writing. I had no idea what terms he was stating in the contract, but I had a feeling they said nothing about regencies, stipends, or the choice in having children and how they're raised being my decision.

"What are you writing?" Rutendo asked, unknowingly answering my internal shouts.

"I wrote what she said. Princess Ainsley claims her throne, but because she's illiterate and uneducated, she leaves ruling Adalinda in the capable hands of her husband, Awnan Elsher. All monies inherited upon claiming the throne to be under my control.

"Her movements are under my control. All decisions for where she lives, her visitors, and her education are up to me. She will bear me five children. More if her body takes to it and she's still comely."

You twisted, miserable, controlling bastard!

"She is to drop out of dragon training effective immediately after the contract is witnessed by the High Council. Her dragon will be put to death."

Deep, freezing horror quieted me, mind and body. I finally stopped breathing.

"Kill her dragon?" Dazai croaked, holding rags to his nose. "You can't do that."

"Well, I can't kill her to break the bond, can I?" Awnan snapped. "I know. Killing a dragon makes me no better than a Druk, but I don't have a choice. On the first day, her dragon almost slaughtered the entire recruit class to protect her. She's too dangerous to have around. The only reason we don't have to worry about her now is because Carlow pretended to go downstairs, and instead went to the Royal Wood and fed the beast a drugged goat."

Those bastards. Tears that wouldn't fall gathered behind my eyes. *Everything. Their friendships. Their support. It was all a lie.*

Lemomi flicked to me. She wasn't grinning like we were at a Calthoon feast anymore. "Mother Zaeah, save us, child, I'm sorry we have to do this. If there were any other way—" She shook her head. "There isn't. I saw the future coming for every unique mage if King General Roark remains in power." She rubbed the booted lizard on her arm. "We have to stop it by any means necessary. One day, I hope you understand."

"Enough," Awnan said. "What else haven't I thought of?"

Dazai flapped a hand. "Write that if any harm befalls you, even if it appears to be an accident, *she* is to be held responsible."

"That's good," he muttered, jotting it down. "Anything else?"

"Shouldn't we write down the laws we want enacted?" asked a nameless one. "Unique mages are superior mages born above the common folk. We're to be given our own province with the right of self-governance. Any attack against us is punishable by death. Half the Golden Guards will be assigned to our province to protect us, and half the palace coffers belong to us.

"We are the next stage in magical evolution. We will not live like peasants. Once a child is found to have unique magic, they're to be taken from their common parents and relocated to our province. Also, bonded unique mages will have their own academy." She gazed at me coldly. "Write that she decrees they go into effect as soon as the contract is witnessed."

"No point, Salena. Laws go through the High Council. They can turn them all down—marriage contract or no. What matters is I'll be the prince consort with the power of the throne backing me, and a gambling-addicted high councilman in my pocket. The laws will go through in time."

"—get out of the way." A commotion hit my ears. "Garvan, what are you doing? Move."

"Go back downstairs, Keely."

"Excuse me? You don't tell me what to do."

"Don't— Argh!"

Crash!

My mind shouted at my head to turn and see, but it didn't respond to the command.

Keely pushed through Dazai and Lemomi. Smiling away, she dropped down next to me and squeezed my shoulder. "Sorry it took so long, guys. Kane and Flynn kept distracting me, then Garvan blocked the door like an idiot. So how's our girl doing?" She saw my coin was gone. "Oh no. I went away for a minute and you lost this badly? Yikes. I'll have to give you tips for the next round."

Their loaded silence quieted even my inside speech. Keely did not know what was happening here.

"What? Mimi, why are you looking at me like that?"

"Keely," Awnan forced through gritted teeth. "You need to go."

"Go? Why?" She straightened her back. "What's going on here? What are you writing?"

He drew the paper back, quickly covering it. "It's nothing."

"It's obviously not nothing or you wouldn't all be acting like freaks right now." She spun on me. "Ainsley, what's he hiding? Hello, Ainsley? Why are you looking at me like that?" She flapped her hand in my face. "You're not blinking."

"Princess, tell her everything's fine," Rutendo blurted.

"Everything's fine."

"What the—? Oh my gods, Rutendo. Are you— Are you using your magic on her?" she shrieked. "Stop it. Stop it now!"

"Keely, will you calm down!" Awnan looked around like one of his accomplices might have a change of heart. "You don't understand what's going on here."

"Then why don't you tell me what's going on here, because unless you're about to say Ainsley asked him to put her under, I'm going to kick his fucking ass."

By all the gods, bless Keely and reward her with the best of fortunes.

Awnan hesitated.

"Speak now, or you're never seeing me naked again."

Awnan's face reddened. "Okay, relax. Here." He handed over the marriage contract. "Before you say anything, this was necessary. Lemomi had a vision that sometime in the future, all unique mages must be reported and registered. Those with magics he finds useful are bound in service to the king general. Those with magics that are too dangerous or useless—"

I knew what he'd say before he finished.

"—are executed."

"No," Keely breathed. "That can't be true. No one would allow it."

"It's true," Lemomi stated. "Again, I don't know when, but a unique mage is going to rise up and wreak havoc on Adalinda. Many people will die. As a result, the survivors will demand King General Roark protect them by stemming the aberrant surge. Those barbaric laws will be the result."

"You see?" Awnan pushed. "We have to stop that from happening."

"Ainsley will stop it from happening! When she takes the throne. You don't have to—to—enslave her," she cried. "This contract is disgusting, Awnan. It's tantamount to rape and imprisonment. I'm ashamed to know anyone who could do this to a woman."

Yes, I would cry, then I would hug Keely so hard her bones would creak.

Awnan wasn't moved. "She refuses to take the throne. We heard it from her own lips. She's going to abdicate, then marry Dominic Roark. She doesn't believe she's worthy to rule because she was raised as a peasant. Her lack of faith in herself will be our downfall."

If I could've reacted, I would've flinched. Why did he say it like that? I wasn't refusing the throne because I didn't believe in myself or care about my people. I had many responsibilities, but I couldn't sacrifice the promises I made for the one thrust upon me. I couldn't rule a country, but I would pass it on to the man who would, and in doing so, I'd save all the children in the orphanage and Rosaleen.

If only the world knew the real Dominic. He may be a lying cheat, but one thing I didn't doubt about him is that he hated his father, and would die in pursuit of undoing his damage to Adalinda.

"I don't care," Keely said. "A woman not doing what you want isn't an excuse to steal her inheritance and make her a sex slave.

You're a monster, Awnan. All of you! This isn't happening." Keely tore the contract to shreds and threw the pieces in Awnan's face.

He lazily flicked parchment off his chin. "You haven't stopped anything. We'll just draw up another one.

"Guys, put her back downstairs."

"Don't you touch me!"

Keely threw out her hands. Threads shot out in every direction. They wrapped around Awnan's throat, secured Lemomi's wrists, and yanked the legs out from under Dazai and Rutendo.

Rutendo hit the ground and his control snapped. Function returned to my body, resounding like a horse kicked my chest.

I gasped—limbs flailing. "Keely!"

"Ainsley, run!"

Keely made a fist, then threw it. Threads lashed around my arms, legs, and waist. I went flying.

Over the heads of the complicit, shouting accomplices, Keely threw me at the front doors. I reached out—palms up. All I had to do was get through, get outside, then run. Run as far and fast as my feet would sprint to Reyna. Those bastards. They'd better pray whatever they fed her wore off fast, or they'd find out what it felt like to be consumed by hellfire.

I'm coming, my beauty. I'm com—

"Ahh!"

The threads snapped. I crashed to the ground, taking three patrons with me. Over their curses and groans, I heard Keely.

"Get the fuck off me! You can't do this, Awnan. It's wrong. You know it's wrong!"

"Get her downstairs!"

Shouts, profanities, the sound of struggle and magic flying. Keely was fighting to free me. I had to get out and fetch the Golden Guards. None of these monsters had to worry about the tragic fate coming for unique mages. They wouldn't be alive to see it.

I crawled over the bodies and shoved on the door. Cool night air hit my cheeks.

My arm flopped on the floor. Jamb swinging shut, it crushed my fingers. I didn't react to move or scream. My body stopped responding.

"Stand."

I stood up.

"Turn and walk back to the booth."

My legs obeyed the commands from Rutendo, not by me. I screamed to run, fight, kick—nothing happened.

I sat down as the door slammed on a shouting Keely and my last hope of this madness ending. No one was coming to help me.

Awnan returned with more parchment, a quill, and a wicked, bleeding scratch over his eye. Wonder of wonders, lovers didn't like it when you revealed yourself to be a controlling, scheming beast who treated women worse than cattle.

Unshed tears blurred my vision as Awnan rewrote the contract with even more vile restrictions and demands over my body, life, future wealth, and station.

Would that be my saving grace? When the gambling high councilman read the contract, he'd know that no one in their right mind would agree to these terms. He'd see that I was forced, and his conscience would win out. He'd warn the king general and accept the reward for saving me.

Even as I thought it, I didn't believe it would happen. Awnan had thought of everything. He knew his plan would succeed, or he wouldn't be so awfully smug.

"Done," he announced. "All there is to do is sign."

"What will you do with her while you wait for the high councilman?" Dazai asked. "No point to any of this if she goes running to the general's son and tells him what we've done."

"Already taken care of," Awnan said, signing the bottom. "I've got a little place for her. Tucked away. She'll stay there until everything's arranged. The wedding, the coronation, her dragon's execution."

Awnan slid the parchment across the table. I fought with everything in me as he forced my fingers around the quill.

"Make her sign."

No, please. I see on your faces that you know this is wrong! The piece of shit could've talked to me, and told me of the future coming for unique mages. Instead he steals my life and body! He's evil and can't be trusted.

He said he had no control over my mind, but for a second, I swore Rutendo heard me. He looked at me and his face changed. I read it clearly.

Guilt.

"I'm sorry, Princess."

"Why are you apologizing?" Awnan demanded. "We're doing this for the good of the country and unique mages everywhere. We will be enslaved, not her."

Rutendo gave no sign that he heard him. "We're doing a terrible thing to you, and I'm ashamed for my part in it. I will not go down in history as any hero."

Hope soared. *Yes, you know this is wrong. Stop this. Let me go.*

"But sometimes in war there are no good, moral choices. There's just staying alive." His face hardened. "Sign the contract."

My hand banged the underside of the table snapping up to obey.

No. No, no, no!

I signed.

Awnan snatched the parchment back—rolling and tucking it safely in his pocket. "Salena, it's time to send my wife to her new home." He dared to take my hand. "I don't know how long it'll take to make our marriage official, but the cabin is stocked with food and supplies for weeks. You'll be fine... as long as you don't try to leave."

Slim, acne-riddled, blonde, and covered in jewels, Salena looked like every other noble I passed on the street. I wouldn't have seen the threat, and I still couldn't see it in her bored expression. Nothing about this woman gave the sense that she cared she was helping to imprison me.

Standing to the side, she pressed her palms together, then spread them apart as if framing the sun.

A black dot appeared. Hovering in the air chest-high, it grew before my unblinking eyes—forming a large and impossible black hole in my understanding of reality.

"Throw her in."

Arms seized my shoulders—Lemomi's, Rutendo's, and the needlessly rough grip of Dazai. They dragged me to Salena and the horrid thing she created, hearing nothing of my screams.

Please, don't do this. Someone help me. Reyna! Dominic, I cried out with my very soul. *Dom, help me. Come for me!*

They lifted me by my arms and feet, swung back, and threw.

Bang!

"Ainsley!"

Lemomi slipped and dropped me. The sudden weight shift knocked my kidnappers off-balance, and we collapsed on the ground in front of the undulating black orb. The surprise broke Rutendo's concentration, and control returned to me with another punch to the gut.

I wheezed—eyes watering and vision spinning from wine and adrenaline. Dominic couldn't be here. My desperate, mental plea couldn't have been answered, but there he was.

Whole, strong... and angry.

"Dominic..."

"What the fuck are you doing to her!"

Awnan's face drained of color. He looked from me to Dominic. "Kill him."

"No!" I screamed.

The silent, purposely oblivious mob came to life, surging on Dominic.

"You get one fucking warning," he shouted. "You touch me or her, you die!"

His head snapped to the side, grunt ripping out of him. Dominic doubled over, clutching his abdomen from a blow he didn't see coming.

An invisible mage.

No wonder the pub was packed. No wonder everyone was involved and aware of Awnan's disgusting plan. He wanted to make sure every array of unique magic would be there to throw at me, or anyone who helped me. He wasn't letting me go anywhere.

Dominic choked. Neck tipping back and heels coming off the floor, his unseen assailant strangled him.

Flames erupted on his body, covering Dominic from head to toe.

"Ahh! Ahhhh!"

Ear-piercing, soul-shattering screams ripped through the mayhem. A man—or I thought they were a man—blinked into existence, burning alive.

"Ahh!"

Thrashing, flailing, running around, the burning man ran into the bar and flipped over the top. The thud of his body, then silence.

Dominic charged the crowd, scattering would-be attackers out of his path to me. Movement out of the corner of my eye turned my head. Awnan shoved through the bodies, running in the opposite direction with the contract.

I didn't think. I ran after him. "Awnan, stop! Come back, you fucking monster!"

Awnan looked back, unglassed eyes suddenly no longer reeking with overconfidence and triumph. His hand slashed the air and I jerked to a halt.

I cried out, falling to my knees. My feet wouldn't move. Why wouldn't they move!

Looking down, my throat squeezed at the hardened earth encasing my boots up to my ankles. *Mud.*

"Awnan, stop this! It's over. You're never going to get away with—"

A body thudded down before my fingertips. My attention tore away, and I beheld Dominic.

He was a nightmare.

Hellfire engulfed him like a burning city. There was nowhere to go. Nowhere to hide. No one coming to save you.

Fireballs swirled around his head, shooting out at will at every mage unwise enough to charge him. The trail of burnt bodies in his wake stole my breath—not for its gruesomeness, but for the fact I knew... he was holding back.

I knew what it was to be consumed by hellfire. If he wished it, every body, plant, glass, and splinter would be a pile of ash at his feet. Dominic didn't have to show any restraint or mercy in dealing with them. In the same way he didn't have to be fair or generous with me for the terms of our marriage.

I swallowed hard, accepting a truth his kiss with Nuala made me question. Dominic Roark was an honorable man. Certainly more than the sniveling, cow-dung coward who stole my life, throne, and body with a single forced signature. Dominic may have once wanted me dead, but he never wanted me hurt.

"Dominic!"

Two burning black holes for eyes fixed on me. I pointed at Awnan.

"Him. Stop him!"

Dominic lobbed a fireball at Awnan without pausing for breath.

Shouting, Awnan grabbed the nearest person and flung them in death's path. Dazai fell bellowing at his feet.

Dominic reared for another strike. His flames whooshed out, leaving him standing bare.

I chilled seeing the hand gripping his arm, and who it belonged to. I guessed his magic during the fake game meant to get me drunk and slow. A magic I thought of because it seemed like mine.

The power to take the magic of others.

Dominic thrusted his arm at him, lips peeling farther back when nothing happened. "What the fuck have you done to me?"

Oskar loomed over him. Six feet tall, pumped with muscles, and brimming with anti-magic.

That was his word for it. Making someone's magic disappear for minutes to an hour with one touch.

Oskar's laugh boomed. "Nothing yet." He punched him in the face, throwing Dominic back.

He recovered quickly and struck back, burying his fist in his gut. Oskar's smile went from smug to pained grimace, doubling over. But one good hit didn't turn the tide. With his power gone, the mages that were running, ducking, and hiding abruptly found their courage. They descended.

"No, Dominic," I cried.

I whipped my head around, frantic and out of breath. Dominic was under attack with no defense, and facing magics he's never heard of. I couldn't lie around on the floor like pub scum when he was only in this mess because I didn't heed his warning. He told me to have any man, but stay away from Awnan.

I no sooner thought the vile man's name than I saw him clinging to the wall. He was trying to skirt around the fighting, make it to the front door, and escape with the contract that would ruin my life and the lives of everyone I loved. That would not happen.

I have to get out of this stuff, I thought, pounding on the mud. *I'm in danger now. Our lives are on the line now. Why won't my magic take over? What do I have to do?*

An anvil appeared over Dominic's head.

"Look out!"

Dominic dove out of the way—colliding with the conjuring mage, and dodging Oskar's punch. Oskar couldn't stop his momentum and sailed into the path of the anvil.

"Argh!"

Metal struck bone and yanked Oskar to his feet. He was still screaming when Dominic kicked him in the face, knocking him out cold.

Right then, I thanked the academy and my instructors for teaching us to fight the right way. Making sure we had knowledge and control solo, before we tricked ourselves into thinking we were ready to fight as a team. Dominic was never more vulnerable than he was right then, but his panicky, uncoordinated attackers didn't know what to do other than wildly throw magic at him, and whoever was caught in the cross fire.

The tiniest shred of hope blossomed in my chest, spurring me to pound harder. We would win this. We'd get out of here, and I'd mount Awnan's head on Reyna's horn like a pike.

The mud encasing my left foot cracked. A hairline fracture, but all I needed to know I'd soon be free.

Grunts and labored breathing sounded from Dominic's corner of the room. He was fighting hard. He would not fight alone.

The crack deepened and I threw myself back, pulling on my ankle till I broke free. Onto the next.

Thud, thud, thud.

I punched until the mud turned red, stained with my bleeding knuckles. A glance up showed me Awnan was nearing the exit.

Mud gave way, crumbling under my fist. I put my head down and pulled, praying to Zaeah, Parthelan, and even Kai for a safe way out of this.

My foot popped free. I jumped up and came face to face with Dazai.

I screamed so loud Dominic spun to me, and was hit with another conjured object that threw him off his feet. I ran to him, pulling him tight against me.

Charred bodies rose—some leaving a limb or two behind. Head barely attached, shuffling gait, unseeing eyes. They converged on us—our nightmares made real.

"What is this magic?" he hissed. His forehead split open, weeping down his swollen eye. "Where are we? How are they doing these things?"

"It's a pub for unique mages." I strained to help him up. "I don't know all they can do, but I do know there are magics worse than this."

I tried to find Rutendo among the horror coming at us. I couldn't see him or Awnan anymore.

"Stay behind me."

"No," he said, holding me back.

"But you don't have your magic. If they try to kill me, my magic will take over, then I can fight back and protect—"

"No one is hurting you!" His look and tone silenced me. "I don't need magic to take down these aberrant fucks, or to protect you. Just be ready."

I nodded, steeling myself.

Turning on our slow-moving opponents, I pressed my back to Dominic's. We were getting out of this. Roan's key to survival was something I'd been doing my whole life. Fighting like a peasant.

Dazai grasped the air, reaching for Dominic. Dancing on the necromancer's strings, he struck and punched Dominic's crossed arms. Dominic rocked back so hard, he almost popped me off my feet.

"They're slow, but they're strong," he shouted. "Fight dirty, you sadistic beauty. The dirtiest you ever have."

It was ridiculous even to me that I was heating up at his weird compliment in the middle of a fight for our lives. But I wasn't used to being praised as easily as he praised me. Under Dazai's truth magic, I called myself worthless.

I will be worthless if I don't stop Awnan's plans for me and the kingdom. A walled and guarded province all to themselves? Unique children stolen from their parents? I may not be worthy to rule a kingdom, but I'm good enough to save it.

A burned corpse I didn't recognize swung at me. I dropped quick, swept their legs, then shoved my boot through their skull. I couldn't let myself remember they were a person who deserved a better death ritual than this. Whoever the hidden mage was that was controlling them should've done that.

"Ahh!" Fingers twisted in my hair, yanking a chunk out at the root ripping my head back. Neck tipped to the ceiling, the mug came down fast and brutal on my face.

Dominic caught their wrist—crumbling charred bits of flesh on the floor—and flipped them over his shoulder, sending the poor being flying into another death puppet.

"On your left!"

Dominic pivoted and kicked a once-mage through the chest. I jumped over his back and leaped on one trying to get him from behind—sending it flying into another and the two of them collapsing in a struggling heap. I had Dominic's back and he had mine.

Wrapping my elbow around its neck, I held my breath and wrenched—ripping its head off. The puppets packed a powerful punch, but with the usual parts that connected their bodies burned away, they were nothing more than char and bones. They came apart stomach-sickeningly easy.

"You think it's that simple?"

I searched for who shouted.

"They're dead, fools. If they don't need a soul to fight"—a fist smashed into my jaw—"they don't need a head."

"Ainsley!"

I didn't need Dominic's warning. The headless body threw their next hit. I blocked, grunting under the force, and snapped my arm in an arc—smashing their bones against the wood. Their hand came apart like children's building blocks.

Dominic lifted and swung me into another puppet, breaking it apart.

They were coming from everywhere all at once. Dominic and I were as one like never before—punching, kicking, tripping, spinning, and taking down every poor person the lone face in the crowd was throwing at us.

I punched one of the last to come at me. As they fell, I landed on Awnan just as he grabbed the front door handle.

"Dominic, we have to stop him!"

Dominic took off—me hot on his heels. Blinding light stunned me, then my vision cleared on a burning Dominic. His magic was back. Awnan would soon be dead.

He bellowed—his scattershot forming in the air, and heading for one target.

An ashen, sweaty Awnan plastered against the corner, screaming his head off. He threw his hands up, and disappeared behind a surging wall of mud. We skidded to a stop but it was too late. We flew into it—mud surrounding and clinging to us.

My hair, my nose, my mouth, my ears. His mud overwhelmed my senses. I couldn't see him to stop him. Only Dominic finding and grabbing my hand let me know he was there.

I threw back my head and broke free for the barest second.

"Salena, now!"

A hard, unforgiving force struck us and we went soaring. I fell back on something soft and pillowy. Icy chill invaded immediately.

I cried out, breaking free of the mud to behold an impossible sight.

The pub was gone. We were surrounded by a sea of white with more coming down—blanketing the world in snow. The only break in the monochrome landscape was a single swirling black orb, hanging in the air above us.

"Wait—!"

It winked out.

Chapter Twenty-Three

I huddled in on myself, teeth chattering. A cold so complete and profound burrowed beneath my skin, turning my blood to ice. I would never be warm again.

"How—? Where are we?" Dominic freed himself from the puddle of mud and ice. It was already beginning to freeze over. "Where the fuck is Golden City?"

"D-D-D—" I reached for him, snowflakes dancing on my blue fingers.

"Shit. Come here."

Dominic scooped me up in his arms. A gentle wave of his hand, and we were cocooned in hellfire. Not his scattershot, but tiny, glowing embers teasing the sky as it mimicked a blanket of starlight.

"Beautiful," I whispered as blessed warmth settled in my bones. "I didn't know that hellfire could be... this."

"It's deceptive in its beauty."

Part of me felt there was more to that sentence, but he didn't voice it.

"Just don't touch it," he said. "The prettiest things tend to be the most lethal."

There was definitely more to that sentence.

"Where are we?" he asked. "How did we get here?"

I relaxed under his hellfire cocoon. It steadily kept the cold out. I could breathe. I could think.

"Awnan bet me that there was a mage in the bar who could move people great distances in a blink. He won that bet."

"Mother Zaeah," he breathed, looking around. "Pray my father never learns of such a mage. Or any of the ones we faced tonight. But first, we need to get out of this cold."

"Awnan—" A lump choked me. I tried again. "Awnan said he was sending me somewhere out of the way while he had Reyna executed and made our marriage official."

His grip tightened on me. "He what?"

I didn't know if that menacing growl was for me, or Reyna, but both outcomes made me want to throw up. "He got away, Dominic." Tears spilled hot and fast. "He made me sign that awful, evil contract. He said he has a high councilman in his debt who'll stamp whatever he puts in front of him. What are we going to do? I can't feel her anymore. I can't warn her. Dominic, what do we do?"

"Ainsley, listen to me. I don't care if he has the entire High Council in his pocket. No one would ever allow the execution of an innocent dragon. They're not simpleminded livestock. Such a betrayal of the dragonkin would not be forgiven. Our bondeds would never trust us again."

"Are—are you sure she'll be okay?" My voice was small.

"I promise. No mud-covered piece of shit is killing Reyna. Matter of fact, I hope he tries." Dominic's face changed. "That contract isn't worth the used baby swaddling it's written on. He won't live to see you walk down the aisle. I told you there're two ways to break a marriage contract. A fine—"

"—or death," I finished. "I absolutely choose the latter."

"We've got to find a way back to Golden City first." Dominic set off, maintaining the cocoon around us. "The mage must've sent us where he intended you to go. Which means there must be shelter somewhere in this snowstorm."

"How do you know this is where Awnan wanted me to be?"

"Because he still needs you alive."

I couldn't fault that logic. A marriage contract would force me down the aisle, but he wasn't my husband or prince consort until we recited our vows before the altar of Tenille. Awnan didn't do all of this only to let his schemes freeze to death.

Dominic tramped the frozen wasteland, leaving floating balls of hellfire in his wake to mark a path he'd already taken. It was another chance for me to marvel his nearly limitless power, but all I could think of were his arms warm and strong around me, and that after the worst night of my life... I finally felt safe.

"There," he said, pointing off into the distance. "I think I see it."

Squinting, I saw nothing, until I did.

A small, modest-size pile of stone stood out in the storm. There was nothing special about the four granite walls and heavy oak door, except that it was four granite walls and a heavy oak door. We rushed inside, breathing the first sigh of relief when the door slammed shut on the snow.

Dominic put me back on my feet as he sent his light ahead, illuminating the small space.

A writing desk shared the same wall as the tiny kitchen while the fireplace sat next to another door, likely concealing the bathroom.

Dominic sent his light further out to the lone bed covered in downy sheets and pelts. One bed.

I looked away from it, and fixed on the crates and boxes stacked against the far wall.

"I hope there's firewood in there."

"I can't use my flame on it if there is," Dominic said, drifting away. "It'll burn out of control."

"That's okay. I know how to start a fire." I said that, but I didn't move.

"Princess?"

"What was it?" I spoke so low, the howling wind tried to snatch away my words. "The night of the party, you warned me away from him, but I didn't listen. How did you know he was rotten?"

Dominic was quiet for a minute. "The baths. I overheard him saying he couldn't wait to find out if royal highness pussy tasted better than noble pussy. He also spoke at length and with unnecessary detail about his sex with a rider named Keely, and that he wanted to do filthier to you while she watched.

"He's scum. I knew as I listened to him talking about you, I was destined to cut off his tongue and hands, then feed them to him. For what it's worth..." I jumped at a large, caressing hand on the small of my back. "I didn't want to be right about him."

I squeezed my eyes shut, willing my tears not to fall. "How did you know I needed help?"

"It was strange. I was in bed, sketching, when threads wrapped around my arm and tugged me. I burned it off, but they kept coming after me until one ripped the charcoal out of my hand and wrote 'Ainsley needs you.'"

"Oh, Keely," I whispered. "I didn't think I could make another great friend in my life. As soon as I'm queen, I'm granting her a title and the biggest land in Adalinda."

"What happened tonight?"

"It was a trick." With his fire spreading warmth to every corner of the room, I moved to the crates, checking our supplies. "Everyone in the pub was in on it except for Keely. Awnan made me sign a contract saying he'd have absolute power over me and Adalinda, and I'd have a prison out of the way with our five children. More if I'm still comely."

"Fucking bastard."

My sentiments exactly.

"Why would he go this far? He must know that assassins will haunt his shadow the moment the contract is known. The loyalists and militarists want the House of Boreen or the House of Roark. They don't fucking want the House of Elsher."

The regret in Lemomi's eyes haunted my memory. "The mage who owns the pub can see into the future. She says a terrible fate will befall unique mages at the hands of your father."

He frowned. "Tell me. I have a feeling it will not surprise me."

"A unique mage is going to rise up and kill many. People will stop thinking of them as aberrant, and start seeing them as dangerous. Your father will take that chance to pass a law that says every unique mage in the kingdom must turn themselves in to him. He will bind the ones with useful magics in service to him. The rest will be executed."

Dominic blew out a breath, carding his fingers through his hair. But he was right. He did not look surprised. "He had spoken of such things, but even he recognized the High Council would never enact those laws. But if a unique mage was slaughtering with magics that seemed unstoppable, the tide of fear and paranoia would change many a mind."

"We have to get back there and stop him. Both of them," I said. "You say no one will give him permission to kill a dragon, but Awnan doesn't have to ask. He already had her fed a drugged goat. The next could be poisoned."

"I'm fairly certain we're in Edjer."

"How do you know?" I asked, lifting off a crate of apples to see the frozen bananas underneath. "Have you been before?"

"Only the capital, but this cold... You don't forget it. We're far up north, and I doubt we're close to a town."

"I do too." I gestured to the crates. "Salted pork and beef, fruit, nuts, seeds, and water. Enough for a long stay."

"Wood?"

"I think that's what this is," I said, patting a large wooden chest under the water crates. "Help me."

Dominic lifted them off with none of the puffing and straining I would've done. I shoved up the lid, and lit on firewood as I hoped.

My eyes widened. "No. No, no, no— That idiot!"

"What's wrong?"

"We can't use this wood." I threw some out only to find more to despair at the bottom. "That fucking fool cut the wood of a Hye-longan poisonwood tree. It's in the name. Burn this and our lungs will be sandpaper in an hour. If we haven't gotten the hint by then, it'll stop us breathing altogether."

"What?" He rushed to my side, looking for himself. "Of all the trees, the fool chooses the one we can't burn? Was it on purpose?"

"I don't think so," I said grudgingly. "Poisonwood is sneaky. It blends in with other berry trees, so it's easy to mistake."

"Can we break down the crates for firewood?"

I ran my hand over one. "Yes, but it's flimsy and will burn fast."

"It's better than nothing. Wash up if you can. I'll take care of this."

It was only then I remembered I was covered in mud and human remains. It was also then I noticed Awnan didn't leave me anything to wear.

"There's nothing for me to change into."

Dominic carried a crate to the small kitchen, emptied it, then stomped wood beneath his boot. Everything was dominated before him. "We'll wash and re-wear our clothes. Is there running water, or do we have to use our drinking water?"

I ducked into the bathroom to check. Prayers went up to every deity when I turned the cold faucet over a small wooden tub.

Water splashed out, beating the basin with strong and blessed pressure.

"Thank goodness. There's water," I called. "This place must be fed by an underground hot spring." I stuck my hand in the flow. "Make that an underground tepid spring."

"Need me to warm it?"

It wasn't lost on me that this was the longest we'd gone without a fight, barb, or heavy silence in days.

"No, that's okay. I grew up bathing in cold rivers and streams. This is nothing." I looked around the dark space. "Do you mind…?"

"Sure."

An orb floated into the bathroom, casting a soft and flickering glow over the bare space.

I washed myself quickly, then set about cleaning my clothes. Despite what I said, I'd gotten used to weeks of warm baths and fancy scented oils. This cold and barren wasteland Awnan sentenced us to was as depressing and humiliating as he intended it to be.

I came out to Dominic feeding a growing fire. He glanced up at me, then quickly looked away—clearing his throat.

"Sorry, I didn't think you'd mind," I said, standing there in not a stitch. "You have seen me naked before."

"In a dream," he told the floor.

"Nothing was changed or exaggerated. My breasts really are this small."

"That much I knew."

I flung my freezing wet pants at him. They smacked over his face, making us both crack up.

Dominic cut himself off, sobering. My smile dimmed as he tugged off my pants and let them fall to the floor.

"Fuck's sake, I don't understand you, Ainsley."

"What? What do you mean?"

"What do you mean!" he cried, stalking to the other side of the room. "You're here laughing, and joking, and standing there like that as if you don't know what even being in the same room as you does to me." He gestured to his middle, and the rising pole making a tent. "All this after you said you didn't want me, you'd have nothing to do with me after the marriage, and you don't want much more to do with me now. Is it this easy for you to play with me? Is it all some game to you?"

"A game? I'm not playing games, Dominic. I'm putting the fighting aside because, if you haven't noticed, we're in the middle of nowhere while an evil bastard tries to take the throne from both of us!" I snatched a blanket off the bed and wrapped myself up. "You're very cute making it out like I'm insincere when you can't tell the truth to save your life!"

"I haven't lied to you!" He grabbed the air like he wished it was my neck. "Not since we made up in that room. Why do you keep saying I did!"

"Are you serious?" Anger and resentment burned my throat. "You stood in front of the whole mess hall and said the idea of you marrying me was a joke."

He blew back, screwing up his face. "I only said that because the abdication and contract are a secret. I was doing it to protect you from the very thing Awnan did! If the loyalists know before the contract is signed, any one of them could try to force a contract between you and their sons. We agreed to keep it quiet, Ainsley. How am I the asshole for passing it off as a joke so no one would take it seriously?"

"You're the asshole because the first thing you did was tell our secret to Nuala. The person who spilled it in the first fucking place," I shot back. "Why did you tell her?"

"She was going to find out first either way. The choices were that she heard it from me, or from my father when he handed her a bag of coins, then told her to fuck off. I thought it'd be better coming from me."

"R-really?" My voice cracked. "You were just being gentlemanly and breaking the news to her yourself?"

"Yes," he cried, brimming with frustration. "Why does it matter?"

I glared at him, boring a hole through his head and wishing it showed me his true thoughts. "I saw you with her that day. Saw you near tears telling her there was nothing you could do to keep your contract with her because you had to marry me. Like it was some fucking chore.

"I saw you kiss her."

"Oh." He dropped his head, pinching his nose. "Shit."

"Yeah. Shit."

"It's not what you think—"

"I think you lied to me again."

"It was a kiss goodbye, Ainsley. It meant nothing."

"Ha!" I shrieked, blowing his brows up. "A kiss goodbye? What fucking bullshit. Tell another joke, Roark. I'm in a laughing mood."

"Of course it was a kiss goodbye. How could it be anything else? I don't want to be with Nuala," he shouted. "I want to be with you!"

I violently pushed down the feelings those words stirred in me. "I don't believe you. You spin everything to your advantage. Not a single thing you do or say is the truth." I scoffed. "Like the folio. I bet you thought giving me that would make me melt like shaved ice in the sun."

He frowned. "It wasn't like that. There was no ulterior motive. I made it for you. I wanted you to have it."

"You didn't make it for me. Keely said putting together that folio would've taken weeks. Weeks ago, you were plotting to kill me." I threw up my hands. "You made it for Orla. Why won't you just admit it?"

"Because I made this for Orla." He snatched something from his pocket and held it out. "I've been working on another one for her. I was when those threads came for me. The one I gave you was for *you*."

"Oh, please. You were wasting your time drawing a reading aid for a woman you wanted dead? Why would I believe that?"

"Because I didn't want to kill you." He put the page in my hand and stormed off. "I wanted you to survive me."

"You—!"

He slammed the bathroom door shut on me and my stifled scream. Dominic always had a reply, but I knew what I saw. He had nothing but regret on his face when he told Nuala he had to break it off, then he kissed her and pretended he didn't know what I was talking about later that day.

"No silly little drawing proves—" The words lodged in my throat as I looked at what he gave me.

The sketch on this page was clearly for a small child. Orla would no doubt giggle at the goofy-faced lizard waving at her... in his shiny pair of boots.

DOMINIC CAME OUT OF the bathroom and didn't say a word to me. Just as well because I had no words for him.

He hung his clothes by the fire next to mine, helped himself to an apple, salted pork, and a slice of bread, then he retreated to a corner of the room farthest from me.

This was Awnan's true punishment—forcing us into the same room together.

Hours, or what felt like hours, passed as I sat by the fire, gazing unseeingly at the lizard in boots. Orla, Lemomi, Nuala, Keely, and the king general ran through my mind on a loop—along with that bastard's accusation.

I was letting all of Adalinda down because I didn't have faith in myself.

Tiredness weighed on my lids, bringing my musings to an end. I picked some blankets off the bed and made my own by the fire.

"What are you doing?" Dominic asked, making me jump.

"I'm going to sleep."

Lying down, I pulled the blanket over my head. It and me were scooped up with a shout.

"Stop being ridiculous. You're not sleeping on the cold, hard dirty floor."

"I'm not sleeping with you either."

"Flattered, Princess, but I wasn't offering."

Dominic placed me on the bed, snapped off a pelt, then claimed my spot in front of the fire.

I chewed my lip, fighting with myself. I didn't want him sleeping on the cold dirty floor any more than he did me, but I couldn't handle sharing a bed with him. No matter how close he was, the anger and lies would widen the gap between us.

Flipping over, I shut my eyes and went to sleep.

DAYS PASSED WITH US exchanging little more than a terse word here or there. On the second day, Dominic left the cabin without a word and didn't come back for hours. I asked him where he went, and he replied, "I'm trying to get us out of here," and not much else. I didn't have it in me to ask more questions, so I left it alone.

By the week's end, we ran out of firewood.

"What do we do?" I wrapped up in another pelt, staying warm while my underclothes warmed in the dying embers' heat. "It's not all the way out yet, and it's already so cold my toes are turning blue. We'll die."

"We won't." Dominic rationed out our food—his back to me. "My flames will keep us warm. I didn't want to drain my magic when there was still wood to burn, but we don't have a choice now."

"What about when you sleep? Your hellfire will wink out, and we'll freeze to death anyway."

"We won't. I can control it while I sleep," he said. "Besides, I should have us home any day now."

"How? What are you doing out there?"

"Sending signals that we're trapped and need help."

I nodded to myself. It was more than I could do. I prayed to the gods that it worked.

"I still can't feel Reyna."

I didn't know why I said it. I guess after days without talking, I just wanted someone to hear my voice.

"Her happiness, her bloodlust, the pain from the bond. It's all gone," I rasped. "He did it, didn't he? He killed her."

Dominic didn't speak for a beat.

"That can't be true. If we'd lost her. If the bond was truly gone, I have to believe you'd know. We must be too far away from her."

"I've never heard of distance affecting the bond. Something is wrong. I know—"

"She's alive, Ainsley," he sliced in—not angrily or impatient. Just firm. "We'll see her when we get home, so let's focus on making that happen as soon as possible."

I sat up straighter. "I should go out with you. Help you find the Edjerians that live in this frozen wasteland."

"No. You can't help me."

"Why not?"

"Because I need to know something," he said, turning on me. "Do you want to marry me?"

I squeezed my fingers under the blanket. "Why are you asking me this?"

"Why are you refusing to answer?"

"I'm not refusing," I said, a bit sharp. "I just don't know why you're asking things you already know the answer to."

"Humor me. Tell me the answer."

I narrowed on him. His blank expression gave nothing away.

"Yes, Dominic. I have to, so it's what I'm going to do."

"No."

"What do you mean no?"

"I said no. I'm not accepting *have to*. Either you want to marry me, and I mean me. Not my throne, or my money, or to remove my father's target off your back. Do you want to be married to me?"

I stared at him. Silent.

Dominic nodded to himself, accepting an answer I never gave. "You know, I've been thinking these last few days about Awnan and what he's done to you. The guy's a festering, maggoty carcass... but I'm not much better."

My brows crumpled. "What? Why would you say that?"

"How is forcing you to marry me any better than what he's doing?"

"It's not the same. I offered to marry you of my own free will. You didn't get me drunk, force truth magic on me, then take away control of my body. Every single one of his terms was inhuman and disgusting. *I* chose the terms of our marriage. That's the difference."

"It's not different. It's still a life you don't want with a man you hate."

Stunned, my jaw worked trying and failing to speak.

Dominic looked me in the eyes—amber orbs pale and steady. "I won't do it. Our deal is off. We're not getting married."

I choked—words punching me in the gut. "But— But— We have to. Your father lost his mind for this deal. He doesn't want me dead anymore, and we'd rule Adalinda together. My heart, your head. This is what we agreed."

"Not anymore."

"So what now!" In a flash, I was screaming. "You think I'm still going to abdicate without the marriage contract?"

His voice was calm. "You will abdicate."

"The fuck I will." I advanced on him quick. "You'll have to kill me and get the job done right this time. If you think—"

"And," he broke in, "you'll have your contract with all your terms. It simply won't be with me."

"Who, then?"

"My brother." Dominic sidestepped me and went to the writing desk. He picked up the drawing of the lizard. "More than a few of my brothers are good men. It's why they don't warrant the attention of my father. Of those few, seven are unmarried and don't have contracts with anyone else.

"Take your time. Get to know them. Fall in love. Choose." A soft *scritch-scritch-scritch* whispered through the room as he wrote. "You'll get your regency, your stipend, and a man you want to raise children with. I'll get the throne. Everyone still wins."

A band constricted my chest, squeezing the air from my lungs. What was he saying? Why was he speaking such insane things?

"No one wins. The key was that *our* children would be heirs to the throne. House Boreen and House Roark would rule. Not a loyalist or a militarist would question it."

"Your children will still be my heir. Adalindian law has always allowed the current ruler to choose their heir. As long as they're of the royal bloodline—which your children would be—they'll be my heirs. Simple."

"It's not simple— For fuck's sake, will you look at me!"

Smoothly, he turned, the parchment dangling from his fingertips.

"Do you think this is how it works? You pawn me off on another brother, then sail off into the sunset? I don't want him, or them, or whoever it is!"

"You don't want to marry someone you love?"

"I am!"

His calm mask broke. "What?"

"Am—am—am capable of deciding for myself what I want and who I choose," I finished quickly. "I don't know your brothers. I know you. I choose you."

"You don't trust me."

"You never stop lying to me," I snapped back.

Dominic chuckled without mirth. "Well, how about this for some truth, Princess? I won't marry you like this, or with those terms. This is our new marriage contract." He held up the back of the parchment. "Sign this, and we go ahead as planned. Don't, and you can pick from my harem of brothers."

I vibrated with fury. I didn't know whether to scream or cry. Why was he punishing me? It wasn't me who kissed Nuala and lied about it. "It's short."

"Yes."

"I'm guessing it says nothing about the regency or stipend."

"Correct."

Cry. When I locked myself in the bathroom, I would definitely cry.

"I can't read it," I replied softly. "I only recognize three words."

He shrugged. "The deal was I teach you to read, and I will. It's not like we have anything else to do in this icebox. When you know what it says, you make the choice to sign. Agreed?"

I slammed into the bathroom. Spinning the faucet, I held my head under the spray and bawled my eyes out. Why was he doing this to me? How did it all go wrong? Were the two people who held each other in a dream just that? A fantasy?

Hours passed before I trudged out and went straight to bed, not bothering to pass him a glance. I was afraid if I did, I'd strangle him.

THE NEXT MORNING, I woke to find him in the same spot—eyes closed, and meditating under a halo of hellfire. A bigger halo surrounded me, keeping me so warm through the night, at one point I kicked half the covers off and snoozed under their burning glow.

"Dominic? Dom?"

Raising his head, bloodshot eyes turned to me. "Yes?"

"Are you okay? Did you get any sleep last night?"

His expression softened. "Did you?"

I touched under my eyes. It was puffier, and no doubt redder than his. "Let's not talk about it."

"We should talk about your lessons instead," he said, getting to his feet. "Sit. I'll make you something to eat."

I did as he said for lack of anything else to do. He was right. We didn't know how long we'd be here, so I might as well work on learning to read Dominic's new contract.

Don't go there. My eyes prickled. *Dominic gave me his options. I'll make my choices.*

"Have you been practicing?"

I nodded. "I'm up to umma."

"You've memorized all the characters before it?"

"Yes."

"Show me. There's parchment in the top drawer."

Quiet smothered our small space, broken only by my charcoal and his shuffling. He brought my plate as I crossed the dash on the last character. He leaned over me, his bare chest brushing the top of my head. With only one set of clothes, we had to get used to being half-naked around each other. I wasn't nearly as relaxed about it as I pretended to be.

"Good. Beautiful handwriting."

I stupidly blushed.

"We'll move on to sentences."

"But I don't have the whole alphabet memorized."

"You do, Ainsley. You're slowing yourself down because you want to get it done perfectly before you move on to the next, but you're already farther than most who learn to read and write later in life."

"I'm not," I dismissed, shaking my head.

"You are. My father forbade my mother from teaching us Old Ghidorian. After he sent her away, I taught myself because fuck him."

Because fuck him. That was the soundest reason for doing something that I ever heard.

"Speaking, listening, reading, and writing. I had to figure it all out on my own, and I damn sure wasn't writing my characters as neatly as you in a few weeks. You not only have speaking and listening down, but your quick and cleverness has you breezing through the final two. You're incredibly intelligent, Princess. I'm always in awe of you."

I gave him a flat look. "Nice try, but flattery stopped working on me around the time you laughed in my face minutes before my execution."

His grin didn't dim. "No it didn't."

"Fuck you."

Dominic laughed. "You can curse me out to deflect the compliments, but I mean them. You've got a system for remembering, don't you?"

"I..." I gazed down at the parchment. "Yes. I have a story for each character. I connect them to people I know. Like this one. It kind of looks like a dick, and you've got the character for dick in your name." I smiled beatifically. "With that one down, it's easier to remember the other two. Dick."

He chuckled. "Excellent. Tell me the story for these five."

"Why?"

"It'll be easier to teach you if I work with your system, instead of making you work with mine."

That was a fair response, so I gave in. Of course, I left out that the stories I was giving him were about my brothers, sisters, Rosaleen, and Sister Aven.

"Alright, so, Vela was chased up a tree by a pissed-off mother goat. This is how you write it." Dominic wrapped around my hand, thoroughly spreading goose bumps up my arm before taking the charcoal. "Practice until you have it down."

Again, silence lapsed between us while I copied the sentence three, five, ten times. When I was done, Dominic wrote ten more sentences based on my stories, then went outside to continue his task of finding us a way out of there.

I wouldn't tell him then or ever, but his way was helping. I felt ten times more confident in what I knew by the time he returned. Broden had no patience with me for not being able to grasp something "so easy." His sighs and eyerolls made me feel stupid every time. He certainly never said I was incredibly intelligent or that he was in awe of me.

Dominic stumbled inside. As in stumbled. He collided with the wall like he didn't see it.

"Dominic?"

"I'm fine," he gruffed, turning away from me when I approached him. "I just overdid it. Used up too much magic. I'm going to take a bath. I'll check your progress after."

I let him go. Sympathy broke through the heart I was hardening against him. Dominic had to keep his fires burning inside for me, and outside while lighting his way, keeping warm, and sending his signals.

I could acknowledge he was a lying asshole threatening me with a choice of another contract I didn't want, or marrying from his harem of brothers... while also recognizing that he was doing a lot to keep us both alive.

Dominic came out a bit later. His eyes were still red but the haggard lines around them softened.

"How is it going?" I pushed the plate of food I made toward him. "Do you think anyone is seeing your signals?"

"I do, but only an ice mage would risk trekking out in this never-ending storm to see who they're coming from. I won't give up until one does."

He sat heavily in the chair, rubbing his eyes. The sympathy burrowed deeper.

"There has to be something I can do to help you."

"There isn't unless you've learned to give power as well as take it."

"You'll be the first to know if I do."

Dominic flashed me a lopsided smile. That was one thing I could do. Make him smile.

I hung back and gave him a chance to get some food down. Climbing on the bed, I hugged my knees to my chest and watched him. This could be our life.

Not stranded in a frozen hellhole in the land Edjer forgot, but the two of us alone after a long day, talking to each other. Helping each other. Relying on each other.

"You wouldn't really let me marry one of your brothers, would you?"

Dominic stilled.

"All that stuff you said..." I held my legs tight. "You didn't mean it, right?"

"I meant every word."

My jaw clenched pressing my lips together tight to stop them trembling. "Dominic, don't do this."

"It's not me doing it. Why should the choice only be yours, Ainsley? If this marriage is just about land, money, and saving you from my father, you don't need me for that. You either want to marry me on my terms, or you'll marry one of my brothers on yours."

"You were right." My voice was colder than the frozen death he held back. "You're no better than Awnan."

Dominic didn't reply. He finished marking my work, polished off the remains of his dinner, then claimed his place in front of the fire.

I was wrong. *This* is what a life with Dominic Roark would be like.

DOMINIC WAS GONE BEFORE I woke up the next day. He left more sentences for me to copy, but without him reading them to me, I didn't know what they said.

I put them aside and continued practicing with the characters after umma. When that was done, I made myself little study cards out of torn parchment, and tested myself.

I was proud I got none of the alphabet wrong, and annoyed Dominic was correct about me being overly cautious and knowing more than I thought I knew.

I stopped, ate a modest meal, then waited around for an hour, maybe two. Dominic had been out there for a long time. When was he coming back?

Having few toys or books in the orphanage meant I had to make my own fun. Every day playing with my borrowed brothers and sisters, running through the forest, climbing trees, and watching Golden City in the distance—that's exactly what I did.

My brothers and sisters weren't there. No trees to climb. No daydreams of a better life in a not-so-faraway place. There was just me and Dominic, and with every hour that passed with the cold absence left behind, I realized he wanted it to be just me.

Eventually, I gave in and practiced the sentences. Sounding them out helped me decipher a word or two. Since they were based on stories of my family, it actually wasn't that hard to make the leap to what the words said.

"Iffa-lat-anko-soum," I read out. "I— Ilem— Ilemka!"

Happiness burst through my tears. My sister's name. Tiny and sweet with the obsidian Nehebkan skin and a smile brighter than the sun. I still remember the day her father brought her to the orphanage with tears soaking his face, telling of a terrible disease that tore through his village—killing his wife, parents, two brothers, and sister.

He told Sister Aven that he had to start over. He was the village farmer, and there was no village or farm. He promised to come back when he had a home and coin again. After all they'd lost, he wouldn't subject her to begging and sleeping in the dirt.

Ilemka wasn't the first child brought to the orphanage because the parents couldn't care for them anymore, or didn't want to. None of them ever came back in the twenty years I'd been there, but there was no doubt in Ilemka's heart that her father was coming back. Truthfully, there was no doubt in mine either.

I told Dominic that story with a few changes that turned Ilemka into an old acquaintance, and the orphanage into distant noble relations. But still, he wrote her history for me, and gifted me the blessing of knowing how to write my sister's name.

My confidence came back, spurring me to sound out more words. "Ilemka... father— Ilemka's father was a... farmer. He... He will..." I didn't know the next word, so I skipped it. "—back for... her. Ilemka's father was a farmer. He will come back for her! Ahh!"

I squealed, jumping up and down. I did it. I read an entire sentence—*two* entire sentences by myself, and I'd only been learning for a few weeks. I could do this.

"I can read."

Grinning, my gaze drifted to the top drawer. Dominic's new marriage contract was in there. Before I knew it, I had taken it out and smoothed it over the desk.

I squinted, finger tracing a line under the characters. Dominic's writing wasn't perfect like he called mine. Not that it was bad. It was swoopy, slanted, and... different. Like him.

"I..." I sounded out the next three words, but that did nothing for understanding them. Skipping that sentence, I went to the next.

"I... will... ser—serve..." My lips went numb. *No... it can't be.*

I forced myself to keep reading. "—serve... w-without... question." I skipped a couple sentences down. "Sae-kim-a. Speak when... spoken to." Frantically scanning down, I searched for the words that said this was all a joke.

"Sl— Slave."

Swiping it off the desk, I threw it in the drawer and slammed it closed. Let the evil fucking bastard freeze to death out there. To think I felt any kind of sympathy or worry for him while he kept another slave contract masquerading as a marriage bond in the drawer waiting for me to sign.

Dominic could go fuck himself and stuff his contract up his ass while doing it. I didn't need him. I didn't need his brothers. The throne was mine to give by blood and right. If this was the true measure of the current and future leaders of Adalinda, then I wouldn't let either of them get their hands on it.

"I may not be confident enough to rule a kingdom or fight a war, but I'm spiteful enough to prove wrong every man who agrees. So teach me how to read, Roark, it just puts me one step closer to taking everything else from you."

My speech was heard by no one and nothing. Sighing, I took my practice sentences to bed and worked on them under a cocoon of blankets. It was getting colder in the cabin. I was afraid to think of what that meant.

Noise stirred me some time later, popping my eyes open. I woke on top of a pile of parchment and pelt. When had I fallen asleep?

Dominic trudged inside and dropped hard before the fireplace.

Shaking his head, he stifled a groan pushing back up. I watched him concentrate, and yes it was the first time I'd ever seen him concentrate to summon his magic. His fire orbs had shrunk to a tenth of the size, and I hadn't noticed.

They grew as he grunted and groaned, straining like... like a peasant.

This was the first I'd seen the great, powerful, perfect Dominic Roark brought to the level I lived on my entire life. I'd gotten into this mess. It was all because I didn't listen to his warning about Awnan, and got myself captured and thrown into an icy pit. He saved me then, and he was saving me now.

He shouldn't go out tomorrow. Yes, we have to get out of here, but we can't do that if his magic bleeds dry. One day to rest is what he needs.

My lips parted to speak.

Dominic stood and went to the writing desk. He flicked through my work, then opened the drawer.

I swallowed through needles when he unfurled it, ran his fingers over the words, then carefully placed it back.

He turned and I flicked my eyes shut. Silence reigned while he did... what? I didn't know.

Soon I heard the bathroom door open and shut. Sleep claimed me before he returned.

I WOKE UP ALONE AGAIN the next morning. New sentences awaited me, but no Dominic.

So this was to be our days? Him avoiding me while I taught myself how to read a bullshit marriage contract I would never sign.

I frittered away my day copying sentences and sounding out new words. Adalindian was a complicated language that changed in the decades since the usurper stole the kingdom, and forced the many lands to come under one.

It was now a mix of Old Adalindian, Old Ghidorian, Old Nehebkan, Old Hyelongan, and Old Edjerian all put together to create a language that had an unbearable number of words that weren't pronounced the way they were spelled, or had a single character with six different meanings depending on who was speaking to who and in which province.

Even so, I felt ridiculously excited about my progress. Dominic's folio gave the boulder the first push, and now it was speeding down the hill. I was learning fast, and it wasn't just Dominic and Broden in my ear. Growing up with siblings from all corners of the kingdom, I learned the many meanings and ways of naming the same thing. I didn't know how long it takes the average person to learn to read, but I'd do it in half the time.

Applauding myself for a job well done, I moved on to my next task of checking how much food we had left. I would say one thing for Awnan, he didn't intend for me to starve. He left me plenty of food to last weeks, but he didn't plan for two of us.

I had to make this food last until we got ourselves out of this place, because if we waited until we ran out or Awnan finally came for me—neither option resulted in us both making it out alive.

I reached for an apple and the flames went out, plunging me in darkness. They returned quicker than I blinked. My peace didn't.

"Damn it, Roark," I whispered. "You're running yourself ragged. Just come back and rest."

If his hellfire was supposed to deliver my messages, the hours I waited with no appearance from him showed they didn't. Part of me wanted to go out there and track him down. The other part knew I'd die on the way.

I didn't have Dominic's ability to channel blistering flames. I couldn't feel my bond with Reyna to channel hellfire. I didn't even have the right clothes to venture outside. I didn't know many things, but I knew how quickly the frozen death claimed all but an ice mage who exposed themselves to this weather. I knew because two of my Edjerian brothers lost their parents in that cold, quiet way.

But I won't lose Dominic, I thought, gazing at the flickering orb above me. *When he comes back tonight, I'll break this wretched silence and make him rest.*

I held on to the resolution as an hour passed. Then two. Then more.

Only my body clock told me night from day, and it was clearly telling me it was the middle of the night.

Blowing out a breath, I gave up and climbed under the blankets. Dominic's arrival was accompanied by a blast of chilling wind roaring through the front door. It also woke me up. When it did, I'd strap him to the bed if I had to for no other reason alone than making me worry when I was pissed at him.

I drifted off, my irritation following me into sleep.

SNOWFLAKES TICKLED my skin—covering me in a glittering, pristine sheet of pure white. The snow wasn't melting. My body had long ago given up the fight, becoming one with the cold.

I should've been scared. Screaming, crying, desperately trying to escape the cocoon of ice that froze around me—trapping me on all sides. Fear was easy. It was right.

I chose peace.

All my life I've fought everything. Hunger, bullies, prejudice, magiclessness, Dominic.

I didn't want my last act of life to be another pointless battle. I surrendered to this one.

My eyes drifted shut, blessed by the flakes kissing my lids.

Death didn't win this one. We'd call it a draw.

I snapped awake, body recoiling into a tight, stiff ball. It was cold.

My teeth chattered to unhinge my jaw from my head. What was going on? Where was I?

Pitch black met my questions, and still my sluggish brain strained to understand. The fire was out? Why was it out? We needed his flames or—

"Dominic?" My voice barely rose higher than a thin croak. "Dominic, where are you?"

I fell out of bed, hugging myself. My eyes strained to adjust while I wrapped myself with blanket after blanket. Pelt and more pelt. "Dominic."

Dominic's fires weren't burning, and they hadn't been burning long enough for our toasty warm cabin to become an icebox. An hour? Two?

Dominic wouldn't leave me without heat for two hours unless—

A chill colder than Edjer could produce stopped me in my tracks. What if Dominic didn't leave me without heat for hours? What if he just left me?

The horrible thought went through my head, and I dismissed it firmly. Dominic wouldn't do that to me. He'd set me up to die—sure. But then he'd look me in the face and tell me what he'd done. Even when he was despicable, Dominic Roark was honorable. Abandoning me in this hell with no wood or heat, knowing what would become of me in mere hours, not days... He simply wouldn't do it, which meant one thing—

"He needs me."

I smacked myself across the face, the pain chasing away the last vestiges of confusion and addled calm that tried to lure me to my death. *Get the fuck up, Boreen. Dominic Roark will not die because of a dirty, pathetic loathsome cockroach like Awnan.*

"Dominic!"

I searched blindly in the dark, hoping against hope he made it inside.

My searching fingers found cold stone, cold stone, a freezing empty tub, and cold stone.

"N-no," I sobbed. "Dom, please, no..."

He wasn't in the cabin. If he wasn't in here with me, he was outside in temperatures so cold, they didn't need a full hour to kill. I was already too late.

"No!"

Wrapping, twisting, covering myself in every layer of warmth we had, I marched to the door and threw myself out.

The whipping wind and blanketing snow rain had stopped, leaving behind an untouched field of white almost as high as my chest. In another life, it would be beautiful.

This penetrating, pressing silence of a land the world forgot. Miles around, there was nothing but snow. There was also no Dominic, but he'd been here. The untouched field was not completely untouched. A trail carved through the ice where my burning man had left his mark.

I set off down that trail without another thought.

My teeth were chattering in seconds. Cold came for the moisture in my eyes, vindictively making them water, then turning my tears to icicles on my lashes. My pelts were nothing. A grain of sand defending against the sea. My fingertips were already blue. My every breath was a ragged knife through my lungs.

Still, I pressed on.

"I'm c-coming." I had to say it. He had to hear it and hang on. "I'm coming for you."

I marched on farther, farther, and farther away from the cabin. Cresting the horizon, I lost sight of it completely.

How far had Dominic gone? All this way to send his signals? And all the way back to get him home.

The land was barren, but it wasn't flat. Hills and ridges that were once living were covered by snow jealous of their green and brown. My Dominic was covered in black and red. Envious snow would not keep him from me. *I'll see him soon,* I thought, *and he'll be alive, laughing, and flashing me that shit-eating grin.*

I held on to that smile, holding it closer than the pelts protecting my skin— No, adding it to my protection. I would not die before seeing that mischievous smile one more time. Neither would he.

Despite my promise, my boots fell heavier the farther I went. Dominic's carved trail held, but it felt like I'd been walking for miles without a sight of him. How far would the promise of his smirk take me before the cold did?

Doesn't matter. I keep going.

"Dominic? Dominic!"

I kept walking. And walking. And walking.

My breaths were ice. I stopped feeling my toes shortly after I left the cabin. By then I couldn't be sure they were still attached to my body. My fingers and limbs were stiff as if my blood had frozen solid.

Still, I pressed on.

"D-D-Dom," I called. "Can you h-hear me? I'm coming for you. I—"

I rounded a mound, following his trail, and there he was.

Resting still and peaceful under ribbons of light in the night sky, Dominic could've lain down to watch and fell asleep for how calm the scene.

"Dominic!"

My scream shattered the quiet. Racing to him, I fell at his side and gasped—clapping my hand over my mouth.

Dominic was blue. But only so in the spots where he wasn't white.

Ice clung to his lashes, lips, and clothes. A jealous mistress, it had already begun to claim him.

"Dom," I whispered. I touched his cheek and cried to find it ice cold.

One look at him, and I knew the truth. Dominic was a liar.

Even in his peaceful sleep, I traced the haggard lines around his mouth and the dark bags under his eyes. Dominic couldn't maintain control of his power while he slept, so when our wood ran out, he didn't do it.

He hadn't slept for days. He pushed his magic past the limit. He spent hours upon hours out here trying to signal someone who could help us... all to save me.

"You stupid fool." Dry eyes wept tears that couldn't fall. "You don't dare leave me after all you've done. Wake up, Dominic. Wake up!"

He didn't stir at my scream. His lids didn't flutter. His breath didn't stir the air.

"No," I cried. "You can't take him, Calthoon. I'm not ready."

I pulled him onto my lap, crushing his chest against mine. "I didn't get to tell you why I hate you so fucking much! You made a fool of me, Roark. Because while you were lying, and scheming, smirking, and laughing, and protecting me... you made me fall in love with you.

"You don't get to leave without hearing that I am," I whispered. "I am marrying the man I love."

Dominic didn't speak. My heart fluttered wildly against his chest. His heart did not answer its call.

"Nooo..." A terrible, keening wail tore from my throat. Dominic died cold and alone while I had peaceful, oblivious dreams miles away.

"What more do you want from me!" I screamed at the heavens. "My parents. The beatings. Hunger. The curses in my ear and the spit on my face. Letting me believe I had no magic in a world that values nothing else.

"The rape that didn't happen." I choked on a sob. "And the one that did.

"You put me through all of that, and I took it. I accepted my fate to be worthless. But not this time. You don't get to have him, you evil, uncaring, bastard gods!"

I laid Dominic down and exposed his chest. Lacing my frozen fingers over his heart, I pumped.

"Give him back."

Pump.

"Kai!"

Pump.

"Mother Zaeah!"

Pump.

"Parthelan!"

I bobbed on Dominic's chest, pushing harder, crying heavier, loving deeper. "This magic that saves my life. Now it will save his. Do you hear me! I will be useless no more! My magic defies death, fate, and you. I defy you!"

I swung my leg over, straddling him. Making a fist, I pounded on his still heart. "You will not take my love from me. His soul was never yours, and always mine.

"CALTHOON!" My fist came down. "GIVE HIM BACK!"

Our skin connected, and the punch went through my chest. I flew back—struck by an invisible blow, and tumbled over wood and snow.

Dazed, I struggled to right myself—get back to him.

"Domi—"

"Uh..."

I froze—heart stopping within my bruised rib cage.

"Ains... ley..."

"Dominic." I crawled through the snow—racing to him, reaching for him. My fingers brushed his, and the ground exploded.

"Ahh!" I was thrown in the air.

Screaming, I cartwheeled through a storm of dirt and snow—not knowing which way was up or down. I was flying, falling, dying. I didn't know.

"Dominic!"

A body smacked into mine. I grabbed and held on tight, wrapping my arms and legs around Dominic with no intention of ever letting go again.

We struck the ground. Softened by a bed of snow, and jarred by our bones and heads banging together.

Groaning, I lifted my head… and lit upon our door.

I didn't know how. It was impossible. Somehow and by some miracle, we were thrown to exactly where we needed to be.

"Dominic, we're here. We—"

He'd gone quiet. Eyes closed, Dominic was slipping back into the depths I grabbed him from.

"No."

I didn't waste another second. Grabbing him under the arms, I dragged him the rest of the way to the cabin, through the door, and over the cold floor.

"It's going to be okay. I promise. I'm here for you now," I cried, stripping him of his cold, wet clothes. "I'll take care of you."

I ripped his last boot off in the dark, then heaved him into bed with a burst of strength I didn't know myself capable of.

My last burst of strength.

Exhaustion bowled me over, dropping me to my knees. Whatever magic I tapped into—if it was indeed magic that gifted me that miracle—it had enacted its price. Blindly, I stripped off my clothes and fell into bed with Dominic—covering us with the remaining dry pelts and blankets.

Resting my head on his heart, it spoke to me weakly, but steadily. A fighting drumbeat following me into a darkness from which I didn't hope to awake.

"I love you."

I couldn't say if it was me or him that spoke the words, but it was true for both of us. Dominic Roark and Ainsley Boreen were meant to be. Eternal enemies. Bitter adversaries. Respected opponents. Destined soulmates.

All my life, I hadn't been waiting for my mother to return, my magic to appear, or Reyna to choose me. It was Dominic. It always was, and it always would be.

"I love you too."

Chapter Twenty-Four

Light pressed on my lids, soft and comforting in its promise. I opened my eyes, but didn't need to. I already knew what I would see.

"Dominic."

He smiled—a strained, tired quirk of the lips, but a smile. "Princess."

"You're okay."

"I'm... alive," he said, glancing up at the tiny balls of hellfire floating in the air. "Tribunal is still deciding if I'm okay."

I understood that completely, because I couldn't move.

Not didn't want to move because I was tangled up in bed naked with the man I love—which would be reason enough. But I couldn't.

Whatever I'd done out in the ice had taken consciousness away from me long enough for hunger to gnaw my stomach from the inside out, and now it had taken my strength. My arms were two pieces of sopping wet toast while my legs were stiff and achy. My chest burned as though I was kicked by a horse—twice. The thought of moving an inch was a spike through my brain.

I dropped my head back on his chest, groaning for just that small act. "You lied to me."

"I seem to do that a lot."

"You told me you could control your hellfire in your sleep."

"Ahh," he murmured softly. "Yes... that was a lie."

Tears pressed behind my eyes, seeing Dominic lying cold and still in the snow. "D-don't ever do that to me again."

"I won't, Ainsley." His hand, gentle and warm, cupped the back of my head. "I'm sorry."

I couldn't say how, but I knew he meant it. I could trust him.

"What happened out there?" His hand traveled lower, fingers skating along my spine. "What happened in here?"

I'm sure he didn't need to see my face to know it was burning hot. "I found you passed out in the snow. I brought you back and warmed you until you awoke and used your fire."

"Passed out?"

I lowered my eyes. "Dead."

Dominic's caressing hand halted. I couldn't look at him to know what he was thinking.

"Dead?" he croaked.

"Yes. I'm... You were gone, Dominic."

Dominic was quiet for so long, I'd have thought he fell back asleep if not for the fires still burning. "So, does this mean your magic shields others from death too? Even though I didn't die by magic, and likely long before you found me."

Biting hard on my lip, I sighed. Of course Dominic came to the same conclusions about how my magic worked that I did. He likely did it before me. He was too clever not to.

"I don't know what this means. There's a lot I don't understand. All I know is you left me, and I brought you back." I lifted my stiff, creaky neck to look him in the eyes. "Don't do it again."

"Yes, ma'am." He brushed my hair from my eyes, lingering on my cheek. "Are you okay?"

"I feel like I was hit by a carriage, then they backed up and rolled over me again."

"I shouldn't have put you through this. I thought I could get us out of here before my magic and strength failed. I gambled, lost, and put you in danger."

I shook my head. "It's not about me. I know now that I'm strong enough to survive anything, because that was my magic long before I had any. I can accept that we'll be here a while"—I grasped his chin and my arm screamed for it—"but I won't accept being here without you. That I won't survive.

"You and I have to be a team. Working together to get home. No more silences. No more staying away all day and night. And no more hiding that you need my help. If we're truly not enemies anymore, we have to start acting like it."

Inexplicably, a grin split his face. "You can't think I'd disagree with any of that? I'm very interested in this phase of our relationship where we're"—he raked me up and down—"no longer enemies."

Goose bumps popped along my skin as he traced a pattern on my lower back. I'd be feeling that touch long after he stopped. Yes, I wasn't shy about him seeing what he'd already seen before, but that was different to having my breasts pressed against his side, and my leg threaded between his. I wasn't so numb that I didn't feel his proudly stiff cock poking my thigh.

"Can you not be you right now?" I cried. "I did this to save your life."

"You already saved my life." It made no sense to say his smirk got smirkier, but that's exactly what it fucking did. "You stripped me down and threw me in this bed to finally have your way with me, Princess. Well, go ahead and take me. I'm at your mercy."

I giggled—a light, free sound that made me feel better than anything else could. How could he do that? After the worst shock and pain I ever experienced, Dominic made me smile.

When I choose a man to love, I choose the best. But I didn't voice it. I couldn't. Not yet.

"Tempting," I teased, "but the carriage came back and ran me down a third time. I'm not kidding when I say I can barely move. Whatever I did to bring you back was big magic. There had to be a big price."

Dominic sobered. "I don't want you paying that price again, but I don't know how to keep our promise. We're out of wood. All that trekking I did wasn't just to find someone to help us, but it was also to find one single fucking tree, or anything under the snow that we can burn.

"But there's nothing. Nothing down there but dirt and more ice," he said. "I have to stay awake so that we stay alive."

"You don't." Moving down, I rested my hand over his heart—beating strong and steady as it should, and would for as long as I had anything to say about it. "You've slept for however much time has passed, and we're alive. You don't need to stay awake. You need me."

The grin was back. "Finish that sentence."

Rolling my eyes, I huffed. "You need me to huddle with you every night for warmth. You're no better than a helpless kitten, Roark," I lofted. "What would you do without me?"

"Well, I wouldn't *be* in this mess without you, so—"

I smothered a pillow over his head, muffling his guffaws.

"Gods, this is good," he said, making me yelp as he pulled me closer. "Why weren't we doing this all this time, instead of fighting over things I don't even remember?"

I grabbed hold of my tongue to keep it in.

"Because I remember." I could never keep control of my tongue anyway. "What we were fighting over was no small thing. It's everything if we both want to make this work."

"What do you mean?"

I raised my brows against his collarbone. "Nuala."

A deep, gusty sigh tickled my crown. "Her again."

"I'm not being petty, or jealous, or ridiculous, Dominic." I tipped back to look at him. "You knew she was in love with you while you spun that fairy story of you two being nothing more than friends. You lied to me when you didn't have to, which makes me think you thought you had to. Because you didn't want me to know you love her too."

"That isn't the reason at all," he replied. "I didn't lie. She was in love with me, but I've always only seen her as a friend. A close friend. I never saw her as more than that, but I'd be a blind idiot if I didn't see she wanted more from me. That didn't matter when we were set to be married.

"I had no problem sharing my kingdom with my oldest friend. Someone I trusted. While she was happy to be with the man she loved. It worked," he stated. "Until you."

"Until me?"

"I'm saying I didn't care who I married or how many until you," he said. "To me, marriage was a means to acquire more land, heirs, and power. I *did not care* until I had the chance to marry a woman who irritates the shit out of me."

I gaped at him. "Excuse me?"

"You heard me. You're a massive, infuriating problem, and you have been since you stole my dragon, and that throne chose you as the true heir. Ever since I was eleven, no one has been stronger, smarter, or more dangerous than me. No one's had the power to ruin my life if only they choose.

"I hated you for it. I meant it when I cornered you in that hallway, and said I'd take your life, because it felt like you were taking mine.

"But then... I watched you. I watched you stomp Keir's balls. Highly trained warrior reduced to a bawling mess at your feet. I watched you pick yourself up and climb back on Reyna's back, over and over again, even after she broke bones.

"You blackmailed that library guy into free tutoring. At the party, those mages were throwing their magic around without a clue, while you sat back, studied the problem, then bested them with a few sweet words to a walking pile of mud. Not to mention, you survive the most brutal training in Adalinda with no magic."

"I only did with your help," I protested.

"Help you weren't afraid to demand even if it meant tenting my pants in the middle of the day."

"The only effect my kumquats had on you was open-mouthed shock, and the thought you wouldn't lose your throne, because I'd soon be under twenty-four-hour care of the healers."

"Trust me." He flicked my chin. "That's not what made me late to the next lesson."

If there was something to say in response to that, I didn't know what it was.

"Fucking hell, Ainsley. Dervin putting me in that dream told me everything I wanted to deny. My dream woman is you. This impulsive, ruthless, clever, quick-thinking warrior who's never been afraid of me, and does whatever it takes to win." He caught a tear traveling down my cheek. "How could I want anyone else? When there's you."

It took a while to trust myself to speak. "Then, it really was a kiss goodbye?"

He nodded. "It was. I was trying not to be a bastard, and break the news to her gently, but all it did was nearly lose me you."

"But then why did she look so pleased with herself that night? Woman was strutting around like the goodbye sex was as good as the goodbye kiss. I thought—" I cut myself off.

"Thought what?" he asked, frowning. "That I told her we'd have an *arrangement* after you and I got married?"

The answer was written on my face.

"Huh. That explains why you looked like you really were going to cut my head off and mount it on Reyna's horn."

"It's not funny, Dominic. Nuala didn't look like someone who just got told they'd never be with the person they love."

Something I now know with absolute certainty. If I had lost you out in that snow, I'd never smile again.

"That's because she is going to marry the person she loves," he replied easily. "But that person won't be me. Nuala loved me for years, but got nothing but friendship in return. She didn't take a vow of celibacy during that time."

"What does that mean?"

"It means she's had lovers, and one of them earned the name," he replied. "Nuala has been with my sister, Tyra, for two years. They thought no one knew."

"Tyra." A memory dislodged from my brain. "Isn't she the sister who saved my life when I was poisoned by the venom?"

"Yes. Tyra's a good person. Kind. Generous. She travels through the kingdom, using her magic to heal people for free. Doesn't ask for a single thing in return. Not even a thank-you. So naturally," he said, "my father despises her."

"Of course he does."

"At the moment, he largely ignores her while basking in the undeserved praise he gets for having such a wise and giving daughter. But both Tyra and Nuala know he'll never approve a marriage contract between them, even if the one I have with Nuala didn't exist."

"But you will."

"Yes," he said softly. "Nuala was happy because I told her after we got married, she and Tyra would be free to live their lives together without losing our friendship, or all the things our marriage would've given her."

"It was that easy for her to trade one love for another?"

"I don't imagine any of this is easy for her, but I think most could find some happiness in trading the man who doesn't love you back for the woman who always has."

My brows crowded together. "What about the next morning? She told everyone about the marriage and abdication, and claimed that I was betraying my people for your cock. Did her possessiveness come back with a vengeance?"

"No. She's my friend, Princess. She jumped to my defense because she doesn't trust you and believes you're taking advantage of me." His touch skated over my hip. "What she doesn't know is I want nothing more than for you to take advantage of me. Use me for my cock. Do what you must. Honestly... whenever you're ready..."

The pillow went over his face again. The man was incorrigible.

"Dominic, if you mean all of these things, why did you try and throw me off to your brothers?"

His chuckles stopped. "Because, Ainsley. It's no good if it's not real. If we're going to spend every day like we have the last few days—two people making a small room miles wide with their distance. I'll have my parents' marriage with a woman I don't love. I won't have it with you."

Breath trapped in my lungs. "You love me?"

Dominic smiled soft and sweet, painting my lips with a runaway tear. "I wouldn't have died for you if I didn't, and that was real and honest. You may find reason to doubt all the things I've said, but you'll know this to be true. If it's a choice between me and you, I choose you."

I was crying so hard, I could barely breathe. "I choose you too."

"I love you, Ainsley Boreen."

"I love you too."

I launched at him, lips crashing on his, and screamed.

Pain racked my body, resounding through every limb and muscle with their vindictive reminder—I used the magic, I would pay the price.

"Okay, that's enough." Dominic climbed out in all his bare-naked glory. He rescued my clothes, dressed me, and placed me on my back. He went to work massaging my achy everything without needing to be asked.

I hissed more than I moaned. It *hurt*. All I wanted to do was hold him, but my arms had no interest in responding.

Dominic rubbed me down slow and thorough. For all his flirting, he focused on his task and didn't push to massage somewhere more interesting. It was the sexiest thing he'd done all night. Caring for me without the expectation of anything in return.

I never had that from a man. I never thought I could have that with a man.

The truth was we had to come together in the way that we did. The lies, the tricks, his trying to get me killed, and me breaking him in pieces. If Dominic had come into my life singing praises of my beauty and ruthlessness, I'd have still thought him a liar. I didn't think enough of myself to believe I deserved anything good.

Instead we got to see the ugly, desperate, scheming, tricky sides of each other, and I would not have fallen in love with him in any other way. Our broken pieces matched. We fit together. We would rule together. We would be together.

Dominic kneaded my foot with the palm of his hand. A soft sigh escaped me. I did not hurt there, but I wasn't about to stop him.

"Tell me something you've never told anyone."

He hummed. "I want to be a writer. Not a king general, or his heir. Just another ink-covered scribe surrounded by a mountain of books, and a family to read them to."

"A writer?" I breathed. "I didn't know. You speak of ruling with such conviction."

"Saving Adalinda from my father is also my dream. But it is because he stole that other future from me. The boy that was forced to slaughter his siblings, and was broken down to nothing so he could fashion his perfect warrior heir..." He shook his head. "He doesn't get to live a life as peaceful and irreverent as a writer. I have to atone for what I've done.

"I can't make it right for Roderick or the others, but I can see to it that my father doesn't destroy any more dreams."

I ached to hug him. My hand slid across the bed and touched his thigh. I hoped he felt the comfort pouring from me.

Dominic traveled up my ankle. "Tell me something you've never told anyone."

"My mother is a Druk."

He stilled. "What?"

Taking a breath, I let the final truth tumble out. "This is what I couldn't tell you, Dominic. What I couldn't tell anyone. I'm not lying about not knowing her, or being raised as an orphan. All I ever had of my mother was the letter she tucked in my swaddling when she abandoned me in the woods.

"It said she had to leave me for my own safety, but one day she'd come back for me because I had a destiny to fulfill for her and the glory of the Druks."

His body angled away, stopping me from seeing his expression.

"Please." I squeezed his thigh. "Say something."

"Queen Kisandra," he said, disbelief lacing his voice. "Does this mean she's a Druk? That's why she stayed away even though she lived for decades after losing the kingdom? She didn't want anyone to know what she'd become."

I blinked, staring at his back. That was the most simple and obvious explanation, and I hadn't considered it for a second. Was this the answer? I truly was the princess and heir to the throne of Adalinda. My mother hid herself away from that throne, because she knew the choices she made would not let her sit upon it ever again.

"I don't know," I said honestly. "You were right, Dominic. I was more surprised than anyone when the throne didn't kill me. All I know is what that letter said. I've been hiding that truth all my life."

He turned toward me. All the disgust, shock, hate that I expected to find... wasn't there. "Why tell me now?"

"I don't want there to be any more secrets or lies between us. I don't want a marriage like your parents either. We have to trust each other." I looked away. "Which means you have to tell me what you're really thinking."

"What do you mean? You— Ainsley, were you worried this news would change something between us? That I'd reject you for the actions of a woman you don't know?" He lifted my chin. "I would never do that. You've met my father. I've always been seen as a copy of the man by everyone except you.

"Your mother made her own choices, and those choices won't stop me from loving you."

My eyes watered. Damn it, it was the hell my heart and body had been put through that was making me weep like a sieve. "You truly mean that?"

"Yes. Wholly and without hesitation."

My voice cracked on a laugh. "I love you too. You don't know what it means to me to hear you say that. All my life, I've been treated like a cursed child for being an orphan. People spat on me, slammed doors in my face, told me my coin was no good when I came with an empty belly. If anyone knew I was a Druk's daughter on top of all that... There's no doubt in my mind that anyone but the sister would've picked me up, read that letter, and thrown me in the river.

"I accepted that I could never tell anyone this secret. But no one is you."

He laced his fingers through mine. "This sister sounds like an amazing woman."

"She is," I said, smiling despite myself. "She never made me feel like I had to be grateful to her. If anything, she treated us like the best days of her life were when we came into it. I... I couldn't have asked for a better borrowed mother."

"Tell me about her." He gave me a knowing look. "And *we*."

"Are you sure? I have more brothers and sisters than you."

"What? That can't be true."

"I'll prove it. First, there's Velez. He's the one that taught me that if I get in a fight with a guy, not to bullshit around and go for the balls first. And my sister, Eala, she's an air mage who uses her magic to fly. When we were eight, we..."

Dominic and I stayed up long into the night, or day. We didn't worry about the passing of time while we laughed, joked, and shared the good memories. The ones we never told anyone else for all the heartbreaking reasons.

We collapsed in each other's arms long after, laughter still on our lips, arms tight around each other to keep out the cold—and for another reason.

I didn't think I could be happier than I was falling asleep with his heart beating strong against me.

Then, I woke up the next morning and found him gone.

Pushing up, I moved my arms and wiggled my legs curiously. I didn't feel completely myself, but the pain had morphed from unbearable to manageable.

Running water turned my head to the bathroom door, then the sound of him climbing in. My mind was made up in the time it took me to get up and walk inside.

Dominic blinked at me, in the middle of washing his hair. Steam rose from the water—heated by hellfire and twice as inviting as the tepid baths I'd been taking during our silent fight.

"Princess?"

"I had a question," I said, leaning against the door.

"Okay?"

"Still want to turn fantasy into reality?"

Confusion furrowed his brows, then understanding flicked on. "Get in here."

I didn't get a chance to move before Dominic scooped me up and brought me squealing into the tub. Our lips connected as we hit the water. Both rough and tender, he nipped my bottom lip, demanding entrance.

I welcomed him happily—tongues tangling, hearts racing, moans filling the small space.

The water deliciously heated my muscles, loosening up tightened coils and relaxing kinks I didn't know I had. Or maybe that was his hand moving up my thigh, burning a trail outside, then inside as he guided my legs apart.

I drew him close, sealing our bodies together so that not even water could get through.

The time we spent together in that dream was fresh in my mind. I still felt his hands gripping my waist, and the heat from his magic losing control.

I loved that night for what it gave us. The first breaks in our armor that made us see we were meant for each other. But it didn't change the fact that we didn't know it was real.

It was impossible to say what Dervin intended when he put us both in the same dream. Did he see our desire for each other and want to nudge us on the right path, or did he think it'd be funny?

Either way, the feeling I had for that night would never come close to the one I had the night before when I put it all on the line to the Dominic I knew to be true, and he gave me nothing but love and acceptance in return.

I didn't question it anymore. My doubts evaporated. Father Parthelan and Mother Zaeah did split our souls and put them in each other. In Dominic, he protected my confidence and faith. In me, I held his forgiveness and belief he was a good man despite his father's desperation to make him anything but.

"I love you," we said at the same time, then laughed.

"What do you love about me, Ainsley? Do you love that I do... this?" He pressed a soft kiss to my throat.

I giggled. "I do love that, yes."

"Do you love when I do this?" He kissed me so hard and passionately, my lower belly spasmed.

"That... is my favorite thing you do," I gasped.

"Yeah?" His grin was wolfish. "That's your favorite? Or this is?"

I didn't get a chance to ask what this was. Dominic dropped below the surface, draping my legs over his shoulders.

My moan caught on a cry, dropping my head back on the rim.

Dominic tasted and tortured my wanton hole, flicking my helpless nub mercilessly, then dropping down when my bucking got too out of control—denying my orgasm.

His ability to hold his breath for a long time was impressive, but not as impressive as his expert tongue dipping in and out of my well.

My nails scratched the tub. The heels of my feet pounded the basin. I was losing control, and it was so much better than a dream.

I'd get to keep the memory of his touch on my skin, and the taste of me on his lips. I'd get to keep him.

Dominic popped out of the water, surprising me, kissing me midgasp, and keeping my breath for himself.

Back under he went, with two companions to bring to the party.

"Oooh, yes, Dom..." I breathed as two fingers slipped inside me and spread—stretching me to make me whimper.

Dominic started moving—slow at first, then picking up the pace. Rising up, he captured my nipple between his teeth and sucked, overwhelming my senses.

I came hard, back bending over the rim, and cries near screams.

"Yep," I rasped, flopping in the tub like a damp sock. "I love it when you do that too."

He chuckled. "It's me." *Kiss.* "Who loves." *Kiss.* "Your perfect body beneath me." *Kiss.* "Loves the way you bite your lip when you moan." *Kiss.* "Loves your fingers pulling my hair and your legs breaking me in half."

Kiss.

"I love that you always smell like morning dew and sunshine." *Kiss.* "That every hug you give is fierce and warm, and every kiss lingers like it could be the last."

Kiss.

"I love that you're ridiculously beautiful and clever, and of all people, you chose me." He kissed me sweet. "It makes sense that my life was yours to claim, because you already stole my heart, little thief."

I bit my lip then, lids heavy with unshed tears. "Wow. My reason that I love how you fuck me isn't stacking up as high as yours now. Can I go again?"

"Why?" He nipped my nose. "Don't you love it?"

"I don't know," I purred, wrapping my arms and legs around him. "Truthfully, you've only done it in our minds. We'd have to repeat everything we did in the dream to make it real. We should repeat it a few times, actually. Just to be sure."

"Oh, is that right? How about this for real?"

Dominic pushed inside, rolling my eyes up in my head. The grand question of if this was as good as our perfect dreamworld was answered.

It was a million times better.

Dominic leaned back, setting me on his lap. I rocked on the balls of my feet, meeting him thrust for thrust. Bouncing pump for pump.

"Fuck's sake, Princess. You're amazing."

"We should settle—uh," I cried out, momentarily losing the power of speech when he hit that spot. "—if Princess is a term of endearment or not."

"It was a term of endearment—fuck!—even when it wasn't." He reared up, splashing half the water on the floor. The room spun and I found myself on my knees. "I called you my princess because I knew one day you'd be my queen."

What I wanted to reply went straight out of my head when he rammed inside, lifting me off my knees.

We were as one, moving in perfect sync. Even our groans were in tune. I pressed my cheek against the cool tub, trying to anchor myself to reality as pleasure like I couldn't believe lit all my nerve endings with untamable hellfire.

How laughable that I called my previous tumbles with those greedy and ashamed lovers sex. This was true lovemaking. The giving and taking of two equals who cared about nothing but making the other feel things they didn't know they could.

Dominic always lit that fire in me. He challenged me where others dismissed me. He named me a worthy adversary where others called me worthless. He saw me when I didn't want to be seen.

He filled me to bursting, stretching my middle until it felt so good it hurt. Moisture pebbled on my skin that had nothing to do with the bath. I was hot, alive, shaky, and in love. My core clenched tighter than a corked bottle. My hardened nipples could cut water. Only Dominic had this effect on me.

"Gods, you perfect, gorgeous, *tight*, amazing creature. You don't have nothing to do today. You have me to do today."

I moaned something unintelligible in response. I hoped it sounded close to a yes.

He struck that spot and pleasure overcame me—crashing over my body as I shuddered and cried out, holding on to the tub for dear life. Millions of colored lights burst behind my eyes—my body his portrait like a light mage painted the sky.

I came down slow, his lips soft and murmuring sweetness in my ear.

"Oh, gods," I breathed, head spinning.

"Better than a dream?"

"That was the best sex... anyone's ever had in a dream or out." I let him seat us both back in the tub, his arm secure and safe around me. "But just to be sure..."

"We should do two more times in this tub, and five more times in bed." He bit my earlobe, then kissed it in apology. He could've skipped the kiss and went back to the biting. "I've a thing for you in animal pelts. Imagine how hard it's been for me to hold that in the last two weeks?"

I laughed. "Is it crazy that I can't remember why we were trying so desperately to leave this place?"

"Oh, that's easy." He tipped my chin, kissing me deep. "I'm fighting like hell to get home... so I can finally make you my wife."

Well, there was no chance of his cock getting a break after he said something like that. We made love in every place and position imaginable. I orgasmed so many times, I lost count.

It was as if the final walls came down, and Dominic and I were free to be ourselves. Every morning, he helped me with my reading, then left me to my assignment while he went out to send his signals for three hours, and only three. I warned him if he was gone too long, I'd go searching for him.

When he came back, we ate and talked about anything and everything. I told him about learning to pick pockets, and the one time I was caught and brought before the magistrate. The only reason I still had ten fingers was because my brothers and sisters launched an attack. Led by Velez, they blew in, throwing their magic around, and causing so much chaos—I slipped out unnoticed.

"Wow. How did you all get away with that?"

"We didn't." Dominic and I curled up on blankets before the fireplace—naked. I practically purred under his soft, teasing fingers traveling where they wished up and down my body. "Watch Guards showed up at the orphanage to take us all. Sister Aven summoned a tidal wave that washed them into the next town. I think they were humiliated to have been beaten by a bunch of dirty orphans and their carer, because they didn't come back."

"She summoned a tidal wave?"

"Thirty feet high."

He gaped at me. "I've never heard of such a strong water mage."

"She is strong. Sister Aven was a noble." His brows shot to his hairline. "When she was a girl, her township was taken over by a group of mages called *Faynari*."

"*Faynari*. God slayer."

My head bobbed, eyes glazing as I peered into the fire. "They had powerful gifts and thought themselves living gods. Sister Aven would say even in a world where everyone and everything is the same, people will find a way to hold themselves above their fellow man.

"The first thing *Faynari* did was invade her home, kill her parents, then they came after her and her older sister. Sister Aven used her gift and filled their lungs with water before they broke through their door. They were choking—dying—when the blow got her from behind.

"It was her sister," I said. "She was with *Faynari* and believed in what they did. Only the strong should rule. She left the back gate open so they could come in.

"Sister Aven has powerful magic, but her sister was even stronger. She couldn't fight back against her, and so she watched her people brought under the rule of tyrants and murderers. The hell she went through in the ten years before the Royal Riders took the town back and killed *Faynari*... she still can't speak about it." I burrowed closer to him, seeking his warmth.

"Fucking hell. How have I never heard of this?"

I hesitated. "Because, Dominic. They paid the Watch Guards off for years to look the other way. Coin, drink, whichever women they wanted to snatch off the street and have their way with. It suited them to do nothing and reap their evil rewards. Sister Aven said it wasn't until the guards started demanding more and more ryus that their alliance broke, and *Faynari* killed them.

"There was no hiding it after the guards never reported back in. So when others were sent to investigate, they discovered what was going on, and the riders were sent. It was such a failure and disgrace to the guards, that they buried knowledge of the entire thing," I said. "After she was freed, Sister Aven renounced magic and joined the order. She devoted her life to caring for the abandoned. Like the world abandoned her people."

"Oh, Ainsley," he whispered, fist balling against my stomach. "I thought I knew the plights of my people. Believed my years running around the streets of Ghidorah taught me something of our kingdom's struggles. I don't have a fucking clue."

"Dominic." I cupped his cheek. "This I promise you. You're not the only one who knows our lives were not made better when your father defeated the usurper. We're just living in a different kind of hell. The only fight you'll have is from those who cling to their power. Those who never had any will support you, and they vastly outnumber everyone else."

"Do you believe we can do it?" he asked, brushing my hair from my eyes. "Take over the kingdom. Bring about a golden era of peace and fairness."

I smiled. "Between us we've conquered death. We can do anything, Dominic Roark. Of that I have no doubt."

Our days together bled into weeks. By our unreliable count, we were gone for a full moon.

"What do they think happened to us?" I rested my cheek on Dominic's head, holding him from behind as he pored over his writings. My love told me he wanted to be a writer. There was nothing stopping him now. "What did they do when Awnan showed up with that marriage contract? I wonder if your father did anything to stop him."

"I'm sure my father did many things to ensure it all went his way. He may have even killed Awnan," Dominic confessed. "Might be why no one came for us."

"But still you go out every morning?"

"I won't give up, Princess. We'll be free of this place any day now. I can feel it."

That was one new thing I learned of my devilish, smirking love. He was an optimist.

I just smiled, accepting his certainty as my own.

Dominic gathered his papers, then opened the top drawer. "Hmm. Now that we're speaking of marriage contracts, isn't it past time we signed ours?"

My eyes popped open. "What?"

"Our marriage contract." He took out the cursed thing and unfurled it. "I do believe the agreement was that when you could read it, we'd sign this. Unless you have decided to leave me for one of my brothers after all."

Before my eyes, Dominic picked up his charcoal and signed his name at the bottom. He handed both to me.

"Very funny," I said, throat tight. "Now put that away."

"I won't. Deal's a deal, Princess."

I pushed his hands back. "I can't read it."

"Yes, you can."

Yes, I could. My reading and writing had improved by leaps and bounds. With Dominic as a constant, dedicated teacher, how could it not?

"I *won't* read it, then. Nor will I sign it. On the fire with that thing and we'll never speak of it again."

He cocked a brow, amusement playing at his lips. I was two seconds away from throwing him out into the snow.

"Ainsley, read it."

"No."

I gave him my back, storming off to the bathroom and the only door I could slam in his face. Why he wanted me to read the words that would lodge another splinter of bitterness in my heart after he worked so hard to remove the first one, was a mystery to me. But I didn't care to discover it.

Footfalls bounded behind me. I shrieked to find myself lifted off my feet and tossed on the bed.

"Mother Zaeah, bless me, woman. You're so stubborn." He pinned me kicking and cursing beneath his body. Taking my hand, he pressed the parchment firmly in it. "Please, my love. Read it."

I don't know if it was the tenderness in his voice, or the knowledge that I wasn't going anywhere that made trembling fingers reach out and unfurl the scroll.

"Here thus…" I swallowed hard and continued. "Here thus details the marriage contract between Dominic Augustus Roark and

Ainsley Boreen. I, Dominic, hereby state that I love Ainsley unreservedly and with every drop of being in my soul," I whispered, breath leaving me.

What? What is this?

I scrambled up, holding the parchment to my face. "I make these vows with a clear mind and love in my heart. I will serve her without question. Worship her without restraint. Be honest with her without holding anything back. And give in to her every desire and need with an obsession that borders reckless." I chuckled at that, eyes filling.

"I've never wished for a wife who only speaks when spoken to. Or withers away behind a selfish, cruel, greedy man who doesn't realize the gift he has in a partner who'll stand by his side for life."

I thought of his father and mother when I read that. I'm sure Dominic did too.

"I wish to be with someone who challenges me. Fights me. Outwits me. Forgives me. Loves me. I knew from the day I met her defiant eyes—ever the rebellious queen even as two guards carried her to her death—that I would be a slave to her for the rest of my days.

"As such, the terms of our marriage are whatever she wishes them to be, and mine is that I get to be with her in this life and the next."

Tears ran down the page, staining his beautiful words. The whole time, this is what the marriage contract said? Written before I found him in the snow and we said we loved each other. Sitting in the desk while I thought the worst of him.

"Why didn't you tell me?" I whispered.

"Because you didn't only have to read the words for yourself. You had to believe them too. I pray that you do."

He dropped to one knee. Reaching into his pocket, he withdrew the ruby-kissed body chain. "Because I'm not giving you up for anything."

I crawled to him, then stopped. Vaulting off the bed, I grabbed the charcoal and wrote my name as fast as I was able.

"Yes, Dominic."

I jumped and he was there. Catching me. Kissing me.

"I do."

He groaned.

I hugged him tighter, wrapping my legs around his waist. Made me shiver that my very touch excited him.

"Ahh," he cried, breaking our kiss.

"I'm sorry. Did I hurt you?"

"N-no, it's not you." He released me, hands flying up to clutch his head. "It's— It's— Ahh! Ahhhh!"

I backed away, terror racking me when Dominic fell to the floor bellowing.

Agony twisted his handsome features, etching pain deep into his soul.

"Dominic? Dominic! What's wrong? What's happening?"

"Ainsley!"

Boom!

The earth rattled, ground heaving as though it wished to throw our little stone cabin to the sky.

"He's… here." Beyond all understanding, Dominic laughed as he screamed. "He's here!"

I didn't think. Racing to the door, I threw it open and beheld the most impossible sight.

"Reyna?"

No.

Even as I said her name, I knew this magnificent creature wasn't her. This dragon was taller, bulkier, and boasted ridges where she had horns. His name came to me as if it was always known.

"Libelle."

"Ainsley..."

I ran back inside and helped Dominic to his feet. Soft hisses of pain escaped him as the bond formed.

"This," I cried. "This is what you've been doing out there every morning."

"You told me there was an unbonded hellfire dragon some-where in Edjer. I signaled him for weeks, hoping my fire would draw his attention.

"It did, and he came. He took one look at me and flew away. That was the night you found me in the snow.

"He knocked me out for daring to use my fire to stop him. As you know, I didn't wake up."

My jaw clenched. I would forever hate thinking of that night.

"Why didn't you tell me?"

"I couldn't tell you that I failed in convincing our only way out of here to help us," he said. "All the same, I kept calling to him in hopes he'd come back."

"He did more than that. He bonded with you."

"I don't know why." He massaged his temples. "I feel his disdain for me even now."

"I felt it too." Together, we made for the door. "Reyna's mother distrusted, bordering on hated humans after her babies were killed by Reyna under their watch. She did not instill a love of them to her next broods. It's why they all remained un—"

"Ah!" He winced. "Yes, I will certainly have trouble with him, but he's here to help us. Why else would he come?"

We stepped out into the bitter winds, facing up to Libelle. If it was possible for a dragon to curl their lip in disgust, I'd swear he was doing it then.

"Will you take us home?" Dominic shouted against the wind.

Libelle snarled—a ferocious, stomach-clenching growl that revealed all of his lethal fangs.

We backed up so fast, we almost tripped.

He sat back on his haunches, snorting and giving the air that he was satisfied that we were afraid of him.

Meeting Dominic's eye with one of his own, he nodded.

"May I ask..." I stepped forward. "I know that you know, Libelle. Please, tell me if Reyna is alive."

He looked at me for an uncomfortable amount of time—intelligence mixing with the dislike in his eye.

Again, he nodded.

I took Dominic's hand, the other still holding tight to our marriage contract.

"Let's go home."

Chapter Twenty-Five

Libelle sliced through the air—a living lance of wind and speed. It was only Dominic's cocoon of hellfire that shielded us from the torrents of ice.

It was a quick trip inside to gather the few things we wanted to take with us, before rushing out and climbing on Libelle's back.

Emphasis on climbing.

He refused to lower his body, shook and stomped the earth when we tried to climb his foreleg, then when we finally got on, he snarled and snapped the air—clearly wishing he could snap us right off. Reyna's nestmate had no desire to be bonded, let alone carry humans on his back. Why he'd done both would remain a mystery to me.

"How long will it take us to get to Golden City?" I shouted back. Dominic held me close from behind. I didn't wear my sticky boots that fateful night I went to the Yellow Tail. I didn't know how to ride a dragon without being magically attached to them. "What do we do when we get there?"

"I still don't know where in Edjer we were, but I expect we'll be home in several hours. A day's flight at the most."

The most magnificent words. I still couldn't believe he was saying them to me.

"When we get there, we go straight to my father. You signed the contract. Law says if you break it, you'll be put to death. There's no way the High Council upholds that law after they find out about Awnan, the puppet mage, and where we've been the last month. My father has every reason to force them to listen."

He pressed a kiss to the back of my neck. "Trust me, Awnan will not get away with what he did. The paper king will not rule, and you won't spend a day suffering under his barbaric terms. This nightmare ends in but a few hours."

Smiling, I leaned back, burrowing in his neck. "Of course I trust you."

None of those horrible things would happen because if the High Council tried to uphold that evil contract, Dominic would kill them along with Awnan, who he already marked for death. It amused him over the last few weeks to imagine how he'd do it. His methods got more and more gruesome by the day. Awnan's action did indirectly get Dominic killed, and directly enslaved me to his contract of rape and treason. Anything Dominic did to him was too kind.

We didn't say much as we flew. Dominic was focusing on maintaining our shell of warmth, and I didn't want to distract him. Something else distracted me.

Adalinda.

I knew nothing of my home outside of Ossian and Golden City. Tales and whispers of the marketplace told me of the great Singing Ice Mountains of Edjer where the wind danced with the peaks in such a way, it sounded like a lovely maiden's croon.

It was while listening to an Edjerian cobbler who paid me a copper to clean his tools that I imagined his capital city. No less grand than Golden City, but its opposite in every way.

Soaring white towers pierced the sky instead of gold. People covered in furs and thick boots skated, yes, skated on blades of iron. Ice frequently slicked the roads. They learned to adapt long ago. He spoke of the bell tower—ringing the noonday call to prayer throughout the whole city. A time of the day when everything stopped, and they gave thanks for all the gods had given them.

My eyes filled as we soared over the singing mountains, their haunting cry beautiful in its natural magic. Those tears dried when the capital came into view. I cried out excitedly when the noon bell rang from the highest white-capped tower, a beacon for miles around.

It amazed me to have already walked these streets in my mind, and still to have reality be so much better. Below, unnaturally quick figures skidded to a stop, found a spot, and kneeled to pray.

"One day we'll come back," Dominic said. "As a wedding present. We'll visit all the grand cities of the kingdom. What do you think?"

Happiness filled me to bursting. "The only thing that would make that offer better is if we fuck in all the grand cities of the kingdom."

"My love, we're going to fuck in, around, and on the way to those cities. That is heavily implied in every offer I make. Even if I say we're going for a walk in the garden. You should naturally assume I mean a tumble in the garden."

"Naturally. We—"

Libelle bucked hard, unnecessary, and *deliberate*. We popped off his back and came down rough, scrambling to hold on.

"He wants us to be quiet," Dominic gritted, holding me firm. "I sense that he intends to pretend we're not here."

Nodding, I pressed my lips shut tight. Libelle didn't have to carry out his threat twice. If he wanted silence, he'd get silence.

Mother Zaeah knew why he changed his mind, came to us, and bonded with Dominic. He didn't want any part of us, so why not leave us in that frozen wasteland to rot? Plus, what did it mean for Dominic to have a bond that wanted little to do with him? Would he join him in rider training? Would he break the bond and fly back to Edjer once we were delivered?

I didn't voice these thoughts as we left the capital behind. Partly because Libelle wasn't interested in hearing a word out of my human mouth. The other part because there was no reason to put doubts in Dominic's mind before Libelle did whatever he was going to do. What mattered was we were going back home, and Reyna was waiting for us.

Even if the High Council allowed Awnan's false marriage contract to be approved, no one would allow an innocent dragon to be killed. Dominic promised me that, and he was right. Trust in his word made the world feel safer for me.

If only I knew why I didn't feel or hear anything of her for an entire moon. I knew from that accidental trip through her memories that Reyna occasionally took off on her own to visit her mother in the firepits, and wherever else her heart took her. Unlike me, she knew Dominic was safe to be let out of her sight.

I felt nothing different about their bond due to distance. Was it because Awnan sent me as far as possible without throwing me across the Dark Border?

I mused as the terrain changed beneath me. Snow and mountains fled before warm, humid temperatures and flat, grassy land. We were over Hyelong. The last province to separate us from Golden City.

The little I knew of Hyelong I learned from my Hyelongan brother, and Velez when he told of the place he was living in his letters from away. And, of course, that Hyelong was where Lemomi was born and lived while she used her gift to win card games and collect coin. I wondered at any point did she see the terrible things she would do to prevent a worse fate, and if she considered her actions would cause them.

With everything out in the open between us, I told Dominic what Lemomi said about the booted lizard and that she prayed that future would never come. We spent many a long night talking about what it meant that he ran into the pub with that very creature riding in his pocket.

He pointed out that just because she rubbed her arm while speaking of the hell coming for unique mages, didn't mean she was connecting the two. There were other tattoos on that arm, so he had a point. He also said that no one had or would consider him a unique mage even if it was discovered that he wielded hellfire.

He'd firmly be categorized as a death mage, and that was long ago accepted to be as natural as the elements. Water evaporated, earth became scorched and cracked, the wind stopped blowing, and fires went out. What was more in harmony with living... than dying?

Dominic was not the harbinger of this fate, and after he assured me of that, he addressed my true fear. That if this unique mage came about before we took the throne, his father would use the new laws to kill me, or bind me to his service.

Despite Drake's outrage over the accusation, it did feel like he was experimenting with me. He put me through gruesome death after gruesome death to find the limits of my magic, and seemed ever more intrigued when there wasn't one. He all but stopped paying attention to the other recruits in special talents and devoted his time to me.

Dominic told me Drake was loyal to his father. Master Whelan admitted he'd been checking up on all the unique mages, even going so far as to track down their parentage.

Dominic swore that future wouldn't come about, but hadn't it already? Putting useless magics and mages to death—the fodder battalion. Binding the mages he covets in service to him—the memory mage, and the mages Maili hinted at when she told me to be careful what I say and think of the general.

Seemed to me that a unique mage rising up and confirming the worst fears in the people suited King General Roark very well. He could continue as he had out in the open with the full support of the High Council and the kingdom.

The true question was why? I knew why he used a memory mage to erase what he'd done to his own children. Everyone would see him for the monster that he was. Not the hero who saved the kingdom from the usurper.

He'd been collecting, and killing them in the fodder battalion, long before I ever came along, so he hadn't feared a threat to his throne then. All the same, making sure he never lost his power could be the reason. It could be, but the reason didn't feel enough. Who did he need to protect his power from?

As he told me himself, even if he didn't have a right to the throne, no one else did either. The golden statues in the throne room proved it. The queen's magic rejected everyone who sat upon it except for her descendant. With no one from the House of Boreen appearing in the last fifty years, the king general had no reason to believe someone would.

I rubbed my head, mind spinning in circles. I believed Dominic absolutely when he said he wouldn't let his father hurt me. Even so, I had a terrible feeling fate was trying to tell me something, and not Lemomi.

She never saw the drawing Dominic did. Neither did the person it was meant for—Orla.

I was the one who saw it after Lemomi hinted a terrible fate was attached to that stupid lizard in boots. Why did it fall more and more in line with the strange feelings I'd been having that something wasn't right, and it hadn't been right for a long time?

Twenty years ago, a woman leaves a babe in the woods who turns out to be the heir to the throne of Adalinda. It asks the person who finds me to care for me as their own, but of all the things they tell this person, they say I'm destined to bring glory to the Druks, not to rule the kingdom. One truth risks my life and heaps upon me a burden of shame and suspicion. The other would've placed me in the care of a loyalist family who would have loved and reared me.

Move forward years into the future, my borrowed brother, Velez, makes a promise to always take care of us. He leaves for Hyelong, disappears, and then reappears in Golden City—following me. Where was he all that time? Why didn't he reach out to me before?

All of that was strange, but none as strange as King General Roark.

Decades ago, he defeats the usurper and takes over the kingdom she conquered. Instead of returning sovereignty to Ghidorah, Edjer, Nehebkau, and Hyelong, he claims rule over them too, and then marries all of their former queens, princesses, and royals so that their bloodlines were his bloodlines.

The message there was obvious: a Roark would always rule these lands.

But his following actions were clear as mud. He outlaws education for commoners, seemingly because the usurper wouldn't have caused the rebellion if she hadn't learned enough to discover forbidden magics. But the effect on the kingdom was devastating.

This I knew thanks to Dominic teaching me more than just reading over the last moon cycle. He also spent a fair amount of time teaching me history and politics—both things I had to know once we took over the kingdom.

The general's ban on education was accompanied by heavy taxes. He drained the peasant class of money, then made sure they didn't have the education to make more. Their only choice was to sell their magic—which was just another way to keep us down. The average peasant didn't have much magical ability to be worth much. As a result, Dominic told me crime had risen sharply in every province. Stealing, egg theft, black markets, and people trading.

If he knew this, and *I* knew this from growing up in poor Ossian, his father certainly did too. Yet, that hadn't moved him to amend a single law. Why worry about your people starving in the streets when your time was better served culling your weakest offspring like a bird throws a one-winged chick out of the nest? Why lower taxes to a reasonable amount when you could focus on hunting down unique mages instead?

It could be said the general simply despised commoners and only thought royals and nobles had a right to live happily, but did his actions truly say so? The general made it punishable by death for a commoner to bond with a dragon. He also passed the law that forced every bonded rider to join the Royal Riders.

Only a quarter of recruits survived training, and then the rest were made to carry the protection of the entire kingdom on their shoulders. They had to defend the Dark Border, fight Druks, put down peasant uprisings, hunt down egg thieves, and defeat gangs like Faynari. Being bonded with a dragon grants you a long life, being a Royal Rider didn't. Most of us died within ten years of service. Our mandatory service time was fifty.

Seemed to be the only people living a grand and pampered life since the usurper was overthrown, were the rich and unbonded nobles that got to live safely in their palace with an army of Watch Guards outside protecting them. The rest of us were poor commoners or battle-worn soldiers.

And then, of course, there was me.

General Roark tries to kill an impostor, and instead announces to the entire court that the princess has returned. He made two plans to kill me. Either Madame Sela found proof I used forbidden magic, or his son found a way to mask my death through training.

Both plans are were happily abandoned when I decided to abdicate the throne. Infinitely more valuable than killing me because I'd be abdicating for the entire House of Boreen. My only condition was that I'd be the one person allowed to marry his son, making my children heirs to the throne once more. Even so, he did not question that or any of my demands.

Why?

That same day, I displayed unique magics beyond belief, but he didn't bring me to the palace for questioning. He didn't have a single accusation to level at me? That I'd been hiding my magic? That I dabbled in the forbidden? That I'd done something to his son that not only made him suddenly give up his vendetta, but also Reyna?

Dominic didn't tell him the location of the other hellfire dragons was a part of our deal. What point was there when there was no guarantee one would bond with him? But Dominic didn't have to lie about it, because his father didn't ask.

His favored son and heir was on his way to either being cut from training, or graduating with no dragon to ride into battle. Did he not care about any of that as long as I handed him the throne free and clear?

I could explain so much of his behavior away by assuming he was simply a peasant-hating, coin-addled, power-hungry, child-murdering monster, but...

My mind flashed to that morning we walked to the palace together.

I sensed none of those things the first time we met. All I felt was the frigid bite wafting off a cold man. Hard, unyielding, logical. Not the kind of person who did something without a good reason.

So what were his true reasons for all the things he'd done to Adalinda, his family, and the people? What did King General Roark truly want?

This is why he doesn't want the majority of the kingdom to know how to read. Can't have us doing it between the lines.

"Dominic," I began, risking Libelle's wrath. "There's something bothering me..."

"I see it too." His grip tightened around me. "Gods, save us."

Confused, I twisted to look at him, but he wasn't looking back at me. His eyes were huge, capturing a strange glow that danced in his pools.

Following his line of sight, I got a proper look at what my wandering mind missed. Golden City rose in the distance... and it was on fire.

"My bond!"

I jerked, hands clapping over my head. The only reason I didn't fall off Libelle's back was because Dominic caught me.

"Reyna?"

"My bond, you must hurry! Bring my boy." Her words and emotions slammed into me, rocking me on Libelle's back. Fury like I'd never known raged through her, and therefore me—ripping a snarl onto my lips. Who had done this to my beauty? To my city? What happened!

"They attack," she roared, answering my internal question. *"The abominations attack!"*

"Druks!"

Bellowing, Libelle dropped out of the sky. Wind rushed into my eyes, nose, and mouth—stifling my scream and blinding me for sport. Pulling up just as suddenly, the nimble, fiery-scaled dragon skimmed the top of the trees, staying as low as possible.

I fought to dislodge my stomach from my throat as Reyna pelted me with information.

"Reyna's been trying to find us the entire time. When she saw in the hive mind that Libelle found you, she ordered him to go back, but he doesn't take orders well—as you can imagine. He only gave in now because the Druks attacked. They need your scattershot."

"When did they attack?"

"Early this morning," I shouted against the wind. "It happened so fast. They broke into the Hatchery and—oh no."

"What? What did they do?"

I squeezed my eyes shut. "They killed the workers and kidnapped all the babies."

"Shit!"

The more information that poured into my head, the worse it got.

"They were coordinated. Planned. They knew when the mothers left to hunt and struck then. When they came back and found their babies gone..."

Dominic didn't ask for more, but more there was.

"They lost it, Dominic. They rampaged through the citadel looking for their hatchlings, and Druks used the chaos to launch the attack."

"But that doesn't make any sense."

"It doesn't? Why?"

The closer we got, the more horror seeped into my bones. Smoke dominated the sky—painting an airborne battlefield dotted with spinning, speeding small figures, and the dragon riders fighting them.

"Doesn't make sense for them to go after the babies. They don't have enough power or magic yet to turn a human into a Druk. They know that. The real prize is all the fully grown dragons living in the Royal Wood. It's like they punched a beehive knowing there was no honey inside. They got the bees to swarm and attack with no hope of a reward."

Understanding dawned. "That can only mean one thing. They're not here for dragons, Dominic."

"They're just here to kill us."

I don't know if Dominic told Libelle to go faster because he picked up speed—wings buffeting winds that smacked us around on his back. I hung on for dear life.

We were heading straight for a battle I was laughably unprepared to fight. I hadn't mastered the bow and arrow. I didn't know how to use my magic at will. I'd never beaten the lone Druk who came after me yearly. How was I to defeat an entire swarm?

"Libelle needs to drop me off," I called. "Let Reyna come to me—"

"No. We're not separating."

"I'm in your way, Dominic! You of all people need to be in this fight. You can't do what you need to do with me screeching and flailing around in your face."

"We're not separating, Ainsley. You can't ride Reyna. You don't have your boots."

"Then, I won't ride her. I'll sneak into the citadel through my usual way." A plan formed quickly in my mind. Who said I didn't learn anything from scholarship? "The riders are in the sky with their dragons. Who's stopping the Druks on the ground who are kidnapping women and slaughtering whoever gets in their way? Any Druk that crosses my path will attack, I'll take their magic, and then I'll cut them down. This will work, Dom."

"Ainsley, the city is fucking on fire! You can't move through that."

"Magical fire," I said with calm I didn't feel. "If Reyna's hellfire can't kill me. Their Druk fire is noth—" I cut myself off, eyes narrowing. "What the? But Reyna said..."

We flew ever closer, and my eyes only confirmed what my mind couldn't accept.

"Dominic." I couldn't be certain he heard my thin croak. "The rumors said the Druks were getting stronger..."

My heart fell through my shoes and to the forest floor as my sight tracked fire Druks, water Druks, kaminari Druks, earth Druks, air Druks, and Druks of so many color-dipped scales, I couldn't begin to guess what type of dragon they slaughtered to steal their strength.

Just think of what would happen if the tiger, the lion, and the panther joined forces. Is there any prey they couldn't catch?

It wasn't possible, but it was happening all the same. Druks had learned to overcome their deep-rooted instincts.

"They're fighting together."

Chapter Twenty-Six

Dominic held tight to my hand—the two of us moving swift and sure through the Royal Wood. The fire hadn't reached the forest, but the smoke had. It suffused the air, stung our eyes, and rushed into our lungs.

Still, we moved by memory alone. How many nights did I run through these woods? How many days did he sneak through them? All for the dragon who needed us now.

"You should've stayed with Libelle."

Dominic weaved his fingers through mine. "I'm exactly where I need to be."

I bit my lip to stop myself voicing relief. It wasn't that I didn't trust him or myself to get through this. I simply knew our chances were ten times better when we were side by side. We survived the unique mages' attack. We survived the cabin. Together, we would survive this.

Screeches and roars sounded from overhead. Were my friends in this fight? Were they allowed to be? Recruits couldn't fight as riders until they graduated.

I scanned the skies for a single familiar dragon. *But they can fight for their lives.*

We reached the spot where the goat pen once stood. The side entrance door hung askew and off its hinges. Slowly, we approached.

"The palace is the only place not burning," I said, gazing up at the crown jewel towering on the hill. "People who can't reach the gates will be running that way. Will your father let them in?"

We weaved through the nests, trying and failing not to see the dead bodies scattered through the room. The Druks were ruthless.

"He will. But who is to say they're any safer there? He employs all manner of unique mages to guard his life and palace, but we can't know how long their protections will hold. We need to evacuate the people into the castle, then defend that single position—Wait."

He pulled up short, eyes on the skies like mine were. "Drake, Roan, Phiala, Sorrel, every single Golden Guard. They all know that's the best plan. If they haven't done it already, it's what they're trying to do. There's no point in us covering the same ground."

"Where do you need to be to use your scattershot?"

"The courtyard. I can take out all the Druks attacking the citadel in an instant, but it's the fires, Ainsley. It's killing more people right now than the Druks are. The smoke is causing confusion in the air. It's obscuring the battle from above, and killing the people below."

I chewed my lip, thinking fast. "We need to stop the fires."

"We'll gather every ice, sea, and water mage we come across."

I was shaking my head before we finished. "That's covering the same ground again. I'm sure they're already out there trying to put the fire out. Druk-boosted magic is too strong for them to do this quickly. What we— What I need are the ice, sea, and water Druks."

"No."

"When they attack me, I'll have their magic," I argued. "Magic as strong as these raging fires. This is what I do that no one else can, Dom. It's my secret weapon. Using a Druk's evil for good."

A war raged on his face—torn between his refusal to allow a single creature to harm a hair on my head, and his respect for the warrior who stood toe to toe with him since day one.

"Okay," he rasped. "I trust you. I love you. I know you can do this."

My heart panged. It'd be decades until those words stopped resonating with the small, scared, lonely, useless orphan that was still within me.

His lips crashed on mine—hard, passionate, and over as soon as it started. We had a battle to wage.

"If you know what a water dragon looks like, you know what a water Druk looks like." The two of us took off again. "Get them to attack you magically. Don't get in range of their claws. You didn't absorb Tizor's death magic when he scratched you. We have to assume it's the same with Druks."

I bobbed my head though he wasn't looking back to see. What I was doing was crazy. It was literal suicide, but I had to do it. My friends were fighting out there. Fucking hell, Rosaleen could be out there too with Mathias.

I'd focus on the fires. Dominic would take care of the Druks. The two of us working together—as it was and was always meant to be.

We moved quickly over crumbled foundations and darkened hallways. The dragon mothers had plowed through these halls. Faint echoes of their roars and desperate cries assaulted my ears. The people of Golden City weren't the only ones we needed to save.

I cared for these babies for weeks. I loved them. Even quiet, off-putting Sarcany, Scartha, and Ur. I would bring them back to their mothers.

Sounds of fighting filtered through the cracks, telling us we were close. Over and over, I ran through what I had to do. Provoke

Druks with snowy, deep blue, or aquamarine scales into blasting me across the city. I'd take all that blessed water and douse these fires. That, miraculously, was the easy part. When I had someone's magic, I instinctively knew what to do with it. The other thing I had to do was not so straightforward.

"Reyna, where are the babies? Are they close?"

"I know not where they are. Hatchlings too young. Their minds too young."

I understood her without more questioning. The babies were too young to join their consciousness with the great dragonkin hive mind. Rescuing them would not be easy at all, but the first step was ending this siege so that the riders could go after them.

We rounded the final corner and burst into hell.

Bodies of dead dragons and their riders covered the cobblestone. Some looked to have died when their dragons did. Others were crushed to death when their dragons fell.

Poet bellowed beside a fallen Valor. A scar that wasn't there the last I'd seen him, marred his handsome face from ear to chin. Bellowing, his fire lashed across the sky—ripping off wings, heads, limbs, and pieces of every Druk it touched.

Shards of glass pierced the air, heading straight for him.

"Poet!"

He moved fast—snapping his whip and knocking some, not all from the air. He cried out as cuts opened on his arms, legs, and ear.

"Ainsley, I know that magic." Something in Dominic's voice stayed me when I moved to help. "It can't be..."

"You're getting better, boy." Colonel Kinryu moved through a cloud of smoke, facing Poet down. "I've taught you everything you know, but not all that I know."

"Why are you doing this?" Poet shouted the accusation in my heart. "You've gone mad, sir. You need help!"

"I am not mad," he replied calmly. "I know exactly what I am doing... for the glory of the Druks."

Poet raised a trembling hand—his fire whip at the ready.

"Stand down, Rider Poet."

Drake and Roan stood in Poet's path.

"This is not your fight."

The four of them were lost behind another surge of fighting, but we didn't pursue. If Roan and Drake couldn't protect Poet, no one could. He was defended by the best possible riders.

Everywhere we looked, recruits were heeding Roan's bellowed order—fight like a peasant.

Benen, the cotton mage, flung his arms like a maestro conducting a symphony. Everywhere he pointed, flying Druks tangled their wings in cotton and fell to the ground. They cracked necks and skulls open striking the stone. Such simple, seemingly harmless magic... was lethal.

Benen threw out his arm, and a flash of silver caught my eye. His arm severed at the elbow—sliced by an iron Druk that charged from across the courtyard. Benen fell screaming—losing all sense of the battlefield.

We moved in his direction but Ormr was already there. They slashed their hand and the barrage of silver scythes hit an unseen barrier.

I blinked and lost sight of all three of them behind Suoh and Keir. The shadow dragon appeared as quiet and unstoppable as its namesake. Suoh snapped off a Druk's head in a single bite.

It was chaos. So much so, it was impossible to tell if we were winning. Druks fell as fast as riders. Dragons swooped and soared all over the place. Swords clanged on claws.

Riders traded parries with the Druks on the ground—sweat soaking their brows, and strain rippling agony on their faces as they weathered each blow of their inhuman strength.

Nuala slashed at an earth Druk, sword sparking off a wall of stone. She reacted quick, hand dropping like a hammer through the air, marking the path for her lightning. It hit the creature who never saw it coming, Nuala's strike obscured by their own magic.

Its screams were terrible.

My relief turned to panic. The Druk wasn't the only one not looking where they were supposed to. A column of stone like a battering ram shot out of the ground and sped at her back.

"Nuala, look out!"

Solace dropped out of the sky. Lightning crackled off her stormy scales—a harbinger of death fallen from the heavens. She crushed the column beneath her feet as Nuala threw herself on the ground. Whipping around, Solace smashed her tail into the stone wall and the Druk behind it. They went flying.

Nuala hopped on Solace and took to the skies before the creature splattered against the citadel wall. This was perfect harmony between dragon and rider.

We ran out. A shadow fell over us.

"Ainsley!"

Dominic threw us both out of the way in time for a mangled mass of wings and claws to crash on the spot we were standing on. One look at the dead Druk told me Roan was still alive. His resounding laughter confirmed it.

"Stay back," he shouted. "I'm finishing this."

Dominic ran out before I could speak. Hands to the heavens, hellfire descended. Those floating balls of fire appeared—narrowing on Druks in the air and on the ground.

"Retreat!"

His fire cut through the air—ripping holes through their chests, setting their wings alight. Hellfire consumed them totally as flaming Druks plummeted to the courtyard.

A hush fell over the riders. A collective intake of breath as the clanging, magic, and dying stopped.

He'd done it. It was over. My Dominic was truly amaz—

"Him!"

Swarms of fire Druks rose from the depths of fires burning the city in tens, dozens, seemed like hundreds. Hiding in plain sight. They planned for every part of this attack—including how to conceal the rear guard in case the front was taken out.

Major Sorrel's warning banged in my head. Druks were not stupid. Never make the mistake of believing otherwise.

"Kill the general's spawn!"

"Dominic, no!"

They were on him so fast. Dive bombing out of the air, they surrounded and overwhelmed him in seconds. Dominic was lost behind a wall of tearing claws and talon-tipped wings. Hellfire blasted them away, but more kept coming, coming, coming.

Their intent was clear. Stop him from using his scattershot again—and kill him trying.

With Dominic occupied, the next wave of Druks flew in from the forest. Their number just as impossible as the Druks Dominic defeated. We were exactly where we started.

I ran to him, then stopped—head whipping around. All getting caught up in their battle would do was imbibe me with fire magic that wouldn't kill them. I needed the same elemental opposite to defeat them that I did to put out the fires raging across the city.

"Ice, water, sea!" I spun around—Dominic's shouts making me frantic. "Where are you!"

There.

Taesha traded magic with a snow-white Druk with dragon's feet, a woman's torso, and a head covered in scales where hair should be. It was easy to place her white scales as meaning snow magic as opposed to Tizor's which meant death. She was raining icicles on Taesha that the rider deflected with her tree magic.

I bolted. Running past fighting, through dragon legs, and leaping over a soaring copper lance, I skidded in front of Taesha as the Druk raised her hands for another onslaught.

"Argh!" I bellowed—readying for the pain.

For death.

I waited. And waited.

Eyes snapping open, I stared in the face of the blinking Druk. She looked me up and down, hands lowering.

"Wha—?"

She took off—leaping into the skies and not sparing me a glance back.

What?

"Thank you." Taesha grabbed my shoulder. "She was wearing me down. I felt my magic beginning to falter. You saved me."

"Of course," I rasped, confusion slowing me. "I—"

Taesha was already gone, running to a rider losing a three-against-one fight with a sand, plant, and bone Druk.

Shaking myself, I returned to my search. The fire Druks were still focusing their attention on murdering my love. He needed me.

I spotted two sea Druks near the front gates, blasting gallons upon gallons of water at a person I knew well.

King General Roark held the line. Sword plunged into the ground, he was brought to his knees, holding on to the hilt with all his might, while the other hand held back the tide. There was already a pile of Druk heads at his feet.

Before that day, I would've sworn wither magic was useless against seawater. Another mistake. General Roark was not to be underestimated.

The water boiled under his magic—reduced to steam climbing the air, and a growing pile of sea salt at his knees. It was simply the mere force of the water blasting him that kept him down. It wasn't that they were killing him.

Screech!

My head snapped up. I knew that sound from a single, terrifying memory. Tizor's war cry.

Circling, Tizor narrowed on his pinned bonded, and dove.

"No," I croaked, feet moving before I gave the command.

If Tizor killed the Druks before I stole their magic, there went another chance to save Dominic. I had to get there first.

My lungs screamed. My legs burned. A full moon cycle we stayed trapped in that little cabin, unable to train and exercise. My body felt that lack keenly. I was slowing faster than I would've before Awnan struck.

No excuses, thief! Running in and out of trouble is what you do. Survival was your magic before you had any.

"Argh!" I willed myself faster, improper sandals striking the stone, and jumped. "General, down!"

He reacted with a soldier's instincts—hitting the ground and rolling out of the way. I leaped in the path of their water cannons and was blown off my feet and slammed into the remains of the gate.

Water rushed into my nose, mouth, and eyes. It filled my lungs and stole my air. This was it. *Hold on a little longer for me, love. I'm com—*

The water vanished.

I crumpled on the ground, hacking and sputtering. Through my haze, I saw the seawater Druks wing up and over the citadel wall.

"What the—? Come back! Come back and fight me!"

"I did not need saving, girl."

My chest heaved as General Roark bore down on me. He raised his hand high in the air. "But I respect the attempt, if not the execution."

He caught hold of Tizor's claw one-handed and was taken away, following those Druks too fast for me to join their chase.

I didn't move for a breath—thinking. What the hell was wrong with the Druks? Was it something to do with my magic? Was it something to do with theirs? Reyna sensed the *wrongness* of the memory mage. Maybe they could tell something was off about me too.

If that's the case, I'll have to provoke them to fight. Give the bastards no choice.

I scanned the chaos for my next target.

I wasn't looking for Maili, but I found her all the same—battling a Druk whose scales were as dark as the deep blue sea.

One look at the torrent of Druks attacking my flaming love made up my mind. I was breaking my promise to him, but only because he'd do it for me.

Running up behind the creature, I jumped on her back. She let out a fearsome cry as my arm snapped around her throat, and squeezed.

"What the—?" Maili's vines spasmed as if the shock traveled through her magic. "It's you. It really is you. Fuck's sake, where have you been! You've been missing for a full moon!"

I couldn't answer if I wanted to. The Druk thrashed and bucked trying to throw me off. Her wings smacked me around. Her claws raked my head and shoulder blades, tearing screams from my raspy throat.

"Get off! Get off me, filthy human!" She gave up scratching and punched me—deadly strong strikes that resounded through my body. I felt a bone in my shoulder snap. "You'll pay for whatever it is you've done to her. Your blood will water these lands for ten generations!"

"Ahh!" I sobbed when she punched the same shoulder.

Switch to magical attacks. Mother Zaeah, switch to magic!

The Druk shot off the ground. Reaching higher than the tip of Reyna's longest horn, she snapped her wings to her side, and dropped.

"No!" I cried. "Noooo!"

Her body flipped, putting me between her and the reaching ground.

"Ainsley!" Maili screamed.

"Ainsley?"

Her wings snapped out, catching the wind and slowing our descent—

I crashed to the ground, head bouncing off the stone. Air punched out of my lungs.

My world was pain. Was I breathing? I'd forgotten how to.

"Ainsley?"

Whose voice was that? It wasn't Maili.

Blurred vision spun on a face hovering over me. Squinting, her eyes came into focus.

No... my eyes.

My lips parted—to scream, to breathe, to ask, I wasn't certain.

Eyes so piercing a green, I'd only ever seen one person bearing the color—the person I saw every morning in the mirror.

My too-big nose. My bottom-heavy mouth. My golden crown.

"What have I done?" she breathed. "Oh, my child."

My child.

No. It simply wasn't possible.

"We thought the human pets had done something terrible. Velez feared the worst when you disappeared, and that monstrous marriage contract came to light."

I heard her, but I couldn't be. She shouldn't be saying these things. Knowing that name. Or looking at me... with love and relief.

"Ainsley, can you speak?" she asked, cradling my head. Her hand came away tacky with my blood, making her snarl. A terrible, ferocious sound so like Reyna, I choked. "Forgive me. If only I could take you away, but you're still not ready—"

A sword blossomed through her chest.

I did speak then. A piercing cry that echoed through the courtyard. "No!"

"Argh," Maili shouted. "Get away from her, beast! You'll not harm another hair on her head."

Jaw working, blood dribbled down my mother's mouth—for she could only be my mother. She fell back, and I reached out my hand to help her, to touch her.

My fingers closed on air.

She was gone with the familiar quickness of a blink. Only the blade remained, a stained battle relic on the cobblestones.

I knew two things at that moment. I mistook her scales. The mother whose name I still didn't know was not a sea Druk. She was a shadow Druk. Rare, dangerous, and gone.

The second thing I knew...

"This is all for me."

"Ainsley?" Maili dropped beside me. "Are you okay? I thought that thing was going to kill you. It sounded like it was saying something to you? What was it?"

I barely heard her. Flipping over, I strained to push myself up. Without thinking, I grasped the sword, leaning heavily on it as I got to my feet.

"Ainsley? Ainsley, you can't fight like this," Maili called after me. "You need a healer!"

I kept on—limping, bleeding from a thousand cuts, skull singing with pain. On my left, a kaminari Druk weaved lightning through its claws like playful string. He swiped, slicing through Keely's threads and delivering the final blow.

"You," I roared. "Stop!"

The creature halted. Not moving. Maybe not even breathing.

Keely staggered away from the sudden killer statue.

"Surrender."

Claws snapping to his sides, he dropped to his knees and lowered his head—wings prostrate. Half a dozen riders and Druks stopped fighting when they noticed him, and me.

"Ainsley," Maili whispered. "How are you doing this?"

My eyes lit on Drake and Roan. Multiple terrible wounds wept freely on their body. I didn't know how Kinryu learned the secret to defending against Roan's bone magic, but impossibly, he was still standing—only a useless, swinging arm at his side and a jagged cut on his cheek showed that they'd gotten to him.

"Kinryu," I called. "With me."

Glass shattered inches from Roan's and Drake's feet. He abandoned their fight without a backward glance and ran to my side.

"Lift me into the air."

"As you wish." He waved his good hand—spinning, weaving over the ground. Glass came together out of pure magic, creating something piece by piece, inch by inch. I didn't know what it was until it was done.

A throne.

I sat down heavier than I intended. My body felt weighted down by stones. I had to do this quickly.

Kinryu lifted me into the air over the battle. I saw everything from the fighting below me to the flames consuming the lower city. Reyna was somewhere down there. Passing through the fire as only she could, looking for people who needed help.

"Dru—" I stopped, taking a deep breath. I knew the name they called themselves for they certainly did not prefer abomination, but no person would ever give them the satisfaction of calling them anything else.

"Dragon slayers, cease fighting!"

They stopped. Lowering their claws, releasing their captured opponents, leashing their magic. One by one, they obeyed.

"Fall in."

Hundreds of Druks took to the air. Lining up with near military speed and precision, this multicolored, impossible battalion hovered before me—waiting.

They would while I confirmed one single important thing.

Freed from the mountain of fire Druks, my love staggered to his feet. Dominic was bleeding, drained, and unsteady. But he was alive.

"Ice, water, and sea Slayers, put out these fires. Fire Slayers, fetch and return the hatchlings."

They flew off in a dozen directions, doing as I commanded. Below and beside me, incredulous cries and whispers raged. *How is she doing this? Why are they listening to her? This is impossible.*

I slumped more than sat on my throne. Dark spots danced in my vision. I heard my Dominic shouting for me, but his voice was getting farther and farther away. I was running out of time.

Soon, the fires were out and I watched the last enraged, shrieking hatchling flown unharmed into the Hatchery.

"Return."

The Druks flew back into formation. If they noticed I slurred the command, they didn't give a sign.

"Listen... to me well," I croaked. "This city, these people, and these dragons are under my protection. You're never to come here again."

They snapped their right arms to their left shoulders, tipping their necks to the sky. I couldn't be sure, but I guessed that was their version of "yes, ma'am."

I will be sure.

"If you understand and obey, bow before your queen."

They bowed.

Even as I ordered them about, I didn't believe they would. Why would they recognize the authority of the future queen of Adalinda when they were at war with our nation? What was I to them?

I flicked down. This was not the time to hear that answer.

"Leave."

They flew away. The flapping of their wings was nothing but buzzing after a minute, pressing silence after two.

Slowly, Kinryu lowered me to the ground.

I froze under the stares of the recruits... and the cold scrutiny of General Roark. Dominic shoved out of the crowd and ran to my side. I sensed in his balled fists and tight shoulders. He was ready to fight.

A strange noise sounded in my ear. Disbelief clouded my head. *They can't. It's not possible...*

"Yes, Ainsley!"

Raucous cheers blew my ears back. Running, shouting, clapping, cheering, they hoisted my throne into the air—bouncing my addled head more than it should be.

"Queen Ainsley, Queen Ainsley, Queen Ainsley!"

In the midst of it all, I sought General Roark. Was he cheering? Was he angry? Was he readying to make my head another for his collection?

Darkness claimed me before I found out.

Chapter Twenty-Seven

I held still while the attendants painted my face and applied rouge to my lips.

"You look beautiful, Princess."

I think I croaked out a thank-you. It was hard to be sure, for my mind was still spinning over the events of the last three days.

Yes, three days since the Druks attacked, then left as quickly as they appeared. Three days since I woke up in the palace infirmary—alone.

At least, I was alone for about ten minutes. Then, the healer came in, confirmed I was recovered, and sent in the Heart Readers. For days and hours at a time, they interrogated me.

Why did the Druks obey me? Where had I been for the last five weeks? Was I across the Dark Border? Did I orchestrate the attack on the capital to demonstrate my power, and strike fear into the people? What were my plans? What was my true history? Was I planning to become a Druk? What did I want with the crown heir, Dominic Roark? Was marrying him a part of my plan?

Tenille, help me, if I knew what plan they were talking about. I told them in all the ways I could spell it that I had no idea why the Druks obeyed me. I wasn't behind the attack and knew nothing about it until I saw Golden City burning on the horizon. That if I had any intention of becoming a Druk, Reyna would've snapped my head off already, and, most importantly, all I wanted to do with Dominic was love and be with him for the rest of my life.

I could only assume my answers weren't enough the first time because they asked me over... and over... and over again.

What they didn't do was answer any of my questions. I asked what happened to Awnan and his rancid marriage contract—they didn't answer. I asked what was becoming of the rebuilding efforts, if the hatchlings and dragon mothers were okay, and how bad was the damage to the city? Again, no response.

I could swallow their refusal to answer those questions. It broke me that they refused to tell me anything about Dominic. I hadn't seen him the entire time they kept me in that small, windowless room.

They released me only that morning, and brought me to another windowless, yet twice-as-large room. Waiting for me were three attendants, a steaming hot bath, my clothes, and the marriage contract. It was only right that everything be prepared... for my wedding day.

The attendants helped me up, carefully guiding me across the room in my voluminous skirts. That day— That hour, I was to be married to the love of my life. A fact I discovered upon walking into the room and hearing the news from my excited helpers.

I didn't know what to feel or think as I read the contract. A few words were unfamiliar to me, but not enough for me to mistake the meaning. I'd been granted everything I wanted and more.

Instead of twenty thousand ryus a year, I was to be given fifty. Instead of the Nithe regency, I would be given the regency of Durga. A small town in Ghidorah. Durga was better for the mere fact that Ghidorah was Dominic's home. I knew it'd mean a lot to him to raise our children in the culture he cherished.

I could stay in training, or drop out if I desired to take up my regency now. I had the right to handpick my household staff and guards. If and how many children I had was my choice. Attending royal functions was my choice. Enrolling in higher education—my choice.

I read it every which way, and did not find a single term to argue. This may have been the fairest and most generous marriage contract created in the history of Adalinda, and it was all mine along with the man who came with it the minute I abdicated the throne.

Deep down, I knew this was happening so quickly because General Roark would not stand for me to be the rightful heir to the throne for another second. The siege of Golden City, as it was already being called, scared him.

He watched our greatest enemy bow down to me. Saw them heed my commands like trained dogs who didn't need a treat. He heard me announce myself as queen, then stood by while the people chanted my name and hailed me as the hero.

My time as *Princess* Ainsley was over. From this day, no one would question who is the rightful ruler of Adalinda.

"Magnificent," Bisha crooned. "How do you feel?"

I blinked at my reflection. She looked just as wide-eyed, confused, and anxious as me. She also looked more beautiful than I'd ever seen myself.

Layers of fiery-red tulle bloomed from my waist and whispered against the top of my toes. It was custom for a rider to marry in a gown that matched her dragon's scales. My tight, beaded bodice clung to me in all the right ways, making something of my modest cleavage. I thought of the blush-inducing, core-tightening things Dominic would say when he saw me in this gown. Gods, I couldn't wait to see him. If only—

"I feel rushed," I said honestly. "Wedding celebrations don't usually happen this fast. I didn't get to plan anything. Choose the flowers. Tell the chef my favorite foods. I didn't get to..." I trailed off, saying the rest in my head.

I didn't get to invite my family or Rosaleen. The fire didn't spread past the gates—the only reason I knew that Sister Aven and the kids were safe. Sadly, I couldn't directly ask about Rosaleen's safety, and they wouldn't let me out of the palace to check for myself.

Happy is what I should've felt on my wedding day, but fear and guilt crowded out everything else. They should be here. I was tired of doing everything without the people who were important to me by my side.

"I'm sorry, Princess," Bisha said, patting my arm. "If it makes you feel better, I've seen the throne room and it's gorgeous. Completely transformed. It's going to be the most beautiful wedding."

"Where is Dominic? I want to see him."

She laughed. "You know you can't see him before you both step inside the altar. This is the time for you both to sit in contemplation with Tenille—asking him to bless your marriage."

I bit my tongue, forcing myself not to say where she could shove her contemplations. She was just doing her job. It wasn't her fault Dominic was kept from me for days. I laid that blame entirely on the general's shoulders.

A knock sounded on the door, bringing a smile to my lips. It was Dominic. He came to see me after all.

Bisha and Nem opened the door to Maili.

"Hey, Ainsley."

"Hi. What's going on? Why are you dressed like that?"

Maili wore a rippling red gown in the same shade as mine, except her bodice was plain and she wasn't weighed down by thick skirts.

"Did no one tell you? Ormr and I requested to be your maiden witnesses. We thought you would like a few friendly faces by your side."

"I would like that very much." I hugged her. "Thank you."

"Do you mind if we talk privately?"

I nodded at the attendants to leave. Maili helped me sit down at the vanity when they left, then pulled up another stool. Her expression wasn't as carefree and happy as I was used to.

"Something wrong?"

"I wanted to talk to you about what they're saying out there," she began, dropping her voice. "General Roark has spread through the palace and beyond that you're abdicating the throne. When Nuala said it, I thought it was jealousy speaking. Then, you, Dominic, and Keely disappeared, and Awnan tried to pass off that fake contract. We had bigger things to worry about."

"Wait, Keely disappeared too?"

She nodded. "That's how the truth came out. He kept her locked up beneath a pub while he kept the High Council hostage. He had one councilman's approval, which should be all that you need, but the terms were so outrageous, the others demanded you appear before them and state this is what you wanted.

"Awnan had the fucking balls to say he wouldn't allow you to return until they set the date for the coronation ceremony. No one knew what to do. Heart Reader after Heart Reader went after him, but they couldn't get your location out of him.

"Threats of execution didn't work because if he died, we didn't know what would happen to you. Weeks of this hell, and then finally Keely was able to get a message to the right person." She tossed her head. "Her thread magic is amazing, Ainsley. She controls them like they're a part of her. Extra fingers.

"Roan got her note, burst into some pub called the Yellowfish or whatever, and rescued her," she said. "It all came out about them forcing you to sign, and her getting a message to Dominic. When all that came out, it was over for him. He imprisoned a noble. Performed forbidden magics on the crown heir, and despite his lying and saying he didn't know a thing about what happened to Dominic, the fact that he disappeared the same night as you after Keely slipped him a message..." Another headshake.

"His execution was set for three days ago."

I bolted upright. "He's dead?"

"No. He was supposed to die, then the Druks attacked," she confessed. "Awnan got free in the confusion. They don't know yet if he's among the dead, or if he escaped the city in time."

"Gods," I breathed, slumping back in my seat. "I don't know which I prefer. For him to have died burning in the flames of his own cowardice, or if he's on the run so I can track him down and kill him myself."

"Both sound good to me."

I nodded. After all Awnan did to me. For all that he planned to do to me. There was no version of the future where he got to live.

"All that to say, I assumed all talk of abdication was just more bullshit spread by people scheming to take your throne, but the general says you're really going to do it." Wide eyes beseeched me. "Tell me he's wrong."

"He..." I sighed. "He's not wrong, Maili. Today I give up House Boreen's claim to the throne."

"Why? Is it about those crazy whispers about you being a Druk spy with plans to turn the kingdom over to them after you take the throne? Because anyone with half a fucking brain knows that isn't true. You'd have to be the worst spy in history to reveal yourself like that in front of everyone."

I smiled mirthlessly. "I didn't know there were any rumors. That's not the reason, Maili. I just have to do this."

"Is that what Dominic told you?" She rose up. "That manipulative shit! He said he wouldn't marry you unless you abdicated, didn't he? I can't believe—"

"No, never," I cried. "Dominic would never do that to me. This was completely my choice, Maili. No one forced me, manipulated me, or shamed me."

She stared at me, no less confused.

"Okay, this is the truth. There's no realistic path to me becoming queen of Adalinda," I said, dropping my voice to match hers. "General Roark has ruled for decades. He's married to every woman of importance in every province. He's fathered half the regents, and chosen loyal militarists to rule the other regencies. He's worked for a very long time to stay exactly where he is..." I looked around. "Here.

"No twenty-year-old girl who came out of nowhere was ever going to take it from him."

"Why would you say that?" she cried. "Don't tell me— Fucking hell, Ainsley. That shit Awnan wrote in the contract wasn't true, was it? You want someone else to rule because you grew up a peasant? None of that changes the fact that this kingdom doesn't belong to the general. It belongs to House Boreen."

I met her gaze steadily. "House Boreen— *I* was not going to live long enough to take it. Think about it, Maili. Conscription is mandatory for every rider—royal, noble, and heir to the throne. Even if I survived training, I'm looking at fifty years of mandatory service, and where do you think a unique mage like me will be placed?"

"The..." She visibly swallowed. "The fodder battalion."

"Yes. That's five more decades I won't be eligible to rule, and five decades the general will spend sowing support, passing more laws, digging his roots deeper into the kingdom, and ensuring I don't survive to take it from him.

"Now, I love Dominic. I want to marry him and spend the rest of my life with him. Dominic didn't hold that over my head, but the general would. It's a weakness, in his eyes, that he'd exploit until he ruined us both. My path to the throne is littered with treachery, betrayal, lost love, and death.

"But if I abdicate, the path clears. I walk it with my love, and we inherit the throne together—peacefully. More so, our children will be from both families. House Boreen will sit on the throne again." I took her hand. "I've thought about this long and hard. Adalinda is in no better state if I die before I ever reach the throne. But thank you," I said, squeezing her fingers. "It's nice to have someone who's looking out for me here today."

"Ainsley, I—"

The door opened and General Roark stepped in. Maili dropped my hand like we were doing something wrong.

I couldn't blame her. He had that effect on people.

"Young Ainsley, what a radiant bride."

I said nothing.

"Are you ready?" He held out his arm. "We're about to begin."

"Where's Dominic?"

"Waiting for you of course." The general slowly turned to Maili. "Be on your way and take your place."

She opened her mouth, thought better of it, then left.

Again the general held out his arm. This was it. What I planned for. What I waited for. There was no reason to be scared. Or that's what I told myself.

Rising up, I slipped my arm through his.

"You seem nervous," he remarked as we traversed the empty hallway. "Quite normal. I was nervous on my wedding days too."

"Oh? Were you also interrogated for days only to be freed and told you were getting married with no explanation?"

He didn't break his stride. "A necessary precaution. I had to be sure I wasn't marrying my heir to a spy or traitor. Master Whelan has a theory that your... unnatural affinity with the abominations is another manifestation of your ability.

"Druks are not human nor dragon. They're patchwork dolls held together by pure magic. You simply stole them like you do all other types of magic."

"That is the most reasonable theory," I said lightly. "I thank the gods for Master Whelan. I don't know much about magic, least of all mine. At least he's here to help me navigate my way through."

"As always, a diplomatic answer. You may not have known how to read, but you've always known how to speak without saying anything at all."

I did not know what to say then. Why was he saying this to me when he should be saying that he knew I was innocent?

"Where are we going?" I asked.

"What do you mean? I'm escorting you to the ceremony."

"My ceremony or..." My eyes narrowed to slits. "Ours?"

"I beg your pardon?"

"You say I speak without saying anything, so let me be clear now. Am I to marry Dominic today, or do you think you're going to make me marry you?"

His brows blew up his face. "Child, that's— That's absurd." The general barked a laugh. I was so shocked to hear such a sound come from him, that my confidence shook. "I have more than enough wives, young Ainsley. I do not desire another."

I studied the side of his face. Of course, he gave nothing away other than amusement. "I had to be sure."

"You were already sure. You read the marriage contract. It is not my name on the bottom."

"Yes, but then I don't know your true name, do I?"

Dark, empty pools captured me. "I shed the name given to a child on the day I became a man. Such is my right. But I assure you, neither the name I had nor the name I hold are Dominic. No one is trying to trick you, Ainsley. You are to marry my son today, after, of course, you abdicate."

"Of course."

I fell silent, letting him lead me the rest of the way to the throne room. It was hard not to be suspicious after I was treated with suspicion for days. This sudden turnabout made my head spin. After seeing the way the Druks and Kinryu obeyed me, traitor had to be on his mind, but Maili was right. If I was a spy, I was the worst one in existence. I gave myself away to the entire city to stop a battle I supposedly orchestrated in the first place.

I knew it was hard for them to understand what they saw, but it was no less hard for me. My mother held me in her arms for the first time since I was an infant, then she was gone again. I didn't know if she survived. I didn't know if I'd ever see her again.

How was I supposed to make sense of her being there? The things she said made it sound like they attacked the city because Velez told her I was missing and something horrible had happened to me. Why did she know my brother's name? Why had he been following me? Why would the Druks burn the capital down to avenge me? Why? Why? Why?

The Heart Readers badgered me for answers when all I had were questions.

"Open."

The guards came to life. Grabbing the huge, ornate golden handles, they swept open the doors, revealing a paradise of gold and red. Rose garlands hung from the city, dancing on living vines. The altar stood under shine of the throne, draped in cloths the traditional colors of Tenille and concealing the person inside.

The horrible statues of the dead were still there, but covered with roses to make less of an unpleasant sight. Everyone was here. All the nobles and royals—or at least everyone that survived and was taking shelter in the palace.

I passed under their gaze—alone. This path I had to walk myself.

Bare feet caressed by a sea of rose petals, I flicked up. They had drawn the curtains on the high windows, giving sight to the dragons perched outside, looking upon the ceremony. Tizor, Suoh, Kenna, Cadmus, and my beauty.

"Are you all right, Reyna?"

"That is for me to ask you. I tried to bite the boy's sire for daring to keep you from me, but he wisely remained indoors."

I cracked a smile. I didn't need to peek inside the hive mind to know there was no dragon out there like Reyna.

"Is everything okay here? Can we trust it? Trust him?"

"I have observed everything that's gone on in this room. I sense no human trickery or unnatural magics."

I relaxed a fraction. *"And Dominic? Is he there?"*

"That is for you to find out."

Of course, now my rebellious dragon wants to follow the rules. If Dominic was waiting under the altar for me, the ceremony would proceed. If he wasn't, then his absence didn't need explaining.

Also under the altar should be Ormr and Maili—my witnesses. And the two witnesses Dominic chose. We had to make our vows to Tenille and each other privately. Only our witnesses were there to make sure they were done.

Afterward, the altar is raised, and the ceremony continues before the blessing of the entire court.

My heart panged, wishing Sister Aven and Rosaleen were in there waiting for me. All my dreams were coming true, and the women who got me this far weren't there to see it.

Ducking my head, I passed through and stepped inside the altar. Dominic smiled at me.

"Hey, Princess. Been waiting for you."

I jumped in his arms. Sobbing, I kissed all over his chin, lips, nose, eyes—anything my lips could reach. "I missed you so much."

"Not as much as I missed you." He kissed me hard. "I set half the palace ablaze, burning down doors looking for you. My father hid you too well."

Looking into his eyes, I cupped his face. "Are we getting married today?"

"Anyone tries to stop us, they'll die screaming. Does that answer your question?"

I grinned so wide my face hurt. "Yes, it does."

A throat cleared. Suddenly, I remembered we weren't alone.

Maili and Ormr stood on the side of the sister of the order. Two men I vaguely recognized as Dominic's brothers stood on her other side.

"Good morning, Ainsley of House Boreen, and Dominic of House Roark. I am Sister Honora. It is my honor to join you as one under the blessing of Tenille."

"Thank you."

"We are ready," she called.

The altar was lifted up and over us.

"Apologies," the general announced. "The natural traditions must be observed, but at this point, we will stop for the abdication, so that the marriage ceremony may proceed."

His speech was a signal for movement. Sister Honora was escorted to the side, and a podium was put in her place. On it was a document that read *Abdication of House Boreen* clear on the top.

"Today, everyone, we honor Ainsley Boreen for she has made the brave, noble, and selfless choice. She has decided to step aside, and allow me, a humble servant of Adalinda, to continue to lead our people in this time of war and turmoil."

I looked around, sweeping over Keir, Poet, Keely, and taking in the faces that weren't there. No one answered my questions while they kept me locked away. They certainly didn't tell me who or how many we lost.

No Carlow, Flynn, or Kane. Were they lost in the battle, or were they arrested for the part they played that night in the Yellow Tail?

"All of you bear witness. Make no mistake, Ainsley Boreen is a hero in more ways than one."

General Roark started the clap that turned into raucous applause.

I didn't know what to think of his praise, or theirs. Did they truly understand and support my decision to abdicate?

Dominic kissed my fingertips, drawing my gaze to him.

It didn't matter if the general's speech was just a winner's crowing. Dominic supported and loved me. That was enough.

"Now, let us sign so that the marriage between my son and this fine young woman can begin."

General Roark stepped in front of us and signed the parchment without flair or hesitation. He handed the quill to me.

Movement out of the corner of my eye turned my head.

Maili shook her head, eyes wide and beseeching.

I smiled at her, nodding. I knew that it seemed I'd been forced into a deal that benefited the general in every way, and me in none. But this was right. I felt it in my heart.

I took the quill.

Stepping up to the podium, I read the first line in my journey to leave one life behind, and begin a new one with Dominic.

Reaching the bottom, I pressed quill to parchment.

It ripped away from me, taking to the air.

"What the—?"

"Ormr."

The parchment sliced to shreds, raining down on my head.

"I told you," Maili said, kicking over the podium. "You're not abdicating."

"What do you think you're doing?" General Roark bellowed. "Guards. Guards!"

"What we're doing is stopping a sham. A trickster's play!" Maili leveled a finger between my eyes. "She has no authority to abdicate the throne for House Boreen."

"What?" I looked to Ormr. They looked through me, face chipped from stone. "Maili, what's wrong with you? What are you doing!"

"This."

Ormr and Maili dodged the coming guards and raced up the steps.

"No," I screamed. "Don't!"

They grabbed the throne.

I rocked back, feet tangling and dropping me in Dominic's arms. How could I feel anything but horror, watching my friends die.

Golden tendrils lashed around their wrists and throats, choking the life out of them without giving them the mercy to fight back.

The twins fell to their knees, their strangled cries lost to the shouting, yelling, and insults pouring their way.

"Maili!" Poet bounded up the steps and was thrown back by the guards.

Gold poured down their heads, covering their bodies, blinding them, smothering their mouths.

My eyes widened.

The gold melted into their skin, forming endless, looping tattoos. Rising to their feet, they shone before the kingdom—resplendent in their golden bracelets, necklaces, and crowns.

"This is impossible." General Roark staggered back. "It cannot be."

"It is," Ormr said. "We are the true heirs to Adalinda, and we'll be damned if that bastard mistake gives our throne to another usurper."

Conversations and accusations broke out from every corner of the room. All I could do was stand there. What was going on? Ormr and Maili were descendants of the queen too? And they knew this by the fervor of which they seized the throne—knowing they wouldn't die. Why didn't they say something?

"Silence. Silence!" the general roared, spinning on the crowd. "This changes nothing. The throne bestowed its rights on this girl"—he pointed to me—"while those two cowered and hid. It chose her as its heir first, and as heir, she forfeits House Boreen's claim.

"Guards," he barked. "Remove these two. The ceremony continues as planned."

The guards converged on them. Ormr sliced the air, and their heads separated from their shoulders.

"You dig your hole deeper," Ormr hissed. "Further treasonous acts against us will lengthen your execution, and increase the pain. We were born twenty years and seven moons ago. That thing was born twenty years and two moons ago. This throne is ours by right of age."

Flames rippled down Dominic's arms. "Call her a thing again. I fucking dare you," he growled. "Succession isn't determined by age. You know that as well as I. Stand aside, pretend heirs. The only ones committing treason is you."

Ormr smiled. "True, but in our case, succession was determined by age, since when we were born, Queen Kisandra named us her future. When *she*"—they still managed to make the word sound like an insult—"was born, Queen Kisandra ordered her put to death."

"Lies. You have no proof—"

"The proof is I."

A strong, clear voice rang out in the throne room. We turned as a feminine figure rose from the back. That was the only description I could give to her. A heavy cloak with a long, shadowed hood obscured half her face. The other visible half was concealed behind a painted mask.

"I am Queen Kisandra," she said. "Your ruler. Your sovereign. Your monarch by blood and by right. I abdicate nothing. I recognize that creature not. How dare you?" she hissed, marching down the aisle. "How dare you presume to stand in my throne room and throw away a thousand-year legacy that was never yours!"

I shrunk under her shout. "But I—"

"No, Ainsley," Dominic sliced in. "Don't give this charade credit. She's not the first charlatan to lie about being Queen Kisandra, and she won't be the last. Guards," he barked. "You were ordered to remove these agitators."

They surged, moving on the twins and would-be queen. She threw out her hands, and the throne room came to life.

The chairs heaved—rising up on forelegs and locking their wooden arms around their captives. Shaking off their eternal slumber, the golden statues sprung on every charging guard, fleeing guest, enraged king general, and me and Dominic. I screamed as a soulless, bearded gentleman ripped me from Dominic and pinned my arms behind my back.

Magical attacks abound, but like General Roark's failed attempt to destroy my tiara, the wither, wind, fire, water, ice, and every other attack had no effect on her magic. Dominic was a burning man—thrashing in a tall, once-woman's hold, yelling my name.

I slipped free and tried to run to him. My feet sank in the stone—suddenly soft and shifting like sand. It dragged me down, pulling, capturing, holding me to my knees. I wasn't going anywhere.

I knew this terrible magic by story alone. Living magic. A blessing bestowed on only one ancestral line, and one queen in our recent history. Kisandra of House Boreen.

"All of you will bear witness," she cried. "For today, House Boreen takes back this land from liars, usurpers, and abominations. Your salvation is at hand. Your rightful rulers have returned."

"Our queen."

"We worship you."

"We are your loyal servants."

The people once cheering my name shouted their allegiance to her with near orgasmic devotion.

Climbing the steps, she sat on the throne and the golden vines twisted and writhed above her head. Forming a gift twice the size of mine, it placed the crown atop her head.

"My queen. You've returned to us."

"I don't understand. Why are you doing this!" I twisted to Ormr and Maili. "Why didn't you just tell me the truth? None of this would've happened. If you wanted the fucking throne so much, why didn't you take it!"

Maili scoffed. "It wasn't supposed to happen like this. We couldn't rush our reveal for all the reasons you gave. We still have fifty years of service to look forward to. That was time we would've spent spreading our good deeds and heroics throughout the kingdom. Winning support of the people. Gaining the trust of loyalists and militarists alike. When we were ready, not a single person would've chosen this despot over us.

"Then, you came along," she spat. "You announced yourself princess on the first day, then didn't have the decency to be killed by the throne. Everything spun out of control. We tried to get rid of you, but you're a slippery fucking minx. Your choice to abdicate was the last straw."

"You..." My mouth went dry. "You tried to get rid of me?"

"Yep," she said. "Venom in your cup at the Calthoon feast. Sabotaging your fights with Keir. Putting Ur in the goat pen knowing you would go out to fawn over the stupid animals, and Tizor would attack. Nothing worked. You. Wouldn't. Die."

"She dies today," Kisandra said calmly, mask still firmly in place.

"But why? You don't have to kill me. I don't want the throne now any more than I did an hour ago. I won't abdicate," I stated. "The throne is yours. Our quarrel is over."

"Our quarrel is far from over," snapped the queen. "Twenty years ago, I ordered you put to death. I was disobeyed and you grew to become the filthy stain on the Boreen name that I knew you would be. It is time I right this mistake."

"I am not a mistake. What do you care about me? I know you're not my mother. I have nothing to do with you!"

"Of course I'm not your mother—that disgusting *thing*! You were my son's sin." She rose from the throne. "The night I was chased from this room and forced to leave my home, I carried something with me. My son and heir.

"We had nothing. Nowhere to go if not for the service of those truly loyal to the crown." She nodded to someone over my head. "For decades, I waited. I trained him—the elite warrior and prince. I found him a strong, worthy wife who gifted him even stronger children." Kisandra grasped Ormr's and Maili's shoulders.

"Then, I lost him to that beast. Your mother—the Druk." Hatred laced her words. "She seduced my son. She addled his brain with forbidden magic and made him believe he was in love with her. She plumbed the same despicable depths to fall pregnant with you. That's right," she said. "Your mother was a fully changed Druk before, during, and after her pregnancy. You should not be possible."

I almost didn't hear her last sentence over the shocked gasps and cries of disgust echoing through the throne room. Dominic's muffled shouts sounded from behind his captor's hand.

"You're a thing," she spat. "A nasty beast spawned by rape and forbidden magic. When my son came to me and told me he was leaving his wife and true children to run away with you and that Druk, I knew I'd lost him forever. There was no healing his mind." Her voice shook. "I was forced to kill my precious only child."

I fell hard, jaw hanging. Her son? My father? She killed him? Her own child and she killed him?

"I decreed you and that monster dead too, but she took you and ran. I had to send assassins after her," she said. "They returned claiming you were both dead. I see now that I was lied to. Unacceptable. My will is law. Any and everyone who helped, concealed, acknowledged, and allowed you to live has forfeited their lives!"

I turned away from her. "Ormr, Maili, are you listening to her? She's insane! Warped by hatred. Obsessed with getting her power back. So obsessed that when her precious son dared to not be perfect, she convinced herself he was taken in by forbidden magic and a Druk. A Druk! That should be all you need to know she's the one who lost her mind. Druk women cannot have children."

I might as well have been breeze blowing in from an open window for all the attention they paid me.

"Listen to me! You know me. You know nothing she's said about me is true," I cried. "We're friends. We... We're siblings—"

"Shut up," Maili snapped. "You're no sister of mine. You're a mark on the Boreen legacy that should've been burned out."

"So it is," Queen Kisandra agreed. "You dare to call me insane. Do you see? Look for yourself, my subjects, how dull-witted and vulgar this creature is. How crassly she speaks to the queen of Adalinda. She can't comprehend that she's in the presence of her betters."

I recoiled. She spoke of me like I was little better than an animal.

"You throw this sham of a ceremony in my palace. Dress that worm in finery, and pretend as if it's capable of love—let alone deciding the fate of my throne. Filthy, putrid, disgust—"

A fireball slammed into her face, knocking her off her feet and flat on the throne. The hellfire greedily consumed its new meal. Screaming, Queen Kisandra threw the mask and robe off.

I covered my mouth, shock freezing me stiff.

"Her face," someone whispered.

Was gone.

Two holes where a nose should be, a slash of a mouth, one staring green eye, and the other eye lost. No hair barring a few black, wispy strands. Her entire head was a mass of burn scars.

In that moment, I realized why she hid herself away for a hundred years. Shame... and pride.

"I warned you." Scorching hotter than the sun, Dominic freed himself of the melting remains of the statue. "If you insult my wife one more time, I'll finish what the dragon fire started and burn your mouth shut."

I choked. Did he just threaten the queen sovereign of Adalinda?

"How dare you!" Kisandra shrieked. "Blasphemy! Treason! Kill him!" She half threw Maili and Ormr down the steps. "Kill him now!"

I almost felt sympathy for her as she tore at her dress, trying to cover her face. Almost.

A ring of flames surrounded the twins, trapping their curses and magic. Charred remains of Maili's vines shot through the hellfire, and crumbled to ash before getting close to him.

"You can't do this to our queen."

"Our rightful ruler has returned. You will step aside, Roarks!"

They were turning on him. On us.

"*Reyna, this is bad. We need to get out of here!*"

"*You have to get outside, my bond. Dominic's sire strengthened this dwelling against dragon attacks after killing the usurper.*"

"I don't care that you sat on that throne a century ago," Dominic growled. "You abandoned us! For fifty years, the usurper unleashed a reign of terror. She invaded Ghidorah, and made my mother a prisoner in her own home.

"Have you all forgotten?" he bellowed at the crowd. "Look at her! Queen Kisandra stands alive and well in front of you now. Why? Is it because Golden City was attacked and countless people killed? Is it because crime has risen in every province? Is it because our people starve? Is it because the Druks have grown stronger and are likely now planning their next attack?

"No. After a hundred long years, she returns to protect her legacy. Not all of you. Her throne."

A hush fell over the trapped crowd.

"She abandoned you for a century, and from their own mouths, they were going to make you wait *another* fifty years! But what has Ainsley done for you in the mere two months since she arrived in Golden City?

"She killed herself training happily and without complaint even though she believed she had no magic. All to fight for this kingdom," he said. "She returned when our city was burning down around us. Not our blessed queen. It was Ainsley Boreen who flew into battle and banished the Druks. And because she thought it was best *for you and Adalinda*, she was willing to give up her birthright!

"One of you cheering sycophants better tell me what Queen Kisandra has done for you in the last one hundred years that trumps any of that."

No one spoke.

"So it is," he mocked. "Don't you dare disrespect your true queen, *my queen*, and her sacrifices for that vain and selfish woman. She could've returned at any time in the last fifty years since my father risked his life to oust the usurper from her throne. I'm sure you realize now that she didn't because she refused to let the kingdom see what was done to her. The loss of her beauty and power was reason enough to abandon her people."

I wasn't certain the queen was even listening. She frantically fastened herself a mask made of stone.

"You may question the House of Roark and our right to rule—fine. But what you will not do is sit there quietly while Ainsley is disrespected. You will speak up for her, defend her, worship her"—flickering hellfire appeared above all of their heads—"or you die too."

I gasped at him. What a wild, dangerous, fearless man that he'd attack and insult the queen of Adalinda while threatening to kill everyone who didn't do the same in defending me.

I don't think I'd ever been more in love with him than I was in that moment.

"Dominic, I—"

"Enough of your insolence!" Queen Kisandra punched the air, and the rafters fell from the ceiling.

"Dominic!"

They collapsed on him—twisting and twining like writhing snakes. The break in concentration dropped the hellfire barriers around the twins. They piled on Dominic—lashing him with vines.

Holding him down. His shouts cut off as Ormr cast a wind shield around him. No sound. No air.

His hellfire petered out.

No fire. No escape.

"Let him go!" I thrashed against the clinging, liquid stone, plumbing my depths for something. Anything! To trigger my magic. "Come on!"

A boom shook the palace once, and twice as Reyna rammed the window.

This is my magic. I use it when I decide! Absorb her living magic. Free yourself and Dominic. I strained, screaming for him. *Do it now!*

"Treason," Queen Kisandra shrieked. "Insolence. Mutiny. Violence against your queen. That disgusting whore's spawn has poisoned your minds as her mother did my son's. Kill them," she ordered. "Every last one of them. Their life is forfeit by order of their queen."

The chairs and statues were only too willing to comply. Bodies hit the ground—their necks snapped. I struggled harder as Keely turned blue, the chair arms squeezing the life out of her.

"Stop!" General Roark broke free of his executioner and kicked it away.

Boom! Boom!

"There is no need of this, my queen." General Roark dropped to his knees, bowing before her. "That boy does not speak for us. The royals, nobles, and soldiers of this kingdom are your loyal servants, and have always been." He swept out a hand. "It's been my honor to serve this kingdom until a time as you were ready to return."

"Yes," voices cried out. "Kill the Druk bastard."

"We serve the one true queen."

"Slit her throat."

"Break her neck."

"We never trusted that Druk's spawn."

"Is that so?" Through the eye space, hers narrowed to a slit. "You're a general now, Ladon Roark. High commander of the Royal Riders." She snapped her fingers. "In my time, the general carried out the execution of traitors."

The doors opened. Dragged in by chairs, wooden beams, twisting rope, and binding metal... were Sister Aven and the children from the orphanage.

"No!" I broke my body in half, clawing and bleeding on the stone. *Magic, do something! Steal her power! Help!*

The last to be dragged in was Rosaleen.

"Ainsley," my best friend cried. "I didn't tell them anything, I swear. Ormr came to the Veil. They asked all these questions about you, but I refused to answer. So my aunt did instead." She burst into tears, cutting through the already running face paints on her bruised and battered face. "She told them everything for ten fucking ryus! I'm sorry. I'm so sor—" The vines climbed her neck, lashing around her mouth.

"Let her go!" I screamed. "Don't do this. You don't have to do this! I'll leave Golden City. I swear I'll never come back." My Ilemka, my Niamh, my Colm. All my brothers and sisters there in clothes that were clean and sandals that were new. I did all this to give us a new life. It would not end here. "Please! Let them go."

Boom! Boom!

Queen Kisandra gave no sign she heard me. "I ordered that abomination dead, and instead, that woman harbored the enemy of my blood," she said, leveling a finger on Sister Aven. "She fed and housed the worthless thing when she should've drowned it at first sight. And that harlot," she spat, swinging to Rosaleen. "Refused to give up the betrayer and attacked my heirs when they sought to carry out my rightful justice.

"Execute them, General, oh loyal servant. All of them. Orphans are cursed children and drains on society. For all we know, she's harboring another demon's spawn in that brood. Prove you will carry out my will."

"No!"

"As you wish."

"Noooo—!"

General Roark waved his hand, and my family crumbled to dust.

I collapsed on the ground—jaw cracked on a choked sob. No… not a sob. A scream. I screamed and screamed, calling out for people I would never see again.

Boom! Boom! Boom!

"See, my queen?" Roark bowed. "It is my honor to carry out your will."

"Hmm. Then, you know you're not done yet." She pointed at Dominic.

"Don't touch him!" *Break free, Ainsley! Stop this. Save him!*

"Your son committed violence upon your rightful ruler and incited a mutiny against her."

Ormr released the air shell and Maili's vines lifted him free. His head fell forward, unconscious.

"Kill him."

General Roark dipped his head. "Yes, my queen."

"Roark, stop. He's your son!"

The general looked right at me and said, "I have plenty more." He touched Dominic's ankle.

Wither magic consumed him greedily—eating his legs, pants, belt, and everything away.

My mind broke.

I clutched my head, shrieking under ferocious, unforgiving pain. The ceiling collapsed under the dragon's final strike. Glass fell like rain. Pouring in, their bonds ripped my mind apart one by one. Kenna, Cadmus, Suoh, Mireu.

Tizor.

Their minds, thoughts, and feelings rushed into me, sending spasming agony throughout my body.

"Tizor?"

"Cadmus? Cadmus, love, what are you doing!"

"I can't feel your bond, Kenna. Kenna!"

They became mine. Mine to command. Mine to love. Mine—for I finally knew what I was, and as Kai said, it was so much more than I thought possible.

I roared as I drained General Roark of power, undoing his vile, twisted magic on Dominic. The man collapsed in a heap, unfortunately not dead. Ripping my hands apart, I tore Maili's vines to shreds, dropping my love whole and alive on the floor.

I looked to the shadow of the podium. Just a single look and I was there, standing tall and free of the queen's magic. I raised my hands to the heavens. To my dragons.

"What have you done?" the queen bellowed. "This is forbidden magic. Usurper. Usurper!"

There was nothing forbidden about my magic. Deep in Elder Tizor's mind, he held the true name for my magic—revered and feared throughout time, my abilities were the origin. Named forbidden to keep the truth of what my kind could do hidden.

"*Dragon mother,*" six voices said at once.

"I am not the usurper," I said with a calm that wasn't mine. "She was a failure. I won't be.

"Kill them all."

Unhinging their jaws, my dragons set the throne room ablaze.

Keep In Touch

Join R.A. Vincent's mailing list for news, teasers, and more:
https://www.subscribepage.com/ravincentpage
Join R.A. Vincent's Facebook Reader Group:
https://bit.ly/3bNuCOq

ABOUT THE AUTHOR

Ruby Vincent is a lover of all things enemies to lovers. From fantasy romance to contemporary romance, she loves saucy heroines, bold alpha males, and weaving a tale where both get their happy ever after.

www.ingramcontent.com/pod-product-compliance
Lightning Source LLC
Chambersburg PA
CBHW061851310726
48972CB00004B/971